The Green Lion

Wildside Press Books by Leigh Grossman

The Green Lion

The Golden Thorns

The Wildside Gaming System: Fantasy Roleplaying Edition

The Wildside Book of Loot

www.wildsidegame.com

The Green Lion

Leigh Ronald Grossman

The Wildside Press

Rockville, Maryland

The Green Lion
www.wildsidegame.com

Cover design by Stephen H. Segal

Edited by Amy Goldschlager
Special thanks to Sean Wallace and Seameus Bethel

ISBN 0-8095-7180-3
ISBN-13 978-0-8095-7180-2

Published by:
Wildside Press
9710 Traville Gateway Drive #234
Rockville, MD 20850
www.wildsidepress.com

First Wildside Press edition: September 2007

10 9 8 7 6 5 4 3 2 1

For John Gregory Betancourt
who dared me to write it, all those years ago

Contents

Acknowledgments

In their earliest form, *The Green Lion* and *The Golden Thorns* were the first books I finished, completed in the mid-1990s. John Betancourt, a friend since college and at the time a science fiction editor in New York, pushed me to write the novel, which grew into two books in the storytelling process. The books landed me my first agent and got some favorable attention from publishers, but ultimately were never published, unlike the ten books that followed. Years later, Betancourt, now head of the Wildside Press (which also publishes my gaming books), asked if the novels were still available, bringing the books full circle.

Over the last year, I've had the opportunity to revisit the writer I was more than a decade ago, at a very different time in my life, while substantially rewriting the books to reflect how I've grown as a writer since that time. As an author I've written a number of collaborations, but collaborating with my own past self is certainly one of the more interesting writing experiences I've ever had.

I owe thanks to many people, particularly to John Betancourt for his roles at both the beginning and end of this saga; my first agent, Don

Maass, who made a number of suggestions for shaping the narrative; current agent Val Smith, who keeps me focused and writing; to Lois Garrett, who believed in the earliest version of this book more than anyone; to Rowena Sandoval for her love and support; proofreader Penelope Stowe; and most of all to editor Amy Goldschlager, who first saw these books as an editor at Avon Books, but had a tremendous hand in helping to reshape them a decade later, and whose friendship over the years has helped even more than her editorial guidance.

The Green Lion

PROLOGUE
The Colors of the Rose

❖❖❖

Autumn, two hours after dawn
983 years After the Death of Mara
Brackenwood Castle

From where she sat at the top of the tower, she could hear echoes of the battering ram hitting the door below. Wisps of smoke penetrated the narrow window of her chamber. Dust motes played along a thin shaft of morning sunlight. By now, nearly all her followers had died or been driven away.

She looked at the table in front of her. Thin cards lay spread over its surface in a complex pattern. The cards looked like plaques of ivory, although she had made them from something else—something far more powerful, which had taken nine years of her life to find and capture and properly kill.

Each card bore an etched picture across its face, as lifelike as all of her skills had been able to make it. Hundreds of precise incisions covered the cards, each line cut by the thorn of a different rose. Painstakingly, she'd cut every mark with her own hands.

Rich pigments filled the lines: dyes handmade from mixtures of blood, spices, and rose petals. She'd spent years breeding the flowers until their colors ran precisely true. A whole winter had passed while she harvested the thorns—grinding them into the precise needles she required—and distilled the special dyes she needed. Now, deep colors flowed through the cuts like channeled rivers, smoothly covering the face of each card. On top of the table, across the center of the ivory pattern, lay a single, long-stemmed red rose.

She ran a hand across her face and felt the beginnings of wrinkles. In the last few weeks, age had finally begun to touch her, after many decades held at bay. Magic drained years from a woman's life, years that she had carefully replaced until the frantic events of recent days. Her vanity hated the thought of aging. She had to remind herself that this body had very little time remaining, and no time at all to be young.

The pounding increased from below. Only the tower door separated her from the armies below. They had breached the outer defenses days ago, and killed the last of her soldiers this morning. She reached down, and fingered the rose. An hour or two remained, perhaps. Long enough.

"Leina?" she said. Across the room, a young woman stirred. She stood against the wall, motionless and nearly invisible next to the gray stone blocks. A gray smock half-covered a homespun blouse and long, faded brown skirt. Pale blond hair fell halfway down her back, straight and loose. She looked perhaps sixteen or seventeen.

"Yes, Mistress?"

"Do you know what you have to do?"

"No, Mistress. Nobody told me." Leina shook a little.

"Come here, then. Let me show you. It's nothing to be afraid of."

"You won't send me away like the others, will you, Mistress?"

"No, Leina. Not you."

A loud cracking noise echoed up the stairs. Shouts drifted up from below as the first soldiers reached the stairway. Someone screamed as one of the traps exploded.

She stroked Leina's hair as the young woman drew close. Goosebumps showed on the girl's arms.

"What will the soldiers do to us? Will they come up here?"

"Not for a while, Leina. We have all the time we will need. Now I want you to lean over the table and look at these cards. Tell me what you see."

She stroked Leina's hair and shoulders as the young woman looked at the table. Her left hand traced the contours of Leina's spine as the girl began to describe the marvelous figures on the table, gradually working its way back up to her neck. Slowly, Leina's shivers began to subside. The older woman reached downward with her right hand while her left continued to soothe the young servant.

With a quick knife stroke she slashed open the girl's throat. Warm blood sprayed over her right hand and the blade it held. Her left hand clutched Leina's hair and pulled the young woman's neck back, so she could be certain the blood would spread evenly over all the cards.

"You will be with me forever, dear girl," she said. As soon as red liquid had covered all the cards, she let go of the body. Leina fell heavily to the floor, her body not quite limp.

Putting the girl out of her mind, she picked up the blood-soaked rose, making sure the cards beneath it were as soaked in the blood as the rest. For a moment, she caressed the flower, touching the petals to her lips. Then she pressed her thumb heavily against a thorn, forcing it into her flesh. Smiling, she withdrew the thorn. She placed the rose gently on top of Leina's now-still form and turned her attention back to the cards.

The woman began to chant in a language few remembered. As she spoke, she squeezed her thumb, forcing a drop of blood onto the surface of each card in turn. Long before she finished with all eighty-four of the bloodied plaques, colors began to glow through the liquid as they started to absorb it.

Blood flowed freely from her hand by the time the chant ended. The shouting from below had gotten much closer. Only a few minutes remained.

She glanced down at Leina's body, and saw the corpse of an ancient woman, topped by a blackened flower. Her own skin now felt cracked and withered. She had little use remaining for it.

Once again, she picked up the knife. No blood remained on the table. Instead, a tableau of swirling colors filled the air in front of her: violent crimson and blue and green and gold.

"I have given you all that I have," she said, to no one in particular. "Someday, I shall ask for it back." The colors expanded, whirling and dancing until they surrounded her, obscuring the gray stone room entirely.

She picked up the knife. Footsteps approached, not far away. She looked once again at Leina's body, and touched her own throat. It was time to die.

"So your son is dead?"

They sat on couches in the big parlor, but there were bars on the windows. A comfortable prison, but still a prison.

"I didn't say that, Councilor."

"Missing, then."

"Yes."

"But you came to know his whole story . . . ?"

"Isn't that why I'm here?"

"Just answer the question, please."

"I think so. Some of it I learned from others, after. Some of it I knew at the time. A few pieces I knew before he was born."

"And your son never knew about your past?"

"No. Never. He still doesn't."

"But he hasn't come home. And he hasn't come looking for you since your . . . apprehension."

"No. That's true."

"So perhaps he does know about your role in the whole affair . . . ?"

"I really couldn't say, Councilor. If he did know, perhaps he would come looking for me, perhaps not. But I think he never knew that I'd helped set things in motion, or how much I'd held back from him."

"If he's alive."

"If he's alive."

The conversation subsided while the interrogator checked something in a massive ledger. Several other books lay on the table in front of him, as well as loose parchment covered with meticulous handwriting. Presumably, a discreetly placed scribe was keeping a similar record of this session.

In the background gulls cawed. Occasionally, their shadows crossed the window glass as they circled the harbor outside.

The interrogator put down the ledger. "Perhaps you should start at the beginning."

"At the very beginning? My son wasn't even born yet."

"Nevertheless. You were there . . . ?"

"I was there. Not in the room when it happened, but not long after. I didn't play a big role in the fight, Councilor."

"But you did play a role in the division of the spoils."

"Yes." A long pause. "I was seen as . . . impartial, since I arrived to the fight late. I chose the shares, but I didn't receive any of the larger treasures. Just a consideration in gold. I knew who had which cards initially, though that changed quickly as feuds broke out among various nobles who had united for . . . you know."

"I see. So you knew where they were . . ." The interrogator seemed to rethink the line of questioning; he waved the question off before it could be answered. "Never mind that." He shifted his considerable bulk on the couch. For all his size, there was something deceptively light and feminine about the interrogator's movements, as if the spirit inside didn't fit with his body's bulk. "It is important to this investigation that we have the whole story. Start at the beginning, as you perceive it."

"You know the beginning better than I do."

The interrogator considered that, and finally nodded. "That is true. From the beginning of your son's involvement, then, if that's what you prefer."

"It will take some time."

"And yet—" The interrogator waved a massive hand at the barred window. "—we will have all the time we need, I think. Unless your son chooses to return from the dead to tell his story. From the beginning, please."

A gull cried out, a long caw-caw-caw-caw-caw, as it wheeled around the seaside tower.

1

The Lion on the Road

❖❖❖

Spring, thirty years later
1014 years After the Death of Mara
The Free Duchies, along the Turnpike

Falorn found the man's body the same morning he left home. Much as he loved his father, something had finally snapped after yet another of the inexplicable non-answers to nearly any question raised over the last few months. Falorn had walked away to blow off steam, and found himself still walking an hour later.

It's almost as if he wants me to leave, he'd been thinking, before almost stumbling over the body.

The corpse sprawled facedown like a drunk on the wide cobble-stoned Turnpike that connected Tidewater with the rest of the Free Duchies. It had only just begun to draw flies in the morning sunlight. Ringlets of polished steel armor glinted as the sun caught them through gashes in the man's surcoat. Rich green cloth flapped in the late spring breeze. The wind barely stirred the long, matted black hair which flopped around his head and oddly canted neck. A dented horseman's helmet, its band filigreed in green and gold, lay on the stones a few feet away.

Perhaps twenty yards off, tail swishing to deter the flies which chased it under the shade trees that lined the Turnpike, stood a tall and powerful horse, saddled and caparisoned in green as if awaiting a battle with some forest creature.

There's no blood, was Falorn's first thought. *Why can't I see any blood?* He could smell it, though. The musky slaughterhouse odors of sweat, urine, and blood masked the scent of pollen from the nearby fields.

After a moment's hesitation, he walked over to the body.

Pull yourself together, Falorn said to himself. *You've seen bodies before. There were three of them in Father's icehouse when you left this morning.* It could take months for a dead man's family to save up enough money to pay a traveling priest. Two or three times a year a Maran priest passed through and performed funerals, and Jayse the cooper would come to collect the bodies. Jayse built caskets and dug graves to augment his basket- and barrelmaking trade. Falorn wondered briefly how many bodies he'd seen. *Certainly not as many as the cooper.*

Falorn's younger sister had died from the gray fever three years ago, before he turned fifteen. Two other brothers had died before he was old enough to remember.

But you've never seen a dead warrior, have you? Soldiers traveled through the Free Duchies often enough, commonly passing nights at his father's tavern: Duke's Men in red and gray surcoats and cracked leather coats; swords-for-hire with their rough-cut beards and white painted shields; archers in brown and green, carrying yew longbows taller than themselves; merchants' bodyguards, in their finely cut clothes and polished armor, always oiling and sharpening their weapons; sometimes emissaries from other duchies, or from the Immortal King of the Seven Kingdoms, serious looking men who drank little and said less; once even a pair of elves, their tight-fitting hose, exquisite silver ornamentation, lilting accents, and delicately alien faces drawing stares and exciting conversations for months after. Soldiers ate, drank, gambled, slept, and occasionally fought drunken brawls within the thick oak timbers of the Rat and Rooster's common room. They whored as well; his father's tavernmaids were never from Tidewater, always foreigners who moved on after a year or so when the town wives drove them away. They never married, for reasons Falorn had only recently begun to understand. The soldiers did a dozen things Falorn barely hoped to understand: They seemed more alive than anyone he knew, free to travel and explore a thousand topics Falorn's father had forbidden to him. In theory, Falorn knew that soldiers sometimes died as well, but after building them into such potent symbols in his mind, the sight of an actual dead one seemed somehow incongruous.

The flies scattered briefly as Falorn bent over the body, but they quickly returned, buzzing insistently around his exposed face and hands. Falorn tried to ignore them while he examined the dead man, but couldn't; every few seconds he had to shake his thick mop of brown hair, or brush his narrow hands against his face.

If you don't do this now, you never will. You might as well go back home and clean out stables for the rest of your life. You left home to get away from being kept in the dark about everything, and now you've found a way to achieve that.

After a few minutes of hesitation, Falorn began removing the armor from the corpse.

An hour later, after he had buried the dead man under a shallow layer of loose dirt and stones from the roadside ditch, Falorn looked down at a pile of supplies, and up at the warhorse cropping leaves from roadside brush. No other travelers had passed him, not unusual on a non-market morning; but someone was bound to come along soon if he didn't move on quickly.

Falorn picked up the heavy steel byrne—he'd wiped blood and grease off it with the rags of the green surcoat—and began to wriggle into it, leaving his tunic and britches on underneath. The dead man had worn a quilted and embroidered coat of gambeson as cushioning under the mail, but Falorn couldn't bear to strip it from the corpse. He pulled on leather leggings covered with sewn-on metal rings, fumbling with the unfamiliar lacing. Leftover green rags filled the space around his feet in the enormous, soft leather boots.

Taken together, the armor fit Falorn like a shell on a clam: protective, but large and difficult to move in. *Maybe I'll grow into it.*

Falorn buckled on the dead warrior's armaments uneasily. *Does he have a family they should go to?* he wondered. *I wouldn't know where to begin finding them, and in the meantime, the next person along this road would take them.* Still, it felt strange to be taking over the life of a man so far above Falorn's station.

The tooled leather baldric he slid over his head so it dangled from right shoulder to left hip, supporting a broadsword with a worn grip of leather tape, sheathed in flaking black leather. Another belt hung low around his waist, with a knife and two pouches suspended from it: the dead man's (still unsearched) and Falorn's own. He slid his own beltknife into his right boot, unsure of where else to put it, but reluctant to leave it behind.

He was done; Falorn mouthed what few words he could remember of Mara's Lament for the Dead, hoping the thousand gods would understand. Afterward he left the dented helmet, most recently used as a makeshift shovel, atop the burial mound, in lieu of a better marker.

The massive black stallion snorted as Falorn approached, shaking its white-splashed head and tossing its thick mane and tail impatiently.

"Good boy," Falorn said. "Come on, boy, let me close." He waited for the stallion to make up its mind. "Come on, boy." Falorn had groomed horses from the age when he could hold a stiff-haired brush, and he'd learned to ride soon after, though more recently his father had discouraged him. In a few minutes the horse let him touch it, then rub its back and flanks. When it let him pat its head, Falorn gave it half of his last shriveled apple, taken that morning from the barrels of dried fruit in his father's pantry. *I hope there's food in those sacks*, he thought, glancing at the bulging saddlebags lashed behind the stallion's wood-and-leather war-saddle.

Ignoring his remaining misgivings, Falorn mounted the horse. His feet felt awkward in the stirrups, which were little more than iron rings with open fronts, unlike the solid-fronted stirrups on the war-saddles he'd seen before. In the loose-fitting, smooth-soled boots, his feet kept slipping through the rings, with no heel to catch on the stirrups' edge. *I guess I'll get the knack eventually*, Falorn thought, after three attempts to sit comfortably upright in the saddle. The horse stood perfectly still throughout. *I wonder how the dead man did it. I wonder where he was from. I've never seen anything like this saddle or these boots.*

Stroking the horse's mane and talking softly in its ear, Falorn urged the stallion forward at a walk.

Falorn rode until past noon. By then he felt broiled in his own sweat, trapped inside the heavy coat of interlocking steel rings. He passed only a few travelers following the Turnpike back toward Tidewater: a farmer with a laden mule, a tinker whose pack towered comically over his head.

He ignored the dirt side tracks and turnoffs that led to farmsteads and villages. There was no reason to leave the main road, since he expected no pursuit. *I'm eighteen years old and a younger son*, Falorn told himself. *Father has no hold on me.* He'd taken nothing that belonged to the innkeeper or to his brothers. Falorn doubted he'd be welcomed back, but then, he didn't intend to return. *I'm tired of watching other people pass through on their way to seeing the world, knowing that I'll never get to do anything except groom their horses. For once in my life, I want to be the one riding the horse.*

Falorn rubbed the stallion's flank absentmindedly. The animal lifted its head as it continued walking, shaking its mane until Falorn moved his hand upward to scratch behind the stallion's ears.

I wonder if whoever killed the man in green is still around. That helmet looked like it was crushed by a mace, not by a fall from a horse. I haven't seen any sign at all of soldiers. But people don't just leave bodies lying in the road, at least not bodies covered with armor and weapons.

No one I know could hope to afford any of this in a lifetime.

He finally stopped where a small grassy clearing opened on the side of the Turnpike, edged by young oaks. A firepit and trampled grass marked a recent camp.

Falorn avoided the sunny center of the clearing in favor of the saplings' shade. He unlashed the oversized saddlebags from the stallion before turning the horse loose to graze on the sweet-smelling grass and clover. Falorn hesitated a moment, running his hand over the oddly laced fittings of the thick wood-and-leather war-saddle. *I'd better not loosen it*, he decided, shaking his head. *I don't know how long it's going to take me to get that thing adjusted again. I'd better wait until I know I have time to look at it.*

The left saddlebag *did* have food in it: dried fruit and smoked meat, even a sack with worn cloth straps sewn on, still half full of oats. The stallion whickered with pleasure as Falorn approached with its familiar feed bag, which slid easily into place over the horse's muzzle and head.

He walked back toward the oaks. Picking the bulging wineskin out of the deep saddlebag, he unfastened its stopper and raised the skin to his lips. Falorn recoiled at the sourness of the dark liquid; it tasted nothing like the sweet local wines. Thirst from the heat and the dry smoked meat made him rethink his initial disgust: He sipped gingerly, in between chews of dried meat and fruit, while he untied the second saddlebag.

A bulky rectangular object sat inside, swaddled in layer upon layer of rough brown sackcloth. Falorn unwrapped it carefully. From the middle of the onionlike layers emerged a massive, leather-bound book, its thick leaves held together by shining brass fasteners.

Falorn held the book delicately, almost afraid to touch its heavy leather cover. Cunningly worked brass talons guarded each corner. They looked so real that he expected them to spring from the book at any moment and attack him. Try as he might, Falorn could find no sign of casting, or lathe, or other metalworker's tools; the claws looked as if they had been conjured from air, or cut from some living metal bird, rather than shaped from base metals.

The leather covers looked somehow ageless, though subtly worn, as if stroked to a polish by hundreds of users. They had the same oily sheen as the thin banister which led upstairs from the commons to the four private rooms at his father's tavern. Raised swirls and curlicues surrounded a central oval embossed onto the cover.

As they caught the afternoon sunlight, the decorations formed dragons and serpents and other exotic shapes which danced across the dark leather—but which disappeared quickly when Falorn gazed at them directly. Try as he might, he could not replicate the trick of the sun.

Within the oval, four brilliantly colored dragons stretched outward and away from each other, their tails intertwining in the center of the book cover, their wings meeting at the points of the compass. A fierce dragon more deeply green than the emerald rings merchants wore strove to the northwest. Beside it, a blue dragon colored as richly as the thickest blue in the sunset sky pulled northeast. Below the blue dragon struggled a gold creature whose wings and scales shone brighter than newly minted coins as it flung itself southeast. Last of all, a haughty crimson dragon fought to escape the oval's southwest edge, its features redder than the jetting bright blood of a newly slaughtered bull.

Falorn's hands shook the first time he tried to work the clasp which held the book shut. He had to pause, but on his second try the smooth brass fastener slid aside easily. After only a moment's hesitation, he lifted the thick front cover.

The elaborate, colorfully illuminated runes that covered most of the pages meant nothing to Falorn—no one in his family could read, although he'd learned to figure with numbers a little. His father, like any religious man, owned a copy of *The Book of Mara*, but Falorn doubted that anyone between his father's inn and the brick walls of Briarcliff's market town could do more than look at the pictures—not even most of the traveling circuit priests.

But the pictures astonished him. Interspersed between passages of mysterious writing lay the most amazing pictures Falorn had ever seen. Their vibrant colors glowed and shimmered in the sun. A scarlet knight sat proudly on a crimson horse, which seemed to prance and caper as if anxious to ride into battle over the reddening horizon, its hoofs dancing over the dark red ground.

Another picture showed a mermaid of glittering aqua and teal, swimming through a ceaselessly moving cobalt sea. Dozens of tiny iridescent fish followed her downward like seagoing mosquitoes as her powerful flukes drove her deeper, through creamy blue foam which washed through her light hair and over her small breasts, deeper. . . .

Falorn pulled himself away from the captivating image. A cloud had momentarily blocked the direct sunlight that had caused the pictures to dance and draw him in.

At least an hour had passed.

Shaken, Falorn closed the book. He felt drained, as if a daylong sleep had left him even more tired upon awakening, and still longing for a lost dream. Carefully, he wrapped the heavy volume back in its layers of fibrous sackcloth and gently slid it into the saddlebag once more. It was time to go.

As he walked toward the horse with the saddlebags slung over his shoulder, Falorn remembered the pouch at his belt. He hoped the corpse had left a few coins along with his armor; Falorn's handful of saved crowns might buy him a few meals and space in the commons of some inn, but they wouldn't pay to stable and feed a warhorse. And the armor and weapons would be an invitation to theft if he slept in a common room.

Falorn smiled ruefully. Much as he liked the idea of himself in armor, he had to admit that he had only the faintest notion of what to do with a sword. *I haven't looked at the sword either*, he suddenly remembered. He smiled sadly. *I'll probably have to pawn all of this soon. The armor and weapons and horse will buy a partnership in a city tavern—but if I'd wanted to follow in my father's footsteps, I would never have left the Rat and Rooster.* That raised another question. *I don't know how I'm going to explain to a pawnbroker how an innkeeper's son came upon all of this money. Maybe in a city, the pawnbrokers won't care. I know there are bigger cities than Briarcliff in the Free Duchies. I've never been to Roicenet, but I know it's not far. All I need to do is follow the Turnpike.*

Without untying the pouch, he lifted it from his belt and felt its weight in his hands. It bulged slightly with the feel of coins and small, irregular objects. Falorn could also feel a smooth, thin, rectangular shape. He loosened the drawstring slightly.

Green flowed from the pouch's interior, glowing through an opening too small to look within.

Startled, Falorn tightened the pouch and let it drop, so that it once again dangled from his belt. The horse looked at him quizzically as Falorn clutched the saddlebag and ran toward it. The half-full bag of oats flopped back and forth from the animal's muzzle as it shook its head.

The stallion stiffened and cocked its ears toward the trees.

Falorn heard heavy footsteps closing the distance behind him.

"Get the card!" a guttural voice yelled from too close.

Falorn pounded toward the horse. The heavy armor pulled at him like river mud. The stallion stood unflinchingly as Falorn pulled himself up and threw his leg over the saddle.

Then they were on him. As soon as Falorn mounted, the horse spun and kicked, never still for an instant.

Three men circled warily, trying to avoid the warhorse's dancing hooves. The men wore brown, hooded shifts which hung almost to their knees, covering all their features. Each one carried a long, curved knife.

The horse wheeled and kicked as the first man slashed at its left flank. The man dodged back from a spear-edged hoof. The other attackers closed in.

As the warhorse fought, Falorn hung on desperately, struggling to keep his feet from slipping through the stirrups. One of the brown-shifted men stepped in close and aimed his knife.

The horse reacted instantly, swinging its head toward the new attacker. At the same time, the stallion kicked out with a back leg at the man behind.

Flying oats filled the air as the knife tore through the swinging feedbag, deflected from Falorn's leg. Freed of the impediment on his muzzle, the stallion reared up on his hind legs and whinnied a challenge.

Undeterred, the man again slashed at Falorn's leg as the warhorse returned to earth. Falorn squeezed his legs tightly into the horse to avoid the blade.

Reacting to Falorn's signal, the horse charged toward the road, plowing over an attacker who tried to close in from the front.

He felt someone pull the saddlebags—with the book inside them—from the back of the fleeing horse. As Falorn shouted in frustration, the third attacker dropped his knife and leaped for Falorn's leg.

Falorn kicked in the loose boots as a hand grabbed his ankle. His foot plunged through the open front of the stirrup. The ring wedged around his ankle and the gripping hand.

Pulled off balance by the attacker's clutch, he almost fell from the horse as it fought its way toward the road. His ankle twisted; he struggled to hold on despite the man pulling at him. Falorn squeezed his knees as tightly as he could into the stallion's flanks. He caught hold of the saddle-horn, barely staying on the horse's back

Someone screamed. Pain shot through his twisted ankle. Falorn's rapidly swelling ankle remained wedged into the stirrup, with his attacker's hand still trapped alongside. As he gained a firmer hold, Falorn tried to kick his ankle free. He couldn't lift his leg with the weight of the man pulling it downward. Ice spread through his ankle as it grew numb.

The stallion galloped onto the Turnpike, oblivious to the struggling weight dragging from the stirrup. Shreds of stained brown cloth ripped off on the abrasive cobblestones. The man screamed and screamed.

By the time Falorn slowed the horse, the pain in his ankle had subsided to a dull ache. The pulpy thing hanging from the stirrup no longer howled in agony, but Falorn could see the man's chest still faintly rise and fall.

Only then, after the chaos of the ambush and flight began to subside, did Falorn remember the broadsword hanging at his waist.

Dismounting proved difficult. Spearpoints assaulted his ankle as feeling returned. Gradually, he worked it loose from the bloody stirrup and the pinioned hand which still clutched tightly.

The dying man slumped to the ground when Falorn freed his foot from the man's mangled hand. The man's head banged into the cobbles with an audible crack. Falorn started at the sound, and a wave of pain flooded his lower leg.

Finally, he slid his good leg to the ground, and gingerly lowered himself from the horse. He tried to keep his eyes clear of the ruined flesh on the ground nearby.

Falorn combed his hands through the stallion's matted mane, and began rubbing its sweaty flanks, ignoring the pain in his ankle.

"You saved my life, boy," he said, over and over again. Falorn forced himself to focus on the horse, trying to keep his body from shaking. "You saved my life."

The horse whinnied in return, and shook its mane. The long ride had tired the animal, but still it wanted to run.

"Good boy," Falorn said. "Good run, boy." The stallion nuzzled him with its foamy muzzle as Falorn continued to rub. Afterward, he led the animal to the side of the Turnpike, where a thin, clear brook ran close and fast, and where clover grew thickly. Every time the fight tried to push its way into his mind he forced himself to think of the horse. "There's a good boy," he said, running his hands through the stallion's mane. "There's a good boy."

Falorn turned his head at the sound of a moan from the road. Leaving the worn horse to graze, he limped back toward the broken figure of the attacker. He stumbled once; pain shot through his ankle as he caugh his balance, almost falling from the strain the heavy armor and uneven cobblestones put on his one good leg.

The man's skin had been scoured off by the rough turnpike. Tattered remains of the shift still covered his upper body, but everything else was a mass of bloody contusions. Thick road dust covered what was left of him like a coat of light brown scales.

Somehow, the man opened his eyes.

They were not human eyes.

The creature's body convulsed suddenly, as if to reassemble its broken self and leap at him. Falorn jumped back, this time remembering to reach for the sword. His ankle spasmed painfully. Falorn's arms flew out for balance as he teetered.

The body abruptly went limp, and sank back down to the cobblestones. The unearthly green eyes remained open.

Regaining his balance, Falorn stood still, clutching the hilt of the sheathed broadsword.

"What are you?" he finally whispered.

The horrible eyes focused on him, transfixed him in their awful, unblinking gaze.

"The card, boy," the thing rasped. "Give me the card. My soul will not rest until you give me the card!"

The body convulsed again, shaking like someone in the grip of religious mania, or someone possessed. The eyes—green emeralds mined from some dark, alien chasm—rolled backward into the creature's skull.

The green leached away, fading into the sickly yellow-white of a sow's teeth.

The body trembled and spasmed for a moment longer, then lay still.

Falorn stood paralyzed. His hand clutched the sword hilt as tightly as the creature had constricted his ankle; he looked down and saw his fingers were bone white.

The body lay still for several long minutes. Falorn finally released his grip on the sheathed sword. He shook his hand to restore feeling.

Before he could decide whether to approach the corpse more closely, it began to *change*.

Thin tendrils of acrid smoke curled upward where blood had congealed. The rolled up yellow-white eyes began to shimmer, then melted into bubbling pools. They steamed furiously, even as the creature's skin itself began to peel away and shrivel. As Falorn watched, the whole body festered, bubbling off into bluish-gray smoke.

Within moments nothing remained. Even the blood which had spilled onto the Turnpike boiled away into nothing.

Only a few ragged scraps from the hooded shift littered the cobblestones. A harsh, acid stench lingered in the air.

Falling to his knees on the rough stones, Falorn retched uncontrollably.

Falorn rode until well past sundown, afraid to camp within reach of the dead creature's companions. He finally stopped only out of fear for the exhausted horse.

Moonlight guided him off the Turnpike and to his campsite, a small clearing within a sheltered thicket of fruit trees. Unsaddling the stallion, Falorn combed and groomed it as best he could without brushes or picks. Only afterward did he begin to feel hungry.

Not daring to light a fire, he made a cold meal of the few pieces of dried meat and fruit tucked in his pouch. Most of his supplies had vanished along with the saddlebags.

Falorn had to leave the armor on when he lay down; he didn't have a prayer of getting it off alone with his injured ankle, which had swollen to fill the oversized boot he wore.

Falorn ached to look at the book again, if only for a moment.

He couldn't sleep for a long time. After an hour of vainly trying, his thoughts still turned and turned again to the mysterious attackers. He wondered what they expected from him, what was so important that they would kill for it.

He remembered the glow in the pouch.

Slowly, Falorn fingered open the laces of the pouch. One by one he picked objects out and examined them in the moonlight.

The pouch held dozens of coins; a few of them were coins he knew from his father's inn, ranging from copper half-crown pieces stamped with the likeness of Duke Raniyen to the gold-dipped hundred-crown coins emblazoned with the face of the Archduke, but there were also strange coins of pure gold and silver.

Now there's something people would kill for.

Falorn had seen gold and silver used in the late-night card games that merchants played, passed back and forth like so many pieces of embossed copper, as if a few such gold coins couldn't buy his father's inn and everything in it. He recognized none of the faces and symbols on the coins. They came from outside the Free Duchies; they held value here for their precious metal content alone.

Reaching inside the pouch again, he fished out a tiny bag made of purple velvet and tied with golden silk. Falorn untied it, sprinkling its contents into the palm of his hand. Gemstones glittered in the moonlight: rubies and sapphires and emeralds and diamonds, and a few he wasn't sure of; any one of them was likely worth all the money the Rat and Rooster took in over a week's time.

A fortune. Somehow, though, Falorn knew that wasn't why he'd been attacked.

Replacing the small sack of precious stones, he reached inside again for the last item in the pouch. The thin rectangular plaque felt slightly warm to the touch, its surface smooth as polished ivory. The plaque glowed translucent green as Falorn withdrew it.

He held what looked like a shimmering playing card, with a picture of a green lion, mane shaking as he roared out defiance to the emerald savannah which surrounded him.

The glow from the card bathed the whole clearing in green. *I could not,* Falorn realized, *be more conspicuous if I built a huge bonfire and danced around it like on Spirit-Catching Day.*

He moved to put the card back in the pouch, but abruptly the glow subsided. He found himself holding the most perfect likeness of an animal he'd ever seen, illuminated by the moonlight and by a faint lingering glow.

Falorn studied the card in puzzlement. It seemed to be made of a hard substance like ivory, but it showed no grain or sign of toolwork. The plaque felt impossibly thin for ivory. Unless it had a sword-blade's flexibility, anything so thin should have snapped or bent from pounding against coins in the pouch during the day's frantic ride. But not so much as a scratch or blemish marked the card. It looked as though it had never left the home of the master craftsman who made it.

No brushstroke or ink mark flawed the green lion. The picture could have doubled for one of the mesmerizing plates in the stolen book. Like those plates, the lion seemed to move within the narrow boundaries of the card, tail flickering, flanks quivering in the moonlight.

The moon had nearly set before Falorn could bear to replace the card in the dead man's pouch. He carefully pillowed his head on the pouch, and clutched his hands around it as he lay on his side. At the edge of the clearing, he could see the sleeping horse silhouetted against the trees by the fading moon.

Completely exhausted after his first day away from home, Falorn fell into a fitful sleep, and dreamed anxiously of green knights pursued by green lions.

"You seem well-versed in your son's part in the story."

"You might say that."

"So all along, your son thought it was *his* quest."

"It was his quest by the end. It just didn't start out that way."

The interrogator let that pass, and took a different tack in the questioning.

"And you maintain that he never knew of your involvement."

"No, Councilor. I think he didn't know."

"But you knew he was leaving home?

"Yes."

"Why did he leave?"

"He thought he left because of the secrets I kept from him. But really, it was because of a secret he never suspected. He left because he was angry at me. But he planned to come back. Ultimately, he left because I killed a man."

"The green knight you mentioned yesterday?"

"Yes."

"Your son never knew that you killed the knight?"

"No. He didn't even know the man was in the area. Or how many men I'd killed before I became an innkeeper. I like . . . liked to take long walks in the woods and commons near the tavern I owned. It brings back certain memories, years of scouting and patrolling."

"And that's when you encountered the knight."

"Yes. He was on his way to the inn, though. He would have had questions for me, about the whereabouts of certain cardholders."

"And that was a problem?"

"Not in itself, no. But I didn't want him to know about my son."

"You have other sons."

"Only one of my sons was a threat to the other cardholders."

"Why?"

"He had . . . a certain kind of curiosity. A dangerous kind, if it had become known. There were talents he inherited from me, that made him . . . an attractive catalyst for the cards."

"And that's why you sent him after them? That's why you precipitated all of the deaths that followed?"

"No. I wanted him to have them, of course. But I didn't give any more thought than anyone else to what would happen in the end. It was just . . . a father's wish for his son."

The interrogator arched an eyebrow disbelievingly. "*Some* of us gave thought to what would happen in the end."

"You're right, of course. I did not."

"What did you hope to get out or it? Why did you send your son out that day?"

"I didn't send him. It was his choice."

"A choice that you manipulated."

"Yes."

"Why?"

"I'd prefer to tell the truth. I don't think I can answer that question without lying. And the answer doesn't really bear on my son's story."

The eyebrow arched again.

"Very well. We can come back to that. Why did your son leave on that day?"

"That's tricky as well. He told people that he was looking for adventure. But really, I don't think it was about adventure."

"What, then?"

"Honestly? I think maybe he just wanted to get away from all of the lying. You see, he'd been lied to his whole life, and I think a part of him was beginning to realize it. He was my son and I loved him—I love him still, if he lives—but I lied to him about who he was and his heritage every day of his life."

The interrogator said nothing.

"I think at some point, a part of him started to expect that people who loved him would lie to him. He just thought was normal and accepted it. I think it's one of the reasons he survived through so much."

2

The Festive Knight

Falorn awoke to the horse's impatient neighing. His ankle still throbbed as he sat up and brushed off clinging blades of grass, but the sharp pain had subsided. *It must not have been as bad as it seemed*, Falorn thought to himself. *I didn't think I'd be able to walk this morning, once it stiffened.*

Carefully, Falorn wiped the dew off his armor before he stood up. Although he still had trouble believing that he wore a fortune's worth of tightly woven steel links, he didn't want his newfound wealth to rust.

He didn't have any more feed for the stallion; it would have to make do by grazing. A warhorse couldn't survive long on forage alone, Falorn knew, but he hoped to find something more substantial on the road ahead.

By noon he had fed and watered the stallion, buying oats from a farmstead which lay close by the Turnpike as the road wound snakelike around a bend in the wide, slow Raryan River. He paid two copper coins for a three-day supply of grain; the farmer scowled at Falorn's haggling, resenting having to lower his price for a boy riding a thousand crowns' worth of warhorse.

In spite of his fear of pursuit, Falorn stopped for a long fifteen minutes to watch the canal drivers leading the mule teams which pulled their heavy flatboats downstream.

Early in the afternoon, traffic on the Turnpike grew heavy with farmers and small crafters carrying goods to market.

Without exception, they avoided Falorn's gaze.

Soon Falorn began to see other travelers: a pair of gossiping peddlers walking together, their packs towering high overhead; a long mule train surrounded by mounted guards in blue and by a family of merchants, who scuttled around the plodding pack animals ceaselessly; five dusty swords-for-hire in leather jacks, their axes and shields slung before them on their tired-looking horses. The mercenaries gave him a long, appraising look as he passed them on the road, before finally turning their eyes back to their listless mounts.

No one said a word to him until he caught up to the hindmost of the circus wagons. Enormous draft animals pulled a dozen massive vehicles, each so wide it filled much of the road. Falorn marveled as he rode past each one. The stallion carefully picked its steps to avoid the ditch by the side of the Turnpike.

The last three wagons in the circus train held animals. Tawny beasts of prey paced within the giant rolling cages, their dull pelts contrasting with the bright paint of the wagons.

In front of the cages rolled five huge freight wagons, covered with drab canvas and pulled by slow, lumbering oxen. Heavy-set, bearded drivers leaned over their reins, brows set in concentration as if their teams raced, rather than plodded, over the cobblestones.

A young boy in a red smock sat beside one of the slouched drivers, his head craned excitedly to take in all the passing traffic and scenery around the Turnpike. He waved at Falorn and called out something in a foreign language—the first thing anybody had said to him since his conversation with the taciturn farmer.

Falorn waved back and shouted a hello.

The boy kept waving as Falorn rode past; the driver never looked up from his team.

In front of the freight wagons, four massive coaches rumbled toward the city. Their bright paint and golden trim glittered in the already-fading sunlight.

He passed a blue wagon first, its sides adorned with dancing gryphons and lions and great winged serpents, all set with rhinestones and painted in gold leaf and burnished till they shone like newly minted crowns. Eight massive horses pulled the coach, their blue tack trimmed with gold cord. The dwarf who drove the team wore blue as well: a teal tunic, sky-blue hose, dyed suede boots, and a blue cap and surcoat—both adorned with cloth-of-gold patches.

Falorn could see shadows inside the coach, illuminated against the stained-glass windows by flickering candles.

The dwarf did not look up as Falorn rode past; he just flicked his bullwhip above the heads of his team, over and over again.

Falorn urged the stallion past a green and a yellow wagon, each as ornamented as the blue coach. Finally, he drew abreast of the lead coach, a monstrous red vehicle pulled by dappled gray horses.

Falorn's breath caught in his throat as he saw the woman who drove the carriage. Long black hair flowed like liquid around her shoulders, though there was hardly any breeze, framing the olive-colored skin of her exposed face and hands. She wore a short leather skirt over dark leggings. A black vest laced tightly over her red, high-collared tunic. Red embroidered roses decorated the vest where it curved over the swell of her breasts.

She looked like a picture from the lost book.

"Hey there, Green Knight," she called in his own language.

Falorn couldn't make any words emerge from his mouth. He couldn't even swallow, his throat felt so tight. For the first time since the previous day, he felt very much like a boy in a man's armor.

"H . . . hello," he finally managed to stammer.

"Off to the festival in Roicenet?" she asked cheerily.

"I suppose. I guess I'll go." The first words painfully out, he found it easier to talk. Falorn hadn't known there was a festival, or even that he was on the outskirts of the great city. *The horse must have galloped farther than I thought*, flashed through his mind, the thought instantly driven away by the voice of the black-haired woman.

"Well, I hope we see you there, Green Knight. You be sure and come to see Sheanna at the circus."

"I'll try," he said. Flustered, he spurred his horse forward. He really wanted to keep looking at her, but he was afraid to stare.

"You don't hide your cards so well, Green Knight," she said in a sultry voice. "See that you guard them better."

Mother of Kerion! he thought. *She knows. She knows I killed that man!*

Panicked, he forced the horse into a gallop. Travelers scattered and cursed the armored man on the giant horse as he barreled down the darkening Turnpike toward the bright lights of Roicenet.

Falorn slowed the stallion as the crowds on the road thickened further. The moon had risen, and moonlight reflected on the horse's sweaty flanks as Falorn slowly walked the animal toward the gates of Roicenet.

Hundreds of balls of light as big as hay bales hung suspended in the air in front of the city walls, flickering from one translucent color to another. Falorn heard music from dozens of clashing instruments, mixed with the sounds of bleating animals, carnival barkers, circuit preachers, and wandering illusionists—and with the ocean-wave hum of crowds. People pushed against each other like tides on sand. The festival had begun.

Falorn had been to country festivals and year-end job fairs, and to the carnivals and traveling camp-shows that made their way through the Free Duchies. None of those things prepared him for the sheer mass of *people* he could see milling about, even just from the city's open gates.

How will I get through those gates?

A dozen guards stood on the Turnpike outside the block-shaped gatehouse, controlling the flow of new arrivals into the city. Falorn could see another half-dozen guards just within the gateway.

The gate guards held long, brass-shod halberds with ornate heads, which they used to direct traffic. The inside guards made do with cudgels and the flats of their shortswords. All wore the Duke of Roicenet's colors: loose sky-blue surcoats belted over black hose and tunics, with the duke's crossed-halberd-and-lion emblem appliquéd in cloth-of-gold on each surcoat. None of the soldiers wore armor, other than quilted gambeson vests beneath their surcoats and polished horsemen's helmets with dyed-blue horsehair crests.

The guards questioned each group of travelers briefly before motioning them through the gates. They seemed to be looking for something.

The crowd milled around him as Falorn sat on the motionless horse's back and tried to figure out what he would tell the guards. *They can't be looking for me*, he finally realized. *I'm sitting in plain view on top of the dead man's stallion, wearing stolen armor. Could they be looking for the card?* He wondered how they could have found out about it, without also knowing about the man he'd killed.

Finally, he made up his mind, and started the horse forward toward the gates. He would just have to answer the guards' questions as best he could. The soldiers looked up as he made his way through the crowd. One guard whispered to his fellow, a bearded man with a gold lion pinned to his surcoat. The officer nodded twice, then wordlessly motioned for Falorn to pass through the gate.

Puzzled, Falorn spurred his mount slightly, jogging it through the long gateway (looking up in amazement at the murder-holes in the floor of the gatehouse above) and past the remaining guards. Only when he passed into the clamorous open square of Roicenet's Lesser Market did he realize that they had treated him exactly as a traveling knight would expect.

I'd better learn to act the part, before I reveal myself as the armored impostor I really am.

A less well-trained horse would have stepped on someone within minutes, Falorn realized, or thrown its rider and bolted from the sudden confusion. The shock of new colors, noises, and scents dizzied Falorn. Only with great effort could he keep from sliding off the stallion's back and into the maelstrom of the festival.

Thousand gods! I can't believe it. He held tightly to the saddlehorn to avoid being swept away as he tried to focus his eyes on all the things going on around him. *Where do all these people come from? It must be all the people in the world.*

The stallion could barely move amid the press of revelers. The Lesser Market—he heard people call out the name—could have enclosed the whole of his village, with room left over for one of the hayfields. People filled the open area completely, a sea of heads drowning in the bright blues and greens of their festival tunics. The sea thickened into waves and reefs around the scattered fragile-looking islands of freshly painted vendors' stalls. Loud haggling in a dozen languages broke above the constant roar of the turbulent human sea.

With difficulty, he steered the horse toward the nearest edge of the square.

It took nearly half an hour to travel less than a hundred yards. At the edge of the square the crowd thinned enough to walk the horse normally, but did not diminish entirely. The hubbub remained incredible.

"Where can I find a place to stay?" he shouted toward a middle-aged man in a bright green tunic and red hose. Half a dozen people answered, all calling out the names of different inns. Falorn understood none of them.

A tall, bearded man leaned close to the horse's sweaty flanks and spoke up to him.

"Try the sign of the Twin Unicorns," he said. The man's deep, thickly accented voice carried over the sound of the crowd in the Lesser Market. "That's where your sort always goes. You'll find a room and welcome there, even in festival time, as long as your coin's good. Follow this lane till it crosses the Street of Swordmakers—you'll see a sign with three swords on the corner—and you'll see it on your left."

Falorn thanked him, then remembered the man's comments about coins. He reached into his purse and pulled out a pair of copper half-crown pieces—about what a generous knight might have given Falorn for grooming his horse at the Rat and Rooster—which he carefully slipped into the bearded man's palm. The man held Falorn's hand for a minute and gestured toward the youth's ear. Falorn leaned over so the man could speak to him without being overheard.

"If you're going to play knight," the man said, "you'll need to pay or not pay without looking like you care about the money. And keep close watch on that purse at festival time. The Twin Unicorns is a safe place, for a newfound knight, but there aren't many places in-city that's true of. When you get there, tell the innkeeper that Tevin sent you." He paused. "The real knights came a week ago for the duke's private games. They stay at his palace when they visit in-city, or at his hunting lodge in the forest."

The man lingered a moment before releasing Falorn's hand. A real knight would have been insulted, Falorn knew, but instead he pushed a silver twenty-crown piece into the bearded man's hand and turned the horse toward the sign of the Twin Unicorns.

The lane which led to the Street of Swordmakers was short, but with the festival crowds, it took Falorn the best part of an hour to maneuver the stallion over the bricked street. A mass of people filled the small square in front of the Twin Unicorns as well. Vendors lined the planked walkway which fronted the inn, thrusting wares in Falorn's face as he dismounted and looked for a stable boy to take his horse. After waiting for a long moment, he began leading the stallion toward the stable behind the inn himself, ignoring the hawkers selling meat-pies, and fireworks, and commemorative souvenirs in the duke's colors, and the thousand gods only knew what else.

I have to think like a knight, Falorn reminded himself, *or at least like a wealthy freeman-at-arms. I guess that's what I am now, anyway, whether or not I know how to use those arms.* He remembered Tevin's warning about pickpockets and felt for his sword and purse hurriedly, making certain that both remained in their places.

The crowds did not extend back into the inn's rear courtyard or the stable behind it. Only a pair of exhausted-looking kitchen maids sat on the barrels stacked against the rear wall of the inn, where they would be sheltered under the same long overhang which protected the woodpile and the kitchen door. The girls saw Falorn and froze, staring at him with terrified eyes like cornered rabbits, only looking away when it became clear he was walking his horse toward the stables and not them. As soon as he turned away from them they scurried back into the kitchen.

A two-story brick and wood barn held the stables. As Falorn led his horse through the open double doors, he saw two teenage stable boys frantically grooming and currying animals. Other mounts waiting to be groomed packed the stalls. A third, younger boy stood in the open upper level, raking down hay for the horses and mules below. Falorn found himself vaguely nostalgic at the familiar scent of the stable, even after only two days on the road. He cleared his throat, and all three boys looked at him and froze, with nearly the same expression as the kitchen maids.

"I want a clean stall for my horse," Falorn said, "and make certain you groom him next after the one you're doing now. I'll come back to check on him after I've eaten." He tossed a copper coin to each of the boys. *I hope I got the tone of voice I wanted—the one the rich merchants and their guards always use, just a little less harsh.* To his own ear, Falorn sounded like a hopeless rustic.

He saw evident relief in the three boys' eyes and posture when he shouldered his saddlebags and turned back toward the inn. *I'm sure I don't sound anything at all like a knight.* He hoped that his voice didn't betray his uncertainty to the serving staff.

The outer walls of the inn were constructed of the same gray-brown brick as all the other buildings in this quarter of Roicenet, dingy despite the crowds and festival. The second and third stories protruded outward on the sides of the building, supported by wooden columns which looked dangerously thin. The overhang came within a hand's width of touching the adjoining buildings in this district of close-set structures. It partially enclosed the elevated walkway of pine boards, as wide as a tall man and painted gray, which bordered the inn on the front and sides.

The brick and stone construction used in Roicenet allowed for tall buildings, and the Twin Unicorns' three stories did not tower over the neighborhood, although it stood slightly above most of the nearby structures.

The crowd at the front of the inn had swollen noticeably even in the few moments while Falorn walked his horse to the stables. He had to push to reach the swinging doors of the inn, although the bulk of the armor he wore made people give way.

The inn's faded sign swung ominously. Its brass-plated rod sagged from the weight of a fifteen-year-old who sat on it, having climbed out the second-story window on whose sill the rod was bolted. Oblivious to the creaking noises coming from the overstrained bolts and supporting ropes, the youth poured mugs of beer on the cheering crowd below. A companion inside the window took the empties away and refilled them from a bucket inside the room.

Falorn shouldered his way into the inn without waiting for the inevitable conclusion of the drama above. The Twin Unicorns' common room contained fewer people than he'd expected at a dinner hour, prob-ably because most visitors were celebrating outside at the festival. The room's dozen round tables sat empty, except for a pair of diners who occupied a corner table. Three men sat at the long bar that stretched across the far side of the commons, none of them too close to each other. Behind the bar perhaps fifty barrels were stacked two-high. They cov-ered the wall except in the corner, where a door led into the kitchens. Rough plank shelves above the barrels held empty flagons, along with bottles of wine and brandy. An enormous fireplace dominated the wall to Falorn's right, where a tired-looking barmaid tended pots of mulled wine and cider. At the same time, she turned a spit on which a whole roasting boar revolved. On the left hand wall, a rickety-looking wooden staircase led upward toward private rooms.

The inn was easily twice the size of his father's establishment.

An aproned innkeeper hurried forward from behind the bar, wiping the grease from his hands before bowing low to Falorn.

"Welcome, traveler, to my humble establishment." The innkeeper waved his arms expansively, in a way that hardly seemed humble, when Falorn requested a room for the night. "But you must realize that rooms are hard to come by at such short notice during festival time. Surely a man of your station cannot sleep in the commons."

No one with any visible property would sleep in the commons. Not if they expect to have that property when they wake up.

"Tevin sent me," Falorn told the innkeeper, so the bearded man could be sure to get his fee.

"In that case," said the innkeeper, "I'll give you the best room in the house, even though I have to turn out a group of pilgrims to clear it for you. I'll have to have fifty crowns for the room though, so I can give something to the temple of Ehres to forgive me for putting the pilgrims out in the cold."

Falorn nearly cursed the man for the ridiculous price, before remembering the part he played. *Would a knight care about fifty crowns paid to a greedy innkeeper?* A thrifty one would, he decided. *Just because a man carries arms and wears a full purse doesn't make him stupid.*

"Flames of Kerion!" Falorn cursed, an oath he'd heard a mercenary use once, "Do you take me for a fool? The best room in this hovel isn't worth fifteen crowns a night, not with hot water and meals besides! I'll give you twenty, only because it's festival time. And don't give me any drivel about pilgrims."

They finally agreed on twenty-five crowns for a room, hot water, and the next morning's meal, half to be paid on the spot. The price was still high, although the innkeeper looked slightly hurt that Falorn had haggled with him, and that he'd refused to give the innkeeper his name.

The question would have been impolite at his father's inn. City customs were different than country ones, Falorn knew, but he saw no reason to tell the man more than he had to. *I don't think that anyone looking for me would know my name, but it's best to keep it that way. If they find out my name they can find out where I come from, and I don't want to send trouble looking for my family.*

His ankle twinged a few times as he climbed two flights of creaking stairs to his third floor room. Two of the kitchen maids walked behind him, carrying a small tub of hot water between them. They waited nervously to be dismissed, and seemed genuinely surprised when he asked nothing more of them. Their eyes widened when he flipped each of them a copper half-crown from the change the innkeeper had given him. The two women, neither one as old as Falorn and both with the unmistakable haunted look of the tavernmaids his father hired, left hurriedly.

The room looked perhaps eight feet square, with plastered walls and plank floors smoothed by overuse rather than sanding. A single window looked out onto the roof of the smithy next door, with only a four hands' width gap between the two buildings. Within the room, the only furnishings were the tub, a low, circular table, and an uncarved wooden bed frame containing a straw pallet. A pair of sputtering tallow candles in iron sconces on either side of the door provided dim illumination.

Falorn dragged the tub over to the table's edge. Sitting on the table, he stripped the boots and wadded rags off his feet, unlaced the bottom fastenings on the ringed leggings, and rolled them up. He sat his feet in the tub to soak. He thought about removing the heavy armor entirely, but quickly decided against it. Underneath, he wore only the clothes of an innkeeper's runaway son. Armored, people seemed to overlook his rustic behavior; in peasant rags, he would hardly receive the same consideration. Oddly, no one seemed to think he had a rustic accent.

I wonder where I can find a used-clothing vendor in the festival. No, that's no good. A real knight would visit a tailor instead. He shook his head, almost laughing out loud at the strangeness of the situation. *You've got a fortune in your purse, and no idea at all of how to spend it. There must be some way that traveling freemen-at-arms get clothes in a hurry, when they don't have time to wait on a tailor. But I don't even know where to start looking, and I can't ask anyone without looking like the country-bred kid that I am.*

Falorn looked around for something to dry his feet with. *I guess the best thing to do is to go out into the festival. If there's anything to be found, I'll find it there. Besides, I didn't come to Roicenet at festival-time to spend all night in a tavern room. I may be a country-bred kid, but this looks like a good place to start learning about city ways.*

Falorn thought about the circus, and the black-haired woman with the roses. *How did she know about the cards?* he wondered. He felt a sudden urge to check on the card he carried. Quickly he fumbled at the pouch by his side, splashing the bath water at the sudden movement. When he slid the thin plaque from his pouch, it bathed the room in a gentle green glow. The green lion capered and pranced on the surface of the card, and this time Falorn knew that no trick of the flickering candle flames caused the movement. Something magical lived within the card's thin ivory, something far beyond his knowledge or understanding.

Magic!

Somehow, he would have to learn what it was and who it belonged to.

When he finally broke his gaze away from the surface of the card and slid it back into the pouch, he noticed the throbbing in his ankle was gone.

3

Night Meetings

An hour later, Falorn walked back down the stairs of the Twin Unicorns. The common room remained quiet as he wandered through it and out onto the street. Falorn had cleaned and wiped the armor as best he could with the bathwater and one of the green scraps of cloth he'd stuck in his boots the previous day. With oil and a whetstone brought from his father's inn, he'd cleaned and sharpened his belt knife. He'd checked the sword he had taken from the green knight's body as well. Its blade shone with a polished, mirror finish, and felt sharp to the touch. *However that man died, he didn't dull his sword defending himself.*

Falorn walked to the stables first. As he'd asked, the stallion had been groomed, and fed well. He flipped another half-crown piece to the oldest of the stable boys, who looked at Falorn with wide, scared eyes.

The crowd in front of the inn remained impossibly dense. Falorn skirted it entirely, walking around the edges of the square and retracing the path to the Lesser Market. Fireworks exploded overhead as he walked, arcing upward from a high tower beyond the square. Falorn couldn't help stopping to watch the brilliant explosions which shattered the sky overhead, exploding into violet whorls and red stars, green dragons that spun around and around chasing their own tails, giant blue puff-balls which spread outward like dandelion spoors.

Only the jostling of passersby brought his face back down to the market in front of him.

At ground level, the Lesser Market seemed less a sea of heads than from horseback, and more an endless forest of moving, brightly clothed bodies. He hesitated at the size of the crowd, and found himself stopping to gawk. *I can't believe the number of people here. They must have come from everywhere.* Another thought struck Falorn. *I bet there must be elves here, too. Maybe I'll be able to see elves again.* He scanned the crowd as carefully as he could from its outer edges, but saw only people in festival clothes. *Well, you'd best act the part of the traveling freeman-at-arms. You can't just stand here and stare forever.* He strode into the forest thicket with what he hoped looked like confidence.

The crowd gave him little choice of direction; he moved whichever way the mob surged. Soon, he found himself walking by endless, twisting lines of stalls—gaudily decorated at the night's beginning, but already looking worn and haggard even this early in the festival. The crowd eddied by a particular row of stalls, enough for Falorn to walk almost freely and to look at the wares offered.

The variety astonished him. Falorn found it hard to avoid buying everything at first, half-drunk with the heady feeling of having goods available and money to buy them. First he gazed at decorative silk scarves, dyed fantastic pastel shades and edged with knotted fringes of gold and silver thread. They looked like fairy-tale garments, scarves to woo noblewomen with, scarves princesses gave to their champions before sending them off to die in faraway wars. *You don't know any princesses,* he thought to himself, *and you're not ever likely to.* Reluctantly, he moved on to the next stall.

He bought a pair of small meat-pies from a second vendor. He hadn't eaten in almost a day, and Falorn ate the pies almost without tasting the pungent spices whose aroma had drawn him to the stall. Only after finishing did he realize he'd never tasted anything quite like them before. Unfamiliar spices edged the lingering flavor of meat, onions, and garlic. Embarrassed, he wiped at the juices which stained his mouth and chin.

A third stand provided him with a matching tooled-leather belt and baldric. The tanner loved to haggle. After exchanging money and pleasantries, Falorn began looking for something to drink.

He felt a tug at his new belt.

A small, hooded man slipped away from him as Falorn looked up, and he realized one of his pouches was gone. He shouted and began running after the man, at the same time thanking all the thousand gods that the thief had taken his old pouch from home, and not the one with his money—and with the card.

I'll never catch him in this armor, he thought, but at the same time, Falorn seemed to be gaining on the thief. The man ran awkwardly toward the edges of the crowd. He turned to flee into an alley formed by the back panels of a row of booths, where they nearly abutted the back wall of a warehouse.

Falorn chased him, furious and excited at the same time.

Halfway down the lumber-strewn alley, the man stopped, turned, and whistled.

Falorn's stomach dropped with sudden realization. Three more men stepped out from behind a pile of thick, weathered boards. All three held long, thin knives, the blades reflecting in the light from the single lantern which illuminated the alley. As he watched, the first thief drew a knife as well, and all four advanced in unison.

Falorn stepped sideways to put his back to the warehouse wall, glancing at the mouth of the alley to make sure no one approached from that side. *Why are they moving so slowly?* he wondered. Then he realized.

Because you're wearing a sword, you idiot. He had almost forgotten again. He didn't know how to use it, but none of these four knew that, yet.

He reached down, and the blade seemed to leap from the sheath and into his hand. He screamed, and swung again and again. Closing his eyes, he put all his strength into his arms as the first two cutthroats came at him.

I missed, he thought, as his blade encountered no resistance. Something thunked against his stomach.

Falorn stumbled to the side. Only the wall at his back held him upright. Liquid sprayed his face and chest. His ears rang from the screaming.

I'm going to die, he thought, tasting blood on his face. *They've killed me in this stupid alley because I was too stupid to stay at home where I belonged.*

Why can't I feel anything yet, he wondered. *Is this what it feels like to die, just numb, no pain?*

Then he realized he wasn't the one screaming.

After a minute, he got his breath back and opened his eyes.

A headless body lay sprawled on the ground at his feet. Not far off, dead eyes looked up at him. The severed head had bounced off his stomach and rolled against the rear of a booth. The screaming came from the second attacker, who clutched at the stump of his knife hand. Blood rapidly pumped onto the ground. The dying thief looked disbelievingly at Falorn and his voice faded. The man pitched forward into the mud formed by the packed-earth street and his own puddled blood.

The other two men had vanished.

Falorn looked at the sword in his hand. Its blade shone in the lanternlight, unblemished except for a few drops of blood. He felt the edge, and found it as sharp as before. Carefully, Falorn pulled a rag from his boot, and wiped and sheathed the sword.

Then he began to shake.

By the time he stopped trembling and regained control of his muscles, a dark suspicion formed in his mind. *This wasn't just about robbing someone who looked rich and lost.* Methodically, he began searching the blood-soaked bodies of the dead thieves. He recovered his own stolen pouch quickly; otherwise the first body yielded only a handful of copper coins and a pair of ebony-hilted knives—one of them a boot knife with its curved blade coated with some viscous substance. Falorn left the knives with the corpse. On the second body, he found what he expected.

Sheathing the second thief's knife in his boot, he walked over to the pile of lumber where his attackers had placed their lantern. Gently, Falorn emptied the man's pouch onto a flat board. He whistled softly at the results. Forty-two gold coins littered the makeshift table, and eighteen stones which had to be rubies and sapphires. A heavy gold ring proved to be some sort of signet-ring, with a curious wasp emblem on its surface. Last of all he found another card, identical to the one in his pouch except for the picture, which couldn't have been any more different.

The blue thief on the card looked as real as the ones who had assaulted him—like a living miniature of a pickpocket or cutpurse. The card emitted a faint cobalt glow as he held it. It felt curiously warm to the touch. After a minute of thought, he put the new card in the green knight's pouch with the other one. The gold and gems he returned carefully to the new pouch. He still wore a leather thong around his neck, where he had carried his key to the Rat and Rooster. Now he tied the new pouch to it, and tucked it in so it hung underneath his armor and clothing, against his skin. Now, at least, he couldn't lose everything at once. He thought about moving the cards into the pouch around his neck as well, but decided against it. *Best to keep them farther from my heart until I know what they really do.*

Rags cut from the dead thieves' clothes helped mop up some of the blood that covered him, but Falorn needed new garments quickly. In the night and crowds, he might be just another wine-soaked fairgoer, but the deception wouldn't last until morning. He took the lantern with him as he left the alley, leaving blackness behind him until sunrise. He supposed the screams had been lost amid the noises of celebration, or at least no one had chosen to investigate back-alley commotions. Hopefully, the bodies would remain undiscovered for a few hours. With a little more luck, in the festive atmosphere no one would think too much about the red-soaked stranger searching for a used-clothing vendor.

Falorn gave thanks to Mara and Kerion for helping him to find the Street of Clothing Sellers, which adjoined the Lesser Market. He bought the first oversized cloak which came to hand for nearly the asking price; only after covering himself with the cloak's layers of musty green fabric did he shop more slowly and carefully.

An hour later, he carried a creditable variety of clothing, better by far than anything he'd ever worn—though perhaps not up to the standards of most wandering knights. At least he now owned what could pass for a freeman-at-arms's traveling clothes. He wouldn't look quite so rustic if he took off his armor. Most important, he paid two hundred crowns for a pair of horseman's boots that fit him properly.

After buying the clothing, Falorn began walking back toward the Twin Unicorns. Fireworks continued to explode overhead. The mob had become even more exuberant than before. Falorn hadn't even begun to explore the wonders of the city at festival-time, much less find the circus— and the black-haired Sheanna. But tonight at least, any celebratory spirit the city inspired in him had died along with the thieves in the alley. Now he mostly wanted the security of a locked room, a warm bed, and sleep.

By the time he actually got back to the inn, Falorn's spirits had revived somewhat. He ordered a pot of ale and a plate of roast meat in the still-quiet commons and took them up to his room with him. Once in the small chamber, he stripped off the mail hauberk and ring leggings at last. Tearing his old shirt into rags, he began using the cold bathwater and scraps of cloth to cleanse himself and the armor.

When he had finally scrubbed himself as much as possible with the means at hand, he began trying on his new clothing, in between bites of meat and swallows from the bucket of ale.

By the time the not-unexpected knock came at the door, he wore soft, snug-fitting doeskin britches, which tucked into his thigh-length boots below and fastened with a leather drawstring at the waist; a black woolen tunic embroidered with green at sleeves, shoulders, and hem and belted at the waist with his new tooled-leather belt; and a short vest, also of doeskin and laced together at the front. Falorn had fastened his old knife and two pouches to the belt. The new pouch hung inside the tunic around his neck. His sword swung at his left side from the baldric. He had shaved away his two-day growth of beard, and pulled his tousled, shoulder-length brown hair into some semblance of order.

Falorn's first impulse was to call out to the kitchen maid to go away, that he didn't want company. *Only I do*, he realized. Not the kind of company she offered, maybe, but for the first time since leaving home two days before, Falorn felt terribly lonely.

Lifting himself from the bed where he sat, Falorn walked over to the locked door and quietly drew the bolt back. His breath felt suddenly ragged in his mouth and his body felt cramped, even in his new clothes. He wondered what he should do.

He thought back to long hours spent in the cramped attic storeroom of the Rat and Rooster, watching his father's barmaids and their customers through chinks in the ceilings above their rooms. He'd even fantasized about such scenes, but he'd awkwardly declined on the several occasions—after other festival times, when his father always treated the staff to a keg of his best Roadwark-brewed beer—one or another of the barmaids had offered to help him celebrate. At other times when he might have taken one of them up on an offer, he had found himself unable to ask. He wasn't shy otherwise, and he never really knew why he had turned them down; he just somehow couldn't bring himself to accept.

How would a knight act? he thought. Steeling himself, Falorn opened the door.

In the hallway, with her arm poised to again knock softly on his door, stood Sheanna, the raven-haired woman from the circus.

"W . . . what are you doing here?" Falorn managed to stammer, mentally cursing at the foolish sound of his own voice.

"Why, coming to see you, of course. Do you think I knock on every door in the city?"

Falorn didn't know what to think. From a distance on the road, she had looked alluring; up close she overwhelmed him. Her poise, her sultry voice, even the scent she exuded, all hit Falorn like rich winter wine. He could barely focus enough to understand what she said, much less to reply.

She seemed to realize as much, and softened her tone.

"Aren't you going to ask me in, Green Knight? I'm going to get cold out here."

Wordlessly, he stepped aside and allowed her to enter the room. She walked around the entire room, trailing a hand against the bare plaster walls, like a cat exploring a new place. She glanced pointedly at the bed, but then walked back to where Falorn stood frozen to the floor. She stood too close in front of him. He felt her breath on his neck, felt the muscles in his chest contract where her breasts nearly touched him. Sheanna was almost as tall as him, Falorn noticed.

She smelled of wild roses.

Falorn felt as if he stood very far away and was just watching events unfold, but at the same time he found himself remarkably sensitive to every movement, every sound, every scent within the room.

She still wore the same clothing she had worn while driving the wagon; but Falorn saw no trace of dust on her, smelled nothing but the scent of wild roses, intoxicating in their hidden presence.

"Close the door," she said very quietly. Falorn reached out his right hand and swung the door shut, throwing the bolt with another quick motion. Almost unbidden, he felt his left hand come up and begin to softly trace the embroidered roses that laced the surface of her vest.

She moaned slightly. Languidly, she pulled him close to her, her breast pressing his left hand, her body touching his chest, legs, arms, groin. His face felt hot and flushed as his blood stirred. His erection chafed where it rubbed the inside of his new britches.

He looked down at her face at the same moment she looked up into his. Their lips met and parted. Falorn felt all his senses melting as their tongues met. In the last moment before he submerged, he thought he saw something in her eyes, something very far away, like a wild rose glimpsed across a distant, thorny field. And then he let go, and immersed himself within her.

He didn't resist when she guided him gently to the lumpy straw mattress. She reached into his tunic and began running her fingers softly over his chest. The fingernails of her other hand gently scratched his back. She nudged him downward, and he began fumbling with the laces of her hose, finally managing to untie them despite the haze drifting through his head and the almost unbearable sensations he felt as she caressed his chest, ran her tongue along his neck and upper back.

He finally freed the laces from her hose and slid the fabric down her legs to uncover the olive skin beneath. He was unsure what she wanted at first as she nudged him downward again but then, remembering hours watching the barmaids through the chinks in the attic ceiling, he realized, and lowered his head to her thighs, nearly drowning in the thickness of the musky-rose scent. Her hand crept down his back as he did so, languorously sliding into his britches, along his buttocks, gently squeezing one cheek, and then around the side, exploring until she caressed him, slowly squeezing and rubbing him. All the while her other hand continued to fondle his chest, massaging him, running her fingers in gentle circles around his nipples.

As his lips met the top of her thigh he saw she had a tattoo: a pair of twined roses, one red and one pink, their thorny stems winding together and wending around her thigh and calf, their blooms side by side on the inner surface of her right thigh. The thorns became clearer and detailed before him as she spread her legs slightly and nudged his head downward. His sweat mixed with her musk, and he tasted salt and rose.

From far away, he heard a pounding. At first he thought it was his heart, or the blood in his head, but finally he realized the echoing, frantic sound came from the door.

He sat up, the mood abruptly altered as if a spell had suddenly broken. A girl's voice came from outside the door.

"Sir! There are soldiers outside looking for you! You have to run away!" The voice belonged to one of the kitchen maids who had carried the tub to his room earlier. Listening, he heard the heavy bootsteps of armored men below, even over the festival noises in the background.

"They're coming!" she called out again, and then ran away. But by then he could hear the armored footsteps on the stair. He quickly tightened his britches and belt, tucked his tunic in, and picked up the baldric and sword from where he'd discarded them near the bed. The olive-skinned woman dressed quickly as well. Her expression looked agitated and turbulent.

A mailed glove pounded on the door.

"This way," Falorn called to her, beckoning to the window. "It's the only way out."

"No, you fool," she said. "Give me the card! Quickly, before it's too late."

Her remark stunned him momentarily, but heavier pounding on the door quickly revived him. The wood around the lock and hinges began splintering.

"This way," he said urgently, as he clambered out the window, motioning once again for her to follow. He leaped to the roof of the smithy and sprinted over it without looking back.

Four roofs later, prone behind the shelter of a decorative cornice, he finally turned around to look.

The woman had not followed.

Somehow, I didn't expect her to, Falorn admitted to himself. He had lost the green knight's armor as well, and the beautiful, spirited stallion. *But I still have clothes, money . . . and the cards, which everyone in this city seems to want so badly.*

A sudden thought struck him. *She said* card, *not* cards. *She doesn't know I found the second one. But I don't even know how she knew I had the first.*

He glimpsed armored men in green surcoats as they passed the window of his old room. He could hear them ransacking the room, the noise carrying over the festival sounds. He hoped they wouldn't find the kitchen maid who had warned him, that she could disappear into the festival before they started questioning the innkeeper and his workers.

He didn't see any sign of Sheanna. *I wonder if she has a way to get out, or if she's already found a way to escape. Maybe the same magic that let her look into my mind so easily can save her against the soldiers.*

One of the men abruptly screamed. A flash of brilliant white light blinded Falorn. By the time the spots cleared from his vision, the screaming had stopped.

Flames licked at the upper floor of the Twin Unicorns. Falorn smelled charred flesh on the night breeze.

He staggered to his feet, and began making his way as far from the inn as he could.

4

Discoveries and Concealments

Falorn could barely hear the festival from the deserted back street. About an hour remained before daybreak, and Falorn had finally escaped the noise of the festival and of the bells which began ringing after he fled the inn. He didn't know if the bells summoned people to fight the fire, or if they called out the city guard to catch him. He continued down the long, empty street, idly counting the street lanterns. *Maybe I can slip out of the city after daylight, after the gates open*, he thought. *The guards did let me through once already.* The odds seemed doubtful, but no better idea presented itself. Even at festival time with all curfews suspended or ignored, the city guard shut the gates after sundown.

A small figure in a dark hooded robe stepped out from a doorway.

"Come here, you idiot!" the figure called out in a boyish voice. This second stranger's insult of the night shocked Falorn less than the first one had, but he assumed the implication was the same—someone else wanted to take the cards away from him.

He turned around and began to run wearily in the opposite direction.

"Come back here!" the stranger shouted from behind him, voice rising in pitch. "Are you crazy? They'll catch you!"

He ducked around the corner and found himself on a street filling with armored men in green surcoats. Three of them stood in his path. Two others came from either side to block his exit. Before he could even find a wall to get his back to, the armored men surrounded him.

Breathing raggedly after hours of running and climbing, Falorn drew his sword for the second time that night. But this time he faced seven trained, armored soldiers carrying longswords—not unarmored thieves with knives.

He began swinging as they slowly closed with him, hoping the magic of the alley would return. He felt stronger as his blood began pumping. Falorn kept his eyes open this time, and smiled grimly as he drew first blood, nicking one of his opponents on the hand.

A moment later a sword slashed across his hand in exactly the same place. He looked across at the man he'd wounded, and saw nothing in the man's eyes at all. He fought three of them at once while the others stood a few yards away and watched. Falorn felt a sense of exhilaration, all fear gone in the first second of combat. He took care to watch all of them, amazed at his own new ability to follow so many things at once. It felt like time itself had slowed down to give him the extra moments he needed to fight off so many men at once.

Falorn cut a second man on the thigh, his sword flickering through the iron mesh of the man's armor as if through ringlets of woven silk. The slash pulled him off balance, and the two other swordsmen pushed through Falorn's guard before he could recover. They beat down his sword as he tried to parry.

"Enough play," one of the watching men said in a deep voice. "Finish him."

Pain shot into his side like an axe into soft pine. Falorn doubled over, spitting blood while his free hand clutched the bubbling gash in his torso. He stumbled to avoid another swordstroke and fell to his knees.

The left side of his body went numb. *They weren't trying to kill me at all*, he realized in the clarity of fading consciousness. *I was at their mercy the whole time. I only wounded the two men because they held back their blows to avoid killing me.*

As his sight faded into visions of other times and places, he thought he saw movement, as if the green soldiers fled from new asttackers. Hallucinations, he knew.

Mouthing a prayer to the fire-goddess Kerion, his favorite of the thousand gods—though hardly the appropriate goddess to invoke at the moment—he sank numbly to the ground. As awareness fled, he wondered for the first time why he had left home.

For what seemed like days, Falorn floated on a cushion of air. For a long time, he just let himself float, arms spread like a drowned man. After a while, he felt someone spooning what tasted like salty chicken broth into his mouth. Still, he didn't move, as if he had lost the will, or his muscles had lost the ability.

He felt the warmth of the sun on him and basked, like a housecat in summertime. Only when the sun shifted did Falorn finally open his eyes.

He lay on the most enormous bed he had ever seen, a gigantic feather-stuffed cushion as long as two men, and as wide as three. Three posts, all as thick as Falorn's thigh, supported the foot of the bed, each post carved into the aspect of a benevolent spirit.

Above Falorn's head, a white silk canopy had been rolled back to let in the sun. He twisted his head slightly to look at the headboard, carved with hundreds of cavorting spirits and faeries, the kind described in children's tales. A quilted goosedown comforter covered him so heavily that it nearly pinned him to the bed. Colorful scenes covered the quilt, which looked more like a tapestry than a comforter.

Falorn winced as he moved his shoulders. He slid his arms over to his chest slowly and felt layers of bandages wrapped around him. His side ached and pulled at the movement. In spite of the pain, he pushed himself upright. Long strips of fresh, wide bandages covered his midsection like a shroud. The bandages looked clean and white, so he supposed his wound had stopped bleeding.

He lay in a rectangular room almost as large as the commons in his father's inn. Two high, arched windows on the wall to his right showed nothing but blue sky. An identical window in the wall forty paces in front of him showed the same, so he knew the room was elevated above ground level. He could see no other buildings, nor the city's high walls and towers. Maroon velvet cushions padded all three windowbays. Tapestries and hangings covered the walls, except for the long wall to his left, which held a massive fireplace, with a large teak armoire beyond it. Four matching teak chairs surrounded a round table with a top of polished pink marble. On top of the table a crystal ball reflected back at him from a gilded tripod. Two armchairs sat against the far wall, one on either side of the window. The wall to his right sheltered a dresser and a large hanging mirror between two long tapestries. Polished brass wall-sconces along all four walls held rich wax candles, unlit at the moment. Thick, woven rugs covered most of the floor.

A bookcase, a cloak stand, and a night-table at either side of the bed completed the room's furniture. Falorn counted nearly forty volumes on the bookcase's five shelves—more books than even Lumni, the scribe in Briarcliff, owned. Rather than the tattered, flaking covers he had seen on books, the gold foil and burnished leather covers of the books on the shelves glistened in the spring sunlight. One of the two night-tables held his clothing, neatly folded, with his sword, belts, and pouches carefully set on top. A number of garments hung from the cloak stand—a heavy fur-lined cape, a light hunting cloak, several formal jackets in sky-blue and black, a heavy black hooded cape.

Falorn recognized the last garment, which bore a distinctively cut front and silver buttons. The cape belonged to the person who had tried to warn him, right before he'd been attacked.

A key scratched in the lock of the nearer door. The door opened slightly, and a woman about his own age slipped in carrying a covered silver platter. She looked unsurprised to see him awake. Quickly, she brought a finger to her lips to motion him to silence. After carefully closing and bolting the door, the woman walked over to the bed, setting the tray down on the night-table, and sat on the mattress beside him.

"Welcome back to the land of the living," the woman said, with a laugh in her voice. She had light brown, shoulder-length hair and a plain face, with strikingly deep brown eyes. A bruise discolored her left cheek slightly. About a hand smaller than Falorn, the woman looked a little less than full-figured—not thin, but not buxom either. A chain of thick gold links belted her blue velvet dress, worn over dark leggings. Up close, she looked a little older than Falorn.

Falorn tried to say something, but coughed instead. Pain flared in his side.

"That's fine, don't thank me. I only saved your life at great personal risk, dragged you back here where my father would kill us both if he knew, and singlehandedly nursed you back to health."

She paused for a moment. "Actually, my father's men did some of that, or at least, some of my father's men who are loyal to me, but I ordered them to, so it's the same thing, really."

"Thank you," Falorn finally managed to say. "Who are you?"

"I think *you* should be answering that question before *I* do . . . but I will anyway, since it doesn't look like you're going to be much of a talker for a while. Here . . . if you can move, eat your soup while we talk." The young woman reached over for the tray and placed it on Falorn's lap, removing the cover to show a matching silver bowl and spoon beneath. She pushed a spoonful of broth into his mouth teasingly, like one would for a baby. She clasped his right hand in both of hers to hand him the spoon, as if they were lovers exchanging a great endearment.

"Where am I?" he asked after several spoonfuls of soup, since she hadn't actually answered his first question.

"Curious today, aren't we? We must be feeling *much* better. My name is Sera. My father is the Duke of Roicenet, which you would have figured out if you'd looked at the cloaks hanging in the corner there." She pointed to the cloak stand, with its sky-blue and black inhabitants. "You're here because—aside from any normal humanitarian instincts which might have caused me to rescue some lost boy from the country-side being attacked by foreign mercenaries—you happen to hold two magical cards which I would like very much to see."

She smiled before continuing. "By the way, my father owns five more of the cards. If he finds out you're here, he will kill you to take yours . . . and also because he found you sleeping in his nubile young daughter's bed."

"I'm sorry if I've put you out," Falorn said, sounding incredibly naive even to himself. "Where have you been sleeping?"

"It's a big bed," she said, smiling again. "Now finish your soup and go to sleep. You still have a lot of healing to do." She walked over to the bookcase, selected a book, and sat with it at the marble table. Falorn noticed that she didn't so much as glance down at the pages in front of her until he finished the soup and lay back down.

He slept and woke four more times before Sera allowed him to get up out of the bed. Again, his body healed with remarkable rapidity; by the end of three days' time—and only five days after Sera's men carried him in off the street—he felt only twinges of pain when he moved his side or shoulder.

Over those days, Sera had encouraged Falorn to tell her his whole story. She spoke little of herself, but listened closely to his account, asking questions frequently. He told her everything, even the parts about the woman with the rose. She even laughed when Falorn explained how her attempt to warn him had echoed the dark lady's language.

"Thanks," he said when Sera helped him up for the first time, "I thought you were going to make me stay in that bed forever."

"Don't flatter yourself," she replied, causing Falorn to blush.

"Actually, I don't have much choice but to get you up and moving. My father's been away at his hunting lodge with a lot of festival dandies, but he's due back today. I'll have to get you out of here pretty soon after that or he'll catch you."

"Why not before he gets back, then? I'm almost healed."

"You're not as healed as you think you are. Do you think you could take on those alley-thieves now? Or the soldiers I rescued you from?"

"I know I'm not all the way healed," Falorn said, a little frustrated at being trapped in the room, despite Sera's company. "But I would like to *live* long enough to finish healing. And from what you've said, your father may not want that."

"I wouldn't worry *too* much about him. He's not that likely to come looking for me here. He just sends for me when he wants me. I have three older brothers, so I'm not exactly vital to court functions. And the maids have been afraid to come in here for months, ever since I caught one of them trying to steal a book." Falorn wondered what she meant, but decided to stick to more important questions.

"But what if he does?"

"If he does, then we hide you. Don't worry, I've made plans. And I *will* get you out of here safely. You're just going to have to trust me and do it my way, though."

"And until then I stay here?"

"Until then you stay here. Did you expect me to call one of the soldiers to give you a tour?"

Falorn sighed.

"Now, don't get that way. I want you to tell me more about your father's inn. You're only going to be here for a few days longer, and it's not often I get to talk to a real, live peasant." She smiled to show she was joking, but the words still stung a little. Falorn had only to watch her reading at night or writing letters to remember that the differences between them went far beyond breeding and money. He found himself much less awed by the room than he was by his rescuer and temporary companion.

He had most of the daylight hours to himself. Sera told him vaguely that she had daytime duties to perform around the castle and city. As soon as he found himself alone again, Falorn recovered his clothing from the night-table and put it back on.

After buckling on his belt, he nervously checked the contents of the pouches, pouring each one carefully out onto the bed. Nothing had been taken—or even looked at—as far as he could tell. Everything seemed as he had left it, except for his tunic and vest, which someone had cleaned and mended.

The cards glowed exactly as he remembered them, blue and green figures capering within their own stages. He held them carefully for a long time before replacing them in the pouch by his side. Sera had not mentioned the cards since that first time she'd spoken to him, and he hadn't felt like it was his place to bring them up.

A cold-blooded thought struck him. *I wonder why she didn't just take them, and leave me to die. What use am I to her alive, and in possession of these cards? I'm glad she went looking for me and saved me, but there has to be something she saved me for, that she doesn't want to tell me yet.*

He began exploring the room. Remembering Sera's mention of the maid, Falorn carefully tried not to disturb anything, particularly not the books. He gazed longingly at the indecipherable gold letters on the bindings until the characters twisted like tiny worms struggling to free themselves from invisible hooks.

Sitting in one of the paired armchairs, Falorn gazed out the window between them. It looked out onto the Greater Market far below, bustling now even though the festival had ended two days previously. Obviously Sera's chamber stood high up in the Duke's castle, perhaps even in one of the towers. The other two windows overlooked the rear of the city walls. Falorn could see green, rolling hills beyond the walls, covered with forest where they neared the horizon.

He looked at each of the tapestries and wall hangings in turn. On a whim, he looked behind the tapestry on the inside wall, and discovered a small opening with a tiny chamber behind it. The chamber contained only a bench, a small writing table, and an inkpot. It exited by a waist-high door into what he supposed was a tunnel beyond. *I guess the Duke pays a little more attention to Sera than she seems to think.* He replaced the tapestry carefully, trying to leave no sign of any disturbance. *More likely she knows about it already, and makes sure her father only sees what she wants him to.*

Falorn moved on to the armoire, curious what sort of clothing a

Duke's daughter would need. The stench of mothballs, dust, and musty clothes struck him. Only half of the armoire held clothes, and many of those looked old, stained, worn, or badly outgrown. Sera clearly used the rest of the space to store anything she couldn't easily clean without the help of maids. Supporting himself with a hand on the back wall of the armoire, he leaned over to explore the closest pile of Sera's disarranged possessions.

Something felt wrong about the back wall. Falorn couldn't quite figure out why. He ran his hands along the veneer which covered it. One seam bulged inward slightly; all the others pushed outward. He felt downward along the seam. Nearly at the base of the armoire, in the middle of the largest pile of rags and unmended clothes, he found the catch. When he sprung it, one of the rear panels slid aside, revealing a second hidden chamber.

The little room had no other outlet. Its furnishings clearly belonged to Sera, rather than her father's spies. Try as he might, however, Falorn could make no sense of those possessions. Drab traveling clothes hung on hooks, ranging from peasants' garments to the sort of freeman's garb Falorn now wore. Two saddles sat on a small, plain rug which covered the floor, along with bags of dried meat and cheeses. A crossbow leaned against one corner, along with a quiver of bolts. The first of two small chests contained four beautiful, black-hilted knives, exquisitely balanced for fighting or throwing, as well as a vial half-full of a thick blue liquid. Falorn put the vial down quickly and moved on to the second chest, which held five colorful crystal decanters. Falorn closed the chest without examining the contents of the containers. Several pouches sat on a shelf along the back wall. The first bulged with thousands of crowns in silver and gold coins. A second pouch held a handful of small gold bars. Within the third pouch, Falorn found the cards.

Sera owned two of them: the first a pair of blue twins in remarkable shades of azure and cobalt, and the second a voluptuous, crimson-skinned woman reclining seductively on a scarlet chair in a room made up of a thousand shades of red.

Something clicked within the wall. Falorn quickly replaced the cards in their pouch on the shelf. He stepped toward the closet door to get back in the room before Sera, then stopped abruptly. The noise came from inside the wall itself—someone had entered the hidden room behind the tapestry, next to the little space where he hid. Falorn carefully pulled the door of the armoire closed. Stepping back into the secret chamber on tiptoes, Falorn silently slid the back of the armoire into place, sealing himself in darkness.

Floorboards creaked only a few feet away, and a bolt rustled in a disused lock. Falorn heard weapons and armor scraping as several people crawled through the small doorway of the secret chamber behind the tapestry. The wall-hanging rustled as someone pushed it aside to enter Sera's room. A harsh voice spoke from within the secret room; Falorn could easily hear through the thin wall beside him.

"Search everything. Don't be afraid to make a mess of the room. I can buy new furniture—I can buy a new *daughter* if I want one—but I have to have those cards back."

"What if she has them, Lord?" a soldier's voice asked.

"Her brothers will attend to that. I'll have none of you rabble touching her until I know she's got them."

"And if she does?"

"If she does, I'll put her on the Hook myself."

Wood scraped and shuddered as soldiers ransacked Sera's room. It seemed to much to hope for that the duke would be unaware of a secret passage within his own castle. Falorn could only hope the secret of the room had died with some previous tenant of the castle, before the current duke's occupancy.

He stood motionlessly in the darkness; under his breath Falorn thanked the thousand gods for the impulse that made him put on all his clothing and take all his possessions before he went exploring. He suspected that any unknown man found in the castle in possession of stolen cards would be put on the duke's Hook, regardless of whose bedroom he occupied.

Falorn heard the thump of books hitting the floor. The wall-hangings tore with shrieking noises like children in pain. One of the searchers began rooting through the armoire itself, tossing out the rubbish and banging a mailed gauntlet on the side and rear looking for secret compartments. The thick wood made a dull knocking sound, leaving the hollow area behind hidden.

How come trained soldiers can't find it, when I found it so easily? He couldn't think of an answer that made any sense.

Falorn lost track of time long before the searchers ran out of furniture. Through it all the duke continued to stand in the spy-passage, his presence communicated by shuffling boots or the occasional cough.

Eventually, even the duke gave up.

"Enough. She doesn't have them. That girl's not smart enough to put them anywhere you haven't looked."

"Where should we look now, Lord?"

"Go torture some servants. One of them's bound to tell you something. I don't care if you have to kill every servant in the place, I need those cards."

"We'll find them, Lord."

"I know you will. If those cards aren't back in my purse in two days, I'll find another captain of the guard. Remember how you got your position, Doran. Remember how long Hasek lasted on the Hook after he failed me."

"They will be found, Lord, and the thief brought to justice," the guard said. Falorn heard fear in the man's voice.

"See that they are."

The guards left hurriedly, using the door rather than stooping to re-enter the secret passage. The Duke stamped his feet once, and entered the room for the first time. Falorn barely breathed within his hiding place as the Duke walked a circuit of the room, much as Falorn himself had done earlier. The Duke searched more quietly than his soldiers had, slowly checking and rechecking every piece of furniture, probing and tapping the walls with a sword or cane.

Once again, the door opened. Falorn heard two new sets of footsteps, one heavy and one light, and heavy breathing from two mouths.

"Father! What have you done to my room?" Sera shouted hoarsely, her voice ragged as if she'd been crying.

"Only what you deserved, I'm sure," a new voice said. Falorn instantly disliked the rich, deep, young man's voice, which must have belonged to one of Sera's older brothers. "I didn't find the cards, but I still think the little whore stole them."

"Maybe not," said the duke. "They're not here. I'm having some servants tortured. They'll tell us the truth."

"She'll tell us. Half an hour with the Minister of Pain . . . "

"Son! Watch your tongue." The duke sounded genuinely shocked. "Say what you want about your sister among family members, but she is not for commoners to touch." He paused.

"If you did steal what belongs to me," he went on, now speaking to Sera, "I'll tear you on the Hook myself. But no commoner will touch you."

"I don't know what you're talking about!" Sera wailed. "I didn't take anything."

"Yes you did, you little slut," her brother said. "You're nothing but evil. Father should have had you drowned like a kitten when you were born—when you killed Mother. You're an evil seed in the castle."

"That's enough of that, son. Let your mother's memory lie. I let the girl live then, and I'll let her live now. Unless she took the cards . . . and the servants will tell us that soon enough. Come with me now. We have work to do." He stomped his boots on the bare floor, no longer muffled by the rug.

"You had better pray, girl," he said to Sera as he opened the door. "I've been too kind to you, spoiled you out of love for your mother. You killed a fine woman, a better woman than you could ever be.

"If you stole my cards, I'll feed you to my dogs after I've cut you from the Hook. If not, I've had enough of your willfulness anyway. You'll be gone from this house within the month—you know where."

He strode out of the room. Falorn heard the dull thump of fist on flesh. Sera cried out as her brother struck her twice. Falorn bit his lip to keep quiet. Her brother stomped from the room, slamming the door behind him with a last muttered insult at his sister.

Falorn waited another hour before emerging from the secret chamber, just to be certain the duke and his soldiers would not return. He found Sera slumped against the overturned bookcase, head in her hands. A torn volume sat in her lap. Tapestries and wall hangings littered the floor, along with disarranged heaps of clothing and paper. The floor and walls near the bed wore a dustlike coating of down and feathers from the slashed mattress and pillows. With the covering stripped from in front of it, the entrance to the Duke's secret passageway stood revealed.

Falorn touched her shoulder gently. Sera looked up, eyes distant for a moment but quickly focusing on him. Purpled skin around one eye revealed where one of her brother's blows had struck. Blood seeped from a cut on her forehead. He thought she'd been crying, but her eyes looked dry.

"Well, I guess you *are* healed enough," she said unexpectedly. "We're leaving tonight. Now, actually. I assume you found my hiding place?" She looked at him guardedly, and he guessed at the right answer.

"Yes. I hid when I heard them coming through the other passage. I couldn't see anything in the dark, though."

She looked a little relieved.

"I'll be back in a few minutes," she told him. "I have a few things I need to get before we go."

"You're going back out there? After what they . . ." he stopped when he saw the look that started to cross her face. "Why?" he asked instead.

"Because I'm not an innkeeper's son who can just pick up and go. I have a life here, and people I care about and who have helped me that I'm never going to see again. I want to say goodbye to them. Is that all right with you?"

"I was just worried. . . ."

"Don't be. You heard my father. He and my brothers will be busy torturing servants all night, and no one else in this place can touch me. I can take care of myself without your worry, thank you."

"Should I hide in the passage while you're gone?" he asked, suspecting now how she was going to answer.

"No! . . . I mean yes, I mean . . . wait a minute." An odd expression crossed her face, and then Sera rushed to the half-ruined armoire and nearly flung herself into the darkened passage, closing it behind her. Moments later she emerged again, wearing a relieved look and a set of traveling clothes not unlike Falorn's own. She noticed Falorn's scowl.

"Look, I'm sorry. I didn't mean to insult your background. I've just been through a lot today. I'm feeling a little short-tempered." She pleaded with her eyes, the blackened one nearly swollen shut.

"It's all right," Falorn said tiredly. "I owe you a lot for rescuing me. I guess I'm just scared that there are all these people running around trying to kill me, and I have no idea why except that it has something to do with these cards that you won't tell me anything about." He hadn't meant to say so much, but the words came out anyway.

"I know I haven't told you everything, but you've been hurt, and I didn't have time. I'll tell you more once we're on the road. We're going to be partners, right?" She reached out for his hand, and he extended it, reluctantly.

"Partners?"

"Of course. You didn't think I was just going to keep things secret forever, did you? It just isn't safe to talk about them here. And believe me, I do want you to travel with me, and I do need your help. Not just because I saved your life and nursed you back to health, either." She squeezed his hand before releasing it.

"Things are going to be fine, you'll see," she said. "Wait in the secret room with the door shut; I lit a lantern for you in there, so you'll be able to see. I'll be back as quickly as I can."

She blew a kiss to him as she turned to the door. Falorn still felt a little confused, but he could do little except wait for her to come back and explain her plan. He walked back to the armoire, looking sadly at the ruined books on the floor before entering the secret room and sealing it behind him.

He wondered what it must feel like to have so much power over the liveds of peasants like him, and so little power over her own life.

A flickering candle-lantern provided dim illumination as Falorn sat and waited for Sera to return. As he expected, the pouch of cards no longer sat on the shelf, although the money and jewelry remained. The vial of blue fluid had disappeared from the chest of black-handled knives as well.

5

Wood-Spirits

The candle burned down before Sera returned. Falorn fell asleep on the rug in the darkness, his head pillowed on one of the saddles. He woke up disoriented and still in darkness, disturbed by the noise of someone moving in the room outside. He clutched the dagger in his boot when he heard someone fumble at the clasp in the armoire. Falorn relaxed only when he saw Sera enter, framed in the narrow doorway by the light from the lantern she carried. Night had fallen outside as well, so he knew she'd been gone for several hours.

She closed the door and began wordlessly pulling supplies from the shelf and chests, ignoring Falorn despite the cramped chamber. Sera placed the now-empty vial on the shelf while she secured weapons, supplies, and money on her person. Falorn kept silent. He thought he saw a tear in the corner of her uninjured eye, but it might have been a trick of the flickering lantern light.

When she finished packing, Sera motioned Falorn toward the wall. As he moved, she pulled the drab rug aside, revealing a trapdoor beneath. Sera lifted it, and the trapdoor opened silently, exposing a ladder which stretched into a dark passage below. Sera tossed down the crossbow and several of the sacks of food. Shouldering one of the saddles, she began climbing downward, lantern in her left hand. Falorn wordlessly picked up the other saddle and followed her descent.

The narrow tunnel wound downward in a broad arc, with stone walls to the left, and brick, wood, or plaster to the right. Thousands of footsteps crossed and recrossed in the layers of plaster dust and wood shavings left over from the construction of the tower's inner rooms. All of the tracks looked like they belonged to Sera. After four circuits of the tower, she stopped him with a touch. Loaded down with the saddle, sacks of food, the crossbow, and his own weapons, Falorn barely kept up with her determined, silent pace. His side ached with every ragged breath he took. For the first time since his flight from the Twin Unicorns, Falorn did not mourn the loss of the green knight's armor.

Sera began running her hands along the wall. Even though she knew where to look, Falorn spotted the hidden door before she did. *Suddenly, I seem to have a talent for discovering secrets*, he thought, remembering the armoire as well. But he said nothing, letting Sera find the seam for herself.

We must have climbed below the base of the tower, Falorn realized. The new tunnel angled off in a straight line, leading downward on a gentle slope. After a hundred yards or so the stone walls and floor of the tunnel abruptly gave way to dirt, shored with ancient timbers. *I think we might have left the castle entirely.*

They walked for what felt like miles, although it couldn't have been that far. The tunnel remained narrow throughout, with only occasional side passages. All but a few of those had been long ago bricked up or otherwise sealed. Sera stopped only once, when the wick from her oil-lantern began guttering. She drew a flask from her pouch and carefully refilled the pan while Falorn sank exhaustedly to the dry earth. When she finished and the flame brightened again, she just stared at him silently with her bruised face and dark eyes until he pulled himself to his feet again and staggered onward behind her.

He didn't notice the transition from tunnel to cave. By this time every movement shot pain into his side. Falorn focused his eyes on Sera's dimly illuminated booted feet ahead, straining his tired legs to take each step forward as they twisted and turned in the darkness of the passageway. He only stopped to look up when he heard a horse whicker.

Falorn stood near the mouth of a wide cave. Two hobbled saddle horses stood a dozen yards in front of him, one quietly grazing from a pile of hay while Sera saddled the other. In front of the horses, Falorn saw the slopes of grass-covered hills, illuminated by moonlight and stars scattered across the clear, cloudless night. Falorn sighed and sank to his knees, his muscles all suddenly relaxing.

"You can rest a little now," Sera said, breaking the silence. "We should be safe for a while. We'll ride as soon as the moon sets."

"Will they know you're gone yet?"

"I don't think so. The servants won't talk." Falorn remembered the empty vial she had set on the shelf of the secret room, and his face felt suddenly cold.

"You didn't!" he said, shocked.

"Of course not. Don't be silly." She turned back to the horse and began brushing it furiously. Her shoulders quivered slightly.

"Why?" he asked.

"I told you, I didn't!"

"No, I mean why are we running away now? Why not wait like you said before? And why with me?"

"Oh," she said, drawing a long breath. "That's because of these."

Sera dropped the brush carelessly in the pile of hay as she turned around and reached into her pouch. Her hand glowed as she withdrew it, brighter than the lamp on the ground. She walked over and knelt beside Falorn to show him the five cards spread luminously in her hand.

Apples covered four of the cards, one each of blue, green, gold, and crimson, all of them looking so remarkably real that Falorn's stomach rumbled to protest its own emptiness. The fifth card held a golden chalice, so marvelously elaborate that only gods would dare to drink from it. The cards he'd seen earlier in the hidden room were nowhere in evidence.

"Four the same?" he finally asked, in wonder.

"All of them are sets of four, like playing cards. The apples bring health, the chalice prosperity."

"How many are there?"

"Five."

"No, I mean how many cards are there in all?" Falorn asked. Sera paused, and looked back to the horses and out into the night.

"We'll have to talk about it later. It's nearly moonset now, and we'd best be going. Don't worry, I'll tell you everything I know about them later—I promised, remember?"

"I remember," he said. "I just want to know what I'm getting into, that's all. Before someone else tries to kill me." Sera began saddling the second horse as she replied.

"Of course you want to know, and you will. This just isn't the right time. I'll need to concentrate, and my mind is on escaping before my father catches us and puts us both on the Hook. You do know what the Hook is, don't you?" she asked.

"No. I don't think we have a Hook where I come from."

"Be glad. It's a big, curved iron pole that sticks out from the castle wall on the Greater Market side. It's about ten feet up the wall, and there's a wooden platform underneath it as a sort of a stage. People are put on it different ways depending on their crimes. If they're Hooked properly, they can last for days. It's considered something of an art in Roicenet. Usually there's quite a crowd, and they hate it if the criminals die right away. Once, my father put his favorite executioner on the Hook himself, to avoid a riot after a woman died too quickly."

"Your father killed the man?"

"Of course. He's a master at it. It's a family tradition. That's how he got to be Duke."

"By being good with the Hook?"

"No. By killing my uncle on it. Before I was born, when they were both boys. My father was the second son. But one day, when they were both playing on the wall, my uncle fell—or my father pushed him—and he landed on the Hook. It's death to take someone from the Hook alive, and even the duke can't break that law. My uncle took three days to die. Even then, my father had a master's touch."

"He pushed him?"

"Of course. Wouldn't you?" She laughed at the queasy look on Falorn's face. "Oh, stop it. I'm just teasing you. Come on and help me load the supplies; it's time to go."

She had finished saddling the second horse and Falorn had no idea how to get the conversation back to the cards. Tired, and somewhat confused, he dragged himself to his feet, wincing as the movement tore like a hook into his agonized side.

As soon as they rode from the shelter of the cave, Falorn could hear bells ringing from the city, over the hills behind them. Sera quickly pushed her horse to a gallop, and Falorn struggled to stay in the saddle as the gelding he rode raced after. He wanted nothing but sleep, and saw nothing but the horse's mane in front of him. One shapeless grassy hill faded into another as they galloped through the thin illumination of the starlight.

Gradually, he became aware of a fuzzy line at the crest of the hills ahead. Then he must have fallen asleep in the saddle, because it seemed like only a moment later and the horses had slowed. The animals picked their way downhill over roughening ground and into the thickening forest at a walk.

Lather covered the gelding's flanks. The horse's sweat had soaked through Falorn's britches, and they chafed against his sore-muscled legs. Mist surrounded them as they descended into the woods. Falorn could barely see Sera's horse in front of him, even though the sleep had mostly cleared from his eyes. He had to trust the now equally tired horse to follow closely on her trail.

It felt close to dawn when Sera halted their mounts in a clear, sheltered hollow.

"We need to rest the horses," she said, as they curried and fed their shivering mounts. "You might as well get some sleep."

"Will they follow us this far?"

"Of course they will. They'll follow us a lot farther than this, until we're well clear of my father's lands. But I think it will take a while for them to assemble the hounds, and by then our horses will be rested. I think we got enough of a head start, and they'll hesitate before they follow us too closely into the woods."

"Why?"

"Because they want to bring us back and put us on the Hook. Why else?"

"Sera . . . please. I realize I'm a peasant and you saved my life and all that, but could you please give me a straight answer to *one* question? You promised to tell me about the cards later and that's fine, but do you have to change the subject whenever I ask anything?"

"I'm sorry. It's a hard habit to break. Of course I'll tell you."

"Why won't they want to chase us into the woods?"

"I would have ridden over the hills if we weren't being chased, but this way I thought we might get clear, even if the ground is very rough for horses. And there are wolves, although they're not as bad in the spring as they are in the winter."

"Why, Sera? Please, I'm very tired."

"Well . . . there are supernatural creatures in the forest."

"You mean like brownies and pixies and things? Do you leave milk out for them at night so they won't spoil your crops?"

"No, *elves*. They're as big as us, and they live forever, and they're ruthless and bloodthirsty. They eat human babies—I know a farm woman who had her son snatched away from her breast at spearpoint. They made her watch while they dashed the poor thing's head on a rock and ate its brains raw. Then they laughed at her when she cried. The blood of human babies gives them eternal life."

"You saw this?" Falorn thought back to the two elves he had seen, stopping at his father's inn as they passed along the Turnpike. *They ate mutton*, he remembered. *They only spoke a few words anybody could understand, and they paid in pure, unminted gold. No one talked about anything else for weeks.*

"One of my servants saw it. She came from the farm country out here. Everyone knows that elves are babykillers." Sera's tone brooked no disagreement.

Nice neighbors, Falorn thought to himself, but he said nothing to Sera. Her brother beat her and her father wanted to kill her, but only these imaginary-sounding elves seemed to actually scare her. *Has she ever actually seen an elf? I certainly didn't see any in Roicenet. But I guess there wouldn't be any in the city, if everyone thinks like Sera does.*

He watched Sera check the hobbled horses, then wrap herself in a heavy cloak and curl up to sleep in the center of the fireless clearing. Falorn's sleep in the saddle had chased away much of the drowsiness and fatigue he felt, leaving him just tired enough to mute the soreness in his side. He sat on a fallen tree, ignoring the dampness, and rubbed his hands together for warmth against the slight morning chill.

The mist gradually dissipated. Falorn counted stars, naming all the names his father had taught him as each bright point flickered into view. Somehow Sera's evasions reminded Falorn of his father. *So much for leaving home to get away from all the lies. Either they're following me, or I'm just really good at stumbling onto liars.*

Liars who I care about, he had to admit. He missed his father, and despite her evasions, there was something very winning about Sera, especially in those moments when she wasn't lying to him.

After he named all the stars he remembered, Falorn opened his pouch and took out the cards, letting their dim glow fill the clearing in the last hours before dawn.

He wondered what their power was—what made people try to kill or cheat each other to obtain them. He wondered if they even had any power. Maybe they just glowed. But as he watched the green lion prancing and the blue thief prowling, he knew they had other strengths, perhaps ones he could never hope to understand, even if Sera did. He wondered if he should give her the cards. Falorn broke his gaze away from their ivory faces to look at Sera, silently asleep. He didn't think he could part with them just yet, though. They had come to him, for whatever reason. And if they had drawn more attention than he wanted, they had also brought him adventure, and more wealth than he had dreamed of, even if not much by the standards of Sera and her family. He decided to hold onto them and see what happened, at least for a while longer.

Tugging at the thong around his neck, Falorn brought his old pouch, the one he'd kept a pet snake in when he was younger—and which was now holding some of the money he'd taken from the dead thieves—from under his tunic. He placed the cards inside the pouch, and replaced it under his clothing, mouthing a prayer to Kerion as he did so. They could sit near his heart, and bring him luck if they wanted to. He wrapped himself in his cloak and lay down in the shelter of the fallen log, as the drowsiness that had fled before cautiously returned. He slept instantly, and once again dreamed of green lions.

The horses' nervous whinnying woke Falorn. He threw off the cloak and rose to his feet, drawing the sword from beside him and tossing its sheath aside.

A gaunt, four-legged gray shape looked up at him, removing its thin face from the sack of dried meat it had been worrying with its fangs. It growled at him, baring yellowed fangs and staring at him with reddened, hungry eyes. Another growl echoed from within the woods nearby.

The animal looked like a big, mangy dog whose nose had been squeezed long and thin. It growled again, backing up a few paces on spindly legs as Falorn stepped toward it.

"Sera?" he said, not taking his eyes off the animal. "Sera, are you awake?"

"I'm awake," she replied. "What is that thing?"

"It's sort of like a wolf, but not quite. There's another one nearby, but I can't see it. Can you tell where it is?"

"No."

"Please look carefully." The creature continued to stare at Falorn, growling intermittently.

"I looked carefully. I'm half asleep and we're being attacked by wolves. How carefully do you want me to look? Should I get up and comb the woods?"

"We're not being attacked, Sera. Our food is being attacked. There's a difference."

"There's a difference until they're done with the food." She quieted for a moment. "Uh, Falorn?"

"Yes, Sera?" he replied, taking another step forward. The creature growled more loudly and flattened its ears.

"Are you sure there are only two of them? Don't wolves travel in packs?"

"Yes, they do. But I think if there were any more we'd know it by now. I don't think this one's going to stick around for much longer either. It looks like it barely made it through the winter." He stepped forward again and the animal lost its nerve, turning its bushy gray tail and loping into the woods. It disappeared almost immediately into the heavy underbrush which surrounded the clearing.

"Do you think they'll come back?" Sera asked him after a moment of silence.

"Depends on whether or not we go to sleep again. And whether or not all of the wolves around here are half-starved and sick. How long did you say we were going to be in these woods?"

"Not long, I hope. Just long enough to shake my father's hunters. They may not even follow us into the forest."

A hound bayed in the distance.

Falorn shook his head and walked over to the horses, while Sera unwrapped herself from her bedroll.

"Well, at least it's light," Falorn said. "I guess we ought to be heading deeper into the woods. Maybe the wolves and the elves will eat the hounds."

Sera shivered at the mention of elves. Falorn, busy feeding the horses, noticed only in passing.

They broke camp quickly, eating sparingly from the food the wolves hadn't touched. They could hear the hounds baying intermittently, depending on the direction of the wind. Within a few minutes after the scavengers disappeared into the underbrush, Falorn and Sera followed in nearly the same direction, leading the horses uneasily behind them.

Late in the morning, they stopped hearing the hounds, although they couldn't be sure if Sera's father had called off the pursuit, or if the wind had shifted. They continued to lead the horses through the forest as quickly as they could. Sun glinted through chinks in the green canopy overhead and reflected off drops of moisture on the carpet of squelching brown leaves at their feet. As the woods warmed, the fear that had driven Falorn all morning began to fade. He had always loved forests, and these oak woods were beautiful, regardless of wolves or elves or pursuing hounds.

They stopped to eat on the bank of a brook, which flowed over mossy rocks and fallen trees, reckless with its infusion of spring runoff. Falorn walked up the bank while Sera tended the horses. The brook thundered downward forty feet in a tumbling waterfall, raising a thin mist which curled around the edges of the half-hidden pool below. A grove of willows overhung much of the pool, hiding all but the misty edge from view. Falorn thought he saw a flicker of movement within the willow branches, a brief flash of pale skin. He sat very still next to the waterfall's edge, waiting for another glimpse of the silent creature in the willow-covered pool.

Time passed. he saw nothing but falling water and the occasional fish breaking the surface. It dawned on him that he might have glimpsed a wood-spirit. If so, she would certainly know of his presence. He didn't want to spy, not even to find out if the tales about bathing nymphs had any truth to them. Sera would laugh at him if he told her about the pool; after all, he didn't even know for certain that he'd seen anything.

He stood up, reluctantly moving his gaze from the willow leaves below to the forest around him, and to the brook which led back to the horses and Sera.

"Sorry if I intruded," he whispered, feeling a bit silly. A faint gust of wind ruffled his hair, but otherwise Falorn heard no response. If he had encountered a wood-spirit, she intended to keep that encounter private.

Falorn walked slowly back upstream toward Sera, wondering if he should have continued his vigil over the pool. *What would a real knight do*, he wondered, *if he hadn't started out as a peasant boy?* Probably stay and catch the wood-spirit in her lair, he knew. Maybe force her to show him the future, or give him some powerful magical protection. Falorn didn't think he could bring himself to do any of those things, but he had none of the years of training nor, he supposed, the toughness that a real knight needed.

He turned a bend in the brook, and the horses drew into sight. Sera sat against the bole of a tree nearby, reading a small book she must have salvaged from her room.

"What took you so long?" she asked, looking up as he approached. "You know we have to keep moving."

"I just wanted to look around. I like forests."

"Well, you would, I suppose. I like nice, warm, dry rooms. With thick walls. And guards."

"And Hooks?"

"The whole world's got Hooks, Falorn. You just have to learn not to wander into them." She gestured to an open sack on the ground nearby. "Better get yourself something to eat. We have to leave soon."

He began eating the dried fruit quickly.

"Did you hear any more hounds?" he asked between bites.

"No. Do you think we should wait around until I do, just so we can be sure my father is still following us?"

He didn't answer; instead he bundled the food back up and stowed it on his horse. He checked his sword without thinking as they started walking again, as if by newfound instinct. Sera saw his baffled expression when he realized what he was doing, and laughed.

"Almost like a real knight, right? You're getting pretty good at playing the role. Let's try not to meet any *real* knights until you learn how to use it, though."

"I was just. . . ." he trailed off, confused.

"Get used to it. You never know what you'll find yourself doing when the cards are around."

"So they do have power."

"Of course they do. Why do you think people are trying to kill you for them? But I wouldn't count on them being much help."

"What do they do?"

"Whatever they want to, I think. I really don't know much more about them than you do."

"How many are there?"

"I'm not sure. Maybe fifty or sixty? More, I think. The accounts I've read are a little unclear."

"You've read about them?"

"I've read about them. Sometimes it seems like the more you read, the less you know. You don't read at all, do you?"

Falorn turned away.

"Not at all, no," he replied. "I'm a peasant, remember?"

"I haven't forgotten. But I didn't think you'd want me to keep reminding you about it."

"What else have you read about the cards?"

"Most of what I know is out of date. They may look new, but they're older than we are. My grandfather fought in the war where they were made. I think that's my father ended up with some of them."

That doesn't explain how you get yours, Falorn thought, but assked a question he thought she was more likely to answer instead. "What are they exactly?"

"I couldn't really tell you . . . at least, it's not that simple. I will try to explain everything I know as soon as we have time, and we're not being chased by dogs, or wolves, or my father, or . . . elves."

She lapsed into silence. They walked quietly for a while.

"Do you know anything about wood-spirits?" Falorn finally asked.

Sera looked thoughtful for a minute, twisting a piece of her hair with her free hand, her other hand loosely holding the reins of the horse she led.

"Do you mean children's stories? I know a few of them. I thought everybody knew them."

"Even peasants, you mean?"

"I didn't say that, you did."

"I think we learned different children's stories."

"That's probably true," Sera replied, still wearing a thoughtful expression. "Let me think for a minute, and I'll see if I can remember one." She furrowed her brow in mock concentration, then began speaking with the practiced cadence of the traveling storytellers who he'd heard at the year-end fairs.

"This is a story my grandfather told me when I was just a little girl. He had it from his grandfather, the first of my family to be Duke in Roicenet, and he swore every word of it was true.

"In my great-great-grandfather's time—which wasn't so long ago as you might think, for the men of my family are short-lived—there lived in the city a young knight by the name of Sebastin. Sebastin's father was a powerful lord in the city, but Sebastin was a younger son, so his father encouraged him to go out in the world and make his fortune, so that he wouldn't have to divide the estate. And Sebastin's father gave him a beautiful white stallion with tack all of silver, and armor of silver to match, and a magical sword called Ladysbreath, which would bring its owner great luck and success in battle, as long as he never mistreated a lady.

"Now Sebastin had beaten a whore or two in his youth, and perhaps made sport with a peasant lass here and there while off on his hunts, but he'd never had anything but kindness for ladies, as you might expect from a younger son who lacked an inheritance. So he thanked his father, kissed his mother and sisters, saluted his older brother, swore an oath to uphold the family's honor, and rode off to find his way in the world.

"He soon found himself lost in the woods, perhaps in these very woods. He searched about for adventure, for battles to fight, for wealthy dragons to slay—for in those days dragons were more common than they are today—but he saw only trees.

"Presently, he began to wonder where he was going to find a bed for the night, and a meal, for he had thought to bring only armor and weapons with him; it had never occurred to him that he would have to find food. As luck would have it, soon after dark he spied a light, and a few moments' ride brought him to a clearing surrounding a large and sturdily constructed woodcutter's cottage.

"He quickly dismounted and rapped at the door, but no one answered. He tried the door and found it unlocked. Inside, a huge plate sat in the center of an oversized table. A large stool stood nearby, but he saw neither food nor woodcutter within. Thinking the owner of the cottage might be behind the house, perhaps carrying in a load of firewood, Sebastin strode to the rear door of the cottage and threw it open.

"Outside, he saw a sight which warmed his knightly heart.

"A naked woman, the most radiantly beautiful woman Sebastin had ever seen, was sprawled against a chopping block, her hands bound and a sack pulled over her head as a hood. Looming over her, axe held high like a lightning bolt ready to strike, stood a vile ogre fully eight feet tall, his warty skin rippling with bulging muscles.

"Sebastin shouted and charged, drawing Ladysbreath and calling for the ogre to meet his challenge. The ogre turned and swung his barbed axe in answer.

"Now Sebastin was a great swordsman, and he had his magical blade to help, but ogres are strong as oxen and cunning as thieves, and this ogre was fast as well. My grandfather swears that they fought for a night and a day, but maybe it only seemed like that long before Sebastin held the ogre's steaming head high in the air, and shouted his family's motto out to the uncaring forest.

"Then he looked down again and saw the beautiful naked woman tied to the chopping block. To be honest, the long fight had excited him, and the sight of her pale, smooth flesh aroused him even further. But he felt the sword which had served him so well grow suddenly uncomfortable in his hand, and decided that it wasn't worth the risk of her being a lady, so he just touched the sword once to each of her bonds, freeing her arms and legs.

"Before he could free her head, she slid the sack carefully off by herself, and turned to face him. She seemed to feel absolutely no shame in her nudity, which made Sebastin doubt that she was really a lady, but he wasn't about to take any chances. Every feature of her body was so perfect that it took several moments before he noticed that she wore a mask over her face. When she spoke, her voice was like a wind in the forest, so beautiful to listen to that you had to concentrate to remember what she said.

"'You have saved my life, Sebastin,' she said, and it surprised him not at all that she knew his name, for he was beginning to realize that a woman who looked like this out in the middle of the forest was not a part of the natural scheme of things, 'and you didn't take me by force when you might have. For those kindnesses, I will reward you to the best of my abilities. I grant you three wishes; ask, and I will do whatever is in my power to grant your desires.'

"Sebastin had been hoping for something like this to happen, so he was not entirely unprepared.

"'Very well, then,' he said in knightly tones. 'I wish for fame, for fortune . . . and for you.'

"'I see,' she replied, looking disappointed, though not surprised. 'You have wished well, if not wisely. Fortune and fame you shall have. You need only take what you find within the cabin and ride back to your father's home with it. I will come with you and be a wife to you, but I will stay for only a year and a day, and you must swear never to look upon my face.'

"Sebastin agreed to this readily, since even he realized he had gone beyond the bounds of knightly propriety in his request. At first light he searched the cabin, and found a chest of gold coins and gems within, enough to buy him a very comfortable life, if not exactly a king's ransom. He set the woman (whom he had clothed in a spare cloak for decency's sake, now that she was to be his wife—although she seemed indifferent to any garment at all) and the gold on the back of his horse and set out for home.

"His father's retainers met him before he even reached the walls of the city. His father and brothers had been eaten in a dragon-hunting accident; the retainers urged him to return to the city immediately and look to his new estate. This he did, pausing along the way only long enough for a priest to marry him to the rescued maiden, who seemed as indifferent to the ceremony as to the clothing.

"A year passed, and he had everything a knight could want: fame, fortune, and a beautiful wife with a mysterious air about her, and with a mask which only accentuated her otherworldly splendor. But then one morning, she reminded him of the terms of their agreement.

"'I have stayed for a year and a day, husband, but tonight I must return to my home in the forest. I leave you your fame and fortune, but I can stay no longer.'

"He hatched a thousand plans in his mind, but could not work his way past the essential, troubling point: He had made a promise. Now that he was a lord, keeping his promises was more important than ever. A man's reputation could be ruined if anyone learned he had broken his knightly vows. So instead he stormed out of the house and spent the day drinking.

"By sunset, he had thought of no way to keep her from returning to the forest, but he resolved on one thing: he would see her face once before she left, to see what horrible secret she hid from him. He ran home as the last of the light faded, grabbed his wife by the arm, threw her to the floor, and tore the mask from her face."

Sera stopped talking.

"Then what happened?" Falorn asked. "You can't just stop the story there."

"I know, but the storytellers in the Greater Market always stop there, so they can collect coins before they tell the end of the story."

"You have plenty of coins, Sera. How does the story end?"

"The way my grandfather heard it, they found Sebastin dead on the floor of his manor, the mask still in his hand, and an awful expression frozen on his face. Naturally, there was no sign of his wife to be found, so the estate devolved on his mother, who did a much better job managing it than he had, you can be sure."

Falorn digested the story for a few minutes.

"It's a good story," he finally said, "and you're a wonderful storyteller. But what does it say about wood-spirits?"

"Don't look them in the eye, don't ask too much of them, and don't ever get drunk and try to take liberties with them, even if you have a magic sword." The expression on her face was so studiously neutral that Falorn couldn't tell if she joked or not. "That's good advice about women in general, by the way."

"I guess. You know more about it than I do."

"Women, or wood-spirits?"

"Both, I think. What's that sound?"

He put up a hand to stop her and the horses. The noise had risen slowly while Sera told her story, beginning as a faint clattering at the edge of his hearing, then growing steadily louder.

It grew louder still as they led the horses onward.

"What is it?" Falorn asked.

"It sounds like fighting. There may be soldiers fighting in the woods ahead."

"Your father?"

"No. I don't think so, anyway. I don't think there's any way my father and his men could have gotten ahead of us." Sera's face held an enigmatic expression.

"What should we do? We can't stop, or go back."

"We'll have to try to go around them. They aren't looking for us, and whoever they are, they're busy fighting each other. If we move carefully, they will never know we passed through."

"I guess." Part of Falorn wanted very much to see the battle. Something drew him toward the fighting, a warmth in his chest that burned like a fever for whatever lay ahead at the source of the noise.

They drew to a stop at the edge of a long clearing, where the woods gave way to a wide expanse of open space. As they stood still within the shelter of a thicket, the trees beyond erupted with the sound of metal scraping and biting on metal, and harsh shouted war-cries, and the screaming of dying men.

6

The Lion and the Hounds

❖

The clearing reeked of stale sweat and blood.

Dead bodies littered the ground, scattered around tufts of scrub-grass and dwarf pines. Here and there, blood pooled into mud puddles. Weapons lay scattered everywhere. Falorn could hear noises from the woods at the clearing's far end, but most of the sound came from the center of the open area.

A score of armored men in gold and scarlet hacked at a knot of swordsmen in brown and green. The five unarmored men fought grimly, astride the fallen bodies of their fellows, trying to protect their wounded. The soldiers in gold and scarlet methodically closed in. As Falorn watched, one of the unarmored fighters went down below the blades of three men in gold.

Only a tall, thin swordsman in the center of the battle kept the few unarmored men from being cut down. He fought like a wild animal, ferocious and uncannily fast, yet at the same time curiously controlled. He seemed to take a fierce joy even in this hopeless fight, his slashing blade forcing the mail-clad men around him to fall back momentarily before resuming their assault.

Something about the sight of the thin swordsman excited Falorn. He wanted to jump into the clearing, to shout out something, to draw his sword and madly charge at the backs of the armored men.

Falorn's head ached, as if he'd been too long in the sun. He couldn't take his eyes off the battle, but the longer he watched, the blurrier the images in front of him became.

Falorn's blood surged along with the tall fighter's, pounded in his ears and flushed face. He felt his heart throb as the swordsman called something to his fellows; they redoubled their hopeless attack on the soldiers who surrounded them.

The tall swordsman surged into the attackers. Behind him, another of his companions went down. Falorn could see the man's thin face and sharp nose and widely set golden eyes. A mane of long, black hair swirled around his tapering ears and flowed over his slight shoulders, which looked inadequate to the hard, swift way he swung his blade.

He's not a man! He's an elf, Falorn suddenly realized. *All five of them are elves.* Except that only three of the unarmored elves still fought, against more than a dozen human attackers.

Something boiled within Falorn, an animal rage directed at the soldiers trying to kill the overwhelmed elves—so much like the soldiers who had chased him. Suddenly, he wanted to kill them all. His hand dropped to the hilt of his sword. Fire filled his veins.

Sera's hand on his arm checked Falorn.

"Don't be a fool!" she hissed. "Do you want to get yourself killed? There's nothing you can do."

Her words brought him groggily back to his senses. Falorn's veins felt too small to contain the blood which boiled within them. A heady energy consumed him, enveloping his head as if he were an addict trying to fight his way free of an opium-house.

He shook his head to try to clear it. Only Sera's tightening grip on his arm connected him to the reality of the battle. The lions in his skull wanted to charge and fight and sink teeth into their prey in the clearing beyond. He crouched like a lion, growling and shaking, only dimly aware that Sera held him down.

The tall elf fought alone now. His thin blade jumped and skidded through the air, flying and cutting and parrying like an extension of his arm rather than a piece of cold steel. *Nothing can stop him,* something sang in Falorn's mind. Exhilaration filled him. *Only a lion could fight like that,* he realized, not wondering at the odd thought crossing his turbulent mind. And the elf looked almost like a lion to him, fought like a slashing, razor-clawed lion, threw himself into the fight with a lion's fierce pride.

Soldiers hounded the elf from all sides now, like a pack of hunting dogs worrying at a fierce predator. An axe blade opened his thigh just above the knee in a slash he could only half parry. A barely avoided sword stroke opened a thin red line in his forehead. Still fighting furiously, the elf stumbled momentarily, and the hounds closed in.

Falorn pushed himself to his feet, reaching for his blade.

"Falorn, no!" Sera called out. She had a knife in her hand for some reason. He took a step forward.

Something hard and metal connected with the side of his head. A second blow slammed into him. Falorn sank to his knees, consciousness fading. All he could see was the elf, falling in front of him, too far away to help.

Falorn screamed in real agony as the first blade pierced the tall swordsman's back. A heavy weight pressed on his head, and his eyes clouded. He screamed again, and then felt himself drift off into nothing.

Falorn awoke to the tapping sound of a raven picking at the skull of a dead man. The bird stood less than an arm's length from his head, alternately thrusting and tugging with its beak, occasionally flapping its wings for greater leverage. It looked in Falorn's direction as his eyelids moved, but soon dismissed him as no threat and returned to excavating the corpse.

His back felt sore and bruised, and his arms hurt as if he'd slept badly in a lumpy bed. Most of all, his head ached where Sera had hit him with the knife butt. Pulling himself to his knees slowly, Falorn swept his eyes from the raven to the carnage of the recent battle. A few dying men still moaned faintly. None of them seemed to have the strength or the will to scream. He glanced around, but saw no sign of Sera anywhere.

The nightmarish lions no longer haunted his skull. He instinctively fingered the pouch around his neck, feeling to see that the cards remained within. Then he realized the source of the sensations. *The elf held another lion card.*

As soon as the thought occurred to him, Falorn knew it was no longer true. The bloody body of the elf lay on top of a pile of armored corpses in the center of the clearing, and Falorn felt nothing but a vague sadness, and anger at the waste. No lions stirred in his blood. He knew the card no longer remained nearby.

He pulled himself to his feet, forcing reluctant muscles to act against their will.

Something moved in the center of the clearing.

The elf twitched. Somehow, impossibly, the thin warrior still lived.

Falorn ran into the clearing, sending a flock of startled ravens flapping into the air as he broke from cover. The birds returned to earth as Falorn sank to his knees beside the shallowly breathing swordsman.

The elf's face shone like waxed paper in the sun. His arm felt brittle where Falorn touched it, and blood colored the elf's torn clothes and skin in a dozen places. Only his piercing golden eyes still looked alive. Those eyes knew him in an instant, Falorn thought—knew the cards he held, knew what he ran from, knew what he wanted, even better than Falorn knew himself.

The elf opened his mouth and rasped something bitter and unintelligible. Falorn reached to his skin of water and opened it, bringing it carefully to the maimed warrior's lips. He wet the elf's lips first, then let him drink, careful to keep him from choking.

"I wish I could ask you about the cards," Falorn said, as much to himself as to the elf, "but it would be enough if I can help you live, I guess."

The elf would never fight or walk again, even if he did live. The fierce golden eyes never left Falorn's face, although they gave no hint of understanding his words.

After he finished drinking, Falorn bathed the wounded elf's face with a little of the remaining water, gently clearing away some of the sweat and dried blood. He searched nearby for something to use for bandages, finally tearing a scarlet surcoat from a dead soldier. The thin warrior didn't seem to be bleeding much.

He began cutting away the elf's clothes and wrapping the wounds in strips of bandaging, talking soothingly as he worked—the way he might doctor a sick dog or horse. The elf never responded, just kept staring at him with eyes as gold as polished coins.

"What's your name?" Falorn finally asked. The elf didn't seem to understand, so he pointed at his own chest and said, "I'm Falorn. Falorn."

The elf seemed to recognize the gesture, and a strange expression covered his wan face. "The . . . lli . . . la . . . fa . . . o . . . li . . . Thellilafaoli," he said, painfully. Falorn couldn't be sure if the swordsman had uttered his name or not.

The elf seemed to gain strength slightly as Falorn worked. By the time Falorn had bandaged the warrior's arms and legs, Sera reappeared, carrying fresh skins of water. She didn't offer to help, but instead stood nearby with a pensive look on her face.

"Falorn," she finally said, "you shouldn't be out here. You're not well, and this place isn't safe."

"I'm well enough," he replied with an exasperated grunt. "And if you'll help me here, I'll be done soon." He gestured for her to support the elf from behind as he lifted. "Hold him up so I can bandage his side."

Sera held the elf's back uneasily with one hand, while fumbling at her belt for something.

"Please try to hold him still. I don't want to hurt him any more." He crouched down to cut the cloth away from the elf's torn side. The warrior shuddered suddenly. His body stiffened beneath Falorn's hand. He looked up at the elf's face but the golden eyes had rolled upward, leaving only hideous whites showing.

A red stain blossomed on the elf's chest.

Sera twisted her knife once more in the elf's back, then removed it, bracing her hand on his back for leverage. The body tilted forward and settled against Falorn, who remained in a stunned crouch. As he pulled himself to his feet it collapsed on the ground.

Sera had cleaned the knife already and replaced it in her belt-sheath.

"Why?" he asked raggedly, not trusting his tongue with any other words.

"They're *babykillers*. All of them." She spat on the corpse. "Good soldiers died here today. Why should he live any longer?"

For all I know she might be right, he realized. *I don't know anything about elves.* He turned away and walked back toward the woods and their horses, because he didn't want her to see him cry.

He felt her hand on his shoulder a few minutes later, as he sobbed dryly against the rough bark of a massive tree. His back stiffened at her touch, but she shushed him before he could say anything and began massaging the knots from his shoulders.

"I'm sorry," she finally said, after he had stopped shaking. "I didn't mean to upset you like that. I know you wanted to save his life, but he wasn't worth it. I like you a lot, Falorn, but you're still just a good-hearted farmboy about a lot of things, and some of those things can kill you. I know you've heard this from me before, but there are a lot of things you're just going to have to trust me on."

"But you just . . . killed him. You stabbed him in the back. . . . He was helpless . . . and those eyes."

"Shhh," she said, "don't try to talk. You're too upset. You'll understand everything soon. Now we have to get the horses and move on a little further, away from the battlefield. We won't go much farther today, but the bodies are going to draw wolves tonight, and maybe more elves. We can't be too close."

She guided Falorn to the horses and started them moving. He walked dazedly, although his senses gradually returned as they moved. At one point, they crossed over a crushed trail where hundreds of booted men had recently tramped.

"That's where the rest of the battle was," Sera told him when he asked. "You didn't think that little skirmish was the whole battle, did you? They just got cut off from the main fighting. There's an army at the other end of that trail."

"Do you know whose army?" he asked.

"I think so," she replied. "Probably a friend of my father's. We don't dare go too close."

The two of them traveled only until they found a secluded clearing where they could shelter themselves and the horses. They watered the horses silently in a nearby stream, before refilling their waterskins and returning to the clearing to make camp.

Sera disappeared as Falorn groomed the horses, only to return dripping wet and laughing just as he finished feeding them. Her expression sobered slightly as she saw his dark look.

"I know you feel bad and we're on the run," she said, "but I really needed a bath. I don't care how many hounds are after us, I feel better just knowing that I'm clean again." She poked around at their food supply. "It's too bad we can't risk a fire. I suppose we'll just have to rough it again."

Falorn remained silent.

"Please don't be mad at me," she pleaded. Wet hair framed her face, her cheeks still bright from the shock of the icy stream. "I didn't mean to hurt you."

He didn't reply. After a minute she went on. "I know you're upset about the way I do things sometimes. I can't help the way I react to things sometimes. I try, I really do, but . . . you've heard my father. . . . That's what I grew up with. Sometimes, no matter how much I try, I find myself sounding and acting just like him."

She hung her head slightly. Her brown eyes looked black and deep in the fading light. "Please let me try to make it up to you. I know I've treated you really badly, and you deserve better. I promise, I'll try my best to do better. And I'll tell you all I know about the cards, like I promised."

"It's all right," he heard himself saying. "You did save my life. I owe you that." He found it impossible to stay mad at her when she looked at him like that. *She saved my life,* he reminded himself. The way Sera's wet hair plastered her face seemed to highlight the deep brown of her eyes. Her lower lip quivered slightly.

"You mean you'll forgive me?" she asked, almost plaintively.

"I'll try," he said. "I can't forgive what I don't understand. But I owe you my life, so I'll try." He wondered what had suddenly made Sera seem so frail and afraid.

"Thank you," she said, and held out her hand.

He took her hand, and reached out to touch her reassuringly. Suddenly, she huddled in his arms, shivering.

"It's all right," he said as she shook against him, "It's all right."

They held each other for a long time. Falorn rubbed Sera's back until she stopped shivering, and she moved closer against him. Her hair smelled like river-cedar as it dried.

She crawled close to him when they finally lay down, wrapped in their cloaks. He started to mumble something, but she put a finger to his lips.

"Please," she said, "no more talking tonight." She held out a bare arm and pulled him close beside her under the weight of her heavy gray wool cloak. He felt her smooth skin against the roughness of his shirt. He flinched when he felt her hand at his belt.

"Don't worry," she said, "It's just that the buckle is biting into my skin." She unbuckled his belt, with its sheathed knife and two pouches, and placed it on the other side of her, where his swordbelt already lay.

"I just like to keep my sword and things close. . . ." he said.

"I know," she replied. "Don't worry; they're safe for now."

She began gently massaging his belly and chest, and Falorn put the belt out of his mind. It would still be there in the morning. He caught her hand when it touched the pouch around his neck.

"Not that," he said. "It's a religious item."

"Oh, really?" she answered lazily, running a finger slowly down his side and around the edges of his scar. "I didn't think you were religious. I'll bet that's where you keep the cards."

"I am religious. I just don't like to talk about it. But I wouldn't keep the cards this close to my heart. They might corrupt me." *It might be true. I never would have lied to the daughter of a duke before, especially not one who saved my life.*

"Maybe they will," she purred, "but they haven't corrupted me yet, have they?" Her hands moved slowly downward.

"Sera, should we. . . ."

"Shhh," she said, moving one finger across his lips while the other smoothed the sensitive skin at the base of his belly. "I said no more talking." Her lips touched his own, and he realized that now he was the one who trembled.

Falorn lay on his back and looked at the moon overhead. Sera slept beside him, one hand draped over his thigh. They still hadn't talked about the cards, he realized, unconsciously putting a hand on the pouch which warmed the skin of his chest.

He finally closed his eyes and willed himself to sleep. He dreamed, not of the pain and chaos of the battle he had witnessed, but of the elven warrior, now healed, riding on a massive blue lion. Beside the elf, his own green lion capered, and Falorn realized that he rode on the lion's back. They pranced through the woods along the trampled path he had seen earlier, until they came to a cleared field filled with dozens of tents flying pennants of gold and scarlet. Armored soldiers filled the camp, eating, gambling, practicing with weapons.

The elf on the blue lion wanted Falorn to follow him into the camp, but his own green lion hesitated. Finally, afraid of losing the elf yet again, Falorn urged his lion onward. Startled soldiers looked up as he rode among them, but quickly they seized weapons and surrounded him. He looked to the elven swordsman for help as the soldiers began pulling him from the green lion's back, but the thin warrior and his blue mount were nowhere to be seen.

7

The Lion's Den

Falorn woke up suddenly, hours after dawn. He sat up, reached for his sword, then remembered where he had left it the night before.

Only he and his bedroll remained in the clearing. The horses, supplies, weapons, and Sera had all vanished. Even the knife from his boot was gone. Falorn's hands immediately went to the pouch around his neck. The cards felt faintly warm against his skin. *She must have thought they were in my belt pouch.* He cursed in disgust.

He wondered where she had gone.

His eye fell on a pair of half-hidden hoofprints in the dirt at the edge of the clearing. Throwing the few possessions he still owned together, he strode quickly over to the prints. Almost instantly he saw another hoofprint, and a crushed branch. He walked over, and Sera's trail practically glowed in front of him, as clearly as a plowed furrow.

"It can't be this easy," he said out loud, to no one in particular. "Why would she want me to follow her?"

He felt a growing heat against his chest.

He reached inside his tunic and unlaced the pouch. Only one of the two cards felt warm, even though they sat together in the leather sack.

He drew out the ivory plaque, feeling its heat seem to radiate into his hand and upward through his arm. The card shimmered with color.

Falorn gazed into the face of the blue thief.

"You want me to track her, don't you?" he asked the silent card. "I think you're helping me."

He looked around the woods which surrounded the clearing as he held the heated card tightly. A thousand paths seemed to intersect at his feet: trails of deer and wolves, cougars, elves, soldiers, even the paths of hawks in the overcast sky. Sera's footsteps leading the two horses stood out from them all, edged faintly with a flickering blue glow that brightened as he approached and faded into nothingness once he passed.

Clearly the card had a more expansive view of a thief's skills than Falorn, whose experience had been limited to card cheats at his father's tavern and the occasional cattle thief. *And one pickpocket*, he reminded himself.

Falorn replaced the card in his pouch. The glow of Sera's trail remained, outlined in blue against the ground and the spring foliage. Gradually, the dizzying array of other paths and spoors receded into the background. They looked like thousands of strings of twine, laid over and across each other along the ground. If he concentrated, Falorn could follow any one of the strings, as if lifting it loose from the confusion of the other trails. Left alone, each string faded almost into invisibility. But the blue filament which marked Sera's path glowed brightly.

He quickly realized that her path intersected the trail of the human army they had skirted the night before. By the time Falorn reached the pounded dirt trail, the warmth against his chest had grown in intensity. When he felt inside the pouch a second time, both cards reacted against his hand.

A surge of fire filled his veins with bravery, and he knew at once that the stolen lion card lay at the end of the trail ahead. Falorn smiled, in spite of everything, and wondered why he didn't feel more upset.

The overcast sky faded into sunset before he reached the outskirts of the camp. Dozens of dirty cloth tents squatted in the middle of a cleared field like mushrooms after a storm. Each tent looked big enough to hold seven or eight soldiers. By the number of fires and the piles of equipment and stacked saddles heaped around the tents, Falorn knew the camp must hold several hundred soldiers—practically an army.

Only a few unarmored soldiers milled around the tents, attending to camp chores. In the wake of the battle and march, most of the soldiers must have been too exhausted even to celebrate their victory. Perhaps twenty armored soldiers stood guard, scattered around the outskirts of the cleared field. Most of the guards concentrated their attention on a makeshift pen to Falorn's right, where a small cluster of elven prisoners huddled. The elves had been stripped of clothing as well as weapons: They looked pitifully thin in the fading light.

From his vantage point in the forest, Falorn could see no soldiers on guard beyond the edges of the clearing. He felt himself quivering like a cat in anticipation, his skin warming in answer to the heat from the cards. He could feel the presence of the other lion card within the camp. He knew exactly where to find it. His eyes fixed on the largest tent, its colors not faded like the others. A painted canvas pennant flapped in the breeze which blew toward Falorn. He could smell the horses, picketed on the other side of the camp, blocked from his vision.

He supposed the blue thief would help him find his way into the camp; if it didn't, the guards would certainly kill him. It took all his strength to stay rational, to fight the urge to charge like a lion into the camp and tear the other card away from its present owner. He thought of the elf-warrior's doomed fight, and wondered how the green lion's previous owner had met his death on the flagstones of the Turnpike. For all the exhilaration of the fight in the alley with the thieves, Falorn was beginning to think the lion card might not be an unmixed blessing.

He tried to think about the blue card as he began to crawl toward the camp. With the heat of the lion practically blazing against his chest, Falorn couldn't tell if the thief card remained warm. He saw no blue outlines or other obvious signs of magical aid. Finally, after pausing for a moment on his belly in the hope that the magical signs were just slow to appear, Falorn resumed his slow crawl.

He dared not look above the short spring grass to see if one of the guards spotted him. He could only continue blindly through the grass in what he hoped was a straight and inconspicuous path toward the camp.

He nearly bumped into the flaking painted sides of the first tent. Staying close against the cloth, Falorn pushed himself quietly to his feet. He slid carefully into the dark, shadowed area between two closely set tents. The cloth walls smelled of mildew, dampness, and rot.

Falorn couldn't see into the middle of the camp from his hiding place, but he didn't need to. The lion card in the oversized central tent pulled at him so strongly that he felt no doubt at all as to its location.

He looked around for patrolling soldiers and saw no one. He had passed through the thin line of sentries. None of them wasted a glance back at their own camp. He could hear the noise of a foot-pedaled grindstone at work to his right, beyond one of the tents he hid between.

He worked his way to the left, feeling along the paneled sides of the tent as he slowly moved toward his goal. He listened carefully for noises that might indicate soldiers at work in front of him, but heard nothing. Before he reached the front, he slipped carefully into the shadow of another tent. Flaking paint colored one sleeve of his tunic a faded yellow as he brushed against the cloth.

Falorn heard snores from inside this tent. He listened carefully for any sounds of stirring but heard only the steady rasp of sleeping soldiers breathing. He needed to get deeper into the camp, before the green lion card burned the heart out from within his chest.

He bent down close to the ground and paused, listening again for another long moment. Taking a deep breath that seemed to barely expand his fiery chest, he lifted the edge of a long cloth panel. Letting his breath out shakily, Falorn looked within the tent.

A half-dozen soldiers lay wrapped in cloaks or muddy bedrolls on the tent's dirt floor. Holding one hand to the heat of the pouch within his tunic, he slipped inside. Falorn stepped gingerly over the nearest soldier. He looked at the sheathed broadsword clutched in the sleeping man's hand and paused, but then shook his head and took another step. A sword would only increase his chances of making noise. It wouldn't help him a bit if the sentries caught him, Falorn knew.

A knife, though, felt like it might be more helpful. He worked his way across the tent, stopping in mid-step as a bearded man rolled over and nearly collided with Falorn's leg. Next to the closed flap that formed the door of the tent, a low camp table held a pile of knives, an oily rag, and a whetstone. He tucked one knife into his right boot and held a thin stiletto in his hand, checking the edge with his thumb. With a last glance behind to make sure the soldiers in the tent still slept, Falorn tucked his head through the front flap, looking for anyone walking the camp nearby.

The camp looked clear and the lion surged against his chest. With a faint smile at the impracticality of an innkeeper's son sneaking into a war camp to chase a magical relic which only caused trouble for its owners, Falorn pushed through the tent flap and began cautiously edging his way closer to the center of the camp.

He stopped at an unwatched cookfire to spear some stew-meat onto his newfound knife. He hadn't thought to eat all day, and barely tasted the meat now.

Near the middle of the camp he found more soldiers awake. He had to pass supply tents to reach the tent he wanted. The camp quartermaster and his assistants bustled around the supply area, darting in and out of tents as they finished accounting for supplies lost in the day's battle and prepared for the next morning's march. Even as he blended into the deepening twilight shadows, Falorn found it difficult to move forward without being detected.

After an eternity of incremental movements, Falorn found himself at the rear of the oversized headquarters tent. Darkness had fallen completely, and only cookfires and sporadic torches lit the camp. A sentry stood at the front of the tent, but as long as he avoided the lantern-lit opening, Falorn thought no one would see him. The guard did not walk a circuit, and the light of his own lantern effectively blinded the soldier to everything more than a few feet away in the darkness.

The lion card pulsed steadily, almost as strongly as during the battle. Falorn recognized the sensation and held himself in check, barely. He dared not ruin his careful advance by moving too quickly now. *If the thief card helped me get this far, I'll have to trust it to help me further. The cards do seem to want me here, almost as if they have thoughts and minds of their own.*

He dropped to the ground and crept slowly around the bottom of the tent, looking for an area loose enough for him to look through without revealing himself. Near the ground, Falorn noticed light spilling out from within the tent, which seemed to be illuminated inside like the festive walls of Roicenet.

Falorn crawled behind a pair of barrels and found the loose cloth he wanted. He couldn't help thinking of the alley where the thieves had ambushed him as he hid between the barrels and the heavy, orange cloth of the tent wall. Burrowing his head and body almost into the dirt, Falorn maneuvered until he could see at least part of the tent's interior without (he felt reasonably sure) being seen from either inside or outside unless someone knew precisely where to look.

He swore under his breath at the contents of the tent, and even the surge of the lion at his breast couldn't offset the sudden sickening feeling that welled up from his heart.

Sera stood on a floor covered with woven rugs. She had bathed and combed her hair free of the knots and tangles from two days of flight through the forest. She wore a man's clothing: white linen britches, a black velvet tunic belted with a strip of silk, soft leather boots. Falorn watched her talking animatedly with a man dressed in crimson.

The man looked only a few years older than Falorn, perhaps twenty years old. He kept his brown hair cropped short like a cavalryman. A thin beard barely colored his chin. Both hair and beard looked freshly washed and combed. The man wore a long puffy tunic of dyed-crimson silk, under a laced vest woven from pure cloth-of-gold. A gold clasp shaped like a striking eagle held a small scarlet cape, worn fashionably over his right arm. Crimson hose covered his legs, and soft doeskin slippers clad his feet. A tooled-leather baldric, also dyed crimson, hung from his right shoulder to his left side. Attached to that belt was the sword Falorn had set aside the night before.

A servant in scarlet livery approached the young man and Sera with crystal goblets and a decanter, carried on a silver tray. The man filled the two glasses with an amber liquid, handing one to Sera and taking the second for himself. He motioned for the servant to leave the tent, gesturing and uttering some witticism which Sera laughed at. Falorn could hear nothing of what they said.

The man carried the lion card stolen from the dead elf-warrior, Falorn knew in an instant. His own card burned with recognition. He wondered how he could possibly get it away from the man. He wondered what Sera was doing in the camp.

The man turned and stared directly at Falorn's hidden face. The heat from the lion card stopped utterly.

"Idiot." The young man sneered, displaying perfect teeth. Falorn felt the point of a sword poking against his back.

As the guards hauled him to his feet, Falorn flushed. *The other lion card must have heated up just like mine*, he realized suddenly. He felt like a fool. *The elf might have been killed for his card, but mine are about to be taken away from me without a fight.*

Two guards hustled him around the tent and into the front entrance, while a third followed behind and held a sword to Falorn's back. A scarlet banner with a gold eagle embroidered onto it hung from a spear propped above the doorway. One of the soldiers forced Falorn's head down as the other guards pushed him below the flag and through the doorway.

The young man smiled at him like a cat eyeing a trapped insect. Sera clung to the man's right arm, but kept her eyes averted from Falorn, to avoid meeting his gaze. At a gesture from the bearded man, the soldiers released his arms and let him stand upright. They stood a pace or two behind him, with the third guard holding the point of his sword at Falorn's back.

"Well," the young man said, in suave, city-bred tones, "what have we here? A spy maybe? But it doesn't look like a spy. It's a bit young and scrawny for that, not at all the sort you'd want prowling around an enemy camp. But what else could it be? A soldier? If it's a soldier, it seems to have lost its sword. Let me think for a moment . . ."

He paused theatrically.

". . . I know! I think it came here *looking* for something. Is that it?"

Falorn didn't answer.

"Isn't the little peasant boy going to answer? Why not, peasant boy? Is it that you're afraid to speak in the presence of your betters? Do I need to call in my horse-grooms to question you? Shall I have my servants fetch the draymaster?"

Falorn didn't dare say anything. He glanced around the wide, carpeted tent. Velvet cushions and a few low tables lay scattered around in place of furniture. A partially open curtain partitioned a huge featherbed from the rest of the tent. Sera's worn and soiled travel clothing sat folded and stacked neatly on the edge of the bed, her boots lying on top of the stack.

"There is another possibility, though. Maybe the peasant boy came here to *bring me* something. Do you have a *present* for me, peasant boy?"

Unaccountably, Falorn felt a warmth stirring against his chest. He looked at the young man again, and saw the sword and a pouch slung behind it had acquired a faint blue glow. The man continued to talk, but he didn't seem to care whether Falorn replied. Whatever he had just said made the guards at Falorn's back laugh.

Falorn thought he knew just what the thief card wanted. The nobleman who had captured him wasn't paying much attention, but he would need to divert the guards somehow. He didn't think he could do that without talking, though, and he knew—from years of watching drunk soldiers at his father's inn—that once he said something the danger to him would grow tremendously.

He looked at Sera, who still avoided his gaze. He wanted to think she hadn't told the man anything about him, but that was probably too much to hope for. He tried to guess what the man expected. He didn't even know who he faced, or why the man had an army here in the middle of the woods . . . unless it was about the cards.

He decided to play the scared peasant, although somehow he felt no fear at all.

Falorn fell to his knees in front of the thin-bearded man.

"Don't kill me, Lord! I'll do whatever you want!"

"Just as I thought. A peasant in a man's clothing."

Sera stroked the man's hair gently with her left hand, and he stopped talking to look at her. She still held tightly to his right arm, and she whispered something into his ear as he turned his head. He smiled in answer and she brushed his mouth with her lips.

Falorn couldn't see the guards behind him. From where he knelt, he hoped his back blocked their view of their master's sword and pouch, if they looked at him at all. Sera nuzzled the bearded man, and he responded by kissing her neck and ear. Falorn saw the man's left arm begin to creep up Sera's side toward her breast, leaving his baldric unprotected.

Sliding his right hand downward to his boot, Falorn palmed the small knife within.

He reached forward as unobtrusively as he could, taking care to keep his arms sheltered in front of his body. His right hand touched the pouch and felt the leather cord which attached it to the wide baldric. He flicked the blade once across the cord and felt it part easily. The pouch dropped into his left hand.

Falorn surged to his feet as the man started to turn. Sera's hold restricted the bearded man's arms as Falorn dropped the knife and slid the familiar sword from its sheath.

Twisting his left hand cruelly on Sera's breast, the man pushed her away. Instead of falling she clung with both arms to his right arm, pulling him partially off balance.

As Sera and the man struggled to his right, Falorn stepped back and faced the guards.

The three swordsmen advanced in unison, spreading out slightly. The one who had held the sword to his back was the same servant who poured the drinks earlier, Falorn noticed. *The bearded man must have sent him to warn the guards in front of the tent when he realized I was out there.*

Falorn felt strong and free, despite the advancing swordsmen. The new pouch made him giddy; he felt excited and controlled at the same time. It warmed his left hand, not with the urgent heat that the green lion had burned with before, but with an oddly soothing radiance. Gentle waves of strength washed along his left arm and through his body. From the pouch at his chest, the green lion gave off a similar warmth.

He raised the sword as the three soldiers came at him. Once again the blade felt natural in his hand. A quick thought of his defeat in Roicenet flashed into his head, but Falorn laughed and the fear fled.

This will be different. I don't know why or how, but I know this will be different.

For all their discipline, the three men advanced too slowly, as if the air had thickened around them. Falorn felt crisp and strong, as if he'd fed and rested in the afternoon, instead of crawling into the camp on an empty stomach.

Stepping into the first guard's attack, Falorn parried the left-hand guard's swing before the man could fully extend his arm. On his back-swing, he drew blood on the unarmored servant's exposed side. The man made a brief huffing noise but held his ground. Falorn stepped back before the third attacker could get behind him.

The sword felt light in his hand, like the birch switches Falorn had cut to play at swordfighting with other village boys. When a soldier stepped in front of the others to thrust at his belly, Falorn stepped around the man's right, pushing the thrust aside with the flat of his blade. Out of the corner of his eye, Falorn saw the bearded man watching, knife in hand. Sera lay across a cushion behind him, blood trickling from the corner of her mouth.

The momentum of the soldier's thrust carried him forward past Falorn, leaving his back unguarded. Falorn saw exposed whiteness where the armor left the guard's neck unprotected. Instead of slashing, he slammed the pommel of his sword into the base of the soldier's helmet.

As the guard crumpled, Falorn turned to face the other two attackers, first checking to make sure the bearded man did not advance on his right.

The unarmored servant moved less quickly than the other guard. *He's slowed by that cut in his side. He's falling a half step behind the other soldier.* The two guards advanced. Falorn took a step back, away from the unconscious soldier. The armored guard advanced on his left, while the servant took the right side.

Falorn stepped left and attacked, hoping to pierce the soldier's guard before the servant could come to his aid. The armored man fought defensively, turning Falorn's slash harmlessly aside. His blade clattered off the chain links on the man's forearm, and then Falorn found himself fighting both men at once.

Now they attacked him. The servant cut at Falorn's legs while the armored guard aimed thrusts at his neck and face. Falorn found he could hold them off with his newfound strength and speed, but he could not attack. He had to find a way to quickly end the fight, before the bearded nobleman summoned the rest of his soldiers. He backed up, moving slightly to his left, toward the bed.

The guards pressed their advance, hoping to throw Falorn off balance on the featherbed, or tangle him in the curtains.

Ducking low at the edge of the bed, he parried a series of blows from the armored soldier. He dropped the pouch into his tunic and came up with the boots in his left hand, their laces tangled and intertwined. He threw them in the face of the armored soldier, and saw them wrap around the man's sword as he parried the toss. Falorn twisted to the right and attacked the servant while the armored soldier struggled to free his sword.

The man parried Falorn's blows desperately. He glanced out of the corner of his eye at his companion, and Falorn's sword bit into his hand in the moment of lapsed concentration. The servant's weapon flew off to the right. Before the man could recover, Falorn slammed the flat of his blade into the side of the servant's head, dropping him to the ground. Turning, he faced the last guard's renewed attack.

They traded blows. Falorn felt the guard moving him backward toward the bearded man, and guessed that the nobleman had armed himself. He stepped forward instead, and put all of his strength into a high overhand cut.

The armored man made a two-handed parry with his thinly ground longsword. The tempered steel shattered. His eye blossomed red as splinters of steel flew into him. Falorn kicked the man's jaw, knocking him backward onto a lavish rug.

He turned to face the nobleman, who held one of the downed soldiers' swords.

"It's all over, peasant boy," the man sneered. "All I have to do is raise my voice, and a hundred men will be in this tent. Put down the sword, give me the cards, and I'll let you walk out of here alive. Otherwise, I'll kill you so painfully you'll wish you were dying from gangrene instead."

"And what sort of death is that, dear?" Sera purred from behind the bearded man. She held a short-bladed knife to the back of his neck, and even from across the tent Falorn could see the discoloration of some sort of coating on the knife's blade.

The nobleman wordlessly dropped the sword to the carpeted floor.

Sera held the knife steadily, smiling at Falorn as he tied the man's hands and gagged him with strips of the bedside curtain.

"I was afraid you'd never get here," she said to Falorn as the noble glared at them both.

"What?" Falorn asked, as stunned as the soldiers on the floor.

"Well, I knew you'd follow, silly. Come on, we've got to get out of here quickly. Bring him along as a hostage." She walked over to the bed and wiped the blood from her mouth on an embroidered quilt. Sera tied something into a piece of pastel-dyed silk cloth and tucked it into her black velvet tunic. Lifting a small chest and an oilcloth-wrapped package from a low bedside table, she carried them under her left arm as they stepped through the tent entrance. The chest clinked with the sound of coins moving as she walked. With her right hand, Sera held a knife to the nobleman's throat. She waved off Falorn's attempt to help her with the bundles, although they looked heavy. Instead he held his sword ready, in case the bearded man tried to cry out or escape. Sera smiled at Falorn as they walked out into the camp, but all the same he didn't turn his back on her or the bound nobleman.

Darkness had completely fallen, and they saw no sentries within the camp itself. They reached the line of horses quickly, avoiding cookfires and other signs of wakeful soldiers. They found four warhorses already saddled and ready to ride.

"They want to be able to respond quickly in case there's a night attack by the elves," Sera told him, "although I don't think they'll be able to attack anytime soon. We'll take all four. Cut the cinches from the other saddles." Falorn walked along the row of waiting saddles and quickly disabled each one with his sword. They mounted, careful not to give the bearded man an opportunity to escape.

They heard no alarms as they left the camp behind. Somehow, Falorn was not surprised when Sera easily guided them to a trail. She led the nobleman's mount, while Falorn held the reins of the spare warhorse.

They rode perhaps two miles down a wide moonlit trail before Sera motioned them to a halt. She dismounted; Falorn waited for her to help their captive dismount before leaving the back of his own horse. In the moonlight, he could see she held the dark-bladed knife blade in her hand.

"What are you doing?" he asked.

"What do you think I'm doing? I'm going to kill him, of course."

"You can't do that!"

"Why not? He's unarmed. I think I can manage it."

"You can't kill an unarmed man while he's tied up!"

"It wouldn't be much of a loss." Sera's left hand rubbed her jaw where the man had struck her.

"That's not the point. Please don't kill him."

"He'll only cause problems for us later. As soon as he gets back to that camp he'll have soldiers after us."

"We'll be gone by then."

"He'll keep looking." She glanced at the chest of coins on her horse.

"Sera, please." She saw the look in his eyes and reluctantly sheathed her knife. The nobleman's hard expression had not changed during the whole exchange.

"All right," she said, pausing to take the oilcloth package from the spare horse. "You should put this on before we go any further, though."

He unwrapped the package and found a coat of light chain mail within. Stripping to the waist, Falorn put it on against his skin, since he had no quilted gambeson to wear beneath it. The mail fit too snugly to hold much padding underneath anyway. When he replaced his tunic, the armor could not be seen. He had remembered to take the baldric and sheath from the nobleman. Sera had already stripped the man of other valuables, including the golden eagle pin which had held his cape in place.

While Sera repacked her loot, Falorn pulled the new pouch out from within his tunic, hoping she would not kill the man while he turned his back. He opened the nobleman's pouch and withdrew the three cards within. Two more lions looked up at him, one gold and one blue, each as restless as the green cat whose faint heat still warmed his chest. A crimson knight rode on the back of a caparisoned red horse, the same scarlet soldier he had seen on the pages of the dead warrior's book.

He wanted to look at them forever, but he soon heard Sera buckling her saddlebags shut, and didn't want to show the cards to her. Slipping them into his own pouch, Falorn quickly pulled the laces tight again. He could feel all five cards even after he had returned the pouch to its familiar place inside his tunic. Each card had its own individual radiance; he found he could distinguish them easily, and feel the presence of each of them against his chest.

He didn't want to keep the nobleman's pouch, but didn't want to return it either. Falorn threw it into the woods by the side of the path instead. He and Sera mounted up quickly and rode on, leaving the bearded young man tied and gagged in the middle of the path. The man was still struggling in the middle of the road when the four horses cantered around a turn in the moonlit path and out of sight.

Sera seemed to have a direction in mind. They changed horses often as they rode through the night, stopping only briefly for rest. Falorn waited until their third rest stop before speaking.

"Sera?"

"Yes?"

"Who was that man?"

"He's the son of one of my father's friends."

"Please, Sera. Who was he?"

"His name is Rorik. He's the oldest son and heir of the Duke of Iron Eagle."

"What was he doing in the woods with that army?"

"Leading his father's troops into battle against the elves. They've been fighting off and on in that forest for generations, but I think he was really there to find that elf's card."

"You weren't *really* surprised to find those soldiers then. You knew he was there all along."

"I didn't know for sure. I thought he might be. He told me he wanted to take his father's men into battle against the elves during the spring campaigning season."

"He told you?"

"Of course he told me. Months ago."

"So you two were close."

"Would I have wanted to kill him if we were close? His father and my father were close. We tolerated each other." Falorn thought of the neatly folded pile of clothing by the bed, and the man's clothing Sera now wore.

"But you talked. And he told you about his plans."

"Of course we talked. He was my fiancé. He had to tell me about his plans."

Falorn stared at her dumbly.

"Come on," she said. "It's time to mount up. If we ride through the night this path will bring us to the King's Road by morning. We have to make good time. Rorik and his soldiers are on our trail by now, and I don't think he's in a marrying mood anymore."

"You had a hand in the insanity in the swamp?"

"In the insanity? No. Unless you're talking about the fighting, which I did help provoke. I wasn't far behind when my son left Rorik's camp, and when I realized where he was going, I thought it might require a diversion to allow him to win free again."

"To save your son? Or to take the cards for yourself?"

"Surely you know that I had no interest in taking the cards for myself, Councilor. If I had, I wouldn't have left that first one for my son to take. My motives may not have been pure, but I love my son."

The heavyset interrogator shifted on the couch, seeming to consider his next question carefully.

"If you had no hand in the insanity, can you perhaps explain it?"

"The swamp was a terrible place to live. It drove people mad, whether from magic or desolation I don't know. But it was also the well-spring of the cards' power, and someone had to guard it. Just because the sorceress died didn't mean that another one wouldn't come. And sorceresses may not stay dead like the rest of us."

The interrogator's gaze shifted out the window for a moment, before his attention turned back fiercely. "Go on."

"One of the soldiers finally volunteered to hold the place with his men. It was a death sentence for all of them, but their children were promised homes and wealth in a better land. A cruel bargain, but a fair one, except that something in the swamp made women barren. Not a one of them had a child, and after enough years passed, that twisted all of them. For a while, people visited, until the baron's folk started preying on the visitors. After that, folk left them to guard the swamp, in the same way a troll guards a bridge."

"A strange place to send one's son."

"Perhaps. But that's getting ahead of the story."

The interrogator nodded. "So it is. Perhaps you should continue from where you left off."

8

Golden Reeds

Two hours before dawn the forest gave way to rolling hills. They finally stopped to sleep an hour later, in a roofless hilltop cottage long abandoned by some freeholder or petty farmer. They stumbled inside, leaving the horses to graze on the hillside, and collapsed from fatigue on the soft splinters and sawdust of the cottage's half-rotted floor.

When Falorn awoke the sun stood a quarter of the way across a blue, cloudless sky. His hand instinctively went to the pouch inside his tunic, even though he could sense the presence of the five cards against his skin. He felt for the sword at his side, then looked around in the daylight. Sera slept, curled up like a cat, at the opposite wall of the derelict hut, against the blackened shell of the hearth. Through the gaping hole of the doorway, he saw the horses steadily cropping grass from the hill; that would do for now, he thought, but they'd have to find or buy more feed for the horses soon. He wondered if Sera had thought to bring his other pouch with her, and if so how he might politely ask for it back.

He decided the politest thing he could do would be to search through her possessions while she slept. He took three quiet steps toward her saddlebags before she rolled over, wide awake.

"Do we have anything for breakfast?" she asked.

"I don't think so, unless you brought it. You took all the supplies, remember?"

"I had to. It was the only way he'd believe my story."

"Which was . . . ?"

"Please, Falorn, it's a little early for this. I haven't had any more sleep than you have. Can we talk about this later?"

"Can I have my pouch?"

"Sure. It's right here." She dug into the saddlebag beside her. After a moment, she rooted out the pouch and tossed it to Falorn. He quickly flattened his cloak on the floor and poured out the pouch's contents. As far as he could tell, she'd returned everything.

"Satisfied?" she finally asked. "Can we get moving now, and maybe get something to eat?"

"Sera?"

"What, Falorn?"

"Where are we going? What's this place that's so important you had to take everything and leave me in the woods to get there?"

"I borrowed your things so I could get close to Rorik. It's got nothing to do with where we're going now. And I didn't take everything. I left you the cards so you could catch up, didn't I?"

"I thought you just missed the cards because they weren't where I said."

"Don't be silly," she said, smirking. "A girl never believes anything a man says when he wants to take her to bed. If I wanted to take the cards I would have taken them."

That's true. And she let me take Rorik's cards. And yet. . . .

He walked out of the hut to saddle the horses, running a hand through his unruly hair and hoping the confusion would go away somehow.

After a few minutes, Sera came out of the cottage with a small packet of something wadded in silk, and began walking down the hillside toward him.

"Here," she called over to him, "I salvaged these last night. They're not much, but they'll do for breakfast." She handed him a soggy piece of meat pastry. Most of the delicate crust had flaked away, except where juice from the meat had soaked through the breading. He looked at her uncertainly for a minute, then began to eat.

"Some of them are meat and some are cheese," she said, spreading the parcel out on the grass. "I think the meat ones are pigeon, but I'm not sure. They were next to the bed, so I just wrapped them in this cloth and stuffed them inside my tunic. I forgot about them while we were riding, so they got a little crushed."

"Thank you," he said, after a long silence.

They finished the pastries quietly. Sera shook out the cloth afterward and stuffed it back inside her tunic. Falorn got up and walked over to the four horses. The animals neighed anxiously, ready to run on the grassy, rolling hills. As he put his hand on the saddle of his mount he felt Sera touch his shoulder. He flinched involuntarily as he felt her close behind him.

"Look, Falorn," she said quietly, "I realize I've done a lot of things these last few days that you probably don't understand, and I'm sorry if I haven't been able to explain. But everything is going to make sense as soon as things settle down . . . I promise." She brushed her hands slowly through his hair. He stiffened as he thought of her hands against the bearded nobleman, but he felt his shoulders gradually loosen as she moved her hands downward to rub them.

"Sera," he said, haltingly, "I'm just not sure what to believe anymore. I mean, you took my sword and left me there."

"I know how it must look to you, and I feel bad," she said. "I really didn't want to hurt you, but we needed to get those cards. And you were great."

"Sera. . . ."

"I like you a lot, Falorn. I want you to know that, no matter what happens."

His shoulders tightened again.

"What do you mean, 'no matter what happens'?"

"I don't mean anything. Just that we've been through a lot, and we're still on the run with my father and Rorik and probably his father and the gods only know who else after us. Anything could happen. And I want you to know I do care about you, no matter what."

"Sera, could you promise me one thing?"

"What?"

"Promise me that you won't run off like that again."

"Would you believe me if I did?"

"I don't know. I'd like to."

"I don't want to give you something else to not trust me about. Just give me a chance and I'll explain everything, and then you can tell me if you still want me to promise that." She gave his shoulders a final squeeze then let go, trailing one hand down his back before she stepped away. "Better mount up. We have a long ride ahead, but if we're lucky we'll have a hot meal and a safe place to sleep tonight."

"Where are we going?" Falorn asked as he mounted the warhorse.

"A place called Golden Reeds. The baron there's an old friend of my father, but they haven't seen each other in years. I'm sure we'll be welcome there, and there's no way he'll know my father's looking for me yet." She spurred her horse to a canter and Falorn had to follow, holding the reins of the two spare horses in his free hand.

The second hill they topped looked out over the King's Road, a younger and more crowded cousin to the Turnpike, as it wound its way southwest through marsh and forest and off to distant cities beyond the Free Duchies. Their destination, Falorn gathered, lay in the marsh.

They rode on the King's Road most of the afternoon. Merchants, pilgrims, and soldiers crowded the paved road, but nobody questioned them, despite the tattered condition of Falorn's clothing.

Once they turned onto the side road toward Golden Reeds, they saw no one. Even the occasional farmsteads vanished after a few miles. Grassy hills gave way to brownish-green marsh grass, and finally to an endless sea of cattails.

Falorn's suspicion that they rode on the only dry ground for miles around grew stronger as the afternoon waned into early evening—only to be finally confirmed as the castle came into view, a sullen gray rock backlit by the spectacular reds and oranges of the setting sun.

A narrow raised path of built-up earth, barely wide enough for a single wagon to pass, provided the only approach to the castle.

"Sera," Falorn asked after they halted the horses where the trail narrowed, "this friend of your father's is a baron, right?"

"That's right."

"I hate to admit to a peasant's ignorance, but where is his barony? This land looks like it's all underwater."

"Mostly it is underwater," she admitted.

"Doesn't that make it hard to live there?"

"I imagine it must," she said slowly, as if the thought had never occurred to her before. She seemed to kick the idea around in her head. "Some of the water probably isn't very deep."

"Even so," Falorn said, "I'm not sure I would want to live here, speaking as a peasant. And I don't see any houses."

"Maybe the village is behind the castle. We wouldn't see it because of the sunset."

"Maybe. But it looks like that water goes all the way around."

"So maybe he's a poor baron. That would explain why my father doesn't have much to do with him anymore. Either way, he's bound to have more to eat than we do. Let's go, before they lock the gates for the night." Falorn shook his head, but walked his horse and the spares carefully behind her, along the elevated trail toward the castle.

They found the gate of the castle already closed by the time they reached the head of the manmade path. A square stone doorway faced the path, and a double door of heavy planks bound with strips of iron sealed the front of the small keep. Alert-looking guards in chain mail and helms peered down from the top of the wall. The guards seemed surprised at the prospect of nighttime visitors. *Or any visitors at all?* Falorn wondered. It took several minutes before anyone so much as loosened the slidehole in one of the doors to get a close look at the two travelers.

"I wonder how they keep the armor from rusting in this swamp?" Falorn mused out loud while they waited.

"Or why they're wearing so much of it out here in the middle of nowhere," Sera answered. Falorn had been thinking the same thing. "Did we miss a besieging army somewhere?"

"He can't be too poor a baron if he can afford all that armor. I wonder where he gets the money?"

"I don't know. I haven't been here for years, and then I was too young to think to ask. Maybe he just started out with a lot of money. A decent-sized family fortune would go a long way out here. The armor might be old."

"Not if you had to pay people to come live here."

"That's true," Sera replied.

Someone finally pulled the slidehole cover aside, and a pair of eyes appeared behind it silently. After only a few seconds' additional delay—but no words—they heard clanking and clattering from inside and one of the thick doors came gradually open.

"Come in, be welcome!" an old man's voice cried out. "I am the steward of this place, and I bid you enter and accept the hospitality of the Baron of Golden Reeds." A small, bald man in frayed brown robes stood beside the open door. The top of his head came only to Falorn's shoulder. The old man smiled up at them almost toothlessly, and pulled at his whiskers with his left hand. With his right hand he clutched his symbol of office, a carved staff fully six and a half feet high, stained a dark yellow and with a long brass head.

That staff looks, Falorn thought, *like nothing so much as an elaborately inscribed giant cattail.*

"Come in out of the night, please." The old man gestured them inside fervently, as if there was a rush to get inside. Falorn and Sera stepped inside one at a time, leading the horses. Two armored guards quickly began turning a massive crank mechanism to shut the door behind them.

Why did they let us in without asking a single question? Falorn wondered. He could see a puzzled look on Sera's face as well. *How can they have so many guards, but less actual security than my father's tavern? Just what are all those armored men guarding against?*

They found themselves on the ground floor of a small keep—a single fortified building rather than a walled castle with a courtyard. The bottom floor seemed devoted mainly to livestock and storage. Dozens of ladders and stairways led upward into what looked to be a warren of narrow corridors and oddly shaped rooms above. Shops, stables, pens, and storage sheds piled one on top of another occupied the first two stories of the castle; two more levels remained above, plus the rooms in the keep's lone tower.

Rough-looking groomsmen came to take their horses away. Falorn wondered that there seemed to be no stableboys about. He saw only adults, mainly men. *Probably,* he thought, *the baron can only hire bachelors and free swords. He'd have trouble persuading families to move into his barony unless he could offer them dry land to live and work on.* He wondered at the number of soldiers he saw lounging about. With the number on duty, there must be thirty or forty men-at-arms in this fortress, a ridiculous expense in a poor barony which seemed to be miles away from any threatening neighbor, looked nearly invulnerable to siege, and anyway had nothing worth taking.

The steward gestured for them to follow and shuffled toward one of the multiple staircases, a rickety wooden spiral shored up in several places by thick beams or iron plates.

"His lordship and ladyship have retired for the night, but they do so love guests. His lordship will be overjoyed to see you in the morning. I'm having some of the servants prepare a suite of rooms for the both of you, and I'll have a meal and hot bath sent up. Will that be satisfactory?"

"That will be wonderful," Sera said. "We've had a very long ride.

When his lordship awakens, please have someone tell him that Lady Sera of Roicenet has come to visit him."

"Of course, milady," the steward said. "Now, if you will both please follow me. . . ." He began slowly pulling himself up the stairs, using the staff for support. The boards creaked ominously under Falorn and Sera's added weight.

The stairs led them to a narrow, twisting passageway. Dozens of doors and side passageways divided its whitewashed plastered walls. Even concentrating, Falorn couldn't follow the twists and turns they took, despite the steward's slow pace. After he gave up on making sense of the passages, Falorn decided to practice with the cards and began looking closely at the things around him instead. *It's weird that I just stumbled onto the first magic I've ever seen a few days ago, and now it feels like I've always had these cards. Shouldn't I be scared of them?* But the cards felt oddly natural against his chest, radiating reassurance as if they approved of his attempts to learn to channel their power.

He noticed places where a space of wall or floor gave off a thin blue glow, like the outlines of a concealed door or secret peephole. More than once, he felt as if someone watched him from behind one of those hidden vantage points. He found himself noticing other things as well: a long-forgotten brass coin half-buried under dust, a thinning floor joint where a board would creak if stepped on, the way the steward tugged his whiskers nervously as they passed certain doors or side passages.

The old man finally stopped in front of a bare door that looked no different from a dozen of its neighbors, or a hundred others they had passed in this wasps' nest of a castle. The steward fumbled at his sash for a moment before producing an impressive ring of brass keys. He seemed to know the correct key immediately, fitting it to the door's lock on his first attempt, and twisting slowly until the mechanism clicked loudly.

"Your rooms are here. Your meal and bath should lie already within. The kitchen staff moves, I fear, faster than these old legs. I trust you'll want nothing until morning, but don't hesitate to pull the cord if you need to summon the servants. The custom here is for guests to lie in, since there is no morning hunt, and his lordship prefers to attend to his dawn religious services in person. I will send someone to minister to you later in the morning, and perhaps you'll care to break your fast with his lordship and her ladyship?" The steward droned through the words, as if he'd been rehearsing as they walked and feared he'd forget his lines if he failed to recite them quickly. He leaned on the door, forcing it open, and nearly pushed Falorn and Sera into the chamber. His beckoning staff of office left them little choice but to move forward. As soon as they entered he bowed deeply from the hallway at the edge of the portal, and pulled the door shut.

"We'd be delighted," Sera said, to the blank doorway she now faced. The door clicked loudly in reply, as the steward engaged the lock from the hallway.

"I guess they don't care for sleepwalkers," Falorn said, shaking his head. "Is this the way all nobles treat their guests?"

"Not the simple peasant courtesy you're used to, I guess," Sera replied, although not unkindly.

"Not the sort of courtesy I'm used to as an innkeeper's son, no. My father never locked people in their room at nights. He locked up the valuables now and again *because* of the guests, but he never locked up the guests."

"I can't say that it's what I'm used to either. You haven't exactly encountered the flower of the nobility since you turned man-at-arms, have you?"

"I hope not," Falorn said, sighing. He looked around their chambers. They stood in the center of an oddly shaped room, its walls cut nearly triangular by the twists and turns of castle passages. The room held a sagging couch covered in worn fabric. Two chairs woven from marsh reeds sat opposite the sofa, their seats cushioned with similarly worn brocade. A heavy carved table of stained-dark hardwood sat next to the sofa but matched none of the other furniture in the room. Several covered earthenware dishes sat on the table, as well as a pitcher of thick-looking red wine, two empty bowls, and wooden spoons. A wooden half-barrel filled with steaming water sat in one of the room's three corners, next to a weathered-looking chamberpot. A scrub brush made from gathered reeds leaned against the makeshift tub. Open doorways in two of the walls led to adjoining rooms, while the third wall held only the locked door. Oil lanterns on all three walls illuminated the room.

"Bath before dinner, I think," Sera said. "You first. You need it more."

"I guess," Falorn said, conscious of his empty stomach.

Sera began stripping off his shirt.

"I can do it," he said, pulling away from her. She looked hurt for a moment, but then regained her composure.

"Afraid I'm going to take your things again? Where would I go with them? We're locked in, remember?"

He pulled off his belt, baldric, and tunic and unlaced the chain mail beneath, putting everything carefully on the closest chair. Sitting on the other chair, he slowly peeled off his boots, knocking away caked mud as he did so. He looked at Sera self-consciously before untying his britches; she just watched him with a neutral expression on her face. Finally, he stepped out of them and left them lying on the floor. Falorn walked quickly to the corner and stepped into the bath. He settled into the hot water and felt his legs begin to relax. He realized he had left the pouch with the cards around his neck, but decided not to remove it. The cards felt pleasantly warm against his skin, combining with the heat from the water and the fatigue from the day's ride to leave him pleasantly languid.

The roughness of the scrubbing brush woke him up.

"That hurts!" he said. "You're scouring me."

"Don't you dare fall asleep in there. I want some of that water while it's still warm." She handed him the brush. "I'd offer to wash you, but I think you'd be too embarrassed. It's nothing I haven't seen, you know."

"It's not that . . . it's just that. . . ."

"Scrub!" she said. "We can talk when you're clean."

In spite of her teasing, Falorn tried to avoid looking when Sera undressed. He focused on toweling himself dry with one of the scratchy cloths provided by the servants.

Sera seemed bothered that he wasn't watching; she went out of her way to be provocative as she took off her clothes. Slowly, she unlaced her doublet. She lingered slightly before removing each piece of clothing, gradually showing Falorn more and more of her pale, light skin. He couldn't read the look in her dark brown eyes.

She's scared, Falorn finally realized. *She's showing off because she's just as scared as I am.*

Naked, Sera looked thinner than Falorn expected. She shivered as she stepped into the bath. Falorn waited until she finished scrubbing the dirt from her skin before he approached the tub. He draped a towel over her shoulders before she rose from the water. He kept his hands lightly on her shoulders as she stood up, shaking slightly despite the warmth of the room. Sera leaned back against him, wet towel against his bare chest, and he gently held her close until she stopped shivering.

She turned her head and lightly kissed him on the cheek before she stepped away to dry herself and dress.

"Thank you," she said, and he had to turn away, embarrassed again.

The food proved to be rice, mixed with weakly spiced sauce and thin shards of vegetables. They sat together on the couch and ate quietly.

Falorn felt self-conscious, unsure what to say to Sera. After dinner, he wanted to talk about the last few nights, but the odd setting seemed to discourage conversation.

Sera stayed quiet as well. So instead of talking, Falorn prowled through the three rooms looking for spyholes. The two small side rooms contained no furniture other than sailcloth mattresses stuffed with soft swamp-grass. He found no trace of surveillance.

"What do you think they're so worried about?" Sera asked Falorn, speaking in a low tone.

"I'd hoped you might know. He has an awful lot of soldiers, and they all seem to be on edge."

"I noticed that, too. I don't remember it being like this when I was younger. I don't know if it's changed or I just didn't notice it then."

"Are they worried about something on the outside getting in, or something on the inside getting out? Did you see the way the steward rushed us past some of those doors?"

"It's very strange. They're treating us nicely enough, though, except for the locked door. I don't think they're planning to hurt us. And I'm sure the steward didn't know my father was looking for me. He didn't even remember me."

"I wouldn't wander around if we could. I'd be afraid of getting lost."

"It's very strange," she said again, then lapsed into thought and silence.

When they talked again they discussed only commonplace things. Sera asked about life as an innkeeper's son, and told him a little about growing up noble in a bustling city. Falorn wondered if either of them listened much to the other. He found it hard to concentrate on Sera's words or on his own, between the strangeness of Castle Golden Reeds and the uncertainty of their nearness to each other. After an hour or so they kissed—briefly—on the lips, wished each other a good night, and went to lie down on separate pallets.

Falorn thought he would lie awake brooding over the fears and violence of the last few days, but fatigue caught up with him. He fell asleep almost instantly, one hand clutched protectively over the pouch of cards.

9

The Feast

The door unlocked with a loud click. No natural light penetrated the windowless room, so Falorn could only guess at how long he'd slept. He rose to his feet quickly, sword in hand.

A dim triangle of light appeared as the door opened.

With a quiet shuffle, an older male servant entered the room.

"Steward's coming." The man grunted at Falorn. The servant placed his lantern on the table, picked up the empty dishes, and disappeared back into the hall.

Falorn laced on his armor, shrugged his clothing into place, adjusted his belt, and ran a hand through his hair to straighten it. He walked through the central room and peered into Sera's sleeping-chamber. He found her sitting up on her pallet, already dressed, combing her hair with an enameled, bone-toothed wooden comb.

"Company's coming, I think," he said. "Anything I should know before we go meet the swamplord?"

"Yes," Sera said, without looking up from her combing. "First of all, you address him as 'your lordship,' if he addresses you first. Don't speak without being spoken to, and only reply to a direct question. As the younger child of a duke, I actually rank five places above him on the Table of Precedency, assuming he doesn't know we're on the run. Or even if he does, actually. He'd arrest me, but he'd have to do it respectfully. You, he'd hang."

"Thanks."

"You asked. Bow very low when you're brought into his presence, and don't get up until I signal you. Don't yawn, no matter how long or boring the ceremonies get. Maybe he'll think you're a knight."

"What's the Table of Precedency?"

"It's a table which lists all people by their order, and ranks each of those orders. It's tremendously important when you need to get people to sit down at court without them dueling over who belongs where. Younger children of dukes rank twenty-third, and barons twenty-ninth— unless they hold some other title as well."

"Where am I?"

"If he mistakes you for a knight, you're thirty-one places further down the table. Bachelor knights rank below baronets, the various orders of knights, judges, eldest and younger children of all the higher members of the peerages, and a few other things. Gentlemen entitled to bear arms are four places further down."

"No, I mean where am I if he doesn't mistake me for anything?"

"Oh. If he doesn't mistake you for anything, then you're not on the Table of Precedency at all. Let's hope he does."

"I thought you said it was a listing of all people."

"I did. You don't understand, though. When I use 'people' in the sense of the Table of Precedency, it just means the nobility. It's a stricter usage of the word."

"And everybody else doesn't count?"

"Of course you count, Falorn. But it's not really necessary to determine whether the younger son of an innkeeper takes precedence over the firstborn of a butcher at a state dinner. I don't mean to offend you, but you are here under rather . . . dubious pretenses."

I'm here because you robbed your father, Falorn thought, *and because I robbed a dead man*. But the arrival of the steward saved him from replying to Sera with more than a scowl.

The old man shuffled into the central room and cleared his throat, waiting for the two of them to emerge. When they did, he began walking them toward the door, even before he had spoken a word.

"If you would be good enough to follow me," he said, tugging nervously at his whiskers, "his lordship will see you presently." Falorn checked to see that he wore all of his possessions, including sword, armor, and both pouches. He noticed Sera doing the same, as they began retracing their way through the maze of halls.

A baffling series of twists and turns led them to a pair of impressive double doors, heavy wood hung on unpolished brass hinges. The steward laboriously pulled one of the doors open, pounded his staff of office twice on the stone floor, and called out: "Lady Sera of Roicenet, daughter to His Grace, the Duke of Roicenet." The steward made no attempt to identify Falorn.

They entered the baron's great hall, and found themselves nearly the only occupants of the expansive room. Light seeped in from dirty skylights in the high ceiling above, but most of the room's illumination came from torches in iron sconces bolted to the bare stone walls. Rough tables and benches sat in stacks against the right hand wall, cleared away until needed for meals. At least ten doors spotted the walls. *This hall must be the central meeting place of all the warrens in this stone rabbit-hutch,* Falorn realized.

The baron and his wife sat at the far end of the hall, in high-backed wooden chairs cushioned with green velvet. The baron filled his chair entirely, an enormously heavy red-bearded man dressed all in silk. His wife, by contrast, looked no larger than a child half Falorn's age. Wrinkles lined her wan face. Her body, nearly emaciated, seemed to need the support of the chairback to sit up. Like her husband she wore silk, but while the baron's tentlike clothing loaned dignity to his girth, the baroness seemed lost in the wispy, ethereal fabric of her dress.

"My lady Sera!" the baron's voice boomed out in a warm baritone. Sera walked forward a dozen steps and bowed slightly, gesturing to Falorn. He bowed as low to the floor as he could, feeling like a drunken soldier at his father's inn.

"I'm pleased to see you, Baron. It's been a very long time."

"Very long indeed. Too long to keep a man away from his goddaughter. Come here and sit on my knee and tell me how you've been these many years since your father last visited." Sera walked toward the baron's chair, gesturing once again to Falorn as she did so. He straightened up shakily, dizzy and red-faced from all the blood rushing to his head.

She reached the edge of the baron's chair and climbed up, sitting on the chair's broad arm to the baron's right.

"You've grown, girl, you've grown. What a comely lass you've turned into, all plump and healthy." Falorn almost expected Sera to bristle at the remark, but she held her face in control. The baroness, sitting to the left of her husband, barely moved at all. She looked like a woman struggling with a long bout of sleeplessness. Deep rings colored the skin around her eyes, as if she'd used paints to try and hide the effects of sickness or lack of sleep. The cosmetics had a rather sad effect on the tiny baroness, making her look like a whore's invalid daughter playing with her mother's box of flesh-paints.

"Thank you, Baron. You look like you've prospered, yourself."

"I have, I have, though not so much as some other nobles that never come to see their old friends anymore. Not even to bring my own goddaughter to come visit. I'm glad to see you haven't forgotten old friends and poor relations, even if some in your family have."

"My father's a very busy man. I'm sure he just hasn't had the time."

"In eleven years he hasn't had the time! I give him my troops, I give him my support, I give him my love like a brother, and not once in the last eleven years have I seen hide nor hair of him. I even had my wife write letters"—he gestured to the left, but the baroness remained still—"which he never answered. Your father's a powerful man, Sera, and a good man, but he's forgotten a thing or two about friendship and kinship."

"I'm sorry to hear that."

"Ah, it's no matter in the end. Just another bucket of water in the swamp. You're here now and we'll celebrate tonight. I've already called for a feast. Tonight we'll feast and celebrate like your father and I did in the old days." For a fleeting moment, Falorn saw a horrified look pass over the baroness's face. But her visage quickly subsided into the same dead expression she had worn since they entered the room.

After an hour of bantering with Sera, the baron dismissed them until the evening's feast. Falorn, stiff from holding himself unmoving, felt glad to leave the room. He had not seen the baroness move or change expression again.

Outside the door, the steward awaited them. He seemed to have grown spry as the morning went on, and walked them into rooms and around hallways at a less tepid pace than before. He took them to a variety of storage rooms, where the baron had asked that they select clothing more appropriate to the evening's feasting. Sera chose dark green leggings and a green-edged black satin cloak, to go with the clothing she had obtained in Rorik's camp. Falorn, deciding that no one was going to pay attention to him no matter what he wore, selected new traveling clothes: a loose-weave white tunic with tight cuffs, brown deerskin britches, and a black cloak. He wondered at the variety of clothing in the baron's storerooms. Most of the clothing looked small, although he'd seen no children at all in the castle.

A chilling thought struck him. *I hope this clothing isn't left over from an outbreak of gray fever or another plague.*

They bundled the clothing and made their way back through the halls. Finally, they descended a flight of gray stone stairs behind the steward, and found themselves back in the wide hall they had entered the castle by the night before. Here the steward left them, pleading the urgency of his duties and promising to return for them an hour before the start of the feast.

A dozen soldiers practiced with wooden swords in the center of the room. Falorn dropped his bundle of clothing to the straw-covered flagstones and squatted to watch. He felt an unfamiliar sensation at his chest as he followed the moves with his eyes, and he recognized it as the crimson knight card making its presence known. He felt the rumbling sensation of the three lion cards in the background as well, though they seemed less concerned with the practice movements he watched than with actual fighting or physical exertion. At other times, they seemed to prefer sleep.

After a while, one of the soldiers dropped out with a twisted knee, and his fellows noticed Falorn.

"Ho, there," one of them called out, "how about a turn or two with us working men?"

Falorn smiled nervously and caught the wooden sword the man tossed over. He shook off Sera's hand as she tried halfheartedly to restrain him. He stepped to the center of the practice ring, across from the man who had tossed the sword, and assumed what he thought might be the proper guard position.

A burning sensation in his chest forced him to take a step back and shift his hands to avoid losing his balance. The heat stopped as soon as he moved. His new position felt natural, somehow; he tried to memorize it, so as to avoid further correction from the crimson card.

"A by-the-book knight, I see, always in that perfect position." Falorn did not move as the man feinted slightly. "Let's see how your technique holds up against someone who learned his swordwork on the streets."

The man attacked with a sudden series of overhand slashes. Falorn rolled his shoulders and effortlessly countered them, wondering at the economy of his own movements. The barest feint caused his attacker to hopelessly overstep. A tap on the knuckles sent the man's wooden sword flying. Falorn's own wooden blade halted a finger's width from the man's exposed throat.

"Maybe there's something to be said for that book after all," the man said gruffly, and Falorn found himself laughing along with the rest. He and the guards worked hard at their swordsmanship for several hours. Other than that first joke the guards were a dour lot, but Falorn enjoyed the exertion, and felt the lions exult in the prolonged swordwork as well. He felt no joy from whatever supernatural spirit animated the crimson card; however; it stung him unmercifully any time he misstepped or erred in position. By the end of the afternoon the scarlet knight alone had inflicted more pain than all of the bruises and scrapes from the wooden blades of the other fighters with whom he'd sparred.

Falorn only thought about the time when the steward returned to take them back to their rooms to change. Falorn realized all of a sudden that he and Sera hadn't eaten all day; he began to look forward to the coming feast—assuming, of course, that the baron remembered to invite Sera's anonymous knight-bachelor companion.

The baron and his household had already assembled in the great hall by the time Falorn and Sera bathed, dressed, and followed the steward (who had slowed again as the afternoon wore on) toward the feast. When they entered the room, the baron raised his gold-banded drinking horn and bellowed a welcome; the rest of the household roared in response.

The steward directed Falorn toward the bottom of the main table, while accompanying Sera to her place of honor at the baron's right. Falorn felt uneasy at being separated from her, although he supposed the safety of the baron's walls left him more protected than he had been since leaving his father's inn.

He found himself sitting between a sergeant of the guard and another soldier, neither of them men he had practiced with that afternoon. Pitchers of wine already passed freely around the table, although food had yet to arrive. Falorn accepted a proffered offer to fill the drinking horn that sat in front of him and sipped the rich red liquid as he looked around the room.

Should I be drinking on an empty stomach? he wondered belatedly.

By this time, people completely filled the benches lining each of the three long tables. Falorn saw no children and few women, even among the servants. Thin, nervous-looking men scurried through several of the great hall's many doors, bringing prepared food and drink from the baron's kitchens. Most of the men at the tables looked like soldiers or retired soldiers. The women looked like soldiers' wives or whores.

Many of the other guests wore the same haunted look Falorn had seen pass across the baroness's face, although she wore her previous dead expression. Falorn saw no farmers or other peasants present at the meal. He looked toward the head of the table, and saw Sera in animated conversation with the baron.

The servants began carrying the soup course out to the tables. Someone placed a wooden bowl in front of Falorn, and ladled it full of a thick, creamy stew. Falorn looked beside him, where the sergeant eagerly wolfed the stew down, using a slab of rough brown bread to shovel it into his mouth. The man looked up to Falorn.

"Lizard bisque," he said. "You'll like it. Damned near the only thing his lordship serves that doesn't have rice in it."

"Lizard?" Falorn asked.

"They live in the swamp. They're damned hard to catch, and they squawk something awful when you shoot 'em, but you've got to admit, they make good eating."

Falorn looked glumly at the yellowish stew. A few pieces of gray meat drifted at the surface, along with a pair of indeterminate vegetables. He pulled a hunk of bread from one of the many thick loaves on the table and went to dip it into the bowl. Laughter from the head of the table caught his attention first. The baron must have told a joke; he saw Sera and the steward convulsed with laughter, although he couldn't hear anything they said over the din of dozens of conversations. He took a bite from the bread absentmindedly, and nearly choked. He had to restrain himself from spitting out the gritty stuff.

The baron proposed some sort of toast. Falorn couldn't hear a word of it, but cheered and drank along with everyone else when the man stopped talking.

He tried not to glower at Sera, who hung on the baron's every word. *He is her godfather, after all,* Falorn remembered. *I wonder what sort of feud could have caused Sera's father to cut the baron off so completely. True, they all seem a little bit crazy and scared of their own shadows here, but no crazier than the nobles in Roicenet with that Hook of theirs.*

When he looked down at the table again his stew bowl sat empty. The sergeant looked up at him with an apologetic expression, like a trusted hound discovered in the henhouse.

"You didn't want that, did you?" the man asked. "You looked like you didn't like it."

"It's all right," Falorn assured him. "I'm just hungry, that's all. I haven't eaten all day."

"Well of course not, it's a feast day, isn't it? Wouldn't want to spoil your appetite."

"Right," Falorn said distractedly, trying to pay attention to the head of the table without seeming to stare at Sera. She hadn't caught his eye once since the steward had separated them.

The servants began bringing out the main course. Four servants apiece carried the three enormous covered platters, laying one down on each of the tables. Falorn could see the heads of steamed cattails poking out from beneath the edges of the cloth covering.

"My favorite," the sergeant said from beside Falorn. "Girl with garlic sauce."

Falorn started to give the man a quizzical look at the oddness of the expression, but before he could, the steward dramatically pulled the cloth from the top of the dish. A nude girl of perhaps thirteen lay face up on a bed of steamed cattails, her hair shaved, her skin browned from the effects of baking and uneven basting. Falorn could see a faint slit beneath the girl's small breasts. A thin line of stuffing showed now, where the kitchen staff must have replaced her internal organs.

Falorn saw Sera's face go white. Only the emptiness of his stomach kept him from retching at the table. Lions surged against his chest. Falorn pushed himself to his feet.

The sword seemed to jump into his hand even before he thought about drawing. He roared in anger and revulsion, more an animal noise than a human one.

This is insanity!

The hall fell suddenly silent, and then a dozen voices started shouting at once.

"You've drawn on the baron!" the sergeant beside him exclaimed. "For Mara's sake, man, you've drawn on the baron."

Falorn swung the sword around blindly, hitting nothing. The haze before his eyes cleared, and he saw a hall full of armed soldiers slowly advancing on him. From the head of the table the baron glared, eyes blazing like a mad wolf. Sera's face looked blank, her eyes as dead as the baroness's.

Fighting the lions' urge to attack, Falorn looked around wildly for a way out as the soldiers crept forward. A blue aura surrounded one of the doorways. He turned and ran toward it, hoping he could outrun the half-drunk soldiers. He felt completely sober, despite the wine he'd drunk.

Falorn pulled open the door and slammed it shut behind him, only a few steps ahead of his pursuers. He threw the small bar into place, knowing it would only hold momentarily.

He saw another blue-tinged door, at the end of a wide hallway. Around a corner he could hear kitchen noises.

Falorn darted down that hall and through the door, sliding the flimsy bar into place behind him.

He stood in a wide pantry. Deep shelves on the walls held thousands of sealed jars and bottles. Stacks of sacked flour and meal sat beneath the shelves. Around his head, long strings of smoked sausages and butts of ham hung from ceiling hooks. Falorn grabbed a string of sausages as he ran down the hall, but dropped it on the floor a moment later. *I'll find food after I get out of this castle*, he decided, *even if I have to starve.*

The pantry ended in a blank wall. He presumed the doorway to his left led to the kitchens, where he could expect no safety. He threw the bar to the kitchen door, although he doubted any of the baron's soldiers had thought of circling around to attack him from that direction yet. Then he looked around carefully, trying to concentrate on *seeing* things, the same way he had in the hallway the previous night.

The walls remained blank.

Falorn willed himself to slow down. He pushed the pursuers and the clamoring lions out of his head. *Stop. Breathe. Look.*

Gradually, a thin blue seam became clear in the wall in front of him. The blue abruptly disappeared as he heard the doorway behind begin to splinter.

With the point of his sword, Falorn slit the plaster in front of him, finally knocking a three foot square panel into a hollow area beyond. The panel fell downward, splashing into water a second or two later.

He looked into the narrow passage and realized it was a sealed-off dumbwaiter, probably for hauling barrels of wine up from the cellar. *Except*, it occurred to Falorn, *the cellar must be flooded.* Faint light illuminated the shaft. *It must lead somewhere.* Carefully, he clambered inward. By bracing his back and booted feet against the confining walls of the dumbwaiter, Falorn could inch downward without falling into the water below.

After about thirty feet of inching his way downward with what seemed like painful slowness, he came to a window. A wide iron grating looked out onto the swamp from what must have once been a loading entrance for boats stocking the wine cellars. He could see marsh grass growing in water only a few feet below the grating.

Noises sounded in the hallway above him. *I wonder what's taking them so long.* Like the guards in Rorik's camp, it felt like everyone but Falorn was moving too slowly.

Not that I mind their slowness right now.

Grunting in exasperation, Falorn pounded at the base of the grate with the pommel of his sword, nearly slipping in the process. He heard a dull cracking sound as rusty bolts gave way, and the grating swung outward.

As Falorn clambered through it he heard shouting from above. Something fell past his legs, splashing into the old wine cellar below.

And then he pushed through, and felt himself falling. He barely managed to throw out his hand as he hit springy ground, soaking himself instantly.

Falorn picked himself up and recovered his sword, which had fallen a few feet away. He checked his pouches quickly; he still had cards, money, and supplies. *Which puts me way ahead of this time yesterday.* He looked up at the high wall of the keep and shivered, dripping water from his sodden clothes. Turning, he walked away from the castle, not much caring about direction.

Soon Falorn found himself wading in knee-deep water, amid a forest of waist-high marsh grass.

I can't believe this, he thought. *I just can't believe this. The man is serving little girls. Sera's godfather. And she's stuck in there.* Falorn looked around, hoping to find some sort of shelter while the moonlight held. *She's stuck in there, and I'm stuck out here.*

Falorn paused and looked around. *I have got to find a place to stop before moonset. I don't think the baron will send out a search party at night, but I might step in a hole or a deep spot. With this mail shirt to weigh me down, they'd never even find my body.*

He laughed at his own grim thought. *Of course, I'm not sure I'd want them to find my body. He'd probably serve me to Sera, stewed on a plate with swamp-grass.*

The thought of the girl on the tray brought him back to reality. Falorn resumed wading through the swamp, unable to get his thoughts off the vision of the dead child in the banquet hall.

Ahead, a lone, gnarled tree rose out of a thicket of cattails. Hoping to find a patch of dry land, he waded for the tree, brushing the cattails aside until he came to a small, moss-covered hillock rising out of the water. He climbed up carefully, his sodden boots slipping a few times on the slick moss. Finally, Falorn reached the top and sat down beneath the misshapen tree: hungry, utterly exhausted, filthy, and wet. His tunic felt clammy, while his boots and britches chafed against his skin like leathery, wet rags.

Falorn found himself laughing at the absurdity of the whole situation. *I hope Sera handled the baron's feast with more grace than I've shown.* He sighed. *I suppose I'll never see her again.*

He missed her, despite everything, and he wondered if she missed him as well. Somehow, he doubted it. He looked at the moon fading on the far horizon and laughed again.

Something thunked into the tree above his head, causing the whole trunk to vibrate slightly. He looked up. The three-foot shaft of a longbow arrow quivered a handsbreadth above the top of his scalp.

A guttural voice called out to him in the darkness. He didn't recognize the voice, or the odd clicks and hisses of the language. Falorn held himself very still, and kept his hands well away from his weapons.

The voice called out again, and this time, Falorn could hear splashing noises from all sides of the little hillock on the heels of the command. Falorn said nothing, too tired to even care anymore. He could only wait for whoever had surrounded the hill to climb up and take him prisoner.

10

The Lost Spirit

❖

Gradually, Falorn pulled himself to his feet as his captors emerged from the swamp. For a moment, he thought the lack of food and his stumbling journey through the swamp had driven him as mad as the castle's inhabitants.

The creatures who emerged from the tall surrounding cattails were not human at all.

At least ten of them splashed out of the cattails and onto the hillock in front of him. He could hear more behind him; Falorn realized with a sudden sick feeling that he had almost encountered them earlier.

Only the sergeant's hunger and his own distraction had kept him from eating one of their kind in the baron's stew.

The smallest lizard stood at least seven feet tall. All of them had golden-brown scales on their backs, heads, and sides. Paler skin covered their bellies, though the patterns and color shading on the creatures' scales varied somewhat from lizard to lizard. They walked erect on clawed hind legs, with long, thick tails dragging behind for balance. A dark, flexible ridge of bone or cartilage ran along their backs and partway down each creature's tail. Their arms looked short in proportion to the rest of their bodies, but Falorn knew they possessed enough strength in those slight-looking arms to draw and fire a longbow. They had long, heavily armored heads, with large eyes set far back on either side, like a horse's head might look if it had scales, fangs, no ears, and no mane.

Most of the lizards carried spears or longbows. One especially tall lizard, who Falorn presumed to be the leader, carried only a heavy mace. Another lizard, smaller than most and with scales flaking in places, carried no weapons at all. None of them wore clothes of any sort, except for belts or cords from which pouches, knives, or quivers hung.

The leader and the flaking-scaled lizard climbed up the hillock toward Falorn. The others remained below, but their eyes never left Falorn and their leader.

The tall lizard towered over Falorn. It looked down at him and said something loudly in a sort of guttural hiss. Falorn could made no sense of the words.

The leader turned to its fellow lizard. The two creatures conversed in hissed undertones, as if afraid Falorn would overhear. He listened to the rhythmic clicks and hisses: They sounded like the wheezing of an old dog with a cold.

The lizards had a curious, salty smell to them, which stood out in the freshwater marsh.

After the two creatures finished conversing, the leader stepped back and to the side. The ragged lizard stood alone in front of Falorn. It stared deeply at Falorn, leaning forward and squinting in the fading moonlight. Although Falorn had assumed the creatures saw well in the dark—based on the longbow arrow that had nearly split his skull—this one apparently did not. He could see scales flaking away, as if the lizard had some sort of skin disease. Even where its scales remained intact, they lacked the shiny coating of the other lizards. The creature gave off a faintly musty odor. Falorn had smelled it before in old seashells brought by traders to his father's inn.

The creature leaned back again until it stood upright, then lashed its tail briefly. As Falorn watched, it began waving its arms in odd swirling and circular motions in the air in front of him. At the same time the lizard began to *howl*. Its voice quavered painfully in inhuman notes, like a tortured, injured animal.

In the space between the creature's hands, a strange reddish glow appeared. Light shimmered in the open space, almost like the light given off by the cards, but less diffuse. The light seemed to thicken as it brightened. Its red color deepened to a brownish-maroon, and seemed almost to solidify in the air. The lizard's voice began to break into what Falorn might almost have called a song, and the light brightened again. Its intensity grew; Falorn could see lizards at the base of the hillock, their scales reflected by the unearthly radiance. The light continued to brighten slowly, eerily coalescing into a ball of gently pulsing illumination, opaque yet without substance. The lizard stopped singing. Silence filled the clearing as the creature's hands fell back to its sides. The ball of light hovered in the air in front of the wizard. The lizard waved slightly and the ball drifted above Falorn's head and stayed there, shining above him like the street-lanterns in Roicenet.

The lizard clapped its hands twice, then began again. This time the notes and the hand gestures changed and shifted in complex patterns. Falorn kept his eyes fixed on the space between the creature's hands, waiting for the darkness to dissipate. The lizard's howling seemed alternately like a priest's chanting over the dead or like a minstrel singing, but the tune sounded more complex than any Falorn had ever heard. Again, the creature wove patterns in front of itself, but unlike the first time, Falorn saw no change in the air. He dared not move or disturb the creature, more fearful of what forces he might set loose than of the creature's fellow lizards.

At the end of the creature's song, Falorn felt curiously disappointed. Nothing changed in the air around them, but Falorn hated to hear the song end.

Then he realized that for the last few minutes, he had been listening to the words.

"I can understand you!" Falorn hissed, then stopped in sudden startlement at the noises emerging from his mouth.

"Indeed, you can," the lizard with the flaking scales agreed sadly. Its skin looked even shabbier in the light. "You can perceive our tongue now, although you little suspect the price to myself or our folk. You humans are a tragic race indeed."

Falorn, baffled, said nothing. The tall lizard stepped forward again and whispered something Falorn didn't catch to the shabby-scaled wizard. The wizard shambled down the slope and back to the other lizards, leaving a few broken scales behind him.

"Well," the enormous lizard began, towering above Falorn, "now you can understand a civilized language. What is your name?"

"I'm called Falorn, sir." He wasn't sure what to call the lizard, but it seemed pleased at the response. The creature withdrew to a slightly less intimidating posture, although its long fangs still showed clearly with every word.

"Well, so you are. Respectful at least, though Falorn's not much of a name. You are a power wielder, are you not?"

For a moment, Falorn had no idea what the creature meant. Then his hand went to the pouch at his chest. "I . . . guess so . . . yes, I am."

"I thought as much. That's what drew us to you. Power. Draws things down on you every time. Wouldn't you agree?"

"Yes. I definitely agree."

"Hmm. Maybe a wise one too, not just powerful. Are you the One?"

"I'm sorry?"

"The One. The One who all the prophets tell us will return to lead us to victory against the invaders who have taken the Empire of the Golden Reeds away from us, and claimed part of it for themselves. The One who will lead us from the forgotten caves and far hidden reaches of our land and back to our rightful role as rulers of the middle lands that are neither earth nor sea. The One."

"I'm not sure. I don't think so."

"Pity. We'll have to kill you, then. At least you can tell us the secret ways in and out of the interloper's castle before we tear you to pieces."

"I mean, I might be the One . . . I'm just not sure. This is the first I've heard about it. And I'm very tired and I'm not sure I'm thinking straight anymore."

"Well. Maybe you are the One. The signs and portents are all there. We must feed you, and shelter you, and let you rest, and then your birthright will be clear to you."

"I guess so," Falorn said. "I'd like to help, if I can."

"And so you shall, little wise one. And so you shall." The lizard turned from him to face its comrades assembled at the base of the hillock. "Hear me!" it said. "He who was lost has returned! Proclaim it throughout the Golden Reeds! Summon all of the warriors and wizards together, for hope has at long last returned to our lives! He who will redeem us by His valiant sacrifice has returned!"

Falorn startled a bit at that last, but hoped it was only a colorful metaphor in an imperfectly understood language. Even though he still stood on his feet, he was already beginning to fall asleep as he leaned against the trunk of the misshapen tree.

Falorn awoke on a bed of dry grass. Warm spring sun beat down on him from overhead. He felt stiff, and his armored torso had begun to sweat in the sunlight. Sitting up, he found himself on a solid grassy area surrounded by swamp and cattails. His sword lay beside him. A few yards away, two lizards stood watch—their eyes directed outward across the swamp, and not toward him. He thought of the cards, but felt their presence against his chest even before his hand could check the pouch.

One of the lizards sniffed the air as Falorn sat up. The creature turned to face him. Its scales glittered with reflected sunlight, shining like polished gold sprinkled with the glistening pebbles from the bottom of a fast-moving brook.

"I am glad to see you have awoken, Hero," the lizard said. "We were afraid overexertion might prevent You from fulfilling Your destiny. The gods have played many cruel tricks on us." The second lizard snorted in agreement.

"They have indeed, small wise One," the second lizard asserted. "This land has belonged to us since the First Grandmother laid her first clutch of eggs. The Golden Reeds are sacred to our people. It saddens us deeply that we cannot drive the interloper from our lands without the help of a Hero; but now You have come, as all the prophets predicted, and You have offered to give Your very life's blood to drive this pustule from the Golden Reeds."

"Thanks . . . I think," said Falorn. "That wasn't exactly what I said. I'm not really anxious to die."

"No, of course not. Even a Hero must have doubts and fears. But You will drive on regardless, for You know the cause You champion is just and right, even though it brings You the most agonizing death. Young warriors will seek to emulate you for all the ages—You who are so small yet so brave—and mothers sitting on top of their clutches will think of You, to bring good luck to their egg-children." The lizard looked at him adoringly, while the first lizard began laying food onto a reed mat.

"You must eat, Hero. Soon it will be time for councils of war and the weaving of strong magics. Soon it will be time for You to tell our leaders how You will lead us to victory against the pestilential ones."

The lizard presented the tray to Falorn. It contained a creditable assortment of small tidbits, none of them cooked. Falorn hesitantly tried a piece of rice and raw fish wrapped in some sort of thin skin or membrane. It tasted oddly spicy. He liked the rice, moist and with a faint tang from the yellow sauce. The fish had a strange, slimy texture, and a salty taste which took some getting used to. After a slow beginning, he found himself liking the food.

He fell asleep again after eating. When one of the lizards finally awakened him, Falorn saw the sun already setting.

"I slept all day?" he asked, embarrassed.

"Doubtless You communed deeply with the gods. Have they given You the answer to Your questions? Will You tell us how You will lead us to victory? When will our homeland once again be free?"

"I can't answer that. It's not what you think."

The lizard looked abashed. "A thousand thousand pardons, Hero. I asked of you questions whose answers belong to our leaders alone. In my thirst for freedom I overstepped the bounds of my duties as a mere servant and warrior. Please grant me forgiveness for my presumption."

"There's nothing to forgive. I just don't really know what to say."

"Such compelling modesty in a Hero. Truly, You are the One, for none else but He could be so utterly free from vanity and worldliness. Others hope for fame or glory, while You thirst for freedom alone, even though it costs Your life. Alas that I could not make such a sacrifice!"

"Why are you all so certain I'm going to die? Do you want me to get killed that much?"

"No! All the gods forbid such a thing! We long for a Hero that can help us to preserve our freedom after it has been hard won from the dreadful foe. But the prophecies forbid it. All the prophets agree, the alien Hero who leads us to freedom shall not walk away from that battle, nor shall He see the attainment of that which He so valiantly sacrificed everything to win. It is a tragic prophecy. So many prophecies are."

As darkness fell, Falorn heard splashing from the cattail fields that surrounded the dry, grassy area. Lizards began walking into the clearing, muttering greetings to the guards as they arrived. Many of the lizards carried dry wood. Soon a bonfire burned in a newly dug-out firepit, crackling in counterpoint to the muted hisses of the lizards. All of them nodded respectfully to Falorn, but none spoke to him directly.

Falorn stopped counting when the fortieth lizard joined the wide circle forming around him. Except for the two who had watched and fed him, and a third who tended the fire, the lizards stood well back of Falorn, conversing quietly among themselves.

An hour after full darkness, the leaders arrived. Along with the warrior and wizard Falorn had met, three other lizards joined Falorn beside the fire. Two looked like warriors, tall and massive with smooth, thick scales that glittered in the firelight. The third lizard limped slightly. Its coat looked tattered and shabby, like a discarded snakeskin. The creature looked old, less from the thinness of its scales and slight odor of decay than from the tremendous *presence* it walked with. The ancient lizard fixed milky, clouded eyes on Falorn briefly, then broke off its gaze.

All five lizards settled by the fire, and the tall warrior motioned for Falorn to do the same. The attendants retreated to the edges of the circle, which by now contained over a hundred watchers. For half an hour, the leaders said nothing, content to sit by the flames and bask, despite the mildness of the spring night. Falorn shared their silence. Soon, the hiss and click of conversation from the surrounding circle subsided into nothingness. Despite the constant hum of crickets, the night felt very quiet and still. Gradually, a sense of calmness filled Falorn, a warmth that seemed to originate within the cards and slowly radiate through his chest and body. An odd languor settled over him.

When the lizards finally began to speak, Falorn felt more at ease than he had earlier. He found the sounds of their words soothing. The cards against his chest gave off a sort of warmth. His own words and thoughts seemed sharper and clearer in his mind, despite the disjointed, languid feeling which relaxed his muscles of their own volition.

"I am glad you have chosen to remain with us, Falorn," the old lizard said slowly. "There is much you will do for us, but there are things we may offer you in return. First, we will give you our names, as you freely gave yours last night. I am Khtheea, the seer. It was I who foresaw your coming here, and I will tell you how before you sleep tonight." The old lizard spoke with a measured cadence that held none of the Hero-worship the guards had shown.

"The warrior you met last night is called Theliah, the bravest one. You also met Sethkheliess, the lonely wizard. Two other great warriors of our people have joined in our council tonight, Hesskhess, the dark-scaled one, and Ithshaess, who has borne a dozen clutches." Each of the lizards met Falorn's eye as Khtheea introduced them. Each time, Falorn found himself slowly nodding in acknowledgment. The old lizard's words felt hypnotic. The rhythmic pattern of the seer's language seemed to pull Falorn in. "I can tell you about the part you will play in the destiny of the people of the Golden Reeds, and I can tell you about your own destiny," Khtheea went on, "but to do so, I must first tell you a story."

"Our people are under a curse," Khtheea began, "a curse that goes back many years, to a time when my clutch-mother's mother was but a young warrior. This was a time long before the humans came to the Golden Reeds, except for a few traders and scholars who were known to our people. In those days, the Golden Reeds was a rich Empire, and we hunted and fished and learned and taught and quarreled among ourselves as all peoples do, for we were the rulers of our own land, we were free, and we lived in a golden age—although we did not know it at the time. Now, when we cower in the corners of our once-broad land and watch invaders drain our vitality, we are not so strong, and we forget how proud we once were. We were a mighty people.

"One day in that golden age, a young woman of your kind came among us. Although we did not know her, some of the human scholars who were our friends spoke well of her, and so we admitted her into our land. She lived among us for nine summers, and studied with Seshienessthe, the doomed one, who was seer in those days. In that time, she learned a great deal about our people, but as time went on, we began to learn about her as well.

"She was a wizard, of course. Although she called herself 'Ailissa,' that was not her true name, and she left us a cursed people before our own wizards could learn her name, and from it, her true nature. My clutch-mother's mother never knew what it was the human woman searched for, but in the end, she must have found it. After we discovered her true nature, when our warriors came to her chamber to eject her from our lands, she had already gone. She took with her the spirit of our people, though; on the floor of our chamber lay the body of our seer, Seshienessthe, the doomed one. The human wizard had skinned Seshienessthe, and taken the skin with her when she left the Golden Reeds.

"Now, you may know little of our people, but I will tell you that our essence is in our skin. I am old, and you can see that as I lose vitality my skin fades. When Sethkheliess, the lonely wizard, casts the spells that drain the life from him, he sheds scales like a cattail sheds spores in the autumn wind. You see the way the skin of the warriors glows, for they are the strength of our people. But this human wizard stole the spirit of our seer, and with it, she stole much of our people's spirit.

"Never before had we failed in battle; now it seemed we could not win. Our warriors melted away, and enemies grew up around us like mushrooms after a storm. Where humans once only came to the Golden Reeds as guests, soon they came as conquerors. In my own lifetime, I have seen the humans build the stone temple from which they prey on our people. But my clutch-mother's mother saw truly, and that vision has passed on through me. I knew that one day a human would come to us with the key to driving the evil ones from our land. That human will be with us only a short time, and when he is struck down, we will be powerless to help. But in that short time, that human will bring to us something of the spirit that was lost. And though what he brings will soon be lost with him, a little of the spirit he returns shall remain with our people. Enough, I hope, to help us regain our freedom."

"How do you know that I'm the one?" Falorn asked.

"We can feel it. All of the people you see around you can feel what you bring to our people. You are carrying pieces of the lost skin of Seshienessthe, the doomed one. The talisman you wear around your neck is made from the spirit of my people. I fear it is a small part of whatever evil the woman who called herself 'Ailissa' sought to unleash on the world."

Falorn touched the pouch of cards against his chest. Warmth filled his blood. "If these are made from a part of your seer, you should take them. They belong to your people." He started to unfasten the pouch.

"No, little one," the warrior Theliah, the bravest one, said, and Khtheea clicked in agreement. "The power found you and it is yours, until it is ready to find someone else. You are the One, and trying to give up the power that has come to you won't change it. You've got a sad destiny ahead, and you'll need all the power you've got to find your way to the land of your gods afterward." Theliah reached forward and pushed the pouch back inside Falorn's tunic.

"Tomorrow at twilight, you'll lead us into the humans' lair. Rest until then," he said.

The last thing Falorn heard that night was the singing of Sethkheliess, the lonely wizard.

11

The Prophecy

Falorn awoke disoriented and sluggish, as if he'd slept for days rather than hours. When the fog lifted from his head, he saw that dozens of the lizards still slept in the clearing, like so many curled golden rocks. A few of the creatures walked around the grass, and one tended the bonfire, which had burnt into a low pit of glowing coals and embers.

The morning felt cool and brisk, with a biting wind and clouds that roiled and menaced each other in the sky above him. He shook his head until it cleared, checked the cards at his chest, then began looking around for something to eat.

He saw several woven-reed mats piled high with pieces of seaweed-wrapped rice, fish, and vegetables. Three lizards crouched around the mats, eating and talking, while a half-dozen others practiced with swords nearby. He walked to the nearest of the mats, stretching and shaking to loosen his muscles as he crossed the clearing.

A heavy-set lizard with black flecks on its scales handed him several of the spiced morsels when he reached the mats. The discussion ceased as the trio of lizards insisted on serving him. One produced a wineskin filled with sweet, syrupy nectar.

"Welcome, Hero," the heavy-set lizard said. "Drink with us now and You will surely lead us to victory tonight."

Falorn grunted noncommittally.

"Surely You see that we can wait no longer, now that all the signs are present."

"Surely." Falorn nodded, uneasily. He finished eating mechanically, the food losing all flavor as he thought about what lay in store for him upon his return to the castle.

The black-speckled warrior looked at Falorn curiously. "Will You practice with me?" the lizard asked. "I am not worthy to cross swords with a Hero of Your stature, but perhaps You will allow me the honor of learning from You?"

"I . . . of course," Falorn said. He certainly needed to practice before the upcoming battle, although he feared revealing his inexperience to the enormous lizard. "What is your name?"

"I am called Sthafsassa, the black," the lizard replied. "Shall we begin?" Falorn and the lizard walked over to where the others practiced. A pile of practice blades—made of thin strips of swamp-wood layered together, glued, and glazed—lay on the grass nearby. Falorn selected one that approximated his own sword in reach and weight, and watched while Sthafsassa did the same.

Sthafsassa bowed low and scraped his wooden blade on the ground three times. "You honor me with Your blade, Hero," the lizard said. It stood up again and looked at Falorn expectantly.

"Thank you," Falorn said, embarrassed. "I'm not sure how to reply. Please tell me what your custom is."

"A Hero needs no custom," Sthafsassa replied, "He need only be a Hero." The lizard assumed a guard position. The black speckles on Sthafsassa's golden scales seemed to crawl and move on the creature's skin as the sun reflected off their glittering surfaces.

Falorn advanced warily on Sthafsassa, who stood nearly eight feet tall. The lizard easily parried his first, tentative attacks.

"You need not be so gentle in fear of hurting my feelings," Sthafsassa said. "I long only to learn from You. Please, attack."

Falorn took a deep breath, and thought of the cards. He imagined the crimson knight in his mind, and felt his posture straightening in response. He imagined the cats' attentiveness within his body, and a surge of energy coursed through his chest. He imagined the quickness of the blue thief, and felt a new suppleness in his hands and shoulders.

He advanced more confidently, his breathing slow and even. Without thinking about the move, Falorn spun and parried an overhand cut, darting under Sthafsassa's guard as he did so. Before the lizard could recover his guard, Falorn turned to face him and tapped the blade gently against the creature's neck.

They began again quickly. Within a moment, Falorn's blade caught Sthafsassa's wrist, sending the lizard's blade flying. The lizard stepped back, and its fellows began chattering excitedly.

"Please, Hero," Sthafsassa said, "would you do us the kindness of showing us that move more slowly. None of us could follow your movements." As the others watched, Falorn and Sthafsassa stepped through the sequence of motions again, and again he sent the lizard's sword flying.

Falorn concentrated on the movements as his body stepped through them, trying to memorize the every step that the cards guided him through. *I need to learn all I can, for as long as I have the cards. I could lose them all at any time, I know, and I'd still have all these people out there trying to kill me. If I'm very lucky and the gods are with me, maybe I can learn enough to keep myself alive before it's too late.*

They went through a dozen more passes. Each time, Falorn quickly cut through the warrior's guard, although he could tell Sthafsassa possessed a great deal of swordfighting skill. The lizard never seemed offended at being beaten. Instead, it asked Falorn to repeat every motion, until Sthafsassa and its fellows could learn and counter them.

Falorn marveled at his newfound abilities. In some way, the crimson knight seemed to channel the energy and ferocity of the lions into a more disciplined path. *It's a pity the elf didn't have this card as well*, Falorn thought, sadly. *Nothing would have stopped him then. I wish I could be half the fighter he was.* He wondered if the strength of the cards and the skills they seemed to give him could keep him alive in the battle to come, in spite of the lizards' prophecy.

After a few hours sparring with two eight-foot attackers simultaneously, Falorn realized that only he and his partners continued to practice in the clearing. A circle of lizards surrounded them and watched attentively. He saw Khtheea among his audience.

The two lizards penetrated his guard several times, although Falorn bested them more often than not. By the time they stopped, sweat covered him completely, soaking his hair and clothing, but an excited energy still filled him. *Best to save that for the battle*, he thought. He didn't want to sleep through the attack—especially given the prophecies which surrounded both the attack and himself.

"I thank You for the gift of Your teaching," Sthafsassa said, bowing low to Falorn after they stopped. The second lizard sparring partner bowed as well. Both creatures traced elaborate patterns in the ground with their weapons.

"I'm grateful for the practice as well," Falorn said, unsure how to respond. "I hope I can live up to your expectations."

"Of course you shall live up to our expectations," said Khtheea, stepping forward from the crowd and placing one heavy clawed hand on Falorn's shoulder with surprising gentleness, "We ask only for heroism, and you will give us that. Our freedom we must win for ourselves."

"I'll do my best," Falorn said, his uncertainty returning as the energy of the cards slowly receded from the forefront of his mind.

"I'm certain that will be enough," Khtheea said in a soothing tone. "We will not allow you to die for nothing. If you were not able to lead us as we must be led, the talismans you carry in that pouch, made from the skin of Seshienessthe, the doomed one, would not have returned with you to give hope and spirit to my people." the lizard paused, and looked directly into Falorn's eyes. "Come. You must eat now, and then rest again. At twilight you will lead us into the stone heart of the evil ones."

Khtheea awakened him two hours before twilight. Despite his anxiety, Falorn had eaten and slept as the seer bade him. Now, he stirred at the creature's touch on his shoulder.

"Arise. Your time has come," Khtheea said, with a touch of sadness. "Your armor has been prepared, and our warriors are nearly ready. We have little time, if we are to act while the omens are favorable."

Falorn sat up and pulled the worn cloak he used for a blanket aside. His newly polished armor sat beside him on a woven reed mat. Beside it, his sword lay sheathed, the leather of its scabbard and baldric newly oiled. Stripping off his tunic, Falorn carefully pulled the armor on, making certain it fit as closely as possible. Sthafsassa helped him lace the mail shirt into place before Falorn pulled the tunic back on over it. He slid the baldric over his right shoulder, and checked the sword's fit in its sheath, making certain it drew smoothly and without sticking. Last of all he felt the pouch around his throat, although only for reassurance. He could feel each of the cards, as if their presence flowed through his blood rather than dangled from the thin leather cord around his neck.

"Come now," Khtheea said, as soon as Falorn finished his prepara-
tions. "the time for my people's return has arrived." They walked across
the grass toward the field of cattails behind. Hundreds of lizards began
falling into place behind them, all carrying bows, spears, or swords. The
warriors spread out as they descended from dry land onto swampier
ground. Falorn heard sloshing noises from all directions, but not the loud
splashing and cursing that an army of several hundred human soldiers
would have made.

They overtook Theliah standing alone in the cattails. Falorn assumed
the warrior had waited to escort the seer and himself. He saw no sign of
Sethkheliess, the lonely wizard. Theliah said nothing to either of them;
the massive soldier walked slightly ahead of them, looking around constantly, all the while cradling a massive stone-headed mace in his arms
like a midwife holding a newborn baby.

They drew within sight of the baron's causeway just before twilight.
Falorn looked at the keep for any sign of discovery, but saw nothing, not
even the guards on the roof and tower. The gateway stood open, looking
ominous.

He climbed onto the elevated roadway, accompanied by Khtheea,
Theliah, Sthafsassa, and three other lizards. The rest of the attacking
army waded in the shallow water around the path, like so many ships-of-
war approaching a besieged island. Falorn waited for the inevitable alarm
from the keep, but as they continued to approach, he saw and heard
nothing. The baron's castle remained calm and silent; the gates continued
to stand open.

They nearly reached the open gates before Falorn heard the first
sounds of metal on metal from within, and the nervous whinnying of
horses. No one guarded the walls at all. The tower and ramparts stood
empty, and the entrance to the castle gaped invitingly.

As Falorn approached the door, excited lizards clambered up the
raised trail and through the open portal. Dozens of horses stood tethered
within, but Falorn saw only a few human soldiers—none of them wearing the Baron of Golden Reeds's colors. Men in scarlet and gold with burnished helmets fled up the narrow stairways as lizard warriors poured
into the castle.

The lizards hissed in excitement. One of them tore a human soldier's
head off as the man stumbled on a rickety stairway. Falorn hoped none
of the lizards forgot in the excitement of battle the special role they

expected him to play in this drama. *Can the lizard soldiers even tell me apart from the other humans?* he wondered. The leaders and the ones he'd worked out with would know him, but most of the others hadn't even seen him closely.

He found himself surging up the stairs, practically carried by the press of lizard soldiers. Sthafsassa climbed upward in front of him, the stairs shuddering under the lizard's tremendous weight.

They stumbled into one of the mazelike second-floor corridors, and into the middle of a battle in progress. Falorn saw men in Roicenet sky-blue surcoats and black tunics fighting men in Iron Eagle scarlet and gold, and both colors attacking the baron's mailed soldiers. Sthafsassa enthusiastically waded into the fight. The lizard beheaded a baron's man with his sword, then crippled a blue-clad soldier's knee with a lash from his thickly scaled tail. He screamed a war cry and charged a clump of soldiers in red and scarlet. More lizards poured up the stairs to join in the fight.

I think leading them into an open castle counts as fulfilling my promise. They should be able to take back their swamp now. Maybe I should focus on avoiding the "tragic death" part of the prophecy.

Falorn suddenly wondered where in the battle Sera might be. Neither her father, Rorik, nor the lizards would be much inclined toward mercy if they caught her, and he doubted the baron's soldiers could provide her much protection anymore, even if the baron was so inclined. Avoiding a thicket of swordsmen and lizards all fighting each other, Falorn began along the passageway. He tried to remember where his and Sera's chambers had been. He hoped the baron hadn't moved her, and that she stayed hidden while the fight went on.

Falorn worked his way around corridors where he heard fighting. He counted on the warrenlike maze to eventually lead him where he needed to go. The battle seemed to have spread throughout the castle, with soldiers in twos and threes searching the halls and killing anyone they found. He concentrated on the blue thief card, and tried to remember the steward's route.

After an hour of careful doubling back to avoid the slaughter in the dimly lit halls, Falorn finally found the door.

"Sera?" he said tentatively. He heard no answer from behind the door. "Sera?" he called out again. He felt the knob and found the door unlocked.

He hoped she hadn't left the castle. If she had, he knew he'd probably never see her again. *I'll have to check in the room,* he thought. *If she's left, she'll have taken Rorik's pay chest with her. She might have left everything else, but not her cards and not that.* He twisted the knob confidently and stepped into the room.

A dozen soldiers in scarlet and gold waited within, broadswords drawn. Rorik stood behind them, wearing a new suit of chainmail and a gold-plated helmet with a high, crimson-dyed, horsehair crest. At his feet, Falorn saw the bloodied corpse of the Baron of Golden Reeds.

He didn't see Sera.

"He's the one!" the young noble screamed. "Kill him! Don't let him get away!"

Falorn turned and ran. The soldiers clattered through the hallway just behind him. He wondered if he could find a lizard or two to help him. Even with the help of the cards, he doubted he could beat twelve trained, armored soldiers and their commander. He had seen what happened to the elf who tried.

He found himself in a hallway which tilted slightly upward, with no way to turn back toward his allies except by going through his pursuers. He climbed as quickly as he could, hoping to at least find a good place to fight from. Only bare stone walls and locked doors presented themselves.

The hall ended with a wooden door in front of him. Falorn heard shouts of triumph from behind, and the sound of Rorik's voice urging them on.

"Kill him! He stole your money!"

Falorn lowered his shoulder and charged the door. He slammed into the wood, sending splinters flying, and bursting the flimsy panels outward onto the stone ramparts of the keep's roof.

Falorn stepped through and looked around for a place to defend himself. A chilly wind swept over the bare roof. Only the bulk of the castle's lone tower broke the flatness, and Falorn could see the dull reflection of iron links in the moonlight chaining the tower door securely. A low, crenellated wall edged the roof, giving the illusion of security from below. The wall only extended as high as Falorn's knees.

The soldiers quickly came through the door and spread out, cutting Falorn off from even the minimal protection of the tower wall. They advanced slowly, forcing Falorn back toward the edge of the wall.

He stepped back uneasily, trying to gauge his opponents. Falorn held his sword before him defensively, and looked around for any place that might allow him to make a stand. *I can't fight them here. The weight of*

*the soldiers alone will take me down if they press their attack. I've got to
find a way to keep them from all attacking me at the same time.*

As if responding to some hidden signal, the soldiers charged suddenly. All twelve men came in a rush, their blades churning in the air. Falorn
tried to hold his ground. He fended off the first flurry of blows, somehow
nicking a soldier on the hand. Quickly, he wounded a second man on the
arm. A third man lost his balance as Falorn slashed. The guardsman
banged into one of his fellows, pushing him aside and blocking both men
from attacking momentarily.

Falorn parried two nearly simultaneous thrusts, but the sword-
strokes forced him to take a step back. A third sword got through; Falorn
pulled his head aside to avoid most of the blow, but the slash opened his
cheek just below his right eye. Another blade pierced his right hand.
Falorn barely held onto his sword as pain blossomed all along his arm.

The attacks strengthened as the soldiers forced Falorn into a purely
defensive role. As in the tent, the soldiers seemed to be moving slowly,
but this time, he faced far too many of them. Falorn tried to ward off
three blades all seeking his belly. He threw up his sword to parry an overhand cut, and felt something slam into his right knee. He stumbled
halfway to the flagstones. His whole leg went suddenly numb.

Falorn tried to push upward and into the crowd of men attacking, so
they couldn't all get at him without hitting each other. His right leg buckled, and he felt something tear as his left leg tried to support the weight
of his armored body. He flailed wildly at one attacker, then tried to throw
himself backward as a long blade loomed in his face.

His arms and head met no resistance where the ground should have
been. Falorn's left leg scraped the wall, and then he felt himself falling.
For a second, he saw bewildered soldiers looking down from the wall as
he plunged toward the swamp. Then his back slammed into the water
with a hard splash that felt more like hitting stone than water and mud.

He writhed once, as red needles twisted into his spine and sides.
Then his whole body went numb.

Falorn gasped for air, but he couldn't breathe at all. He felt a wet
sting on his face and in his eyes as his head slipped into the water. For a
moment he saw dim colors, muddy orange and green and red. Then he
saw nothing.

The world darkened in front of him. He saw the same proud lion he
had ridden into Rorik's camp in his dream, now slinking away riderless.
The water closed over his head, and he saw nothing at all.

12

Rain and Rescues

※

Falorn only realized that he still lived when he began coughing up water in violent, hacking rasps. Something held up his head, although Falorn had no idea what. He felt himself shaking violently, but other than that, he felt no sensation in his body at all. He couldn't see at first, but as the spasms subsided, his vision began to clear slightly.

A round white blur in front of him slowly coalesced into a fuzzy outline of the moon, high overhead. No more than a few minutes could have passed since his fall from the tower.

A horse whickered nearby. He opened his mouth and tried to talk, but no sound emerged. His tongue seemed swollen and too thick.

"Shhh," a voice said from beside him. "don't try to talk. Just stay still until you get some strength back. We have a long night ahead of us." He remembered the voice somehow, but it sounded tinny and distant, even though he knew it came from right beside him. It took him a long time to recognize Sera's voice, and to remember who she was, and who *he* was.

He felt a faint sense of pressure against his back, and realized she must be supporting him. A slight tingling began in the tips of his fingers and toes. Gradually, the feeling spread, until his whole body ached from painfully returning sensation. Sera held him firmly, and kept him from writhing in agony.

"Stay still," she said quietly. "You'll hurt yourself."

He felt the cold stones of the elevated roadway underneath his legs. He coughed again, and now he could feel his tongue move within his mouth.

"How . . . how did I get here," he finally managed to croak.

"You fell from the roof. I pulled you out of the water and dragged you to the road. I have horses waiting, but you're not in any shape to ride."

"The battle. . . ."

"They're all still fighting. I have no idea who's winning, but I think we'll be safe here for a few minutes. Now lie still."

"But I have to help. . . ."

"You're not going to help anybody right now, Falorn. Lie back and try to relax." He struggled briefly, but found himself too weak to move. Finally, he settled back into her arms, and waited for the feeling to return to the rest of his body.

Nearly an hour passed before he could get to his feet, even leaning on Sera for support. He couldn't walk at all, but Sera half-carried him to one of the horses. With her providing most of the strength, Falorn mounted. He clung dizzily to the mare's neck as Sera carefully tied him into the saddle.

From behind him, he heard the faint sound of metal clashing on metal.

Sera climbed onto her own horse and took the reins of his mount in her hands. She walked both horses until the path widened enough that Falorn would not fall, and then she increased their pace to a canter.

They reached the King's Road again before moonset. Only then did Sera pause to rest and water the horses, and to check on Falorn. The ropes holding him in the saddle chafed and cut his ankles. Claws of pain raked his whole body as sensation continued to return.

After a few minutes, Sera mounted again and they rode on, not stopping until the moon dropped below the horizon and it grew too dark to ride any further. Sera led the horses to a small, sheltered grove within view of the road and carefully untied Falorn. He smiled feebly at her as she moistened his lips with a few drops from her waterskin and then gave him a drink of water.

He tried to turn his head to say something, but instead of Sera's face he saw three lionesses standing side by side. He watched them rub against each other, and groom each other and play together, and he remembered nothing else until morning.

Falorn awoke stiff and groggy, as if he'd been drugged. He lifted his head slowly and opened his eyes. Sera stood nearby, halfheartedly combing one of the horses. He tried to sit up, and found his body moved with surprising ease. Most of the pain from the night before seemed to have vanished.

Gradually, his head cleared. He stood up and stretched, gingerly at first, but more forcefully when no pain accompanied his efforts. Sera turned to look at him curiously.

"What are you doing up?" she asked. "For that matter, what are you doing alive?"

"You dragged me out of the swamp last night, didn't you? Or isn't that what you mean?"

Sera shook her head. "You weren't in very good shape last night, Falorn. I thought you had a broken back."

"I guess not."

"I'm glad," Sera said, and smiled weakly. "I couldn't stay there much longer, but I didn't know how I was going to get out. And then when my father and Rorik showed up, and everybody started fighting, well, I grabbed horses, but I didn't want to leave by myself."

"And then I fell out of the sky," Falorn said, forcing a faint laugh.

I wonder what she ate while she stayed at the baron's castle?

"And then you fell out of the sky," Sera agreed.

Although Falorn felt fine, Sera would not let him near the horses until afternoon, and then only because of the danger that her father or fiancé might emerge from the swamp to capture them.

They rode slowly along the King's Road, which became gradually more crowded as they entered a belt of rich farmland. Falorn could see several villages in the hills which rolled gently around them, although few lay close to the road; more frequently, small wagon-roads connected farm villages to the highway. Now and again they passed an inn which abutted the road. As evening fell, they stopped at the third such establishment.

Exhaustion had fallen away from Falorn as he rode. He felt better at the day's end than he had that morning. He sniffed the air in the courtyard of the Duck's Head as he handed the horses over to a stablehand.

"What are you doing?" Sera asked. "If I didn't know better, I'd think you were trying to smell the air."

"I am trying to smell the air. I like the smell of inns. This one reminds me of . . . of my father's home."

"It reminds me of an old stable." Sera paused, as if considering her words. "If you like it so much, why did you leave?"

Falorn thought about telling her the truth, about trying to explain how a silly fight that sprang out of years of evasions and half-truths from his father had caused Falorn to stalk away from home without a plan, then decided he couldn't explain it in a way that sounded plausible. He finally settled on an answer that wasn't untrue, exactly, but wasn't the whole truth either.

"It was time to go. I wanted a life that I couldn't have in the village."

"What kind of life is that?"

"You're going to think it's funny. I wanted adventure, excitement, all the things people passing through along the road seemed to have. I wanted to know what it was that made them want to travel."

"Well, you found adventure." Sera's expression remained blank.

"I found adventure," he echoed. They walked toward the inn's front entrance, carrying saddles and saddlebags over their shoulders.

"I wonder," Sera said, just before they passed through the open doorway, "when the people in this inn see you, will they wonder why it is that you travel, and wish they could be like you?"

"I'm traveling because if I stop moving, somebody is going to kill me."

"They don't know that."

"I guess they don't."

A silver coin from Falorn's pouch bought the best room in the house, along with heaping plates of roast lamb and heavy tankards of warm, strong beer. Sera seemed unusually thoughtful as they ate, as if trying to digest Falorn's words along with the food.

Two young barmaids fawned on Falorn as he sat in the common room. Every time he looked up, one of them refilled his drink, or touched him to keep her balance as she brought another tray of food. The two of them smiled prettily every time he glanced upward. They ignored Sera.

Sera glared blackly at him from across the table. Falorn felt uncomfortable, although not because of Sera's dark mood. Until now, he had always envied the rich-looking men-at-arms who passed through his father's inn, and marveled at the way serving women seemed irresistibly attracted to them. Now, he found the attention a little sad in its obvious insincerity.

He looked away in embarrassment when a henna-haired girl of sixteen or seventeen—nearly Falorn's own age—bent over the table with yet another tray, exposing her breasts to his view through the low neckline of her loose white blouse. The girl had clear skin and a wide mouth. She wore no powder or other cosmetics that Falorn could see, except for a touch of black paint to thicken the lashes over her light brown eyes. She had large breasts, revealed all too clearly through the thin white fabric of her blouse, even when she stood upright again. Falorn found himself glancing at her, despite his discomfort. The girl noticed his attention, and winked at him.

After eating heavily but drinking only a little, Falorn excused himself. Several other travelers invited him to play cards, and a pair of prosperous-looking local tradesman asked him to sit and talk with them over a mug of beer, but Falorn declined both invitations as politely as he could. Although he didn't feel tired at all, sleep still seemed like a good idea.

In fact, Falorn felt surprisingly strong and alert as he walked up the wooden stairs to their second-floor room. His injuries no longer bothered him at all, and even the afternoon's ride had failed to sap his energy. Sera followed behind him quietly.

Sera slid the small bar into place to lock the flimsy scrapwood door behind them. As she did so, Falorn began looking around the room, which covered about a quarter of the inn's upper story. Wrought iron bars shielded the three small windows from invaders, although they also cut off escape by any route except through the door. An oversized brass bedstead, tarnished and worn from years of constant use, supported an uneven mattress of canvas-covered straw. A quartet of three-legged stools surrounded a round table, its wooden top marred and discolored by burns and knife scars. A chamberpot occupied one corner, while two buckets of water sat on the bare floorboards next to the door. The walls and ceiling had been whitewashed recently, leaving the whole room smelling faintly like a lime-pit.

Falorn sat on one of the stools, but found his strength suddenly beginning to fade. His vision blurred, and he had to steady himself with his hands to keep his head from hitting the table. He shook his head woozily to clear his sight.

Sera touched his shoulder gently with one hand. After a moment she began kneading the stiff muscles in Falorn's neck with both her hands.

"Are you all right?" she asked, massaging his neck and shoulders.

"Just tired, I think. I felt fine until a minute ago."

"That cow of a barmaid probably put something in your beer," Sera said. Falorn could hardly tell whether she joked or not.

"I don't think so. I think I just tried to do too much today."

"I don't think you could do too much for *those* sluts."

Falorn said nothing.

In a few minutes he felt a little better. He stood up and walked over to the bed. For a moment, he wondered about their sleeping arrangements, but he felt too drained and tired to think about it. He pulled off his boots, belt, and baldric and dumped them all onto the floor next to the bed. He settled back, letting himself sink into the lumpy straw of the mattress. One hand lay on his pouch of cards, but he could feel little else; his body seemed to float weightlessly on the canvas-covered sea of straw.

After a while he sensed the warmth of Sera lying beside him, her body not quite touching his skin. She breathed evenly but not slowly, still awake.

"Falorn?" she said eventually.

He paused, wondering if he should feign sleep. He knew he wasn't more than half awake.

"Falorn?" she asked again.

"What, Sera?" he replied, his voice sounding thick and unfamiliar in his head.

"Do you think that barmaid is prettier than me?"

"Huh?"

"Do you think I'm pretty?"

Falorn thought for a minute. He didn't know how to answer.

"I think you are," he said, finally.

"Thanks," she said after a pause. "You'd say that anyway, but at least you tried not to look at the barmaid."

He didn't know quite what to say. After a moment she reached over and squeezed his hand. He squeezed back, and then felt himself drifting irresistibly into sleep.

They left early in the morning, before the night's coolness fully lifted. Their horses' hooves clattered on the clay that surfaced this part of the King's Road.

By the time the dawn haze faded into bright blue sky, they found themselves on a rougher road surface, as the horses descended into a long valley where winter flooding had washed away much of the paving.

Floods had left other damage as well; heaps of refuse lined the edges of the road, some of them higher than mounted riders.

They watered their horses in an abandoned village around midmorning. Floodwaters had swept away the thatch roofs and clay plaster from the walls of the houses. Only rotting logs and brushwood remained. Their horses seemed nervous in the quiet, decaying place, so Falorn and Sera rode onward as quickly as possible.

Falorn wondered where all the people had gone. He hoped the flood hadn't washed them away as well.

The day grew steadily more overcast as they continued. Early in the afternoon, the sun clouded over. A cool, steady breeze tossed Falorn's hair around his face. The horses remained skittish as they rode through the empty country, startling when a rat moved from a pile of refuse, and nearly throwing their riders at the sound of clattering, windblown wood from some derelict cottage.

A few raindrops struck Falorn's face. Soon he and Sera rode forward into a steady drizzle. The horses whinnied in discomfort as they continued through the long, deep valley. Falorn and Sera saw only drowned grass to the sides of the road now, except where the huge heaps of flood-washed rubbish obscured all view.

Something blue flickered at the edge of his vision. A blue haze now edged the top of one of the refuse-piles.

He reined in his mount, wondering if it would be safe to leave the road and investigate the heap. *What could the card want over there?* he wondered. *There's nothing there at all, except what the flood left. Could there be a cabin or shelter behind there, maybe?* Beside him, Sera reined in as well.

Something moved at the edge of a heap. A shout broke the silence, and a horse whinnied. Falorn reached for his sword, feeling the blade jump into his hand at the merest touch.

Falorn's horse reared and nearly threw him as five riders in green cantered onto the road from behind one of the piles of scrap. Three of the armored men rode at Falorn, while the other two moved to cut off Sera's escape.

Heavy, green-painted helms covered the riders' heads and faces. Green surcoats without insignias or coats of arms flapped over thick hauberks of chain mail. Falorn lifted his sword as the three riders bore down on him.

The first attacker closed quickly, swinging a studded mace with both hands. Falorn spurred forward to meet him, and thrust with his sword before the green warrior could fully extend his arms. The attacker parried with the shaft of his mace, but before he could bring the crushing weapon to bear again, Falorn chopped at the wooden pole, severing it six inches below the head. The four-sided piece of studded iron fell to the ground with a heavy thud. As the green soldier reached for a saddlesword, Falorn drove his broadsword through the eyeslit of the warrior's helm.

He could feel the cards pushing him, but this time, Falorn felt himself anticipating many of the correct movements before the knight card directed him. *Maybe I am learning something. I hope so.*

He scraped the blade clear as the green warrior fell from his saddle, and the two remaining swordsmen closed with him.

One swordsman attacked from either side, hoping to open up his guard by forcing him to defend both sides at once. He batted down a quick thrust aimed at his horse's flank, and recovered in time to parry a slash at his neck. The gelding stepped back, giving him a slightly smaller area to defend, but the two green riders continued to advance, fighting smoothly in unison as if from long practice.

Falorn barely deflected a cut at his unarmored head. The other warrior drew blood on his left wrist at the same time. They continued to force Falorn and his horse backward, as if they wanted to delay him more than defeat him.

Sera! he suddenly realized. *They're going after Sera and her cards!*

He spurred his horse suddenly, pushing forward into the attacker on his left. New energy seemed to flow into him as he battered the green warrior's guard down, and thrust forward with all the strength he could muster. He felt a sword clatter off the armor on his shoulder as Falorn's own weapon rammed through the rider's armor and into his neck. He turned to face the third rider quickly.

The green rider turned his mount and galloped away. The other two riders, Sera, and her mount had disappeared. A faint drizzle continued to fall as he dismounted and bound his wounded wrist. In the misty air, steam seemed to rise from the bodies of the two green warriors. Falorn half expected the two dead men to melt away like the creature who attacked him on the Turnpike. But even after Falorn had checked his horse for injuries, the bodies remained where they had fallen.

Falorn quickly rifled the dead men's clothing and saddlebags.

It doesn't bother me anymore, Falorn realized. *I can touch the bod-*

ies and it doesn't bother me that they're dead—that I killed them. He found the thought very disturbing, but he still felt nothing toward the two blood- and rain-soaked corpses lying on the edge of the King's Road.

He felt vaguely disappointed when neither body yielded up another card. *I guess if one of them had a card, the others wouldn't have left so quickly. Or maybe one with a card would have killed me, instead of dying himself.* He shook his head as he stood up, but nevertheless added the dead soldiers' coins to his own purse. Most of their money was unfamiliar to him, round silver and brass pieces stamped with the images of nobles he didn't recognize. Not surprisingly, they matched some of the coins he'd found with the dead knight on the Turnpike, just as their colors matched his.

Within a few minutes he remounted, this time riding the least exhausted of the two captured horses. The other two horses trailed behind, the second green warrior's mare as a remount and his own gelding, more tired than the others, carrying the dead men's armor and swords.

He began down the wet road at a trot, concentrating as hard as he could on tracking Sera. Once more, thousands of intersecting blue strings appeared along the road in front of him. His head hurt as he tried to sort them out. Sera's trail did not separate easily from the others this time. He had to work at pulling it away with his mind, holding the flickering blue trail separate from all the others. The intersecting lines took a long time to disappear, and when they did, Falorn's head continued to swim. He had to dismount for a few minutes and stand by himself in the rain, waiting for his head to clear of everything but the one blue line which marked his only connection to Sera. As soon as the overcrowded feeling in his skull receded, Falorn remounted.

He followed the trail as quickly as he could, changing mounts frequently to gain time.

The King's Road finally reached the end of the valley, and Falorn felt glad to leave the dead land behind. By late afternoon the rain increased to a steady, soaking onslaught. The downpour thoroughly wet Falorn and the horses; the animals walked slowly, with their heads downcast. Only the blue trail guided him in following Sera. As evening set in, the rain and encroaching darkness reduced visibility nearly to nothing. He only knew that the horses remained on the road because of the clop of hooves on the slick clay paving, which had returned once they left the flood-ruined valley.

Falorn didn't dare camp that evening. He continued riding through the night, stopping only to rest the horses briefly.

An hour before dawn, the rain finally tapered off into a faint sprinkle. He followed the blue line doggedly, even when everything else seemed to blur with fatigue. The blue seemed to burn across the center of his vision; he guided the horses straight along its course. He could see nothing else around him. For all he knew, the line could be leading him to the edge of an abyss. The cards could be leading him straight into Kerion's fires—in his current state, Falorn no longer cared.

By morning, he got a bit of a second wind. He found himself on a tributary road, winding through uncultivated hills and pasturage. Scattered inns and small villages lined the road every few miles, but Falorn stopped only once, to feed and water the horses and buy trail provisions for himself. He ate in the saddle, hoping to cut into the green riders' lead.

That afternoon he glimpsed them for the first time, only a single hill ahead of him. He had just changed horses, and he spurred his mount into a gallop. He screamed out a challenge as he rode, hoping it would make them turn and fight. The green riders paused briefly to look back at him, then pushed their own mounts to a greater pace. By the time Falorn reached the hilltop, they had disappeared from view.

He saw them again just before sunset. This time he could clearly see that one of the horses carried a squirming bundle instead of a rider. Again, Falorn accelerated to catch the green riders, but this time he lost them in the darkness.

He had to slow down that night. The card might illuminate the path toward his prey, but it wouldn't keep his horses from injuring themselves on the steep slopes in the darkness. Although he continued for most of the night, this time he slowed the horses to a walk, and he rested them more generously. Close to morning he had to stop for two hours of sleep, too overcome with fatigue to continue.

At dawn he awoke again and continued the pursuit. The slight wound on his wrist had vanished completely.

Why won't they turn and fight? Falorn wondered. *They have to know I'm a fool for following like this. They could kill me together. Two of them wounded me before, and these three could pick their own ground for an ambush. The cards might help me, but underneath all of the magic, I'm no fighter. I'm an innkeeper's son with a sword and a tired horse. And they have cards, too—Sera's for sure, and probably others, too.*

He wondered why he even continued the chase. *Sera saved my life twice, that's why. I may be a peasant to her, but I pay my debts. I don't understand her, but I am in her debt. Besides, she's the only one who can tell me anything about these cards.*

The road thinned to a narrow trail that morning. He caught brief glimpses of the green riders twice before noon, the second time only a few hundred yards away. Around the next hill, the ground abruptly flattened into a field of switchgrass and purple-bloomed prairie clover. Shrubs dotted the field, and at its far end, less than a mile away, Falorn could see the edge of a thin scrub-forest.

The three green riders—with their fourth, bundled, horse—rode through the middle of the field, less than halfway to the safety of the woods. Falorn charged toward them, new strength surging into his blood.

One of the horsemen started to turn toward Falorn, but his fellow caught the warrior's arm and gestured toward the woods. The third rider quickly pulled a knife and reached toward the large bundle on the riderless horse.

"No!" Falorn screamed, and pushed his horse even faster; but he had no chance at all of reaching the soldiers in time. The bundle dropped heavily into one of the shrubs, its straps cut. The three riders and the empty fourth horse galloped toward the forest and escape.

Falorn reined in his horse next to the bundle, which had fallen into a now-crushed leadplant, scattering gray-covered foliage for several feet around. He jumped to the ground and drew his own knife, which he used to slice the burlap sack open.

Cutting away the cloth, he found Sera—bound, gagged, and unconscious. He found her pulse easily, and only after he realized that she still breathed normally did he even look up to make certain the green warriors had truly gone, and not doubled back to ambush him. Falorn sawed off the ropes that held her, and poured water from his wineskin onto her forehead and face to revive her.

Sera sputtered slightly, but then her eyes opened wide and she sat up abruptly, looking around wildly and clawing at her belt.

"My cards!" she screamed. "What have you done with my cards? How could you take them?"

"Sera, they're gone. The soldiers in green took them."

For a moment she looked at him blankly. Then her eyes went even wider and she began to sob.

13

An Ambush in Green

Sera cried uncontrollably for hours. Falorn held her and let her cry, even though it seemed like she would never stop. Finally, he had to get up from her side to groom and feed the horses. The animals grazed uneasily and whinnied continually throughout the night. But the storm had spent itself, and the night passed peacefully, if not quietly.

In the morning Sera could not ride by herself. She sat in front of Falorn as his horse walked through the grasslands and brush which skirted the belt of upland forest. Sera sobbed as they rode, then shivered endlessly after her tears ran out.

At sundown, they stopped to camp on a lightly wooded hilltop. The hill looked down into a vast, green valley, broken into criss-crossed strips of cultivated fields. Falorn counted fourteen villages along the river which bisected the valley. At the opposite end sat a walled city, its outskirts sprawling onto wooded hills. A paved road ran through the valley, probably the same King's Road Falorn had left behind while chasing Sera's captors.

Sera said nothing all day. After the sun set, she and Falorn sat close together. He kindled a small campfire in a clearing on the hill, out of sight of anyone watching from the valley. They huddled together in front of the fire, his arm around her shoulder, gently holding her. Her shoulders continued to shake under his fingers. Falorn wondered if she would ever speak to him again.

Sera had washed her face in a spring at the foot of the hill, but her eyes and face still looked red and swollen, even in the uneven light from the fire.

"I'm sorry I couldn't get your cards back," Falorn finally said. "I was afraid you were hurt. I didn't even think about the cards."

"You knew about the ones I had all along, didn't you? Even though I only told you about my father's cards."

"I saw them in your secret room, while I was hiding from your father. I didn't want to say anything, though. You might have thought I wanted to take them."

"Oh, Falorn," she said, burying her face in his shoulder, "I've been so awful to you. How can you ever forgive me?"

"You saved my life, Sera."

"And I almost got you killed, too, and I tried to steal your cards. I don't know why you saved me. You should have left me in the dirt there and gone after the cards."

"I wouldn't leave you," Falorn said. "Why would I do a thing like that?"

"I don't deserve to be alive after the way I've treated you."

"I'd be dead if you hadn't rescued me in Roicenet."

"I only did it so I could get you to help me, and I wanted your cards."

"I'm sure that's not true. You would have taken them then if you wanted them."

"I did, as soon as I thought we were safe, or at least I tried to. I left you alone in the woods without any food or weapons. How could I do that to you, when you've been so good to me?"

"Why are you telling me this?"

Sera sniffled for a minute, and her voice caught as she started to answer.

"It's . . . it's just that . . . now that the Crimson Temptress card is gone, I'm starting to see things as they really are. I've been so blind, so stupid. I don't know why you ever helped me."

"Your father was going to kill me if he caught me in your room, Sera. I couldn't really *not* help you. But mostly I helped you because I like you."

"You shouldn't. I'll only hurt you again."

"I'm sure you won't hurt me on purpose," Falorn said, only half believing his own words. He couldn't help wondering how much he should believe her.

"Oh, Falorn. Please don't say that. I'm not a good person. I've done a lot of bad things."

"We all do things we're sorry about later, Sera. All we can do is try and learn from them."

"Falorn, I've had people killed. I've killed people. Those aren't just normal bad things. I can't just go to a priest and ask for forgiveness. I don't think you realize what kind of a person I am."

"You're a duke's daughter, trying to convince a runaway innkeper's son that she isn't good enough to break bread with him. Sera . . . I've killed people too. I don't feel good about it, but I had to do it. I may have to do it again. I'll never get used to it, but if I have to, I'll defend myself, and find a way to live with it later."

"You don't understand, Falorn. I *liked* it. It made me feel powerful. For once in my life, I was in control of other people's lives. I didn't have to answer to my father, or my brothers, or to anyone. I did some terrible things while I had that card. It made me into a terrible person. And the worst thing is, I'd give anything at all to have the two cards I lost back."

"I think I know how you feel," Falorn said, holding her a little tighter. With his other hand he checked the pouch around his throat, even though he could feel the warmth of the cards at his chest. "I don't know what I would do if I suddenly lost these cards. I've gotten so used to them, it's almost like they're a part of me."

"Would you kill to get them back?"

"No," he admitted. "At least I don't think so. The cards are important to me, but I don't think they're important enough to be worth someone's life. I've seen too many people die for them already."

"I *would* kill for them. I'd lie, I'd steal, I'd betray a trust or a friend. That terrifies me, Falorn. Those cards have changed me, and I don't know if I'm ever going to change back." He held her silently and stared into the fire.

The next morning, Sera rode on one of the captured warhorses. She would have ridden with Falorn again, but he felt uncomfortable doing so; riding double left him unable to defend them if the green soldiers attacked again. He spent much of the day walking ahead and picking a trail through the hills, while Sera rode behind and tended the packhorses. When they stopped to rest, Falorn practiced uneasily with his broadsword, nervously looking around the wooded clearing which hid them.

He wanted to work their way down the hills and back onto the road which led through the valley. No one seemed to be watching them, but he couldn't help wondering when the green riders would return to take his cards away.

"Can they find us, do you think?" he asked Sera, as they led the horses through scrub woods.

"I'm not really sure. If they found us through one of my cards, they might not be able to. Similar cards seem to sense each other, the way you and Rorik could each feel the other lion cards nearby. But *all* the cards want to come together, so even if they don't know where we are, they might stumble into us by mistake, or just follow a hunch which leads to us."

"Oh. So if all the cards want to come together, then this is going to keep happening."

"Probably. As long as you have the cards, at least."

"There doesn't seem to be an easy way to get rid of them. If I buried them by the side of the road, you'd just dig them up."

"You have to keep them. They found you, and they're yours."

"What do you mean 'they found me'? Did your cards just find you? Did they come knocking on your door one morning, or follow you home?"

"My cards had some help."

"Well, mine didn't."

"You did go out of your way to get those last few."

"I was looking for my sword. And for you. Your friend didn't leave me much choice."

"He's not my friend. He was never my friend. Right now, he's probably looking for me with a whole army behind him."

"You did want to kill him."

"Not exactly. The temptress card wanted me to kill him. That's what got me into all the trouble."

"I guess," Falorn said, not quite believing. "After all, the lion cards have led to a bit of trouble for me."

She looked at him and laughed, sounding a little forced. "You have come a long way for a peasant boy, haven't you?"

"I think so, but sometimes I'm not so sure. I have money and weapons now. But I ate better at my father's inn, and nobody was trying to kill me."

"We'll find someplace to hide soon, and then we'll be safe. We have enough money to eat well. You can buy another inn if you really want one. You could probably buy a dozen of them."

"But we won't be safe," Falorn said, "as long as I still have these cards."

"No, we won't."

The hills became steeper and more heavily wooded as they descended. By late afternoon, Falorn began walking ahead of Sera and the horses, using the thief card to help pick a path while she waited with their mounts under cover behind him.

As he crawled along the flat, mossy top of one massive rock, he saw a patch of green cloth below. He dropped to his belly, and slid carefully to the edge of the rock. Twenty feet below, two soldiers in green sat in a thicket overlooking the road. Both men held crossbows, and Falorn could see a stack of spears nearby.

He backed away from the edge of the rock, concentrating on keeping his movement silent. He didn't think the soldiers could see him, even if they looked up, but he couldn't tell if others nearby might not have better vantage points.

He looked around carefully, and finally spotted four other soldiers, and a thicket which rustled suspiciously with concealed men or horses. Any of them might be attracted by the slightest movement on the exposed rock above them.

Falorn froze in place and waited. The soldiers looked alert, as if they expected someone to pass by momentarily on the empty road in front of them. Unless they awaited other prey, the green warriors clearly had found Falorn and Sera's trail and anticipated their direction; the only way to avoid the ambush would be to go through the most thickly wooded hills and avoid the road into the valley.

Falorn didn't want to skirt the valley altogether. He wanted better food, and new clothes, and he thought a night at an inn would do Sera good.

None of the soldiers moved appreciably for half an hour, and Falorn thought about trying to retreat despite their vigilance. He felt a sudden cooling against his chest when the thought crossed his mind. So instead he froze in place. He dared not move even when mosquitoes began to swarm around and land on him; he could only ignore the bites and the itching, cursing silently to himself while the soldiers continued their quiet watchfulness below him.

After an hour, he saw one of the green-clad warriors walk onto the road itself. After a moment the soldier came back, and said something guttural, in a language Falorn could not understand. They seemed to immediately relax their vigilance. Falorn scurried backward off the exposed surface of the rock and into the bushes before he could find out why.

He felt safer once the thick bushes enveloped him. Within a few feet, forest noises and colors erased all traces of the green soldiers. The woods seemed to come to life around him as he finally dared to stand up and stretch his cramped legs and shoulders. He picked out a dozen different birdcalls before he stopped counting, and small animals rustled through the brush on all sides. Falorn found he could see them when he stood still and concentrated.

In twenty minutes he retraced his steps on the makeshift deer-trail that had led to the unsprung trap. Sera sat in the clearing where he had left her, while the tethered horses quietly nosed among the underbrush. A carpet of musky, half-rotted oak leaves covered the ground.

She looked up as Falorn walked silently into the clearing, creeping noiselessly around the underbrush and avoiding the thin claws of oak and hickory branches with growing ease. Sera rubbed a hand under one red-tinged eye, and Falorn could see that the swollen, abraded skin beneath her eyes had returned in his absence.

"Sorry I was gone so long," he said. "I had trouble finding a passable trail and had to backtrack. We're going to have to cut around some of this thick forest ahead; the horses won't be able to get through it."

"If you say so," Sera replied listlessly.

"When we get through the rough ground, the road's not far. I'm not sure how safe the road will be in the woods, but we ought to be able to follow it once we get into the valley. It would be nice if we could hide in that city for a few days."

"That would be nice," said Sera quietly.

They camped deep in the woods, but Falorn slept lightly, listening for green warriors in every forest sound. He rose before dawn and began grooming the horses; Sera looked so sad as she slept that he didn't have the heart to wake her. She stirred as the first faint sunlight penetrated the clearing, then sat upright suddenly.

"Why didn't you wake me?" she asked.

"I thought you needed the sleep."

"We need to get moving. They'll catch us if we don't get going soon."

"Who? The green soldiers? Your father? Your fiancé?"

"All of them. Whoever's closest. Any of them could be on our trail."

"Not sleeping isn't going to help get away from them. We both need more rest than we're going to get in cold camp. I think we'll find the road today, and the city tomorrow. Do you know anything about the place?"

"I . . . think so," Sera said hesitantly. "If it's the place I think it is, we can hide there. It looks the same from a distance, anyway, but I can't be sure from the angle we saw."

"What do you think it is?"

"My father took me to a place called Windford once, when I was ten. It was a city-state at the far end of a long valley like this one, and it was about the same distance from Roicenet, traveling by the King's Road. I remember it as being a much bigger place, but I think everything probably looked a lot bigger to me then. I was a pretty small child, and I hated to travel."

"Will your father think to look for us there?"

"I'm sure he will, but he probably won't find us."

"Because your cards are gone?" Falorn asked. "That's got to make you harder to track."

Sera winced. "That's part of it, I guess, but it's not what I meant. Windford's one of those bizarre religious places with odd laws and customs; that's why my father took us there. He was always taking my brothers on trips to educational places, and I got to tag along sometimes. The thing about Windford is that the religious authorities can't stand vanity. Humility is a cardinal virtue, and anything too ostentatious or aesthetically pleasing is likely to run you afoul of the religious courts. A couple of generations ago, one of their ruler-priests (I don't remember their actual titles) decided to go a step further. He decreed that all unmarried persons over the age of ten would be required to wear masks, so marriages would not be made on the basis of beauty and vanity. Supposedly, it makes people pay more attention to inner beauty. I remember some people in pretty fancy masks, though."

"So it doesn't work?" Falorn asked. The idea had a sad sort of appeal, somehow.

"How should I know? I was ten years old. All I cared about was looking at the masks. What did I care about inner beauty? We should be able to hide there, though.

"It does sound perfect," Falorn admitted. "Where will we get masks?"

"They sell them to foreigners from stalls outside the gates, and they buy them back when you leave. There's a thriving little market just outside the walls, if all you want is a plain black mask. Fancier ones you commission from master craftsmen."

"It doesn't sound very humble."

"No, it doesn't," Sera replied. "But we don't care if they're sincere or not. We just want to hide, remember? Maybe we can even get a decent meal for once. I've been eating nothing but vegetables and swamp-roots since we got to my dear, wonderful godfather's castle, except for a little bit of tasteless dried trail meat, which I ate in between being robbed, tossed into a sack, and galloped down the road on the back of a horse."

"I hadn't forgotten," said Falorn. "I'm just not used to cities. And the last one I was in people tried to kill me twice."

"Well, that makes it safer than the road, doesn't it?" Sera said with a forced-looking smile.

"Maybe. We'll find out this afternoon, I think."

They reached the road sooner than Falorn expected. By late afternoon, the rocky hills split open into a long, shallow rift with a brook at its center. Beyond the rocks he could see the green of a field of clover, and beyond that the gray stone and yellow-gold thatches of a village.

They rode out of the rift in the late afternoon sun. Falorn felt his shoulders relax involuntarily at the familiar smell of fresh-mown clover. They reached the distant village just before sundown, at the same time the farmers began walking in from their fields. An unpaved wagon road led through the village and beyond—presumably all the way to Windford, at the far end of the valley.

An inn and a small cluster of craftsmen's shops marked the center of the village. Falorn handed the reins of the three horses to a stableboy and hefted the saddlebags onto his shoulder. He looked up just before stepping onto the wooden walkway which led to the door of the inn. The sign showed a red horse and a pair of red dogs on a black field; the sign of the Horse and Hounds, Falorn supposed.

They ate in the corner of the commons room, the only outsiders in a room filled with farmers and crofters. He drank from a pewter flagon of spiced beer as the barmaid put a slab of roast pork and a loaf of dark bread in front of him. The innkeeper had not yet appeared to haggle over money, but the sight of their warhorses evidenced his and Sera's funds. Thankfully the barmaid here seemed more discreet than the women at the last tavern.

They finished their meal before the innkeeper came to see them. He placed three fresh tankards of beer down on the center of the table, then sat down heavily across from Falorn. He reached for one of the pewter vessels himself, using his other hand to slide its companions over to Falorn and Sera.

"Not many travelers come across this way," the innkeeper said after a long drink. "The mountain trails can be dangerous." He wiped his hands on the grimy white apron which bulged over his belly.

"They're dangerous enough, I guess," said Falorn. "Tough to run an inn without any travelers, though, isn't it?"

"Fair answer to an unfair question, that is!" The innkeeper smiled, smoke-yellowed teeth showing through his full brown beard. "I'd no right to ask something so personal of a paying customer."

"No offense taken. As it happens, we did come through the hills." Falorn put two silver coins on the table. He'd counted them out from his pouch during the meal, and two more remained hidden in the palm of his hand. "Will you accept something for our meal, room, and care of the horses?"

"I'd be glad to, young lord. Much as it pains me to say it, though, you're offering me too much. I couldn't ask half that much hereabouts without bringing trouble on my head from the city."

"Far be it from me to cause trouble, but I'd like you to take it," said Falorn. "Maybe we'll stay here again on the way back, and this can be payment in advance. Or perhaps there's something we ought to know about the city."

"Perhaps there is, at that. But I can't take your money now. The Church has rules about usury, and the Golden Wasp packs a big sting." He slid one of the coins back across the table, and Falorn took it, being careful to briefly flash a view of the other coins to the innkeeper as he did so.

"Thanks for a good meal and service at a modest price, then," Falorn said. He caught the innkeeper's slight glance at where the spies sat.

"Always my pleasure," the innkeeper replied. "My daughter will show you the way upstairs to your room when you've finished. Until then, eat and drink your fill; you've paid for it, and for your morning meal as well."

"Thanks," said Falorn. The innkeeper stood up and walked back behind the bar, whispering something to the young woman who'd served them earlier as he went. As soon as he left, Sera leaned across to whisper into his ear.

"What was that all about?" she asked. "Were you playing some kind of game with him?"

"Later," Falorn whispered back. "We'll talk in the room." They finished the beers in silence. Sera avoided Falorn's eyes when he turned to look at her.

The black-haired barmaid looked up from cleaning mugs and wooden plates when Falorn and Sera rose from the table. She gestured for them to follow and walked to a staircase in the dark corner of the commons room, away from the fire and tables where the farmers drank and laughed.

They followed her up the staircase quietly. The woman held a finger to her lips when Sera started to ask a question.

The second floor contained only three rooms, one with a door closed. Falorn and Sera walked behind the innkeeper's daughter to the opposite end of the hall, above the loud end of the commons. Noise spilled into the room from below, the words indistinguishable except for the sound of guttural laughter.

The woman entered the room behind them, using the candle she carried to light the lamp which hung from a black iron hook by the door. She looked younger than Falorn had thought, perhaps fifteen or sixteen years old, with a round face framed by long, thick, satin-black hair. She had olive skin, coarsened by years in the sooty common room, and rough hands.

Sera turned to face the girl, hands on her hips. "Tell me what's going on," she said grimly. "I want to know *right now*."

"Sera, don't," said Falorn. The girl stood her ground.

"Don't tell me what to do—until you've got enough background to make up for your lack of breeding."

"Sera, *don't*."

"Why not? Why should I start listening to a couple of peasants? Is this a meeting of the innkeepers' fellowship? Is that why you've been excluding me all night?"

"Sera, if you say anything else like that, or even keep speaking as loudly as you are, we could both be dead by morning. I told you I'd explain later, and I will. Please, let's not get into this now."

"Once an innkeeper, always an innkeeper," she muttered. But she turned away as she did so, ostentatiously stripping off her belt and cloak and settling onto one of the room's two straw pallets.

"You knew Zaren, didn't you?"

"Yes. He and his brother Rorn both. We'd all served together in the past, and the crown had given us charters as innkeepers in the Free Duchies. They thought having a lot of former soldiers would give them eyes and ears throughout the Free Duchies, but it didn't quite work out that way. What ended up happening was that a lot of us looked out for each other, and sent word to each other when trouble was brewing. I'd sent word to Rorn and Zaren that my son might come their way, so they knew to look out for him, and to keep him from harm if they could. I sent word to a few others as well, in directions he never passed. Neither of them told Falorn that they knew me."

"You sent them letters? So you can read and write?"

"Certainly. But the letters were written in a sort of innkeeper's code."

"But your son can't write?" The interrogator seemed to think that a significant point.

"I think he can, now. But I never taught him."

"Why not?"

"It would have been a death sentence to him. There were lies I was telling him that he would have seen through. Questions he would have asked that I couldn't have answered without endangering him further."

"Endangering him more than putting him in Zaren's hands?"

"I think perhaps you confuse the reputation with the man. Zaren never harmed him, or put him in harm's way."

"Unlike yourself."

"Was that necessary, Councilor? Would you prefer that I stop this conversation?"

"No. Please continue. I only sought clarity."

"You won't find what you're looking for."

The interrogator nodded. "I think perhaps you misapprehend what it is I'm looking for. But please go on with your son's tale."

14

Betrayed by Tiffanies

❖⁘⁘❖

"I'm sorry," Falorn whispered to the girl.

"It's all right," she said. He liked the sound of her voice, deeper than Sera's, but with a slight hint of nervousness.

"Can we talk here?" he asked.

"Maybe, but I'm not certain. Would you mind if we went outside?"

"Would that be safe?" He looked over at Sera.

"My older brother is in the next room, with his crossbow. He'll watch her through the spyhole."

"I'm not sure that's comforting."

"Better him watching than someone else. Shall we go? No one will think anything of a rich knight walking with an innkeeper's daughter," she said, quietly.

"I'm not a knight," he replied, just as quietly.

"That doesn't really matter, does it?" she said.

"I guess not." He walked over to where Sera huddled on the pallet, turned away from Falorn and the innkeeper's daughter. "Sera, we're going to walk outside for a little while. I won't be long, and there will be someone watching the room." Sera said nothing, only curling herself more tightly and burying her face more deeply into the straw.

He walked from the room with the dark-haired girl, glancing into the other open room as they passed. He saw nothing within, and wondered where her brother hid. He supposed the other, closed room was where the spy her father had pointed out downstairs was staying.

I wonder why they're warning me? Why risk getting into trouble themselves for a stranger?

The girl reddened slightly as they passed the foot of the stairs and the noise from the men by the fire stopped momentarily.

A half-door on the wall led into the kitchen where two apron-clad boys and an older woman worked; Falorn followed the young woman inside silently. She waved at the woman but walked quickly through the hot room and to an open door on the far wall, which looked out onto a long, fenced yard.

They walked to the far side of the yard, beyond a shed and outhouse, to where a wooden bench leaned against the split rail fence. She sat casually on the bench; after a moment's hesitation, Falorn sat beside her.

"My name's Falorn," he said, unsure of how else to begin talking.

"I'm Anthea," she replied. "Why did you tell me you're not a knight? You didn't have to do that."

"I didn't see any reason to lie to you. My father's an innkeeper. I didn't want to spend my life at his inn, but I'm not ashamed of him."

"Then what your . . . what that woman said is true?"

"True enough, anyway."

"But . . . how does an innkeeper's son . . . did someone squire you?"

"I left home, and I've been a little lucky. There's nothing else."

"There's always something else," she said, and Falorn thought he saw her shiver slightly.

"Wait, I almost forgot," said Falorn, taking out the three silver coins. "These are for your father."

"No," said the girl, "that's too much! Do you know what you can buy with that much money?"

"Take it, please. You've helped me, and nobody else has lately. Everybody else is glad enough to have it."

"Won't she be upset?" Anthea asked, glancing toward the upper floor of the inn.

"It's my money, Anthea. She's got her own . . . more than I ever will."

"That's not what I mean. I mean. . . ."

"Please," he said, putting his hand on top of hers, "just take the money."

"All right," she said as he slid the coins into her palm, and this time she did shiver.

"There's something my father asked me to tell you," Anthea said. "Someone came here looking for you. They described you and the horses, and they offered us a reward if we found you."

"What did they look like?"

"Like soldiers, but not from around here. They wore chain armor and green surcoats. None of them took off their helmets, not even the one who did the talking. He had a thick accent—and a strange voice, like he wasn't quite there."

"How do you mean?"

"Have you ever seen a puppet show where the voices didn't quite match the movements? He talked like that, like his voice belonged to someone else."

Falorn nodded, trying to match them up in his mind with the men in green he'd encountered. It sounded more like the creature that had atacked him the first day than the green soldiers he'd encountered later. "That is strange," he said.

"Do you know who they are?"

"Not exactly, but we've run into them before."

"We?"

"Sera and I. Sera is the woman I'm traveling with."

"Oh. I didn't know her name. They didn't know your names either, and they didn't describe you well—they did a better job describing the horses. My father and I wouldn't have known you, except. . . ." She trailed off, as if she couldn't explain it.

"You didn't betray us?"

"No one here would . . . not my family or anyone in the town. You're safe from outsiders here."

"What about whoever your father was worried about?"

"The priest, you mean? He won't trouble you, unless you threaten the Church. He doesn't care for strangers much, if they're not of the Faith, but my father will vouch for you." She made a curious motion with her right hand as she said *Faith*, and Falorn realized he still held her left hand.

"He'll be in the other upstairs room by now; he usually stays with us on this part of his circuit. Most people are religious here, so he comes here often, even if my father isn't as faithful as he'd like."

Falorn nodded "I can't stay long if the green soldiers are this close. Sera and I will start for the city in the morning."

"I thought you would," she said, with the trace of a sigh. "What will you do with the horses?"

"I'm not sure. If they're that well known, we may have to leave them here, or even turn them loose. I hate to give up horses like those, but they're not worth dying for."

"You can't just leave them! Those horses are worth as much as this inn! The Church would forbid it!"

"You could give them to the church after we left," said Falorn, not quite certain of what he could safely say. "Just say we left them behind; it would be true, after all."

"We could do that, if you swear you didn't gain them by foul means. If you did, the wasp's sting might come back on us."

"No, I came by them honestly. The ones those soldiers described I captured after some of them attacked me. They're fair prizes."

It was her turn to nod as if she understood.

"There's something my father said we might be able to do for you. He has a brother, my uncle, who lives in the city. I could take you there. You wouldn't find him without a guide, and the city can be dangerous if you don't know it well. You'd have to take the main road, and those soldiers will be waiting for you there."

"I don't know the city at all. I've never been there. Sera's been to Windford once, but she was just a girl."

"Then you'll let me guide you?"

"Unless Sera objects, yes. I would be very happy to have you as a guide."

"Thank you. You honor me." She squeezed his hand slightly. "There is something else . . . I . . . if you. . . ." Anthea trailed off uncertainly. Falorn looked at her, unsure of her meaning. She took a deep breath. "If you would . . . I mean, if you want. . . ."

She leaned back, until her back touched the rail of the fence. She reached up to her muslin blouse and began untying its laces. Falorn thought he saw the beginnings of tears in her eyes.

"Anthea. . . ." Falorn began.

"I'm not good at this," she said. "I'll try, though. I promise. I'll do my best not to disappoint you."

"Anthea, I can't . . . I mean, we can't."

"You don't like me? I can't . . . what did I do wrong?" She began crying in earnest.

"No, Anthea, it's not that. You're very pretty, and I *do* like you. I like you a lot. But that's not what I want. I mean, I want that, but not. . . ."

"Is it her?" she looked desperately toward the dark wall of the inn. "But the things she said about you? You can't. . . ."

"No, that's not it. I mean, that's part of it, but . . . I like Sera, some-how, but not the same way I like you. I don't think she'd understand at all, but I can't, not this way."

"But the money you gave me . . . let me give it back to you. You paid me. If you won't do. . . ."

"No," Falorn said gently, pushing her hand back into her lap with his right hand. He put his left hand lightly on her shoulder and squeezed gently, then carefully cupped her chin and brought her face up so that she had to look in his eyes. Tears streaked her face, and she blinked rap-idly in a futile attempt to stop them. "That's not why I gave you the money, Anthea. That's for you and your father, for the use of the inn and the room, and for caring for our horses, and for not telling the green sol-diers about us. That's all I paid for."

"Then let me give you. . . ."

"Please, Anthea, no. I can't."

She dropped her face away from his, and her head shook. He reached up and stroked her neck and shoulders until he felt her relax slightly, and she stopped shivering. She placed one of her hands on top of his for a moment, then sighed, and began retying her blouse. She looked up at him and smiled wanly.

Apparently, the wasp dislikes usury, but doesn't care about chastity.

After a few minutes of silence, she stood up, using the rail of the fence for support. "We'd better go to sleep," she said. "We'll have to get an early start if you want to make it to the city before sundown.

When Falorn returned to the room, Sera had rolled over on the pal-let. She lay on her back, with one arm thrown over her eyes. He stood and looked at her, unsure whether he should try to wake her or not. Finally, he pulled off his sword and baldric, pinched off the lamp-flame, and lay down on the second pallet. He closed his eyes and hoped to dream of lions again. Instead he dreamed of Anthea and Sera, walking together down a long grassy path, holding hands and talking like sisters, or lovers.

Anthea's light knock on the door woke them at dawn. She entered with a bucket of water and said nothing, but Falorn caught her quiet gesture: It was safe to talk, for the moment.

Sera's eyes looked darker than usual as she rose to wash her face.

"Was she any good?" Sera asked Falorn as soon as the girl left the room.

"Sera! It wasn't like that."

"Right. You just sat up and talked, I'm sure."

"That's exactly what we did. Her father asked her to tell me a few things that weren't safe to talk about downstairs. And today she's going to guide us to her uncle's inn in Windford, so we'll have someplace safe to hide."

"She's *what*?"

"She's guiding us to Windford by a back road."

"So you're telling me you expect me to spend all day on a horse next to that half-grown trollop?"

"We're going to walk. The horses aren't safe."

"Aren't *safe*? What, are you afraid I might fall and hurt myself? Or did she convince you to give those to her on top of the money? Must have been quite a night."

"The horses aren't safe because we're being looked for, and there's a reward out for us, and it includes very good descriptions of the horses. Warhorses are a lot more noticeable than we are."

"So just because this hussy claims we're being followed. . . ."

"We *are* being followed, Sera. I spotted them in the mountains on our way here. We avoided at least one ambush on the road."

"Oh," she said. "Nice of you to tell me my life was in danger. Were you planning to say anything?"

"I didn't want to scare you, when you were already upset." He stopped, and thought for a moment. "I'm sorry, I should have told you."

"Yes, you should have." Sera began rapidly looking through her saddlebags, consolidating the most valuable items into several pouches, which she then strung on her belt. "I hope you're right about this girl," she said when they heard Anthea's footsteps approaching in the hall, "because if you're not, she could be leading us right to them."

They walked from the inn as the sun rose, leaving behind horses, saddles, and tack. Sera ignored Anthea and barely spoke to Falorn. The sky lightened from purple to red to light blue streaked with pink, marked only by a few wisps of cloud. Despite the early hour, Falorn felt the sun's warmth almost immediately. The day promised heat to come, and the cards at his chest gave off warmth in seeming accompaniment. They seemed to give him energy as well: Despite the weight of his mail shirt and weapons, Falorn found himself gaining strength rather than tiring as they walked.

They turned off the village road almost immediately, and walked along a succession of winding dirt tracks and goatpaths. The empty ground around the village soon gave way to cultivated fields. They passed through high stands of spring wheat, nearly ready for the season's first harvest. By early afternoon, tall orchards surrounded them, and they stopped to rest and eat beneath a stand of fruit trees. Falorn looked around nervously all morning as they walked, but saw only the occasional herder or field worker.

They walked more slowly in the heat of afternoon. Falorn and Anthea talked a little about the woods and fields they crossed, but that seemed to darken Sera's mood even further. After a while, Falorn heard an unfamiliar birdcall, and began looking for birds and animals around them as they walked. He found when he concentrated, he could spot them easily, everything from field mice to a single, sleeping cougar hidden in a flattened cluster of long grass on the edge of a rocky field. Sometimes the animals bore a blue nimbus around them when he first saw them, and at other times they did not.

At first it made Falorn's head hurt to concentrate so hard on seeing things. Over the course of the afternoon he experimented with different levels of attention. With effort, he found that he could see a vast panorama, although it made him dizzy. When he focused less intensely, he still saw a great deal, although the blue tinges faded away almost entirely.

Falorn enjoyed the heightened awareness, if not the dizziness.

By late afternoon, they drew within sight of Windford's granite-faced walls. The spring heat remained intense, despite the sun's fade toward the horizon. Sera, more used to city life than either of the others, looked particularly exhausted after the long day's walk. She said nothing, however, and grimly fought to keep up with Anthea's brisk pace.

"Will we be able to pass through the gates?" Falorn asked Anthea, when they finally stopped to rest again. "It doesn't look like we'll get to the city until well after dark."

"We won't," she said, "but we should be able to get in anyway. The Charity Gate is always open, as long as you're wearing a mask."

Falorn looked over at Sera, who glowered back at him and then looked back down. She had removed her riding boots, and Falorn could see that the leather heels had worn badly, and unevenly.

Sera rubbed her filthy, blistered feet with grimy hands. Tears streamed down her face, leaving tracks in the gritty dust which covered them all, but she made no sound at all.

"Maybe we should camp here tonight, if this isn't a bad spot," Falorn said, waving at the orchard that surrounded them. "We've made good time today, and we can get to the city in the morning. We'll blend in better if we get there with the morning market crowds, instead of alone at night."

"That's a good idea," said Anthea. "We can all use some rest."

Sera looked up. "I'll rest if it's safe," she said, "but if we can make it to the city tonight I wouldn't mind a clean bed."

"Clean beds tomorrow, I think," said Falorn. "Rest tonight." He expected Sera to bristle at his making the decision for them, but she just nodded. *There's no way she can go any farther today, but she'd never admit that out loud.*

They made no fire, but the night stayed warm long after the sun set. They ate bread, dried fruit, and cold sausage from their packs, and then Anthea and Sera settled down to sleep, rolled up in their cloaks. They slept far away from each other, one on either side of a cluster of heaped stones that stood as high as Falorn's shoulder.

For a long time after the two women fell asleep, Falorn sat on top of the rocks, hands wrapped around his knees, and kept watch. He only partly worried about the green soldiers, who he suspected had lost the trail for the moment. But many other thoughts pranced and capered through his mind, like so many showhorses or circus-bred dancing lions.

He wondered about his feelings for Sera. He wondered about the cards, and his growing power over them. Did they have a power over him as well? How many were there, and would he keep encountering them forever? What made them worth killing for, or worth dying for?

Finally he tried to push all thoughts from his mind. He looked down from the rock, first at Anthea's sleeping form, then at Sera's. In the darkness, they looked much alike.

Clambering down from the mound of rocks, he sat down on the ground halfway between the two women, with his back against the piled stones. There he slept, with his sword across his lap, hoping for happy dreams that would help him to understand the cards, or would help him to understand his feelings for a woman who seemed to hate him half the time and desperately need him the other half. Instead he dreamed about his father's inn; about the sights and smells and noises of a smoky tavern crowded with soldiers and travelers in winter bundles; about the silent, hopeless look of the dark-eyed barmaids.

15

Masks

❖❖❖❖

The polished granite of the city walls glistened and sparkled in the morning sunlight. Near the center of the immense, silver-gray slabs the wall opened in a giant archway, lined with pink granite. A wide river flowed entirely through the city, exiting on the other side of the wall. As Falorn looked around, he could see signs of the massive earthworks, now subtly disguised as natural terrain features, which had reshaped a segment of the swift river that flowed down the rocky hills at the edge of this valley and then looped back through a jagged cut serrating the valley's end. An enormous iron portcullis thick with rust hung above the arch, waiting to plunge down and seal off river traffic in case of attack. The city looked strong, rich, secure, and placid.

Several roads led to the city, all feeding like tributaries into a single avenue—ten wagon-widths across and paved in pink stone—which led to Windford's enormous central gateway. The gates, covered in huge carved wooden panels bound with iron, stood wide open, and looked like they had not been closed in years. From the size of them, and the elaborateness of the decorative inside panels, Falorn had trouble believing the gates *could* be closed.

The open fields which surrounded the central avenue into the city had blossomed into a sort of permanent fair, filled with brightly colored booths selling food, clothing, and omnipresent masks. Musicians, clowns, mimes, jugglers, and storytellers strolled around the market-grounds, occasionally staking out clear areas where small crowds of curious travelers or farmers on their way to sell goods might be diverted by a performance. Some of the entertainments had assumed a more permanent nature; Falorn saw elaborately constructed puppeteer's booths, a round stage with dressing-room huts on either side, and an odd, four-segmented platform shared by a contortionist, a snake-charmer, a trio of young dancing girls in threadlike wisps of transparent silk, and a pair of large, muscular men who alternately wrestled members of the crowd and swallowed flaming swords.

Falorn looked around in amazement, and found himself wondering about the whereabouts of a certain circus wagon. He daydreamed as he walked, keeping an eye on his pouches and other possessions, but otherwise just basking in the energies and emotions of the growing crowd. A dancing bear growled as he nearly walked into it, bringing him abruptly back to the reality of the morning.

"Masks here! Get your masks here!" a hawker cried out from nearby, and Falorn remembered their primary purpose in visiting the fair. He quickly caught up with Sera and Anthea, who had wandered ahead. Sera looked through a seemingly endless variety of piled cloth masks on the hawker's table. Stiff painted masks, made of boiled leather or laminated strips of wood, hung from hooks on the wooden panel which backed the table.

Sera looked up at Falorn, holding a domino-mask of soft black velvet. "I liked it here when I was a girl," she said, sounding wistful. "Sometimes it's very comforting to wear a mask."

She paid the hawker his asking price for the mask and walked away from the stall quickly. Falorn tossed the man a small coin for a plain brown catseye-mask and ran to catch up again.

"Sera, wait!" She stopped and turned around, smiling, with the black velvet of the mask concealing the top half of her face. Glittering silvery sequins lined the edges of her mask.

"See," she said, "I can be anyone I want." She blew him a kiss, then pouted at him, then frowned, then flew through half a dozen other expressions in quick succession. Her eyes sparkled to match the sequins, and they held his attention like she had when he had been trapped in her bed.

Anthea appeared on the other side of Falorn and gave his arm a little tug. "Come this way," she said. "There is a gathering in the market square.

He looked to the gates of the city, and noticed most of the crowd headed toward them. The fair outside the walls was thinning noticeably.

"Come on," Anthea said again, pulling him forward.

Armored and masked guards at the gate seemed to be doing little beyond checking that people who entered the city wore masks. The three of them were waved in without incident.

The market inside the city gate looked far more somber than the colorful booths outside the walls. Plain gray flagstones paved the large square, without trees or fountains to break the relentless symmetry. At the far end stood a large wooden stage, its planks painted a dull black. Monotonous stone shops and taverns lined the sides of the square, all slate-roofed and whitewashed, the doors of every one shut tightly. The only splashes of color came from bright circular badges nailed to the doors of all the buildings. Falorn counted eight different colors, which seemed to be randomly distributed among the otherwise indistinguishable tradesmen's houses.

He wanted to ask Anthea what the colored badges meant, but she hushed him and pointed to the stage when he touched her shoulder. She had donned her own mask, a piece of deep blue suede which covered her entire face, except for eye cutouts and a triangle which left her mouth and the tip of her nose exposed.

A long procession snaked across the far end of the square, walking slowly toward the stage. Falorn heard cranking noises from within the stage. Some sort of large metal implements, looking like giant wrought-iron caskets, began rising through the floor of the platform.

The procession split in half as it reached the rear of the stage, and began to walk up the stairs located on either side of the platform. Most of the men who mounted the stairs looked like priests or government officials of some sort. They wore flowing lavender robes, with silver torques at their necks and tall, elaborate hats. None of the men looked young, and few looked middle-aged—although none wore a beard or facial hair of any sort. All wore thin black masks, which covered only the area around their eyes. Behind the officials came three younger, barefaced men in thin white robes. The third of the young men could not walk unassisted; two armored soldiers held him up, and streaks of blood showed plainly through the back of his robe. Eight soldiers in all accompanied the procession onto the stage. They looked like an honor guard, with lavender surcoats over their polished armor, silvered helmets on their heads, and full masks which covered their entire faces.

The crowd fell silent without any urging from the men on the stage. After a few moments in which no one made a sound, not even the dozens of children in the audience, the oldest looking of the lavender-robed men stepped forward. He began to chant in a clear tenor; Falorn understood none of the words, but the tone and cadence marked them as a prayer. Behind the high priest, the underpriests began chanting as well, in a soft bass counterpoint to his words. The prayer continued, almost unvaried, for nearly thirty minutes. No one in the crowd seemed to stir at all in that time.

Finally, long after Falorn thought the man's voice would fail him, the priest's chant slowed. As soon as he fell silent, the crowd began to stir and buzz. Falorn heard the sounds of vendors in the rear of the crowd, hawking meat-pies and sweetmeats, or parasols to keep off the heat.

The guards pushed one of the white robed men forward, cuffing him across the face when he resisted. The pitch of the crowd noise increased, and Falorn could feel excitement building around him. He looked across at Sera and she shrugged slightly. Anthea seemed riveted on the spectacle in front of them, and no longer noticed her companions at all.

The white-robed man finally reached the front of the stage. He stood unsteadily on his feet, wobbling as if he might lose his balance at any moment. He looked a few years older than Falorn, probably in his early twenties. The robe flapped loosely around his gaunt frame.

The soldiers allowed him to stand for a moment, then pushed the man to his knees. The priest loomed over him.

"Who comes before the face of the Golden Wasp, whose sting is the scourge of sin?" the priest intoned.

"I . . . do . . ." the man said in a barely audible voice. "I . . . am . . . a sinner."

"And what is the nature of your sin? Speak, that you may be judged."

"I . . . stole . . . a pair . . . of candlesticks." The man sagged forward on his knees. Falorn could clearly see the criss-cross red marks of scourging on his back.

"You robbed your fellow man of the fruits of his labor. You robbed the true gods of the fruits of your own labor, by forsaking honest endeavor for the life of a skulking thief. You have forsaken the gods for the sake of your own vanity. It is time to atone for your sins." The priest turned to the guards. "Immobilize him. It is time to begin the atonement."

Two of the guards pulled the man to his feet, while another leaned over the back of the stage to say something to the workmen beneath. The cranking noises began again, and one of the coffinlike metal containers began blossoming outward. When it opened fully, the metal shell still looked like a coffin; two-inch iron thorns studded the inside, except for two narrow corridors on either side of the opened front.

The man began to struggle and thrash, but the guards held him securely. Once they dragged the man to the open metal casket, two of the underpriests stepped in to help secure him. They bound his arms and legs into the channels on the open sections, using leather straps. When they finished the man stood nearly spread-eagled in front of the iron box. A guard gestured and the cranking began again, pulling the sections farther outward. The man screamed hideously as the muscles, bones, and tendons in his shoulders and knees ripped apart.

The priest gestured, and one of the underpriests passed a device that looked like an oversized iron baby's pacifier into his hand. He tested the screw on the back of the mechanism to make certain it worked; when he turned it, the two pieces which made up the head began to widen and separate. He walked over to the man, who continued to scream and flail within his bonds. At a look from the high priest, the two guards stepped forward and forced the man's jaw open. The priest inserted the device, and immediately the screaming faded to nothing. He began turning the screw with agonizing slowness. Falorn shuddered as he watched. He glanced at Sera and Anthea, who both looked entranced. The priest continued to turn the screw, forcing the man's mouth impossibly wide. Falorn flinched at the loud crack as the man's jawbone snapped. The priest turned to face the crowd.

"Here is a man who will never blaspheme against the gods again," he said. Behind him, one of the underpriests hastily unscrewed the expanding device. Another used a white cloth to wipe it off before passing it to a third, who replaced it in its velvet-lined sacramental case. The high priest reached out, and one of the underpriests handed him a second implement. This one looked like an iron mask, its interior studded with rusty metal thorns. A rod at the top of the mask allowed its two segments to be screwed together. The priest placed the mask around the prisoner's head and began slowly twisting the rod. Streams of blood quickly ran down the sides of the tortured man's neck as the thorns bit into his face. The priest stopped tightening before the mask could crush the man's skull. His assistants removed it, revealing a hideously disfigured face beneath. The high priest again turned to the crowd.

"This face will never again seduce the innocent," he intoned.

He looked to the underpriests, and one of them opened a wooden case containing a row of small silver-bladed knives in its velvet interior. With the first knife he slit the tendons on the man's wrists, carefully handing the weapon back to one of the underpriests to be cleaned and replaced in the case.

"This man shall never again rob from the innocent, nor deprive the gods of their due."

He used the second knife to put out the prisoner's eyes, carefully slicing so as not to accidentally kill the man. "This man shall never again look on another man's possessions with covetous eyes," the high priest said.

Falorn nearly vomited when the priest reached downward with the third knife. Only the strength that he drew from the lion cards allowed him to retain any self-control at all. The priest slashed open the blood-stained white robe the prisoner wore, leaving him naked before the crowd.

"This man shall never again pollute the world with his seed," the high priest said as he severed the man's testicles. The high priest stepped back, giving the knife to an underpriest to clean, and turned to face the crowd once more.

"What say you? Does this man repent?"

"No!" the crowd roared.

"I ask again: Shall I spare this man?"

"No!" came the roar, even louder, and Anthea shouting as fervently as all of them.

"We find this prisoner unrepentant," the priest said. "He shall feel the sting of the Golden Wasp." The audience cheered. Anthea roared along with them. The cranks began again, this time closing the coffin instead of opening it. The spiked iron doors forced the battered prisoner inward as they closed, compressing his body into an ever tighter space. Blood began to pour from the vents in the side as the iron casket shut. The audience continued to cheer and yell as the cranking finally stopped.

The high priest acknowledged the crowd with a nod of his head, and then beckoned the second prisoner forward. Falorn couldn't watch anymore as the ritual began again, with the second man confessing to burglary. He looked around, but the square had filled entirely with cheering townspeople; even the vendors selling meat-pies and pastries had given up, and now stood atop their carts for a better view of the executions.

Sera seemed to have lost her enthusiasm as well, Falorn noticed. They could go nowhere, however. He suspected it might be dangerous even to take his eyes off the proceedings for long. Anthea certainly paid rapt attention, and Falorn found himself forced to watch, and to suppress the growing sense of queasiness within.

Two hours later, the last of the three criminals finished dying. After some additional chanting, the guards and priests turned and filed away, leaving the blood-soaked stage and caskets to be cleaned by others. The crowd began to gradually dissipate, some wandering out the gates to the fair, others entering one of the taverns or tradesman's establishments which lined the square, while others remained to buy goods from one of the tables or stalls which merchants began setting up. Falorn noticed that the stalls bore colored badges much like those on the doors of the buildings, but in no pattern he could readily ascertain. He thought to ask Anthea but decided against it, a little fearful of offending her religious sensibilities.

Anthea seemed energized by the morning's proceedings. If she noticed the unsteady way Falorn walked after the executions, she said nothing. He recovered quickly, however, and Sera seemed none the worse for what they'd all seen. He thought back to the Hook in Roicenet, and kept his thoughts to himself.

It seemed strange to Falorn that she would help unbelievers like Sera and himself. *Her father's not a believer, though, and he's the one who told her to. Maybe obeying parents is more important than obeying the church.* He thought about the way he'd left his father's inn in anger, and was glad he hadn't told Anthea that part of his story.

He and Sera needed more clothes. Their own garments were now worn and fraying—and the green soldiers had seen them as well. Sera's other clothes had been lost to the green soldiers along with the horse, and Falorn still wore the travel clothes he'd drawn from the Baron of Golden Reeds's stocks.

Browsing the tables of used clothing, Falorn haggled for several tunics for each of them, some plain and some colorful. He bought new britches as well, and a quilted vest for Sera. Every time he spoke, Anthea clung to his shoulder, as if fearful that he would accidentally blaspheme. Early in the afternoon they left the square, and Anthea began guiding them through the twisted streets of the city's Old Quarter.

"Are we being followed?" Sera asked Falorn some time later.

"I don't know," he answered. Falorn glanced back but saw nothing.

He tried to concentrate as he had on the trip to the city, but no lines grew up in front of him, as if something blocked the effects of the thief card.

They came to the river where it roared through the center of Windford. They passed several bridges, but did not cross; instead, they walked along a paved avenue which lined the near side of the river. Falorn looked down at the fast-rushing greenish water. It flowed through a manmade channel of dressed stone, almost like a giant cistern.

Anthea seemed to become preoccupied as they walked farther into the Old Quarter. She said nothing to Falorn or Sera as they walked, trusting them to follow her through the odd turns and narrow alleys of the city's back streets. The river avenue never seemed to continue in a straight line for very far; they kept leaving it and returning to it, or glimpsing it from nearby streets.

The inn stood no more than fifty yards from the river's edge. They could hear the loud chatter of the racing water clearly from the door of the building, although an irregular row of houses blocked the river from sight. Falorn looked around again, concentrating as hard as he could on the cards within his pouch, but he saw nothing, not even the hint of a blue glow anywhere. He saw no one following, no hint of pursuit at all, but he shared Sera's disquieting feelings anyway.

The one-story building hardly looked like an inn. No sign decorated it or hinted at a name, and only a colored badge—orange, in this case— adorned its gray stone face. The inn had a narrow, windowless front, although it stretched far back.

Falorn reached for the brass knocker on the door, but Anthea caught his hand.

"Don't knock," she said. "Wait here and I'll get my uncle." She strode quickly around the corner of the inn and turned out of sight.

"Don't knock?" Falorn said quietly. "At an *inn*? What is going on here?"

"Whatever it is, we're too far along to turn back now," Sera replied, just as quietly. "I just hope your little friend isn't turning us in to the morality police."

"Was it like this when you were ten? I'm not sure this is as wonderful a place to hide as you thought."

"I don't *think* it was like this, but I *was* only ten. Maybe they just didn't have any executions that week. You're right, though. I think we'd better try to get out as soon as we can. Tomorrow, if nobody turns us in tonight."

"Definitely."

Anthea reappeared at Falorn's elbow. "Come this way," she said. "You don't want to go in the front way."

"We don't?" Falorn asked. Anthea ignored him, and began walking toward the back of the inn again. Falorn and Sera followed, glancing at each other nervously.

At the back of the inn they found a heavy oak door shod with iron. The peephole had already been slid aside, and someone watched them from within. Anthea walked up to the door confidently.

"Uncle Zaren," she said, "these are the ones I told you about. Take good care of them, please; Father will vouch for them."

She turned to Falorn and gestured toward the door. "He'll let you in now. This place is safe, but be careful about wandering the city, even with a mask. This place isn't safe for unbelievers."

"Thanks, Anthea," said Falorn. "Thanks for the help and the hospitality. I hope we pass your way again."

"You won't," she said, "but thank you anyway." She leaned upward and kissed Falorn on the mouth.

He passed her another silver coin, which she accepted without protest. "It's for guiding us to the city," Falorn said, "nothing else." She didn't reply, but smiled slightly. In a moment she turned away and began walking purposefully. As he watched, the lengthening afternoon shadows swallowed her.

16

An Old Soldier

The door cracked open slightly, and a large hand waved them inside.

"Don't be all day about it," a deep voice said. "Get in here *now*. I've got no wish to explain you to the Wasp."

They hurried in, Falorn and Sera both glancing at each other uncertainly as they did so. They found themselves in a long, narrow hall, with plaster walls and ceiling and a pine floor. Only a pair of lanterns in wall sconces, and one in the hands of their host, lit the corridor.

Their host had enormous hands: heavy and callused with thick nails, dark, hairy backs, and dozens of thin white scars criss-crossing otherwise tan skin. Falorn saw the hands first, and would not have been able to take his eyes off them, had it not been for the man's face.

The innkeeper's head had been shaved smooth, and three large scars covered parts of his face and scalp. He had heavy brows and dark eyes, nearly black in their intensity. His thick black mustache showed no gray at all, although the man looked as old as Falorn's father. His body betrayed no hint of fat—just wide, corded muscles which his loose, open tunic and tight deerskin britches revealed. A blue sash wrapped around his waist and heavy jackboots finished the costume. He carried no weapon, not even a knife, and wore no adornment at all.

"Well? Are you finished staring yet? I'm in a hurry, even if you two want to get killed. This way." He turned and strode off. They followed him halfway down the corridor, but he ignored all the doors. Instead, he kicked a hidden lever of some sort, and a three foot square panel appeared in the plaster, where before Falorn had seen no seam.

Why is the blue thief not working, Falorn wondered, not for the first time.

The big man gestured and they crawled through the hidden door into a narrow room beyond. The innkeeper didn't follow, but thrust his head in after they'd gotten inside.

"You'll have to keep quiet in here; you can whisper, but nothing louder. I'll bring food, but don't open the door for anyone, no matter what. If you're caught here, you're dead, and so am I. No foreigners allowed in this district, and they only barely tolerate unbelieving old-timers like me. Here's a lantern," he said, handing it to Falorn. "You can keep it lit here. The common room's on the other side, but it's always lit. Use the spyholes to look out if you want, but don't talk if you're facing them. Understand?"

"Yes," said Falorn.

"Good. You've been vouched for, so I'll keep you alive if you're not stupid. If you are stupid, it doesn't matter what you do; you'll never get out of here alive anyway."

Why would his brother vouch for us? I'm confused.

The innkeeper looked at them again, taking in their features for the first time. "I'm Zaren," he said, thrusting his hand forward.

Falorn extended his hand to shake Zaren's, but the older man held up his other hand before he could speak. "Don't tell me your names," said Zaren. "That would be stupid, and if you're stupid I might have to kill you myself. Stay here. Keep quiet. Wait for me to come back. Don't do anything else. Nothing." He withdrew his hand. "If you listen to me you *might* make it out of this city alive, although why you'd want to come here in the first place is beyond me."

The door shut, sealing them in the room, which would have been too small to hold four barrels of Falorn's father's beer.

They sat quietly for a while, neither one knowing what to say.

"Why *did* we want to come here?" he asked Sera, finally.

"We wanted to hide, I think."

"Well, we are hiding. So I guess we got what we came here for. I'd hate to think we'd wasted a trip."

"Falorn, we gave up three warhorses to come here. We could have *bought* an inn with that."

"Not one with charming accommodations like this, I'll bet." He forced a smile. Sera's smile looked just as forced. "I wonder how the guests who come in through the front door get treated." He leaned forward and peered through one of the many peepholes which dotted the room.

The common room looked as grim and starkly functional as the inn's exterior. Wooden tables and benches sat in neat rows. Men in coarsely woven gray shifts, local workers of some sort, ate their meals from plain wooden plates, without apparent enthusiasm. They talked among themselves, but only in low tones, as if the inhabitants of each table conspired against all the others. No one joked, or laughed, or talked loudly. A wide fireplace sat against one wall, but it contained only a charcoal brazier, rather than logs. The food seemed to be prepared elsewhere.

The sole concession to ornamentation hung on the walls. Above the fireplace, an enormous two-handed sword lay on a pair of wooden pegs. Its blade and brass fittings glistened as if polished constantly. The leather tape on the grip looked new, although the blade showed a good deal of wear. A battle axe hung on similar pegs on the wall opposite the fireplace. Above the axe a heavy footman's helmet sat on a small, unpainted shelf.

The door held no rings for a bar or bolt on the inside. If it had a lock of any sort, Falorn couldn't see it. Curious, he tried to concentrate on seeing hidden locks and doors. A whole network of lines suddenly divided the walls of the common room; seams and joints leaped into view with remarkable clarity, all edged with a faint blue aura. Whatever force prevented the thief card from working its enchantment earlier no longer remained active.

After a few more minutes of watching he leaned back, and sat down on the floor next to Sera.

"It doesn't look like the people who come through the front door get treated any better than we do," Falorn said.

"They have food," Sera pointed out.

"So do we." Falorn nudged his pack with one of his boots. "Nothing but the best beef jerky, dried fruit, and watered wine. Besides, Zaren promised us food."

"His niece promised us a place to stay, too, and look how that turned out."

"It is a little small," Falorn said, "but the view is terrific."

"You should have stayed at your father's inn, Falorn," Sera said, although this time without malice in her voice. "You would have made a natural innkeeper."

"And miss all of the wonderful times I've had on the road? And all of the wonderful people I've met?"

"Most of them have tried to kill you."

"That's true." They sat quietly for a little while, not quite touching.

"You really didn't sleep with her, did you?" Sera finally asked.

"No."

"You wanted to, though." The way she said it wasn't quite a question or a statement, but something in between the two.

"I thought about it," Falorn said, after a pause. "Part of me wanted to. But I just didn't think it would be right."

"Right for who? For you? For her? For me?"

"A little of all three, I think. I didn't really think about it that way at the time. It just didn't feel right."

"That's very noble of you," Sera said, and Falorn couldn't tell whether or not she meant it sarcastically.

"Last night I thought that she and I were a lot alike, that I had a chance to leave and she didn't. I felt sorry for her, and I guess maybe even a little bit homesick. Not that I wanted to go back to my father's, just that it brought back memories. Today, after what happened in the square, I'm not so sure. She seemed to *like* what was going on."

"She seemed to believe in it, Falorn. It's not the same thing. Religion's a funny thing that way. Sometimes I think we shouldn't look at what we believe in too closely, and other times I think we should throw everything out and start over, invent a new set of gods and heresies, and see if we can't do better."

Falorn caught his breath. "You don't believe in the gods?"

"Of course I do. I'm just not sure we ought to worship them."

A splintering crash from the common room interrupted their discussion. Falorn stood up quickly and put his eye to a peephole. Soldiers poured through the doorway to the common room. The unlocked door had been kicked in, and now hung precariously from a single hinge.

Mother of Kerion! he muttered to himself. The soldiers quickly began rounding up the inn's customers and pushing them through the front door. Within a few minutes, no one remained in the room except Zaren and perhaps twenty armored soldiers with mask-fronted helmets, their surcoats emblazoned with the symbol of the golden wasp.

A semicircle of soldiers surrounded Zaren, who had backed against a wall—not the wall with the sword or the battle axe, Falorn noticed. An officer stepped forward to face the innkeeper.

"You're not masked, Zaren," the soldier said, "We could have you for that."

"I'm in my own home," Zaren replied calmly, ignoring the cordon of armored men. "I don't have to wear a mask here. I know the law."

"You're an innkeeper. This is a public place."

"But also the place where I live. I fought in Garrister's wars, before he was an archbishop. He gave me this land, before anybody'd thought to put colored piety ribbons on people's doors. One of these days you're going to finally take me, but you're going to have to do better than that."

"You're not the hero you used to be, Zaren. People forget."

"But you haven't."

"Not yet, Zaren. But I will. And so will his eminence. We're not here for you tonight though. We're looking for a couple of fugitives."

"Look away. I've got nothing to hide."

The hell he doesn't, Falorn thought. He looked around for a more secure place to hide. From the main room, he could hear pounding and thumps as the soldiers began to search, moving furniture and probing the walls with their spearpoints to detect hidden rooms. Soon, they moved into the hall as well.

"Come here," he said to Sera. "I want to try something. If it doesn't work they're going to find us anyway."

She crawled over and they huddled together.

"It's been a good run, Falorn," she said. "If we don't make it, thanks for everything."

"We're going to make it." He concentrated as hard as he could on the thief card. Thankfully, it warmed at his thought. Whatever force had stopped it from working before seemed to be gone.

Instead of trying to see things, Falorn focused all his energy on *not* being seen.

His head began to ache as the walls shifted around him. Floor and ceiling seemed to waver and compress until they filled the world, as if he and Sera held each other snugly in a cocoon of soft, shifting plaster.

Falorn awoke to Sera's tug on his shoulder.

"Wake up, Falorn," she said, but it took a few minutes for the meaning of her words to permeate his clogged head.

"Wake up," she said again, pulling harder at his shoulder. He tried to move, but his body failed to react. "Falorn, they're gone. It worked. Now get up. Please?"

He heard a scraping noise as he finally managed to pull open his eyes. He turned his head sluggishly, only to lose all control of his neck; his head flopped helplessly onto his shoulder. He saw Sera hovering over him, looking concerned. The walls of the secret room looked unchanged, as if nothing had happened. Here and there spear-holes in the walls betrayed where soldiers had somehow missed discovering them.

He heard the scraping sound again. As his eyes began to fully focus, Falorn saw Zaren's head poking through the small panel that led into the secret room. Blood colored the innkeeper's forehead from several fresh cuts. A bruise discolored one of the man's cheeks.

"Well, you didn't give us away," Zaren said. "Better than I expected from someone fool enough to come to this city."

Falorn pulled himself upright to a sitting position, ignoring the waves of dizziness in his skull. "You came here," he said to the innkeeper. "Why am I any more a fool than you are?"

"Almost true," the man agreed. "But I came here before the archbishop took over everything, and before he knew what wonderful things magical cards are, especially for a churchman with ambition. Cards like yours, boy. And that's what makes you a fool."

Recognition suddenly dawned on Falorn. "You're a cardholder too, aren't you? How did you know I have them?"

The man's face tightened. "Don't make accusations you can't support now, boy. I might just lose what little respect I have for you. I know you're a cardholder because nothing but these cards would have made you run blindly into this foul place, when you ought to be home sitting on your mammy's lap."

"I might have been running away from something," Falorn said, tersely.

"You might, at that. But there are better places to hide. I know you have the cards because *they* know you have them, even if they can't find you yet. If you bring that sort of toy under the archbishop's nose, he's going to smell it. I don't know what you were running away from to come here, but you're running right into something else. And you'd better get used to it. They're going to keep coming after you until they kill you, and that will be it for you and your precious cards."

"They?" Falorn asked.

"Everyone. Anyone who knows you've got the damned things."

"Even you? Why aren't you trying to take them if you know so much about them?"

"I don't want them. And I don't want to have something the archbishop wants."

"Like another card?" Falorn felt certain now. When Zaren's face tightened even further, it only confirmed his certainty.

"Now you're starting to make accusations again. The archbishop might *think* I have one of the damned useless things, but that doesn't mean I do. Doesn't mean a damned thing. The archbishop's troops search this place every week, and they find nothing. Just an old soldier still a little too famous to kill."

"But you've got one."

"I think you should look to yourself, and let an old soldier guard his own skin. If you want to get out of here alive, you're going to have to listen. I'm only going to say things once. Understand?"

"Yes," Falorn answered. He felt a gentle pressure from Sera's hand on his arm. His head felt clearer with every moment they talked. The innkeeper tossed something into the small room, where it fell near Falorn's feet.

"There's food in that bag. You're leaving tonight, and you won't have time to eat first. You won't have to go outside again, but if something goes wrong and you do, avoid anything with a wasp on it. Archbishop Garrister of the Church of the Golden Wasp owns this city, and he wants your cards. He knows you're here, and he's looking for you."

"Do you mean that Anthea . . . ?"

"No relative of mine would ever betray you." He seemed very sure of his words, and Falorn wondered why. *What am I to them?* "Anthea left because she doesn't approve of my religious beliefs. Garrister knows you'e here because he's got cards, and he can feel other people with cards."

Something clicked in Falorn's mind. *I knew that. Or at least, I should have. I knew the lions could call to each other. Maybe unlike cards can, too, if you know how to use them. That must be how Sera and Sheanna and the things in green found me. And it's probably why the thief card wasn't working earlier.*

Zaren noticed Falorn's surprised look. "You can do it too, you just haven't figured out how yet. Learn how to use the things you've got and maybe you'll live a little longer."

Falorn felt more pressure from Sera's hands as his muscles stiffened. Zaren ignored Falorn's reaction.

"Garrister knows how to use his cards; he's spent years learning. I knew him before he lived in this city, back when he was just the captain of a mercenary horse-troop. He got this city with the cards. He turned a quiet religion into the militant church he always wanted with the cards. And he'll get your cards with them too, if you give him a little time." Zaren chuckled, then went on speaking.

"There are sewer tunnels under the city. They drain into the river, but they're only filled when the river's at flood. One of those tunnels runs below this building. In about half an hour you're going to be in it. I have a boat hidden which you can take downstream—I hope you can manage a boat, because the river gets rough the way you're headed. If you stay on the river it will take you to Cathan in three days. Once you're in Cathan, you can look for a man named "Steel" Stennet—he's a general in the royal army of Cathan. He's a cardholder too, but you can trust him as much as you can trust anyone. He's an old friend and a good man. He can tell you what to do if anyone can. Do you understand all that?"

"Yes," Falorn said, and beside him Sera nodded.

"Good. You'd better. Now listen while I tell you how to find the boat, and give you a few landmarks to look for on your way to Cathan."

Something crashed in the front room. Falorn heard the sound of heavy boots trampling on the floor.

"It's all over, Zaren," a loud voice called from beyond the wall. "Come on out and bring the strangers with you."

Zaren looked at Falorn and Sera. "Well, never mind the instructions, then," he said. "We don't have time. I'll have to show you myself. Come on out of there now."

They crawled from the secret room into the hall as quickly as they could. Zaren carefully replaced the hidden panel behind them. The noises continued from the front room, gradually localizing into a heavy pounding on the other side of the door to the hall. The heavy bar across the door shook with every sound, but held within its iron frame.

"That will take them a few minutes yet," Zaren said. "We still have a little time." He reached over to the near wall, where the sword, helmet, and battle axe Falorn had seen in the common room all lay in a neat stack, along with some sort of leather harness. Zaren picked up the leather straps and buckled them on carefully, ignoring the noise from behind the door. When he finished, he looped the straps over his shoulders and attached them to a heavy sword-belt. He picked up the huge sword and slid it over his shoulder, where it fit neatly into a pair of loops and hung within reach on his back. The battle axe hung at his belt, and a pair of thin-bladed throwing knives slid into the straps across his chest. The helmet fit snugly over his head. A knife and several pouches on the belt completed his accouterments.

Finally satisfied with the fit of his equipment, Zaren looked up at the others. "Are you ready?" he asked, and they both nodded. Falorn had already checked his sword and cards. Sera picked up the bag of food, and they followed Zaren silently as he padded quietly down the hall, toward the back entrance.

"Don't you think they'll be watching there?" Falorn asked.

"Of course they will. We're not going there," Zaren answered. He stopped two-thirds of the way down the hall and swept a small rug out of the way to reveal a trap door. He pulled on the heavy brass ring which served as handle on the wooden hatch. On the third try, Zaren heaved it open, letting the hatch thump down on the bare floor.

A corroded metal ladder led down into the darkness.

Falorn stared into the blackness below.

"Are we supposed to go down there without any light?" he asked Zaren.

"I don't really care what you do. Give my regards to the archbishop if you decide to stay. Otherwise stay close to me."

Before Zaren could take the first step into the tunnel, the rear door burst open, and half a dozen masked soldiers charged into the passageway.

"Damn," Zaren said, "I knew I should have fixed that bar." He saw Sera standing nearby and shoved her backward without a word. She went flying into a wall, making a slight surprised cry.

"Stay clear of the fight, girl," he said, as an afterthought, and lifted the battle axe from his belt.

Falorn drew his sword and stood nearby, so they blocked the hall between the two of them. The soldiers slowed at the sight of the drawn blades. Cursing loudly, Zaren charged into them.

The first soldier swung a broadsword at the innkeeper's head. Zaren bent his knees and ducked underneath the blow. He thrust his head forward and smashed his helmet into the man's stomach. The soldier grunted and doubled over. Zaren straightened his knees abruptly, tossing his attacker back over his shoulder as he rose to his feet. Falorn looked to see where the man fell, only to see him plummet downward through the hole in the floor. A second later, he heard a loud splash.

Falorn turned his attention to the other attackers. Zaren fought with two of them, and Falorn stepped forward to meet a third. He parried the man's thrust and aimed a cut at the masked soldier's face, only to see it blocked. He fought warily, with little room to maneuver even in the wide hallway, unless he wanted to risk getting in Zaren's way. He traded thrusts and cuts with the masked soldier, neither of them drawing blood. Falorn tried to open his mind and follow his instincts, letting the card guide his moves as he had while practicing with the lizards. He parried a series of quick thrusts and then lunged forward himself, going on the attack.

The soldier gave ground before him, hoping to find a clear area where one of his fellows might come to his support. Falorn's opponent stepped to the side quickly, but Falorn anticipated the move and broke through the man's guard as he moved. His sword flashed across the back of the man's hand. The soldier's sword clattered to the ground as he clutched his mangled fingers, the blood welling upward through his unwounded hand.

Falorn glanced across at Zaren, who still fought with two men. A pair of bodies lay on the hall floor.

A sudden, piercing shriek came from beneath the floor. From down in the tunnel, Falorn heard the sound of water churning rapidly. The man shrieked again, and then the noise cut off suddenly.

One of Zaren's opponents hesitated for a moment at the sound of the shriek. Before he could move his sword, the innkeeper knocked it away with the flat of his axe, and then swept the axe blade back across the soldier's throat. Blood sprayed in a wide swath around the room as the man staggered away.

Zaren turned to the last man and laughed. The dying man's blood ran down the innkeeper's chest in rills and rivulets, mixing with the sweat which coated his bare skin and shone in the lanternlight. The soldier growled desperately, and aimed a cut at Zaren's head. The innkeeper caught the soldier's blade with the head of his axe, and sank to his knees as if driven to the floor by the force of the blow. Zaren's left hand shot forward as he held the man's sword above his head. He reached under the soldier's mail skirt and twisted fiercely. The man screamed horribly and crumpled to the ground. Zaren's axe dipped again, and blood fountained from the downed soldier's throat.

"Fool," Zaren said as he rose from the ground. He looked around to be certain no one else threatened them, then walked over to help the stunned Sera.

"Come on," he said, "we've got a long way to go tonight, and we can't get there with you gawking."

He turned his attention to Falorn, who stood watching the open back door, sword at the ready. "Come on, help her down the ladder. They'll be a few seconds yet. We've got plenty of time if you stop daydreaming and get a move on it."

While he talked, Zaren wiped off his axe on one of the bodies.

"We're going down there?"

"Where do you think we're going? Are you stupid or something?"

"But I heard. . . ."

"So? Would you rather stay here? If you stay close to me, you'll be fine. *Very* close."

Without another word, Zaren fastened the battle axe back onto his belt, walked over to the open hatchway, and began climbing down the ladder. Sighing inwardly, Falorn put his arm around the still-groggy Sera to support her and began to follow. He saw nothing but utter darkness below. Outside, he could hear the sound of more soldiers arriving.

"Hang on," he told Sera. Clutching her tightly around the waist with one arm, he began climbing down the corroded metal ladder.

17

The Blue Serpent

The water reached nearly to Falorn's waist before he felt the stone tunnel floor beneath his feet.

Sera grew more alert as the cold water touched her. At first she just shivered and clung more tightly to Falorn, but she quickly found her own footing in the darkness. He took her right hand with his left so as not to lose her. Drawing his sword, Falorn held it high above the water to keep it dry.

The current flowed sluggishly near the walls. A carpeting of dark, sticky moss covered the stone sides of the tunnel almost completely. Falorn saw a faint glow a few dozen feet away, near the wall. Squeezing Sera's arm slightly to warn her, he began to walk forward.

They came to Zaren a few seconds later. He leaned against the wall nonchalantly. His axe glowed with a pale green light, faintly illuminating them.

"Took you long enough," he said.

"Why is your axe glowing?" Falorn asked.

"Because I took it away from a princeling who paid a wizard to make it glow. Four years later, I tracked down the wizard and paid him to tell me how it worked. It's useful in dark tunnels."

"I guess so."

Something smooth and scaly brushed against Falorn's leg. He remembered the soldier's scream and raised his sword.

"I wouldn't," Zaren said. "That's a bad idea."

"Something touched my leg."

"Ignore it and stay close to me. It won't hurt you."

Zaren turned his back and started walking away from them. Falorn and Sera hurried to follow, sloshing awkwardly through the chilly water. As they waded forward, Falorn felt more of the water creatures brush against him.

Falorn heard the clank of boots on metal, as soldiers began to descend the ladder behind them. He looked back, but could see nothing in the darkness.

"Zaren," he asked, "what happened to that soldier who fell into the water before?"

"The same thing that's about to happen to this bunch. Keep moving."

They kept slogging through the water. Behind them, the noises of descending soldiers continued.

"You weren't bad up there," Zaren finally said, his face faintly illuminated by the glowing axe, "but you should really learn to fight right."

"I hate to admit this, but I never really learned to fight at all. I've practiced a little since I got the cards, but most of what I know is from them."

"Then either you're really lucky, or you've got too many cards. How many do you have?"

"Falorn," Sera broke in, "you don't have to answer that."

He could see on her face that she wanted to know the answer too, though.

"It's all right, Sera. He's the only person that's asked about them instead of just trying to kill me and take them. He might as well know, if we're going to be traveling together." He paused, then looked at Zaren. "I have five of them: three lions, a knight and a thief. I don't know what their real names are, but that's what they look like."

"Close enough," said Zaren. "Don't let the girl worry, I'm not going to take them. Or hers either, if she has any. Those cards'll help you fight all right, even if you don't know what you're doing—the lions'll make you fast and strong and aggressive, and the knight will help your technique. But there are things they won't help you with. Like they won't teach you to fight *right*."

"What do you mean by 'right'?"

"Look at that soldier you fought up there. You cut off a few of his fingers and then left him. Nine times out of ten, that will stop him. But that other time, he'll kill you as soon as you turn your back."

"That's not a problem the way you fight, I guess."

"No it's not. You may not like it, but if you don't learn, you might not even make it out of this tunnel."

"What are you trying to say?"

"You want to fight fair. It will get you killed. *Never* fight fair."

Falorn heard the sound of splashing behind them, as the soldiers waded toward the light of Zaren's axe. The innkeeper turned around to face them. Falorn looked at him quizzically, trying not to flinch as something large slithered against his legs.

"Why did we stop?" he asked.

"I'm going to show you something about fighting fair," Zaren answered. He cupped his free hand around his mouth and shouted at the oncoming soldiers. "Hey! Fishbait! What makes you think you can catch us down here? Or did you just come down because you like to wade in the piss?"

The splashing increased. Soon the soldiers came into sight, at the edge of the area illuminated by the axe's faint green light.

Kerion! There are an awful lot of them, Falorn thought to himself, but he said nothing. Sera let go of Falorn's arm and shrank backward along the wall, only to have Zaren catch hold of her shoulder.

"I said stay close," he growled.

"Why, so we can all die together?" she asked.

"Because I said so," he replied, not letting go.

The soldiers splashed closer. Green light reflected off their drawn blades and the metal of their helmets and masks. The water roiled around them. Even the water where Falorn stood seemed agitated and rough.

As the armored soldiers drew within a half-dozen yards Zaren abruptly raised both arms above his head. He shouted and brought them down, pointing them toward the soldiers. A blue tinge surrounded Zaren's hands and axe as he looked at the advancing warriors and laughed.

The tunnel suddenly felt close and confining. A thick, harsh smell filled the air, like a fish market at the end of a hot summer day. The water began to churn and foam around them all.

"Stay close!" Zaren shouted, although Falorn could barely hear him over the roaring water in the confined tunnel. "In the name of all the thousand gods, stay close!"

An ugly, pointed snout at the end of a long, thick neck broke the surface of the water. Grayish-silver scales glinted in the light. Another head, stretched on an impossibly long neck, broke through the foam and hovered. Then a third shot up out of the water, and plunged toward one of the soldiers. Needle teeth tore into the man's neck and pulled away a chunk of flesh. The man screamed and stumbled, flailing with his sword. Instantly, something pulled his leg out from under him and he splashed into the water. A dozen snake-heads plunged after him, and he never resurfaced.

The soldiers began to fall back uncertainly, but not before the gray coils pulled another man under. He screamed hideously until his face hit the water. Falorn felt Sera flinch beside him. He put out an arm to support her. They both stood as close as they could to Zaren without getting in his way.

As the men backed away, a large gray mass rose behind them, in between the soldiers and the ladder which led back to the safety of the inn. A solid wall of sinuous, snake-headed bodies waved out of the water. Falorn looked away at the first scream. When he looked back, he saw nothing but white, churning water.

"*That* is the way to fight," Zaren said, putting his free hand on Falorn's shoulder. "Just remember, *never* fight fair."

They turned to walk away, Sera trailing slightly behind them. "Don't forget to stay close," Zaren called over his shoulder.

They walked through the tunnels for a while, wading at first, and then sloshing through knee-deep water as they reached a central walkway adjoining the river. The path paralleled the river underground, and they followed it toward the far city wall where the river exited.

"How did you do that?" Falorn finally asked.

"I think you know that," Zaren answered. "I used this." He held up an ivorylike card, which glowed in brilliant shades of unworldly blue, sending swirls of light coruscating through the tunnel. A scaly serpent of cerulean blue writhed on the card, its sapphire eyes fixed on Falorn as if he alone could free it from its ivory prison.

Sera gasped from behind them. "You . . . you showed it to him," she said. "Why did you do that?"

"He asked, Lady. And he told me when I asked." He twisted his wrist, and the card disappeared. Zaren turned his attention back to Falorn. "That's just one card, remember, but I know how to use it. See that you learn how to use yours. You're going to meet a lot of other people who want them, and most of them will be pushier about it than your girlfriend here."

"She saved my life," Falorn said, "and she's a nobleman's daughter. I don't have any claim on her."

"Whatever. You can do what you like. Now there's a couple of things you ought to know before we get out of here. I've got a boat stocked with supplies moored up ahead, and the river gate's open where the water leaves the city—ever since it clogged up and flooded out the palace one time. The Archbishop's got at least six cards, two of them mates to this serpent. That's how he got the river-snakes here in the first place. He's always known I have one, but he could never prove it or find it, and if he killed me he knew he'd never get it."

"What are his other cards?"

"I'm not certain, but I know they got him this city. I also know he's got at least one wizard in his pay, and I expect them to be waiting for us. If they're not watching the river gate we should make it all right, but hold onto your sword just in case. Once we get on the river, his power won't reach much beyond the city."

The tunnels began to grow lighter. On their left, the stone walls opened outward to reveal the river and a glimpse of the night sky above. The noise of the river grew loud as they approached.

"The current is very fast where the river leaves the city," Zaren shouted. Falorn could still barely hear him over the noise of surging water. "The boat's over here. I hope you know how to handle one of these. It'll be all we can do to keep her off the rocks when we hit the real rapids downstream."

Ropes at both ends of the pointed craft held the boat to the walkway. The force of the current would carry the boat through the last few yards of tunnel and into the river as soon as they released the stays.

The boat had three benches, with waterproof packs stowed under each of them, as well as in compartments at either end. The bow and the stern each held a small seat as well. A collapsed mast ran down the center, although it seemed useless for river travel. A pair of paddles sat across the benches.

"She's a lake-boat," Zaren said, pulling one end of his mustache reflectively. "I bought her cheap from a drunk who had come too far downriver and couldn't pay his tab at the inn. That was a long time ago, before the laws were quite so tight, and I kind of hid her, just in case something like this ever happened. I come down here every week or so just to make sure she's still in good repair."

Falorn noticed the slightly faded green letters on the prow of the white-painted boat. "What's her name?" he asked.

"I never got around to renaming her. The letters say JHENINAH, the name of the drunk's wife."

"It's a pretty name."

"If you say so. I don't put as much stock in names as some people. But if we get out of here, you really ought to tell me yours." He held up his hand before Falorn could say anything. "Not yet. We're not out of here yet."

They climbed into the boat, Zaren in the rear, with Falorn in front and Sera on the middle bench. Falorn drew his sword and held it ready to cut the line at Zaren's signal. The big man waved and Falorn slashed downward. The taut rope parted immediately and the boat surged forward, like a colt running for an open paddock door.

Falorn held tightly to the bench with one hand, and to his sword with the other. He had no hope of grabbing the paddle beside him, unless he wanted to be thrown overboard. Zaren somehow seemed to have replaced the battle axe on his belt and gotten hold of his paddle. The big man dipped the paddle into the water as they reached the river, steering the boat into the main current with seemingly practiced ease.

River spray soaked Falorn from where he sat near the prow. The river roared and buzzed loudly, like some mad animal, even though the stream didn't seem all that wild. The boat moved quickly but barely bobbed at all now that the river carried them below the open night sky.

"Falorn, look out!" Sera shouted.

He turned around as a wasp the size of a sheepdog swooped at him; he ducked just below the sweep of its sting. The giant insect paused in midair and came around for another pass, buzzing loudly. The noise increased as Falorn saw more of the creatures approaching.

Falorn stood up in the bow, nearly falling overboard in the process. Zaren shouted something at him, but he couldn't hear what. He let himself focus on the cards, and felt energy welling up from inside his chest. He brought his sword up as the giant wasp dove, and sliced at its thorax, knocking the vicious stinger away.

The boat began to rock as Zaren stood up to fight as well. The current still carried it quickly toward the outer wall of the city, but it looked as if most of the wasps would reach them long before that point.

Two wasps hovered above his head, buzzing ominously. The wounded one circled nearby, as if waiting for him to take his eyes off it. Suddenly all three flew at him at once, their sound rising to a piercing keen.

Falorn swung his blade twice without thinking about it. The steel cut in a compact arc and severed half of one giant insect's wing, sending the creature plunging into the river right next to the boat. A second insect swerved to avoid his blade, tangling it and its companion and nearly sending them into the river as well. They rose and separated, then dove for Falorn's head again.

He dodged the first of the creatures and lost his balance in the wildly rocking craft. He fell and banged his right knee, and had to put his left hand on the lip of the boat to avoid falling overboard himself. He stuck his sword up as an insect buzzed by where his head had been a second ago, and sliced a long, thin line along its belly. The creature wobbled as Falorn's blade reached its stinger; it hit the water on the other side of the boat. A pool of bright blue ichor spread thinly over the surface of the river for a moment and then dissipated rapidly.

Falorn's knee ached with each wobble of the boat as he rose to his feet. A nearby wasp swerved when he pulled himself up, and slowly descended to his level. The insect he'd wounded still hovered slightly above and to his left, just at the corner of his field of vision. He didn't dare look toward the back of the boat to see how Sera and Zaren were doing.

The creature accelerated toward him, its blurred wings giving off a numbing whine. Falorn extended his sword in front of his body in a guard position, just flicking it slightly as the creature swept toward his face. The insect plummeted into the water, half of its head sliced away.

He looked around quickly, but all the insects seemed to be gone. Only the single wounded insect still flew parallel to the boat, its buzz rising and fading as it labored to stay in the air. Sera huddled in the bottom of the boat near his feet, and Zaren stood in the rear of the craft.

"Good work," Zaren said. "You'll be better when you learn to do it right, but good work for now."

"Thanks," said Falorn. He crouched down and touched Sera's shoulder. "Are you all right?" he asked. She looked up slowly.

"I'm fine, I think. The bottom of the boat seemed like the best place not to get stung or stabbed."

"I think you're right. They're gone now. Thanks for the warning."

"Any time, Falorn. Just keep the bugs off me."

"Of course," he said, and kissed her on the cheek.

He looked up to make sure the last wasp still kept its distance, and saw the wall looming ahead of them.

"Mother of Kerion!" he shouted, "Get down! That gate is low."

The boat swept toward the river gate. The water roared around them, gaining force as it funneled through the narrow entrance.

"I think we're going to make it," Zaren shouted. "Just keep your head low."

The wasp slammed into the wall ten feet ahead of them and careened into the boat, striking the planks between Sera and Zaren with an audible thump. Falorn dropped as the thick wall towered beside them. The boat drove through the rushing water where it poured through the gate. Something popped loudly from the rear of the boat, and he heard Sera cry out. And then they passed through, and he saw the night sky above them again, and the roaring water pushed them away from the city. Falorn could only hold on as the boat bobbed and spun and tilted. Waves splashed, soaking his face and upper body again and again, but he didn't dare try to move for fear of being thrown overboard.

"Zaren!" he called. "Zaren! Help!" He heard nothing but the roar of the river. If the innkeeper answered, the noise vanished into the water.

18

Spray and Mist

After an eternity the boat came to a calmer stretch of river. It still moved quickly, but no longer rocked or threatened to overturn.

Gradually, the noise of rushing water subsided.

Falorn pushed himself up slowly. All the muscles in his arms ached, and his knee throbbed painfully.

He no longer saw city lights behind the boat. They had traveled quite a distance along the racing water. "Zaren? Sera?" he called. The two of them were sprawled in the base of the boat, unmoving. Bluish liquid stained the planks beneath them, although the body of the wasp had vanished into the river.

"Are you two all right? Sera?"

He limped over to Sera and turned her over, wincing at the pain in his knee. She thrashed against him as he moved, and he saw blue coloring on her face and hands.

Kerion! He held her as still as he could until the thrashing stopped. After her violent fit subsided, he limped to the side of the boat, tore off his already-damp shirt, and soaked it in the river. He limped back to her, and began wiping the remaining wasp venom from her skin.

Sera breathed shallowly, and her skin looked very pale. He didn't dare check if she felt feverish, for fear that he would touch the venom himself.

After he wiped away all the venom he could see, he soaked the torn shirt-cloth again and made his way over to Zaren. The pain in Falorn's knee and the muscle aches within his arms had already begun to fade by the time he reached the innkeeper's side. He touched the pouch of cards gratefully and then went to work on the big man. After a moment he realized something, and his hand went to Zaren's belt. A quick check showed that the serpent card still lay within the man's pouch. Falorn looked at it briefly, then closed the pouch again without even touching the thin plaque.

"Poor Sera," he said out loud to the two unconscious bodies. "She'd really hate to know about the chance she missed."

Zaren didn't move as Falorn cleaned his skin, and mopped the rest of the remaining venom from the floor of the boat. The big man breathed more deeply and steadily than Sera, but showed no sign of returning to consciousness. By contrast, she tossed constantly, and Falorn had to watch carefully to keep her from throwing herself out of the boat.

When Falorn finally lay down, utterly exhausted, in the dimness of the early false dawn, he held Sera close beside him to keep her safe. She had begun to mumble and speak incoherently at the edge of consciousness, although her eyes never opened.

As he tried to sleep, he half-listened, trying to make sense of her fever-dreams. He already felt the first stirrings of sun on his eyelids before he heard anything he could understand.

"Alex," she said. "Alex, come here. I need you."

Falorn awoke to the early afternoon sun in a blue cloudless sky. Zaren lay unmoving in the base of the boat, while Sera still slept uneasily. Now and again she said something under her breath.

The boat moved swiftly, with little help from Falorn. He considered trying to unstrap the mast, but decided against it. He'd never been on any water craft larger than a rowboat before, except the ferry which crossed the lazy river a dozen miles from his father's house, pulled back and forth across the placid brown water by ropes that also kept it from leaving its course.

He ate sparingly from one of Zaren's sacks of supplies, and did his best to give Sera and Zaren something to drink. Falorn wiped their faces with moist cloths periodically, but he could do little else except keep the worst of the sun off them.

Late in the afternoon, the river began to make noise again. A subdued grumble from up ahead grew louder and louder, finally becoming a wild roar. After a few minutes, he realized the source of the new noise, and began looking for something to secure Sera and Zaren into the boat with.

The boat shook and bobbed in the water as the river increased its speed. Falorn saw dark gray rocks jutting from the water at uneven intervals. The water whitened into foam where it tumbled and ran around them. Some of the stones reached as tall as a man's height; Falorn wondered if smaller, hidden rocks lay just below the river's surface. Forcing himself to ignore the ominous rocks, he tied down the two unconscious passengers as best he could, trying to arrange the lashings so they wouldn't strangle or drown if the craft took on water.

The thunder grew louder as the water pushed past the thickening rocks on either side of the boat. Moss gathered on some of the rocks, but most of the wet stones glistened in bare slate-gray.

Falorn looked for some way to steer the boat as it swept onward through the foamy river. The river or the fight in the city had long since carried away the paddles.

He checked the ropes holding Sera and Zaren again, but the boat began shaking too hard for Falorn to move around. He crouched down on his knees rather than try to make his way forward again. Falorn held Sera with one arm and Zaren with the other, and mouthed a prayer to all the thousand gods.

The boat bucked through the choppy water, like an unruly horse in the rain. They pushed through curtains of spray which seemed to hang in the air, filled with shimmering rainbow colors and hidden rocks and snags.

An old tree trunk swept against the boat, driven by the swirling currents. It scraped the side of the craft and shattered into a mass of splintery rotten wood. Bits of flotsam clung to the edge of the boat before being carried under and away by the churning water.

Falorn clung tightly to the two unconscious bodies. He tried to keep watching the river ahead for danger, although he had no way to steer even if he could move. The spray blocked nearly everything from view, soaking the boat with wave after wave of biting, icy water. Falorn began shivering, although the afternoon sun still shone brightly in the cloudless sky.

As Falorn held tightly to her, Sera began to twist and writhe again, fighting the ropes which held her in the boat.

"Alex," she called out loudly, "Alex, where are you? Where have you gone? Alex?"

She thrashed violently against the soaked cords that bound her. Spray and mist soaked her, plastering brown hair against her face and forehead and molding her clothes confiningly to her body.

She called the same name over and over, then broke off abruptly.

"Where are my cards," she asked a little later in a weak voice. Falorn looked at her face, but Sera's eyes remained closed. "My cards are gone. Where are they?" She threw her head back and forth, but soon that movement subsided as well. After that she said nothing, and seemed to slip back into deeper unconsciousness.

Falorn sat as close to her as he could, letting the spray wash over him. He wondered who Alex was. He wondered if Rorik Iron Eagle knew. Maybe she had a second fiancé. *That's not very nice,* he thought to himself. *Think what you want, but she's saved your life at least twice. She may want your cards, but she doesn't want to hurt you.*

Falorn smiled grimly and looked ahead into the blinding spray. He checked behind as well. Zaren still remained safely lashed and unmoving.

Something bumped into the front of the plunging boat, and he heard the loud splintering noise of boards crunching inward. The boat spun around after the impact and the stream continued to pull the damaged craft onward, now facing backward. The boat gained speed rapidly.

Falorn looked in front of him toward what had become the back of the boat. Crushed boards gapped inward on the right side, where the rock had smashed into them. Water flowed steadily into the boat.

He looked around for some way to plug the leaks, but saw nothing. Turning his head forward, he saw nothing but mist. A cloud of moisture enveloped the boat in an endless translucent mist. Something roared below and in front of the boat, at the other side of the blinding gossamer fog. Without warning, the boat shot out from underneath his feet, and Falorn found himself falling into the insubstantial mist.

Falorn splashed into the water heavily, losing his breath and nearly cracking his skull. Somewhere nearby, he heard the boat crack against rocks. He flailed around for purchase on the slippery river bottom. Only gradually did he realize the water only reached to his chest. The current no longer pulled at him, either. He wiped his eyes clear and looked around.

He stood in a wide, shallow pool at the base of a waterfall, which churned up clouds of spray far above its fifteen-foot height. The shattered wreckage of the boat lay a few yards to his right, impaled on a cluster of rocks. Only luck or the thousand gods had kept him off the rocks—and the boat off him—as he fell. A pebbly beach covered the shore to his right, while the ground beyond the boat looked swampier. On both sides, forest quickly swallowed the clear ground; he could see only a few feet of shore before the trees took over. Beyond the pool, the river flowed on, wider and slower than the rapids above.

Falorn reached to his throat and felt the pouch, still intact around his neck. His sword still hung at his side, although its leather baldric had been soaked and frayed beyond repair. He began wading toward the splintery ruins of the boat. The pain in his knee and arms had entirely vanished.

Climbing the rocks proved difficult with no leverage and ruined boots. He finally gave up and waded around to the other side of the wreckage. There, he found the two bodies tumbled together, still lashed to the collapsed wreckage. He couldn't tell if either of them still breathed.

It took another few minutes to work his way to the entwined figures. He reached for his knife, but found only the second pouch at his belt; knife and sheath had disappeared into the waterfall. Drawing his sword, Falorn awkwardly sawed at the wet, twisted ropes.

Zaren sagged free as soon as he cut the first ropes. Falorn caught the man before he could slide into the river. He hauled the innkeeper upward onto the rocks temporarily, and went to work on Sera's bonds.

She felt cold and stiff under his hands. He maneuvered her awkwardly from the crushed planks and onto his shoulders. Wading back around the rocks, he carried her slowly toward the gray pebbly beach.

He felt her shake slightly against his shoulders. She began to cough up water. Her shuddering increased as the water grew shallower against his legs. Gently, he laid her on the smooth, rounded stones, careful not to injure her further. Her eyes flew open as he brushed the hair out of her face. She looked at him without seeing anything.

"Alex," she said, "you came." Her eyes shut again.

Zaren proved more difficult to carry to shore. Falorn could barely lift the bulky man's weight, even with the help of the lion cards. Only the cards had kept him going as long as he had already, Falorn felt certain.

After he finally did manage to bring the big innkeeper to the beach, Falorn returned once more to the wreck. All the supplies had been swept away in the river—not surprisingly, since Falorn had used their lashings to bind his unconscious companions. He searched the area around the wreck, but found no sign of Zaren's sword, battle axe, or helmet.

By the time he made his way back to shore, his vision began to blur and swim in front of him. Falorn sank to the smoothly pebbled ground as soon as he staggered above the tide line. Turning onto his back, he closed his eyes and slept.

The lions returned to his late afternoon dreams. This time, three of them pranced at the riverside, sniffing him while he slept. When he didn't stir, they settled around him. One of them groomed a paw briefly while the others dozed. Soon that lion closed its eyes as well, and Falorn remembered nothing else.

Night had fallen when he awoke, but a dim glow illuminated the pebbly beach. Falorn heard the crackle of a fire behind him, and smelled meat cooking over pine branches.

"Zaren?" he asked sleepily, "Sera?" He opened his eyes fuzzily, but Zaren's unconscious body still lay beside him, now covered with a tattered blue saddle blanket. Something glinted in the firelight. Falorn focused on the glittering shape, which, as his eyes focused, solidified into a blade sticking upward from the ground only a handspan or so from his head. He turned his head to follow it upward. A thin, long-fingered hand held the blade, a hand belonging to an oddly familiar-looking man who stood above his head.

Falorn thrust himself to a sitting position. The eyes of the swordsman shifted to follow him, but otherwise the man didn't move. Three equally lanky men, all armored in links of glistening mail, sat around a fire. Roasting skewers filled the air with the rich scent of cooking venison. The men paid no particular attention to Falorn, nor did they look particularly vigilant. Spears and swords lay stacked near the fire, but not so close that the heat might damage the shafts or cord-wrapped hilts.

"You . . . you're an elf," he said to the man with the sword.

"And your point is . . . ?" The man replied in Falorn's own language, although with an unfamiliar accent.

"But . . . I mean . . . I . . ."

"I understand. I don't suppose you speak a civilized language? Or do we have to continue in this barbaric tongue?"

"It's . . . it's all I know."

"I sincerely hope not. But perhaps the river has, shall we say, damaged you a bit." The elf glanced out at the water, then back at Falorn. "Did you go over that waterfall on purpose?"

"I didn't know it was there. And I couldn't steer anyway."

"Then what were you doing guiding the boat?" The elf put up a hand before Falorn could answer. "Wait. Do not tell me yet. I sense a long story coming on, and I would rather hear it all at once when you have rested than in bits and incoherent pieces now."

"Thanks . . . I think," Falorn said, nodding. He looked at where Sera and Zaren lay, both unmoving. "Are they . . . ?"

"They will both survive, I suppose. We'll take you all someplace civilized in the morning, where they can be taken care of properly. For now, their condition has been . . ." the elf reached for a word, "stabilized, you would say."

"Thanks again, I think." He walked over to where the two of them lay, staggering briefly before his feet got used to being on solid ground again. The elf made no move either to help him or to block him. Falorn crouched down next to Sera and bent his head over her face. She breathed more evenly than before, and seemed to sleep more deeply. Satisfied, he stood back up and looked at the elf. "Thank you for helping them."

"We prefer you not die here. Under the circumstances, it seemed appropriate to help. For the same reason, may I offer you some food?"

"Yes. Please."

The elf walked over to the fire and took one of the skewers. One of the armored elves looked up at him and said something in a lilting tenor. None of the three around the fire bothered to look at Falorn. The unarmored elf walked back toward Falorn and handed him the skewer, which held a sizable chunk of meat.

"Thank you," Falorn said, and sat down to eat. He tried to glance surreptitiously at the elf while he ate, but found it difficult, since the elf's gaze never left him.

"Do not bother staring," the elf finally said. "You cannot see in the dark, and I will still be here in the morning. Why not eat your dinner before it gets cold, and then sleep a little more?" Falorn looked back down at the skewer and continued eating, embarrassed. After he finished, he rinsed his hands in the river and unobtrusively brought them up to his pouch.

"You need not bother with that either," said the elf. "Your cards are all still in there."

19

The Hunting Lodge

When the elves awoke Falorn just after dawn, Sera and Zaren remained unconscious. The elves placed the two bodies on travois-style litters. A few feet into the forest, a half dozen horses waited for them, next to a well-marked trail wide enough for a double file of riders.

"One hopes you steer a horse better than you steer a boat?" the unarmored elf asked Falorn.

"Better than that, yes." In daylight, and after a night's sleep, the elf no longer looked identical to the swordsman he'd watched Rorik's men cut down in that other forest. The elf stood a few inches taller than Falorn. Gold tinted his hair light brown when the sun caught it, and his yellow-gold eyes matched the reflection. His thin hands never stopped moving.

Falorn watched carefully while the armored elves fastened the two litters behind a pair of horses. Two of the elves mounted, while the third armored man packed the neatly butchered remains of the deer they'd been eating the previous night on a third horse. The golden-eyed elf motioned Falorn to an already saddled horse.

The chestnut-colored mare stood perfectly still while Falorn mounted. It remained unmoving until the elf said something in his own language, after which it obeyed Falorn instantly.

"Your horses are very well trained," Falorn said to the elf after they'd been on the trail for a few minutes.

"Possibly. Or maybe you are just used to badly trained animals." That silenced him, and they rode quietly for an hour or so until the elf spoke again. "I apologize for the rush and the lack of breakfast this morning, but I think it is important we get your companions to a place where they can be properly cared for. We will eat well this afternoon, I assure you."

"Thank you. I appreciate your care for my friends."

"Helleinen are many things, you may find—but in Delerian at least, we are not bad hosts."

"Helleinen? Delerian?" Falorn had never heard either term.

"Delerian is the country you stand in. I am Hellein. All of us together"—he gestured to the other elves—"we are Helleinen. It is what we call our people. What you call *elves*."

There was a particularly scornful inflection on that last word.

"I'm sorry," said Falorn. "Does the word offend you?"

"There are Helleinen who would draw steel on you for using it."

"But not you?"

"It matters little to me. I have lived in many places and been many things. Once you have occupied a cat's body for an afternoon, the distinctions you make between races seems trivial."

I'm not quite sure what to make of that. He looked again at the elf. *At the Hellein. Get used to the word.* "I will try to remember to use the word you prefer. I appreciate your hospitality."

"As I said, Helleinen are not bad hosts."

"You've certainly treated me fairly enough. Better than I might have expected."

"What, may I ask, were your expectations? Or is that part of the long story I asked you not to tell me until this evening?"

"Mostly it is. I've seen elv . . . Helleinen treated badly by humans before. And while I don't know much about Helleinen, what little I have heard is . . . not . . . um, comforting." Falorn thought of the pen in Rorik's camp, where naked elven prisoners had huddled together.

Stop it. Stop using that word. Don't even think it.

"You mean you have heard that we eat babies?" the Hellein asked, smiling oddly.

Falorn startled in his saddle. "You mean it's true?"

"It is widely believed in some . . . provincial circles. The belief does not speak well for your education, I am afraid. But if it gives you comfort to think so, by all means go ahead."

"What makes you think I'm educated?"

"You are in possession of a great deal of money and a thin patina of civilized behavior. Neither is directly indicative of education, but the one is helpful in its attainment, and the other often a by-product."

Falorn barely followed the meaning of the Hellein's words, although he spoke in Falorn's native language rather than his own. I *guess the money actually fooled somebody for once.* Sera had certainly seen through his disguise easily enough. Somehow, Falorn thought that continuing the Hellein's misapprehension would be a bad idea.

"I'm an innkeeper's son, actually. I have no real education at all, except for a little bit of religious teaching from traveling priests."

"That speaks well for your country's priests, then, or perhaps for its innkeepers."

Falorn flushed. "For its innkeepers, I think. My father taught me as much as he knew. And Zaren," he pointed to the litter dragged behind one of the horses, "was an innkeeper too, until he gave it up to save Sera and me."

"It is good to know that your publicans are upstanding creatures. They do seem to play a central role in your society."

Something occurred to Falorn. "Do you have a word for us? The way we call Hellein . . . um, Helleinen, elves?"

The Hellein bowed his head. "We do," he finally said. "But it just means *non-Hellein.* It's no more polite than *elves,* really. I prefer not to use it. It would be like calling you a baby-eater."

Falorn kept quiet. He didn't understand Helleinen at all. This Hellein might be making fun of him, but he seemed nothing like the demonic elves of Sera's descriptions. *But then, I don't really understand Sera at all, either.*

"Can I ask where we're going," he finally asked, "if it's not some kind of secret?"

"It is no secret at all," the Hellein answered. "If we think you might tell anyone we do not want to know, we will kill you long before you leave the country. We probably will not eat you, but the possibility exists." He smiled at Falorn with the same odd smile as before. "We are going to a sort of hunting lodge that my family administers. I think you will like it there."

They rode through thickening woods all morning. By noon, the ancient trees surrounding them towered hundreds of feet above the ground. A thick layer of moss and wintergreen carpeted the woods beyond the path. Falorn had never seen trees this old, or growing this thickly. Most of the older growth in the thin stands of woodlands near his father's inn had long since been cut down. He saw beech and maple in abundance, with white and copper birches mixed in nearly everywhere. He could identify a few of the other trees which he had seen before, ash and black cherry and other hardwoods—all expensive and hard to come by in the village where he'd grown up. A scattering of spruce and young hemlocks thickened the forest as well. The musty smell of decaying leaves and mulch mixed with the scent of cherry and cedar to give the air a thick, woodland aroma.

Early in the afternoon, the trail widened further, until four or more horses could ride abreast. The trees grew smaller as the path sloped slightly upward. Honeysuckle and trumpet vines twined around the trees, now that more sun came through. The trail finally broke through onto a long, grassy meadow cleared of trees. Falorn could see nothing on either side of the hill because of the height of the woods on its slopes. Several long, low buildings of gray stone and wood filled the near half of the clearing. Beyond the structures Falorn saw horses grazing, and practice fields for archers and swordsmen.

"That's a *lodge*?" Falorn said out loud, without meaning to. "It's huge."

"It is rather larger than the typical hunting lodge," said the Hellein, "but then a great deal more than hunting goes on here. The lodge is a sort of informal meeting place, where one can come and go with less concern for family protocol than elsewhere in Delerian."

"What is 'family protocol'?"

"Everything. In Delerian, family is everything." The Hellein turned to his armored companions and said something in his own language. The one with the unencumbered horse immediately spurred toward the lodge. The other two dismounted and checked the unconscious figures in the litters before leading their horses onward.

The door of the nearest and largest building opened. A bizarre mix of humans and Helleinen, males and females, approached the slow-moving travelers. The newcomers wore an astonishing variety of clothing and colors, as if they came from dozens of principalities, rather than a single oversized hunting lodge. It looked more like a festival than a gathering of hunters; such a profusion of colors would scare away any animals who saw them.

A number of humans and Helleinen quickly surrounded the litters and unhitched them from the horses. They carried the unconscious bodies back toward the buildings—not toward the structure they had emerged from, but to a lower, smaller structure behind it.

"Where are they taking them?" Falorn asked the elf, interrupting his conversation with several of the newcomers.

"You will see," he answered. He turned back toward his conversation, but then added as an afterthought, "It might be the smokehouse, you know."

Several Helleinen and humans laughed; others besides the golden-eyed Hellein spoke his language, or at least understood some of it. He flushed slightly, but dismounted as the Hellein directed.

A red-bearded man led the horse away as Falorn walked toward the largest of the buildings, amid a crowd of Helleinen and humans.

The building was larger than Falorn had thought from the hillside. The stones and mortar of its base rose above his head, and logs rose above that for another story. Wide, arched windows broke through the logwork at frequent intervals, their heavy shutters open against the walls beside them. A sloping roof of cedar shakes peaked high above the top of the building. Clearly the structure had been built with an eye toward airiness, rather than defense.

Fine stonework surrounded the door, bordering the heavy, polished cherrywood panels with carved deer and bear and other woodland creatures. On the door itself, smaller patterns carved in lighter-colored wood framed eight large panels: raised borders of leaves and wildflowers and twining stems of ivy that wound around the glistening hardwood of the panels as if grown naturally that way.

The door pushed inward easily, opening onto a stairway that led downward into a dug-out level below. The whole group trooped down the stairs with Falorn at the center, most of them chattering in their lilting language—human as well as Helleinen. Falorn had assumed it was the Helleinen tongue, but he wondered if it was just the language everyone in Delerian spoke.

Falorn stopped short as they entered the underground room.

He found himself in the center of a massive atrium which ran for the length of the building and rose upward for the structure's full three stories. Shafts of light streamed downward from the open windows above.

Floorboards extended outward perhaps ten feet on either side of the two floors above. Partitions formed three-sided rooms on those floors, open to the main room. Woven privacy screens of split black ash had been pulled aside to allow light to flow through to the massive central chamber. Ladders bisected the upper floors at intervals, for access between levels. The central room filled nearly all of the bottom level, except for four rooms with closed doors along the near wall.

On either end of the lodge, enormous stone fireplaces dominated the walls, their inner edges lined with the same sort of carvings as the doorway outside. The fireplaces looked large enough to roast an entire deer along the massive spits which ran through their centers. Only low coals burned in them now—enough to keep the room dry and ward off a late chill at the end of a spring day, but no more.

The long floor had been constructed from cherry and walnut boards, interlocked in a mazelike parquet. Etchings of groundfern and periwinkle and other plants covered some of the boards. Woven rugs and thick furs littered the floor, along with a profusion of mismatched chairs, stools, and small tables. Against a side wall, Falorn saw stacked planks that might make up banquet tables when assembled. Above the planks, painted portraits of dozens of Heleinen hung along the paneled wall, covering the whole length of the building.

He looked behind, and saw that the stairs opened out of a huge carved tree trunk that also encompassed the chamber's other four rooms. Branches spread outward like supporting pillars for the floors above, covering the whole near side wall. All along the branches, in hundreds of forks and splits, Falorn saw gold lettering engraved into the tremendous carved tree.

"It is a family tree," the golden-eyed Hellein said from beside Falorn, "a depiction of the history of all the twelve families of Helleinen, all the way back to the gods themselves."

He took Falorn by the arm. "Come this way. Sit, be comfortable. Someone will bring food, and after you have eaten and rested you can tell us your story. I think perhaps there are some others who should meet you then as well."

"Thank you," Falorn said, "but can I see Sera and Zaren before I sit down? I'd like to make sure they're all right."

"They are being tended to. All you would do now is distract our healers. You will have time to visit with them later, while they recover."

"I just wanted to see . . ."

"I quite understand. But would it not be better to wait until they regain consciousness?"

"I guess." Falorn wondered how he would tell Sera about the armed elves tending her.

The Hellein with the golden eyes led him toward the fireplace on his right. "That is my family," the Hellein said, pointing to a wide, gold-inscribed branch on the carved tree as they walked past it, "the sixth branch of the tree, and the sixth in separation from the gods. Neither the most powerful nor the least, but we do keep a fine hunting lodge."

He gestured toward a low chair, its two plush velvet cushions colored in deep forest green. Vivid carvings of ivy and wild grape twined over the back and sides of the chair, which looked more like a finely worked hardwood ornament than a functional piece of furniture. Falorn could see the faces of small carved animals peeking out from under the edges of ivy leaves. A low table with similar carvings sat alongside the chair.

Falorn sat, and found himself sinking into the soft plush forest of the cushions. He sighed and leaned back, forgetting himself for a moment. The Hellein smiled at him, a real smile this time, not the enigmatic expression of before.

"I am glad you like the chair. It is the work of one of my family's master carvers."

"It's beautiful," Falorn said. "This whole building is beautiful." The Hellein smiled again, but said nothing. He must have gestured without Falorn noticing, because suddenly a light-skinned Hellein with long, dark hair braided down his back stood beside the chair with a pewter tray in his hands. The long-haired Hellein set the tray on the low table and walked away without saying a word.

"Eat, please," said the golden-haired Hellein. "I will return later, after you have had time to rest." The Hellein walked toward the stairway by which they had entered the building. Several others joined him as he left the building. Falorn could hear them speaking their lilting language as they walked up the stairs and out of sight. A number of other people and Helleinen remained in the room, sitting on chairs or rugs, reading or talking among themselves. Falorn wanted to look at the heavy, leather-bound books a few of them held. The volumes reminded him of the book he'd had and lost in his encounter with the awful creature who had gotten caught in his stirrup. He shook his head to clear it of the memory and turned to his food. *You can talk later*, he thought, *but who knows when you'll get to eat again. You won't be able to help yourself or the others if you can't think straight from hunger when they come to question you.*

Falorn looked at the tray. A scalloped pewter plate contained thin slices of cold venison. Next to it sat a knife and a small cheese. A wooden bowl held mushrooms. To one side sat a sculpted glass bottle of thick red wine, along with a skin of water to dilute it. A scalloped pewter mug matched the plate; inset within the mug sat a glass cup to hold the wine.

He poured some wine and watered it. *I hope it's not drugged*, he thought, then laughed to himself, *but that's silly. They have you here, you're not going anywhere. If you're going to worry, why not get fussy about the mushrooms, too?* Falorn didn't like mushrooms much, but he ate everything else. He almost gulped the food down until he caught himself and forced himself to slow down. He had forgotten how little he'd eaten lately, but his hunger returned in a rush now. Falorn drank as well, but watered the wine heavily; he wanted to feel clearheaded when the Helleinen asked him to explain himself later.

Falorn wondered briefly what he should tell them. Sera would make up a story, he knew, something convincing and utterly plausible. He hated to lie, especially since he didn't know his ground here and there were other lives beside his own at stake.

He hoped they wouldn't kill him if he told the truth.

He hoped Sera wouldn't kill him if he told the truth.

After he finished the food—except for the mushrooms—he stood up and stretched. The meal left him satisfied, but not as tired as he expected after a day on the trail. He felt for the pouch against his chest and wondered if he owed his store of energy to the lion cards, the way he suspected he owed them for his recent recuperative powers.

He looked around the room, and wondered what the Helleinen would think if he walked over to one of the readers. *Probably not a good idea*, he thought, *at least not until I know a little more about what's going on.*

He sat back down in the chair to wait for the interrogation to come.

After a while he closed his eyes, and dreamed of three lions rolling and playing in the sun on a grassy hilltop, surrounded on all sides by thick forest which blocked his view of the world around them.

He awoke to a light touch on his shoulder. Falorn's eyes opened instantly. The room had darkened, either because the shutters had been closed or because night had fallen. Many of the screens had been pulled across the rooms above, blocking their interiors from view in the dimness. A graceful candle lamp on the table illuminated his surroundings. Coals from the fireplaces glowed at the edges of the room, but much of the rest lay in shadows.

Three chairs had been pulled close to his own. He couldn't tell if anyone else remained in the hall beyond the occupants of those chairs, one of whom had just awakened him. In the center chair sat the golden-eyed elf who had rescued him. On his right side sat a Hellein with hair that looked like burnished gold in the thin light of the lantern. He had blue eyes and a wider face than most of the Helleinen, who tended toward thin, sharp features. He wore a black velvet doublet belted in twisted gold cord and embroidered with gold thread, as well as close-fitting black hose. He wore black suede boots as well, with finely wrought gold spurs attached. The elf had taken off his sword belt, but his longsword leaned against the side of his chair, in a scabbard faced with black leather and trimmed with gold. The hilt of his sword glittered with gold wire, and a large cabochon-cut star ruby glinted from the pommel.

The third Hellein wore a dark green vest with black laces over a light gray tunic. The same sort of close-fitting hose covered his legs, though in dark gray instead of black. He wore a knife in a plain sheath at his belt, but otherwise carried no weapon. Black hair hung far down the back of his chair in a neat braid, tied with a green ribbon. He looked at Falorn with blue eyes, lighter colored than his companion's but piercing in their gaze. Like the golden-eyed Hellein, his hands moved constantly in unconscious patterns.

After a few moments of silence, the Hellein with the golden eyes spoke. "I am glad you slept. I think we may have a great deal to talk about. Do you feel rested?"

"Rested enough, I guess. I'm ready to tell you everything I can. But I'd like to ask first, if I can, how are Sera and Zaren?"

"They are sleeping. You will be able to see them in the morning if you wish to."

"Yes."

The black haired Hellein spoke in a smooth, low voice. His accent mirrored Sera's, that of the aristocracy of the Free Duchies. "There's no need to be afraid. We've fed you and shown you hospitality; that leaves an obligation on our part. We wouldn't have done that if we meant to harm you."

"An obligation on your part? I'm the one who's in your debt."

"But we have an obligation as hosts."

"I'm sorry. I don't think I understand."

The golden-eyed Hellein motioned his companion to silence. "Later. He is correct, but I do wish to hear your story. We can talk of hosts and guests some other time, but there are obligations that should be met. You know little of who we are, and we know nothing of you beyond the cards and weapon that you carry."

"Oh . . . of course. My name is Falorn. I'm just an innkeeper's son from the Free Duchies."

"I suspect there is more to you and your introduction than you say, or than there appears to be, but one introduction deserves another. My name is Danbhe, and I am of the Eraina, sixth in the families of the Helleinen. I keep this lodge for my family. My companion and fellow Eraina," he gestured toward the black haired elf to his left, "is named Lherryal, or Ryal. The other who you see before you is named Cirque," said Danbhe, motioning to the elf in black and gold. "He is a member of the Seyrene, first among the families of the Helleinen, and a direct descendent of the gods themselves."

"I'm honored," Falorn said, and bowed his head, uncertain of the correct response. Cirque laughed, causing Falorn to look up in bewilderment.

"We won't eat you," Cirque said. "You look like you're afraid we'll throw you in the stew pot if you say the wrong thing."

"Which we rarely do," Danbhe added.

"Well," said Falorn, "I guess I'm not sure what I should think."

"Fair enough," replied Cirque, "but I've been a guest of Danbhe's many times, over seven or eight of your lifetimes. Eraina hospitality— and Danbhe's in particular—can be *lively* at times, but it's rarely ife-threatening. Tell your story, however you see fit. You and your friends are as safe now as you would be in any of your own homes."

"That's not very comforting," said Falorn.

"Why not?" asked Ryal. "Tell us."

20

The Sea of Clouds

❖

Falorn talked for most of the night, interrupted frequently by questions from the three Helleinen. Some of the things they asked surprised him, but he found himself giving a better, fuller account than he might have otherwise.

He thought to just briefly mention his father and the inn, but Ryal asked question after question about his daily routine, the guests he saw, the other members of his family, and a half-dozen other things Falorn thought barely worth hearing about. The Helleinen listened as if he described palaces and princesses instead of stables and barmaids.

When he mentioned his leaving, Cirque wanted to know why he ran away. "It wasn't the life I wanted, I guess," Falorn answered, although that sounded hollow even to his own ears. *I was tired of being lied to*, he wanted to say, but it was hard to quantify abrupt subject-changes and evasions. *I wanted to find a world where I could get answers to questions, instead of having to work my way around the real topic. Which is exactly what I'm doing now, of course.*

"So you wanted . . . ?" Cirque asked.

"I don't think I really thought about it. I left pretty abruptly, without much of a plan. I wanted adventure, I guess. Maybe a little money, at least enough to give me a few choices about what to do with my life. Something other than living and dying in the same village as everyone else I ever knew, while hundreds of other people with more interesting lives passed through on their way to more interesting places."

"So you have gotten what you wanted?"

Falorn paused to think. "Some of it, I guess. I think I'm on my way to something now, but I'd like to know a little better what it is. Everyone else seems to know all about these cards except me. I still don't see what makes them worth killing for."

"The fact that there are people willing to die for them," Cirque said. "But you still haven't told us how you found them."

"I found the first one on the body of a dead knight on the Turnpike—I think he was a knight, although I guess I don't really know that for sure—the morning I left my father's inn. He had a book, too, but I lost that." Falorn described the card and the book, and the attack which had followed. The elves questioned him, but seemed less interested in that part of his story than in his life at the inn.

When he came to his description of the trip to Roicenet, he found himself telling them everything, not just about his encounter with the thieves and their card, but even about the woman with the rose tattoo, which he thought he'd be too embarrassed to describe. Something about the elves' manner made him want to be truthful with them, despite Danbhe's sarcasm. He described his rescue by Sera in as much detail as he could remember. Cirque questioned him about her father and the castle, while Ryal seemed more interested in her bookcase and cards. Danbhe asked for more details about the Hook, of which Falorn knew thankfully little.

He became more nervous when talking about their flight from Roicenet. He left out his discovery of Sera's poisons entirely. Talking about it wouldn't reflect well on a woman who remained unconscious and unable to speak for or defend herself. What came after, he found much harder. He described what he had seen of the one-sided battle the lion card had led him to, and his own barely suppressed physical reaction. None of them asked any more than he told them about the Hellein's death, but he sensed that they knew he withheld information. As he talked, he realized something, and reached for the pouch at his chest.

"These are yours, aren't they," he said to Cirque, handing him the blue and gold lion cards, "One of them is, anyway."

"No," said Cirque, pulling his hand away as if he'd touched a flame, "I don't want them. The Hellein you saw is distant kin of ours, I'm certain—although from another line of Helleinen altogether. I want revenge for his blood and that of his people. But the cards came to you. They are yours. I don't want any part of their magic."

"'Are you sure?" Falorn asked. "It doesn't seem right to get them that way. Over someone else's shed blood, I mean."

"But you didn't take them from the Hellein," Ryal said.

"No," Falorn replied. Quickly, he moved on with the story, grateful to get away from the Hellein's death without the need for further evasion. He tried to minimize the role Sera's disappearance played in his discovery of Rorik's encampment and subsequent capture of the three cards her fiancé held. Again, the elves' questions took him away from the areas he wanted to avoid. Ryal asked about the appearance of the tent, while Cirque wanted details of how Rorik's men fought, and how he organized his soldiers' camp.

I suppose I'm giving them details they could use to kill humans, Falorn realized. But the humans in question were far away, and all of them had tried to kill him. The thought troubled him, but Falorn continued the story nonetheless.

Falorn moved with some relief onto the story of the cannibal Baron of Golden Reeds and the lizards whose land he lived on, happy to be past the need for deception. Mostly Cirque and Ryal seemed interested in the lizards and the tale they'd told Falorn. Danbhe asked a number of detailed questions concerning the girl with garlic sauce. "Do you think it would work with human babies?" he asked Falorn, before Cirque quieted him.

The story of Sera's lost cards and their trip to Windford went more quickly. Falorn ignored Danbhe's request for more details on the auto-de-fé, and none of the Helleinen seemed to care. Even Danbhe, perhaps tiring of the joke, didn't push too hard. By the time he finished describing their meeting with Zaren and the escape along the river, he felt utterly drained. Nearly every drop of memory had been wrung out of him, except for the few he'd deliberately held back.

"Well," Danbhe said after Falorn concluded, "that is quite a lot to think about. You certainly found the adventure you looked for."

"I did," said Falorn, "but I think I need to sleep now."

Danbhe gestured to his left, and Ryal spoke up. "This way," he said, motioning to Falorn, "I'll show you to a place to sleep."

"Should I bring the lamp?" Falorn asked, as they stepped into the shadows, away from the thin circle of light.

"No need for it." The Hellein gestured, and spoke an odd word of many twisted syllables, and a yellow glow grew around his hand, gaining intensity until it rivaled the lamplight. "That should be enough for you to climb the ladder by."

Falorn followed him upward to the second level, where they left the ladders. The two of them walked along the outer edge of the floor past a number of partitions, all with screens pulled in front. Falorn counted six before they came to an open room.

"This should do fine," Ryal said. "There's no window, so it will stay dark enough for you to sleep into the day once you close the screen. Sleep as late as you like. When you wake up, I'll show you where the bathhouse is." He stepped into the room ahead of Falorn, and touched his hand to a candle on the low table within. The light on his hand coalesced around the candle, and sank into an ordinary candle-flame. When he removed his hand, the magical glow had vanished. Only candlelight illuminated the small chamber.

"Sleep well," Ryal said. "I'll be downstairs if you want anything."

"You'll wait up all night?"

"I will have time to sleep later. I need very little now."

"You're . . . a wizard, aren't you."

"Among other things, I suppose I am. Not the wizard Danbhe is, but a fair transmutationist nevertheless."

"Transmutationist?"

"In the morning, Falorn. There will be plenty of time later. Now you need sleep." Ryal stepped out of the small room, pulling the screen shut behind him so that walls enclosed Falorn on all sides.

He's putting me off the same way Sera did, Falorn realized, but he found himself too tired to care.

Falorn undressed and lay down on the pallet within, pulling the thin blanket over himself for warmth against the slight chill. The candle flame went out normally when he blew on it.

He slept more deeply than he had since leaving home, and dreamed that lions guarded him.

Falorn awoke to the sounds of people moving and many voices from below. Only a few glimmers of light passed through the screen into the partitioned room. Rain beat noisily against the outside timbers of the lodge. He sat up in bed and checked his cards and sword. Standing up, Falorn stretched and recovered his clothing. The fabric looked somewhat the worse for its river adventures. He beat off the worst of the dirt as best he could and then dressed.

When he pulled the screen aside and looked below, he saw about thirty people in the enormous room below, human and Helleinen both. Most talked with each other in small clusters. A few read, and one or two ate quietly at the low tables. Falorn looked at them and suddenly felt ashamed of his filthy travel attire. Most of them wore comfortable-looking tunics with close-fitting breeches or hose. Men and women dressed largely alike.

"Falorn?" a voice beside him said. He looked and saw that Ryal had arrived unannounced. "I'm glad you're up. I thought we might take a trip to the bathhouse before we eat. After that, maybe you'd like to meet a few of the others."

"I think so," Falorn said. "I feel kind of out of place. And my clothes are. . . ."

"Don't give it a thought. I will take care of it. And besides, you are a cardholder. You shouldn't feel out of place anywhere."

"What does that mean?"

"It means you are in very select company. There aren't very many cards, and most of the people who have them are very powerful."

"Sometimes it seems like everyone in the world has them. Or at least wants to take mine." He paused for a second, reminded of Zaren by the thought of his card. "Are Sera and Zaren all right?"

"They are still sleeping, but the danger has passed. They will not be up and moving for days yet, but they will awake and talk within a day. Much of the healing is done. Now they must rest and recover their energy." Ryal motioned toward the nearest ladder. "Shall we go to the bathhouse?"

Falorn followed without answering. They climbed down the ladder and walked to the stairway without anyone seeming to take much notice of them. No one had bothered to throw the bolt to the outside door; it opened freely for Ryal.

Outside, rain flew down in sheets from a roiling gray sky. The Hellein stepped calmly out into the storm, walking as if undisturbed by the slashing rain attacking the suede of his boots and doublet.

"Won't they be ruined?" Falorn asked, striding head down beside Ryal. The storm instantly soaked through his clothing, making him feel like he had never left the river.

"I doubt it," said the elf, "they're waterproofed. Even if the spell failed, I could just fix them again."

"Oh."

"I'll explain more when we are out of the rain, if you like."

"Thanks."

They approached one of the smaller buildings, a two story stone square with a flat slate roof and a pair of chimneys. Although dwarfed by the lodge itself, the bathhouse looked nearly as large as Falorn's father's inn. Like the entrance to the lodge, the bathhouse doorway bore carvings—thorny wildflowers that looked dissimilar to any of the carvings he'd seen in the other building. The cherrywood-paneled door itself bore no ornamentation, just a large brass knocker in the shape of a scrub brush.

Ryal knocked twice with the scrub brush and they waited.

"Why is this one locked, when the door to the lodge is left open?"

"People come and go from the lodge at all hours. Here, they might want some privacy. It's just a courtesy, really. I doubt there's anyone here but the keeper."

The door opened, and the two of them stepped in, Falorn soaked and Ryal wet-haired and shedding water in droplets from his clothing, which appeared undisturbed.

"Hello, Nia," said Ryal, to an Helleinen woman standing behind the door. She had a thin face and long, straight blond hair, which she wore loose and unbraided. Her white tunic, belted at the waist, hung down just above her knees like a skirt. A single sapphire in a golden setting dangled from a gold chain around her throat.

"Hello, Ryal. Are you Falorn?" the woman asked, turning to look at him.

"Yes." She spoke his language with a musical lilt. "Does everyone here know my name and speak my language?"

"No," she said, "but we thought you might feel better if you could talk to the people around you. Danbhe asked me to watch the bathhouse today because I speak Denbar."

"Denbar?"

"Your language. That's what it's called."

"Oh." It had never occurred to Falorn that his language had a name, although now that he thought about it, it seemed like a stupid thing not to know.

"Can you understand me all right? I haven't spoken Denbar with a native speaker in a long time, probably thirty or forty years. My accent must be awful."

"No, it's perfect. Did you say thirty years?" He looked at her, and she laughed. He thought Nia looked about his own age, perhaps a year or two older. Her face looked sharp but unlined, with pronounced cheekbones.

"About that long. Don't try judging Helleinen by human standards. I'm young, but I'm probably seventy or eighty years older than you. And Danbhe and Ryal are older than your country." She laughed again at his look of bewilderment. "Don't blush," she said. "A lot of humans make that mistake when they first meet the Helleinen."

"And besides," said Ryal, "your country is not very old, as countries go."

"Come this way," Nia said. "Don't just stand there soaking wet. The baths are waiting." She led them through a short passageway. Unlike in the lodge, they remained at ground level. The hall opened into a central room, which contained two large, rectangular pools of water. A tiled path led around the edges of the two pools. On the other side, six doorways in the wall indicated rooms beyond. Colored tiles covered the walls, forming a mosaic that seemed patternless, though pleasing to look at.

Steam rose from the nearer of the two pools, beading into droplets on the edges of the tiled walls.

"The first pool is hot water," said Nia, "and the second is very cold. It can take some getting used to."

"I realize you think I'm uncivilized, but I have *bathed* before."

"Oh, I'm sorry," she said, smiling slightly, "I didn't mean to offend you."

Ryal laughed. "Nobody thinks you're an unwashed savage, Falorn, even if Danbhe talks that way sometimes." The Hellein stripped off his tunic, dropping it on the tiles at his feet. Falorn looked at the wet floor doubtfully. "Just leave your clothes," said Ryal. "Someone will be through to launder them in a little while. There are fresh clothes in the next room."

Falorn glanced at Nia as he started to undress. She looked at him without blushing, and laughed when he flushed. "You embarrass so easily," she said. "Are all your countrymen like that?"

"I don't know," Falorn grumbled back. Hurriedly, he slipped into the steaming pool. The hot water felt wonderful against his skin. Days of trail dust and river mud begin to seep away in the scalding water of the bath. Ryal slipped into the pool. The Hellein sat down to Falorn's left on the bench which lined the pool.

Falorn looked up and saw Nia unfastening the belt to her tunic. The woman slipped the garment over her head, and carefully hung it on a previously unseen wall hook. She wore nothing beneath except the sapphire pendant. She stretched, flattening her small breasts against her chest as her muscles tautened. Nia shook her head, and blond hair flowed over her shoulders. Extending a lean, muscular leg, she touched one foot to the water, pulling it back from the heat. Then she shrugged—her breasts bouncing slightly with the movement—and walked down the stairs into the far side of the pool.

"Now look who's staring," she said, looking up at Falorn and smiling.

"I . . . I'm . . . I didn't mean to. . . ." He felt his face flush as the words stuck in his mouth.

"Stare all you like. It doesn't bother me. Just don't equate the external for the person inside."

"I'm sorry?" Falorn asked.

"What she means," Ryal said from the bench beside Falorn, "is that the body is a very mutable thing. What it looks like on the outside doesn't always reflect anything very important, but you humans like to take it as a reflection of the soul within."

"I'm still not sure I know what you mean."

"Do you know what transmutation is?"

"No. The first time I heard the word was when you said it last night." Falorn's blood stirred as Nia sat on the bench on his right side. He found himself having difficulty concentrating on Ryal's words. He squirmed on the bench, and focused with difficulty. Beside him, Nia smiled innocently.

"Transmutation means change. It's one of the fourteen schools of magic. What I do is change one thing into another."

"What does that have to do with her?"

"Watch," Ryal said, and gestured with his hands. Falorn turned to look at Nia, still embarrassed at the way she smiled at him. As he looked, her features altered and wavered. Her hair shortened and her cheekbones became less pronounced. Her breasts grew slightly more full, and her face filled out and rounded slightly.

"Sera!" Falorn called out.

"No," said Ryal from behind Falorn. The elf spoke a word in an alien language. The changes faded abruptly into Nia's skin, and her Helleinen features returned.

"Wouldn't she be upset to know you were staring at her that way?" Nia asked.

"But, it wasn't her, was it? How did you know what she looked like?"

"I was there with the healers, assisting. I might just as easily have changed Nia into the likeness of your other friend, but I thought that might be a little more alarming. Some of the features were approximations, but you seemed to think the likeness was close enough."

"It was . . . unreal. It looked just like her."

"It was real," Nia said. "That's what he's trying to tell you. That changed flesh was just as much mine as what you see now." She looked at Falorn pointedly and he blushed again. "It just doesn't tell you any more about who I am. Sera's appearance is no more a reflection on her inner soul than mine is."

Falorn remained confused as he watched Nia climb from the tub and dive into the frigid water of the second pool. She began swimming around its edges with long strokes as he and Ryal joined her in the cold water. The sudden drop in temperature made him shiver, but the water felt invigorating—more so as his skin and muscles got used to the change.

By the time the three of them climbed out of the cold pool, Falorn felt cleaner than he had since his first day on the road. He went to follow Ryal into one of the back rooms, but a slim, wet hand touched his shoulder first. "Not that room," Nia said. "This way."

She walked through another of the open doorways. Falorn caught himself watching the rhythmic sway of her naked buttocks as she moved in front of him, and shook his head to try and break his focus.

The small room contained a wide, low table in its center, but little other furniture. Shelves covered all of the walls, with cabinets beneath them. Some of the shelves held towels, while others contained dozens of strangely shaped glass bottles and other stoppered containers.

"Here," said Nia, and gestured toward the low table. She held a thick, white towel in her hands, and began drying Falorn's back with the soft cloth. He felt himself beginning to react as the towel moved lower.

"Uh, Nia, I'm not sure if this is. . . ."

"Relax," she said. "The towel is for drying. The table and oils are for massage." Her hands moved lower as she toweled the backs of his thighs. With difficulty, Falorn kept still. "We Helleinen are a very long-lived people," she continued. "We age and mature differently than you. There are not that many of us, and our families are everything. When someone sleeps with someone else, it is not a casual thing. It is rare for a Helleinen woman to have a child before the age of two hundred. We have no need to hurry the way humans do; we build relationships more deliberately."

Nia finished drying Falorn's back. Stepping in front of him, she began to run the towel slowly over his chest. "Enjoy a massage for what it is," she said. "For a few days at least, slow down your frantic human pace. Try to understand a little of what it means to be Helleinen, as the humans who live among us do." She continued to dry his torso, rubbing the towel in gently circular motions as she moved it downward. Light glinted off her wet hair—illuminated by a translucent globe which hung from the ceiling, and glowed with the same sort of magical light he had seen on the walls of Roicenet.

Slowly, she finished drying him. His groin ached, no matter how much he tried to relax and listen to her words. "Lie on the table," she said, finally, "face down." He stepped over to the low wooden table, and settled himself on its cushioned top. Embarrassed, he tried to shield his erect penis from her eyes, although she had seen—and dried—it moments before.

"Relax, Falorn," she said, soothingly, as he felt her hands gently touch the muscles of his shoulders. "Relax and accept what is here, instead of fretting over what isn't."

"I'm sorry. I don't think I can."

"Relax," she said. He felt a warm liquid on the skin of his back, as she continued to knead his muscles with her fingertips. The warmth slowly spread over his skin, and his muscles loosened under it. A diffuse sort of energy seemed to emanate from the touch of her hands. In spite of all his tension and confusion, his body began to relax. He felt himself beginning to drift, and his eyes closed. When she asked him to turn over, he did so; he no longer felt anything sexual at all, just a languorous, sensual pleasure which infused his body and left his mind floating on a lake of thick, billowing clouds.

He realized, somewhere in the back of his mind, that he no longer wore the cards. He had taken them off without a second thought before entering the bath. He knew that should trouble him, but he only wanted to float forever on the endless sea of clouds.

21

Troublemaking

❖

Falorn awoke with a start and sat bolt upright on the table. The room still glowed unnaturally. Nothing looked out of place, except for a pair of lightweight wooden chairs which had been brought in from elsewhere. Nia and Ryal sat on the chairs talking quietly, both dressed as they had been before the bath.

"Where are the cards?" Falorn asked.

"Over there," Ryal said, and pointed. A pile of clothes sat on one of the cabinets. Falorn's two pouches lay on top of it, underneath the lowest shelf. On the floor in front of the cabinet, Falorn saw an unfamiliar pair of boots and his own sword and knife, both unsheathed. He saw no sign of his scabbard, baldric, and belt—nor of the clothing he had worn into the bathhouse.

"What about the rest of my things?"

"In the laundry, or gone. Your belts and sheaths were too water-damaged to keep. Your pouches don't have much life left in them, either, but I thought you might be alarmed if you didn't see them when you woke up."

"You could have asked before you took them."

"You were asleep. And we *are* providing you with new things. Take the clothing as a gift from my family."

"I don't have a lot of choice, do I? It's this or go around naked."

"Will you feel more comfortable if we leave while you dress?"

"Do what you want," Falorn mumbled, then checked himself. "I'm sorry. I'm your guest, and I appreciate your taking me in, but I'm getting very tired of surprises."

"I understand," said Ryal. "We don't wish to be rude." Wrapping a towel around himself, Falorn walked over to the cabinet and opened the first pouch quickly. The cards remained inside. Their warmth spread immediately to his hands as he touched them. He replaced the cards within the pouch, and hung it around his neck so they lay against his chest once more.

He looked up, and saw Ryal standing alone by the chairs.

"Where did Nia go?"

"She thought you looked embarrassed, so she left. Her duties here are done, anyway."

"Please, if you get a chance, thank her for me. I'll try to myself, but I'm not sure if I'll see her again."

"If you don't see her before you leave, I will be certain to mention your wishes."

Falorn sorted through the pile of folded clothing. He slipped on the pair of soft, light gray doeskin breeches, which fit closely against his legs, almost like hose. A loose white tunic felt comfortable on his skin, as if he'd been wearing it for years. Three ebony buttons lined the upper front of the tunic, where it lay open at his neck. The vest, in a muted maroon color, fit perfectly over the tunic. Supple fabric hugged his skin without constricting. He buttoned the tunic and tied the laces of the vest, then looked down at the boots and weapons.

Sitting on the edge of the table, Falorn slipped on the first of the thigh-length, dark brown boots. The leather looked new and unmarred, but felt softer than suede, as if the boots had been broken in already without creating a single scuff on their surface. They fit perfectly, as if the finest cobbler had painstakingly measured his feet and calves.

"These clothes are wonderful," Falorn said, "How did you find them so quickly? They fit perfectly."

"It wasn't that quick," Ryal said, "You were asleep for a while."

"How long?"

"About three hours, I suppose. Long enough."

"Long enough to bring in a cobbler? I've never owned boots like these."

"Well, it's about time, then, isn't it? You are rich. You can afford them."

"That's not what I meant."

"I know. Actually, I have a confession to make."

"What do you mean?" Falorn felt an edge returning to his voice.

"Those are your clothes."

"Well, thanks, but. . . ."

"No, you don't understand. Those are the same clothes you wore when you came in here."

"They certainly aren't."

"Yes, they are. I am a transmutationist, remember."

"What does that have to do with . . . oh."

"I felt a little bad. You seemed so embarrassed by the bathhouse, and you were trying so hard not to show it. And your clothes were in pathetic condition."

"It was raining out!"

"Now they are waterproof. I wanted to make you a cape, too, or at least a cloak, but I thought that could wait. You won't need one around the lodge."

"Thanks," said Falorn, uncertainly.

"Oh, I enjoyed it. It helped pass the afternoon nicely, and I do like to stay in practice."

"So what happened to the sheaths?"

"I threw them out, just like I said. There's a leatherworker here who does much better work than I could. I may be a wizard, but she's an artist. Human, too, believe it or not."

"It happens, you know."

"I'm sorry," said Ryal, "Humans in Delerian aren't always . . . oh, never mind. That's not going to come out sounding right. Anyway, you will have to pay the leatherworker, since of course she is not an Eraina, but I don't think that will be a problem."

"I'd be glad to pay."

"Wonderful. I'll let her know to start work immediately."

"But don't I need to tell her what I want?"

"Of course not. She's an artist. You take whatever she gives you."

The rain had stopped by the time they left the bathhouse. Thin lines of blue showed here and there between layers of sleek gray clouds. In the west, Falorn saw the red of sunset through scattered breaks in the trees.

"It's late," he said.

"You looked like you needed sleep more than food or company," Ryal answered. "Do you feel better now?"

"I do," said Falorn. The bath and Nia's touch had relaxed him. Aches had vanished from muscles where he'd gotten used to near-continual soreness.

"If you feel up to it, dinner will be served soon. You can eat separately if you don't want to be around so many Helleinen."

"Thanks. I'd like to eat together with everyone, I think. I don't want to put you to any more trouble."

"That's laudable, although troublemaking is one of the more developed human talents."

Falorn stopped and looked at the elf.

"Did I do anything to deserve that?"

"Deserve what?"

"None of us has asked anything from you. You've all been very helpful, but you as much as kidnapped us after Zaren's boat wrecked, and you haven't even let me see the others. How are any of us causing trouble?"

"I'm sorry. I should have said that differently," Ryal said. "Your presence and the presence of the cards is troublesome. It will attract unwanted attentions, but there's little you can do to stop that."

"And my friends?"

"You will see them as soon as they awake. I hope that will be tomorrow."

Grudgingly, Falorn followed as Ryal pushed open the thick cherrywood panels of the lodge's door and walked down the stairs. Bright globes of light illuminated the central chamber. Plank tables had been set up in the room's center. The furniture and rugs must have been pulled aside; Falorn did not see them anywhere in the room. Small knots of Helleinen and humans sat along the tables, talking. It looked like most of the Helleinen had not yet arrived. Energetic fires burned in the hearths at both ends of the hall. The smells of roasting meats and of spices filled the lodge.

Ryal led Falorn to where three humans sat, and gestured him to a place between two of them. Falorn took the offered spot on the bench without saying anything. He still felt angry as the rest of the dinner guests arrived. But as the leisurely meal began, he found the edge on his feelings began to dull. The dinner seemed more like an occasion for conversation than for food, despite the trays of meats, breads, fruits, and vegetables that kept passing by.

Falorn sat between a blonde woman of about forty who wore her long hair in dozens of thin braids, and an older man with worn skin, thick black hair, and a beard going to gray. Both of them spoke Denbar with an easy fluency. They chattered happily on about everyday life in Delerian. Falorn felt relieved that they asked few questions, and those mostly out of politeness. He listened carefully while he ate.

Soon he discovered the woman was the leatherworker Ryal had spoken of. That led to new areas of conversation, and Falorn found himself able to let his guard down a little bit for the first time in many days. By the time he finally climbed up the ladder to his sleeping chamber, his head somewhat thicker from rich food and good wine, he no longer feared the elves, or seriously believed they wanted to kill him.

He hoped desperately that they would somehow fail to discover Sera's role in the death of the Hellein warrior.

Ryal roused him just before sunup with the news that Sera had awakened. They left the lodge in the half-gray light and walked through the brisk morning air toward one of the far buildings, near the practice fields. Ryal noticed Falorn shivering in his thin tunic.

"It is cool here in the mornings and evenings," the elf said sympathetically, "even in the summertime. I'll get you a cloak or something by tonight."

"Thanks. I think I'd settle for something hot to drink now."

"There may be tea in the healer's house. Otherwise, you will have to wait for mulled cider in the lodge afterward. It will warm up soon enough."

"I know," said Falorn, "but I'm cold now." They both laughed as they approached the door of a square stone building, about the size of a tavern or prosperous city tradesman's house. The house had wide windows, their red-painted shutters all open. The door glistened with red paint as well, in contrast to the unpainted wood and carvings that he'd seen elsewhere in the elven settlement.

"The healer's name is Chirye," Ryal said. "She's a distant cousin to Danbhe, although from a different branch of the Eraina family."

"Is she good?" Falorn asked, a little surprised at his own rudeness. The traveling physician whose circuit included his own home town had once bled Falorn in an attempt to bring down a fever caused, the man explained, by an excess of blood which had reddened and heated his skin. The procedure seemed to have no great effect for good or ill, unlike cupping and other medical procedures, which left permanent scars even when successful.

"She is a wizard like Danbhe and myself. Probably she is better than I am, if not quite as good as Danbhe. When I talk about healing, I am referring to another school of magic, like transmutation. She may use herbs, salves, or powders where they are appropriate, but the basis of her powers are magical."

"Oh. She won't bleed them, then?"

"Whatever for?"

"I'm not sure. A physician did it to me once when I had a fever." Ryal opened his mouth as if to say something, but then closed it again and shook his head. He knocked twice on the door, which opened before his conversation with Falorn could resume.

The Helleinen woman who stood in the doorway looked barely Falorn's age, if that. Short-cropped brown hair extended half a finger's length above a narrow, striking face, with high, prominent cheekbones. At first he thought she must be the healer's apprentice, but then she and Ryal embraced closely, and the dark-haired Hellein called her by name.

After a moment, she broke the embrace and looked up at Falorn.

"You can see them, but only briefly," she said. "Both of them are still in need of rest. Tomorrow, you can spend time with them; today you can only visit a little."

"I understand," said Falorn. He followed into the house behind her, his foot creaking on the unpainted hardwood floorboards.

Sera and Zaren lay on adjoining beds in a small room off the main hallway. Wide windows allowed for plenty of light and air, despite the early hour; heavy quilts covered the invalids and protected them against the accompanying chill. A small round table sat between the beds, its surface covered by a vase of flowers, a bowl of soft-skinned fruit, a black-painted pitcher, and two wooden mugs.

Sera sat propped up on the nearer of the two beds, her head supported by a mountain of white-cloaked pillows. Her eyes followed Falorn as he entered the room, but she said nothing.

She seems so tired, Falorn thought.

Sera's face looked drawn and lined with utter exhaustion, like a woman emerging from a daylong childbirth.

A similar mound of pillows held up Zaren, although his eyes remained closed.

"Hello," said Falorn, reluctantly. *What am I going to say to her? Is she ever going to talk to me again?*

Sera said nothing. Her eyes continued to trace Falorn's movements.

"She can't really talk yet," said Chirye. "Both of them still have a lot of healing to do. The major damage is gone, but they had to draw on a great deal of their strength in the healing process. They will get stronger quickly in the next few days, but they're very weak now."

As Falorn watched, Sera's eyes sagged closed. He walked over and took her hand. It felt warm, but sat limply within his palm. He replaced Sera's hand over her chest, leaned down, and brushed a few straggling hairs out of her face. He kissed her forehead gently, and then stood up again.

"I think I'd better go," he said. "Thanks for letting me see them."

He followed Ryal out of the healer's house silently. The Hellein turned away from the buildings and walked toward the tree line. The ground sloped slightly downhill as they walked, and as they left the cleared area, the ground became rockier.

"This way," said Ryal. He led Falorn to a partial enclosure formed by an overhanging rock on the hillside. Two small sacks lay on the ground, on top of a folded cloth.

"There is food in the bags," the elf said. "I thought you might want to sit alone for a while this morning. After you eat, there will be others around the lodge and at the practice fields if you want company." The Hellein paused, and looked around the little rocky area as if searching for something. "I think that sometime after your friends are more recovered Danbhe will want to speak with you about your plans."

"I thought he might. Thanks for the food."

Ryal turned and walked slowly up the hillside, his black braided hair swinging across his back. Falorn watched until the Hellein passed out of sight over the crest of the hill, and then turned to look at the supplies within the shelter. He spread out the cloth and sat on it, and began unpacking the food and wineskin within.

I guess I'm not getting that hot drink, Falorn thought to himself, but the wineskin proved to contain hot mulled cider, presumably courtesy of the transmutationist's magic.

He ate slowly, looking downhill into the thickening woods while chewing absentmindedly. The cards warmed Falorn's chest as he thought over the events of the days since he had left his father's home, wondering if he might have done anything differently. He wondered how his father and the rest of his family were doing; he hadn't had time to think of them much these last few days, but a part of them missed them, for all that he didn't miss the half-truths and evasions that were an everyday part of living at his father's inn.

I wonder if I'll ever know what it was that my father was hiding, or if there was anything at all. Maybe life just made him secretive: I've certainly told more lies and kept more secrets these last few days than I did in years at home. But I hope I never get used to lying, that it never becomes a part of me the way it did with my father.

Finally, he packed the empty bowls and wineskin into one of the sacks, carefully folded the cloth again, and walked up the hill toward the practice fields, looking for exercise and distraction.

22

Bedside Tales

Falorn practiced hard each of the next three days, only leaving the practice fields for the bathhouse after sundown. Although he soaked himself in sweat and worked his muscles into a state of near-constant soreness, he couldn't seem to exhaust or distract himself entirely.

Every night before dinner, he visited with Sera and Zaren. They looked a little more lucid each time he saw them, but the two of them still talked only in short, disjointed phrases—like fever victims. Chirye refused to allow him to visit more often.

When he awoke on the fourth morning, the soreness in his muscles had vanished. Falorn dressed quickly; his clothes seemed almost to shed dirt since Ryal had transformed them. He saw no one else on any of the practice fields, so he began running around the cleared edge of the hill-top, letting the heat build in his legs while he circled the woods' edge in the early morning mist.

As he finished his third circuit of the settlement, he saw Nia standing in his path. She motioned for him to stop and he did so, breathing hard but evenly as he slowed his pace to nothing. He had only seen her at a distance since their first meeting in the bathhouse.

"Good morning," he said. "Were you looking for me?"

"You're not hard to find," she replied. "Chirye asked me to tell you that your friends are awake. You can talk to them any time you like."

"You mean, now?"

"Anytime you like."

"If you'll excuse me . . . ?"

"I'll walk you there, if you'd like. Chirye wanted someone else around once she moved them to different rooms."

"They had a fight?"

"No. Why would they? I thought you said they were friends."

"They are. It's just that . . . they can both be a little short-tempered."

"Chirye thought they might like more privacy now that they are both awake. The woman has asked for books, while the man asked about you."

Falorn coughed back a response. "Well, I'm very glad they're feeling better," he said. "I owe many thanks to the healer."

"Not so many as they do," said Nia. Blond hair flowed over her shoulders and down her back in a golden cascade. She wore the same one-piece belted tunic as on the day in the bathhouse, or another just like it. Falorn tried not to be distracted, but caught himself looking at her nonetheless.

"That's true enough."

Nia opened the healer's door without knocking, and led Falorn down the hall to the same room he'd visited every night. This morning, only Sera occupied a bed. The other sat empty and neatly made, although stripped of its mountain of pillows. Nia shut the door behind Falorn after he entered, leaving him alone in the room with Sera.

Sera sat propped up in bed with a thick, leatherbound book open in her lap. Her face remained thin and drawn. She looked up as the door clicked shut.

"I'm so glad you're awake," Falorn said, walking to the edge of the bed. "I was worried."

Sera's unfocused look coalesced into a dark stare.

"Falorn, these are *elves*!" she hissed at him in a loud whisper.

"I know," he replied with a shrug. "They call themselves Helleinen, actually."

"How could you *do* this to me?"

"It wasn't really what I had in mind. I didn't have much choice at the time. You know, they did save your life."

"*You* saved my life. Now you have to get me out of here."

"I think it might not be all that bad, Sera."

"What do you mean, 'not that bad'? We might as well have stayed in Golden Reeds!"

"I hate to say this, but I really think they're not going to hurt us."

"You are so naive."

"That may be true. But I was conscious and you weren't. I did the best I could."

Sera sighed. "I know. You saved my life. But waking up has been a bit of a shock. And they speak our language!"

"A lot of them do, anyway."

"What did you tell them?" she asked, her tone abruptly fearful.

"Everything, almost. Let's leave it at that." he looked around, unsure if someone might be listening. Sera caught the gesture instantly.

"Thank you," she said, letting out her breath nervously, "although I hope you didn't tell them about Rorik. I don't come off well in that story."

"I'm sure you did what you thought you had to. And they know all about the cards you had."

"What about . . . ?" She held her hand at her chest, at the height his pouch hung.

"They're fine. But they know about those cards, too. They knew about them before I said anything."

"It figures." She sighed again. "Why did it have to be elves?"

They talked for a while longer, until she started to tire. Sera only asked once about the cards she had lost, and seemed unsurprised when Falorn told her that he'd heard nothing about them. No one disturbed them or checked on her, which made Falorn certain they were being watched surreptitiously. As he turned to walk to the door, he remembered something he'd meant to ask all along.

"Sera, who is Alex?"

"Alex?" she asked. Her eyes widened almost imperceptibly.

"Alex. You kept calling out that name when you were delirious in the boat."

"Oh, Alex. I must have been thinking of Alex of Rohn. He was the first cardholder I ever met, when I was about twelve or thirteen. Everybody talks about him as some kind of a fierce fighter, but he was very nice to me. He gave me books, and wouldn't let my father hurt me while he was around."

"I'm surprised your father put up with that. Doesn't he use the Hook on people like that?"

"Not for Alex. He's the greatest swordsman in the world. Besides, his brother is the God-Emperor of Rohn."

"He's a god?"

"His brother's supposed to be, anyway. I think it's just a hereditary title. I'm not sure anyone actually worships him. Rohn is a pretty big country, though."

"So you were praying to Alex in the boat."

"No. I must have been calling for help. Other than you, Alex is the only person who's ever tried to help me."

Falorn found Zaren in an adjoining room. The former innkeeper sat upright in an enormous bed, sharpening an axe with a hand-held whetstone. A flask of oil and several rags sat beside him, and Falorn could see oil stains marring the pristine white bedspread. The man's head had been freshly shaven, but Falorn saw little evidence of any other gear recovered from the wreckage of the boat; even the axe looked unfamiliar.

"I wondered when you'd come by."

"I came as soon as I knew you were up."

"As soon as you'd checked on the filly in the other room, you mean."

"Yes, you're right."

"Good for you. I'd do the same thing. Although that slip of an elf-doctor's not bad at all, or her friend." Falorn looked uncomfortable. "Don't tell me you didn't notice?"

"I tried not to."

"Waste of time." He rubbed the edge of the axe-blade with one of the greasy rags, and then set the weapon down on the bedspread. "Now then, I said once we survived the city you could tell me your name. What is it?"

"Falorn."

"Just 'Falorn'? Not 'Falorn of Somewhere' or 'Falorn the Something Really Impressive'?"

"Just Falorn."

"Never heard of you."

He's lying, Falorn knew. But he didn't know why, or how Zaren could possibly have heard his name before.

"Of course not. Why should you have?"

"You're a cardholder, and you've got a lot of them. I thought I knew most of the important ones."

"You do?"

"Are you stupid? Or just deaf?"

"It's just that it's a little hard to believe, that's all."

"What, you don't believe that a mercenary officer gets around? Just because I ended up in a shithole doesn't mean I was always there. And it wasn't a shithole when I moved there."

"I'm sorry."

"Stop apologizing so much! Do you want me to tell you about the cards or not?"

"Of course, if you feel up to it."

"It's either that or I'm going to grind the edge completely off this damned elf-blade. I'm bored and I can't get up, and the sarcastic elf tells me you saved my life. Pull up a chair."

"You met Danbhe?"

"He was in here before you, to make sure our stories matched. I just hope your girlfriend didn't try to lie to him too much."

"I hope so too." Falorn dragged one of the heavily cushioned chairs from across the room to the edge of the bed.

"This story starts a long time ago when I was still fighting," Zaren began, "but I don't feel like telling you that part, so I'm just going to tell you what I know about where the cards come from and what they do."

"That's fine."

"You're damned right, it is. Anyway, they were made by a sorceress. From what I understand, she was pretty tough, and had a lot of enemies. She finally did something that made them all join forces against her— killed and robbed one too many wizards and scared all the others, I think—and between all of them, they were more powerful than she was. And they were rich enough and well-connected enough to bring an army against her. If she had any friends, they weren't about to show themselves until the smoke cleared.

"It took a while to close in on her, though—like I said, she was tough, and she'd spent a long time building up her defenses. She killed a lot of people in the process, but it must have been pretty clear to her that the end was on its way.

"So before they got too close she managed, somehow—and I don't know enough about magic to tell you exactly what she did—to pour her-self into a deck of enchanted cards she'd already made. I don't know if she made them especially to escape with, or if she just had them lying around, but by the time the last of her enemies broke down the door into her final stronghold, all they found was a pile of books, a deck of cards, and her empty husk of a body, along with a dead servant woman.

"The other wizards knew what she'd done, more or less, and they talked a little about destroying the cards and finishing her off. But it seemed safe enough leaving her split up between all the cards, and no one really wanted to destroy such powerful magic—especially after what destroying the sorceress had cost them all in blood and treasure—so they split the cards and books up along with the rest of the loot, and all went their separate ways. This was a bit over thirty years ago."

"How many cards are there?" Falorn asked.

"Eighty-four, I think, unless any of them have been destroyed. I don't know all of them, but I've seen books with pictures of them. My old commander, Steel Stennet, had a book like that.

"The thing about the cards is, there's more to them than meets the eye. Each card is related to whatever picture is on its face, but the same card can do different things for different people. I don't know that they actually give out any powers at all."

"What do you mean?" Falorn asked, thinking of the effects the lion and thief cards had had on him.

"I think most of what the cards do is magnify powers that are already there. The lions might make you tougher, but there's got to be a core of strength already inside you, or they wouldn't do anything. Probably you'd never have found the cards if you didn't have what it took to use them."

So how did you end up with a snake? Falorn wanted to ask, but he substituted a more tactful question.

"But what about the crimson knight card? I never knew anything about using a sword, and now I can't stand it if my posture isn't perfect. It's almost like the card uses me more than I use it."

"There may be something to that, but I'll bet you had the makings of a knight inside you. Nobody'd look at you now and think you hadn't been using that sword for years, and you're what, a few weeks away from the farm? I didn't start calling snakes by myself either, but the card must have found something snakelike inside me." Zaren laughed a little, and made sinuous snake-gestures with his hands.

He's concealing something. Whether it's about me or about how he got the card, I'm not sure, but there's something Zaren's hiding.

"What do you mean, the card found you?"

"I don't think they wind up with a particular person by accident. I think they chose you in some way, although I'll be damned if I know what or why. The cards want something, and they're going to end up with someone who can do what they want."

"Do you think they're controlling us?" He thought about the way Sera's moods changed, and how she vacillated between love and betrayal.

"No. They're powerful, but not like that. I think they can change owners when they want, and they may stop working for you if they decide they don't want to help you anymore. But I don't think they can control people. They just pick out people they like. Each of them is like a little piece of that sorceress's mind. Who knows what each of those pieces want, or whether they all want the same thing? The only thing I do know, is that they all seem to be coming together, and quickly."

"Why now?"

"Who knows? Maybe there's nothing to it, just some powerful people who've all decided it's time to fight each other over the cards. Maybe they want to have a reunion. Maybe the sorceress found some way to have the last laugh after all. All I know is that you hear a lot about the cards now, and you never used to hear anything. And a lot of people are getting killed over them now, when it used to only be a couple of people a year.

"You've got a bunch of them, and the more you have, the stronger each of them are; they seem to work together that way, especially along the same color or suit. They seem to like you, for whatever reason. Use them all you can, learn from them all you can. They might suddenly change their minds and leave you, and you wouldn't want to be stuck with nothing. Me, I'd just be out one card and an inn. You, you'd have a fortune in gold on your belt, a sword you barely know how to use, and a lot of enemies. If I were you, I'd practice with that sword a lot."

"Thanks. I have been."

"That's most of what I know. Steel and I worked a lot of it out between us, but I haven't seen him in years."

"Are they all in suits, like playing cards?"

"Most of them are, but not all of them. They're all in groups of four, but sometimes not all four are identical. There aren't more than four of any of them."

"Thanks for telling me all this."

"You earned it. I figure a few elves listened in, too, but this is nothing new to them. Maybe they'll tell us a little more later."

"Maybe."

They talked for a few more minutes, and Falorn got up to leave. A thought occurred to him, and he turned back into the room. Zaren had picked up the axe again and resumed grinding its blade.

"Zaren?"

"I'm busy."

"Who's Alex of Rohn?"

"He's the best swordsman in the world. Never met him personally, but we were on the same side in a battle once. Why do you ask?"

"No special reason."

"Whatever you say."

He turned and left the room again.

The sun beat down hard from a cloudless sky by the time he left the healer's house, but Falorn went straight to the practice fields anyway. He worked out with various partners until everyone else left, long after dusk. After that he began running circuits of the hilltop again, only coming in for dinner after the last traces of sunlight had vanished from the sky.

23

Unpaid Debts

Two more days passed before Danbhe summoned Falorn.

Falorn visited Sera and Zaren each morning before going to the practice fields; by the second morning both of them could walk easily. Zaren accompanied Falorn out to his workout, though he could only participate by badgering and heckling Falorn. Sera remained mostly within the healer's house, and said as little as possible to anyone besides Falorn. She seemed cowed by the presence of the Helleinen.

Falorn wandered back to the lodge long after dinner had ended. He'd gone running in the hills after the others left the practice fields for dinner, and then washed the sweat off in one of the dozens of icy streams which flowed through the rocky slopes. His chest, arms, and legs ached from hours of exertion, but he felt no weakness or exhaustion. Quickly he climbed the ladder toward his room; he'd left bread and sausage there in case he missed dinner.

He entered his cubicle to find Ryal sitting in the lone chair.

"I wondered when you were coming back."

"I wasn't very far away. You could have sent someone to find me if you wanted."

"Danbhe didn't want to interrupt you. But he would like to see you tonight, along with your friends."

"I figured he would, soon."

"It's nothing to worry about. You are a guest here. We wouldn't hurt you without good reason."

"When would he like to see me?"

"As soon as possible. He's with the others now, and I think he is afraid your friend Sera will be weakened by the strain of continually lying to him."

Falorn glanced at the plate of sausages, but said nothing as he followed the Hellein down the ladder and out of the lodge. He didn't know how seriously to take Ryal's words. He hoped the Helleinen had discovered nothing about the fate of the swordsman Sera had killed. Other than that he could think of nothing she might say that would jeopardize them.

Danbhe sat in an overstuffed, red-colored armchair in the front parlor of the healer's house, on the other side of the hall from Sera and Zaren's rooms. Falorn could see five matching chairs scattered around the room. A deck of cards lay spread on the shiny surface of the polished hardwood table in front of Danbhe. Falorn felt a moment of fear and then realized the cards wore only the usual suits and faces—although the pattern of the game looked unfamiliar. Danbhe studied the layout of the cards for a moment, and then swept away the careful pattern, collecting the cards back together and sliding them into a leather case.

"I have hated that game for fifty years now," Danbhe said. "I do not know why I still play it."

Ryal laughed. "You keep hoping you'll get better at it."

"Not much chance of that."

Danbhe seemed unaware of Falorn, until Falorn realized that the Hellein could only be speaking in Denbar for his benefit.

"You wanted to see me?" he asked.

"Sit down. Pull up a chair."

Falorn dragged one of the heavy armchairs from a corner of the room and pulled off his baldric and bare sword, still worn from his day at the practice fields, hanging them from the chair back. He sat down, sinking into the thick cushioning.

"Still waiting for the new scabbards, I see."

"They'll be ready soon, I think. Your leatherworker wants to be certain they're perfect."

"You should appreciate her work. She is a true artist."

"I do appreciate it. I'm not sure artistry is the first thing I want in a scabbard, though."

"Not the first thing, no. But it is important." Danbhe looked at the cased deck of cards again, as if thinking of removing them for another hand. "I did not ask you here to talk about cards or scabbards, as you may suspect. But there is a thing or two that bears discussion before I ask your friends to join us." He paused. "The first thing is, why does your friend Sera keep lying to me?"

"I think she's afraid of you." Falorn had expected the question.

"Whyever would she be afraid of me? I have treated her with nothing but the greatest of kindness. My folk have healed her, and fed her, and cared for her."

"She . . . has a few misconceptions about Helleinen, I think."

Danbhe looked at Falorn expectantly.

"I mean . . . she thinks you eat babies."

"Is she pregnant?"

"What? I mean . . . no, of course not." *I don't think so, anyway.*

"Then she has nothing to worry about, does she?"

"I'm not sure she sees it that way."

"I am not convinced that is why she is lying, either. But you might want to dissuade her from further prevarications. Go talk to her now, and we will all meet when you return."

Sera sat up in bed when he walked into the room; he couldn't tell if she'd been sleeping or not. Her hair hung in wild, scattered tangles around her face. Blankets lay disheveled around her. She wore a nightgown of some thin, glossy, silklike material which clung to her body in shimmers of pink cloth, glittering from the reflected light of the room's two candle lamps.

"What are you doing here? You startled me."

"Sera, we have to talk."

"Now?"

"Now."

"You know they're listening to us?"

"I know they're listening. They're waiting for us in the front room, but they asked me to talk with you first. They say you've been lying to them."

"Why should I make it easy for them to take your cards away?"

"Sera, if they wanted my cards, they would have taken them when I was asleep on the beach. That makes no sense at all."

"Just because you believe every word they say doesn't mean I have to."

"Sera, we're guests. They won't hurt us."

"What's to keep them from it?"

"Why would they have nursed you and Zaren back to health otherwise? And they let me run around wherever I want, with my sword."

"Maybe they want something from us that we haven't given them yet. That doesn't mean they won't kill us later. Why shouldn't I be on my guard?"

"Be on your guard if you like, but at least be polite. You've got no reason to lie to them."

"Yes, I do. You may not, but I do. Please be careful, since you do have my life in your hands." She spoke very softly, so no one else listening could hear.

"Sera, I would never say anything," Falorn replied just as softly. "I would never do that to you."

"I hate to have my life in your hands. One day you'll say something, and that will be it. They'll come and kill me."

Falorn held one of her hands as he spoke. "Never," he said, "I would never do that to you."

"Why did you save me?" she asked, sniffling a little. "Why didn't you let me drown?"

"I saved you because . . . because I care about you. A lot. You've saved me twice, and nursed me back to health. I'll do all I can to pay you back. I wouldn't hurt you. And I know you don't want to hurt me."

"But I *will* hurt you again. I'll only keep hurting you. It's the only way I seem to be able to treat the people I care about."

"Hush," he said. "It will be all right. We won't be here much longer."

She buried her face in his shoulder for a moment while he rubbed her back gently in soft, soothing motions. When she lifted her head from his tunic, her tears had ceased.

"I'll be fine," she said. "Let's go talk to our jailers."

"They won't hurt you, Sera."

"They're not going to help me, either."

The chairs encircled the table when Falorn and Sera reentered the parlor. Zaren and Cirque had joined Danbhe and Ryal at the table. All of them spoke together in low tones.

"That certainly took quite a while," Danbhe said as they sat down.

"Danbhe, please," Falorn said. "Can we get on with it?"

The Hellein looked as if he wanted to say something, then decided against it.

Ryal broke into the conversation. "We were talking about your next move, about where you want to go when you leave here."

"When can we leave?" Falorn asked.

"As soon as all of you are healthy," said Danbhe. "However, there are a few things you may not know that we can tell you—things that may be important to your choice of destinations."

"Such as?"

"This hunting lodge lies at a juncture of three lands: Delerian, Cathan, and the Seven Kingdoms. One mountain pass leads to Cathan, another to the Seven Kingdoms. The river also leads to Cathan, but I think that would not be safe for you, even without rapids. The river is a very exposed route, and you have many enemies.

"Zaren here," Danbhe motioned, "has suggested that the three of you proceed on to Cathan, where he could meet with his old friend and fellow cardholder General Steel Stennet, who is in the service of another cardholder, Her Majesty the Queen of Cathan. That plan would take you at least momentarily away from your enemies, but it fails to deal with any of them, and leaves all of them free to chase you.

"The enemy I would most like to see eliminated is Rorik Iron Eagle. I *will* have payment for his slaughter of my cousins, however distant. But I will not ask you to help us destroy him—yet. You have another, closer, more pressing enemy, by the name of Prince Jhodric of Northfall."

"Who?"

"He is a nobleman within the Seven Kingdoms, and a direct descendent of their Immortal King. The soldiers in green you met belonged to him. We could help you to take the cards away from him, or from whomever he takes his orders."

"So the dead knight with the green lion card—that was one of his men?"

"I think so. The sendings which chased you afterward did not belong to him, though. They may have killed Jhodric's knight, and been disturbed before they could retrieve his cards from the road. Or killing the knight might have worn out the sendings' masters."

"Sendings?"

"Conjurations—sent by a summoner to bring something back or punish someone."

"A summoner?"

"Summoning is a school of magic, like transmutation or healing."

"You want me to attack a prince? We barely made it away from the archbishop alive."

"You would have help. And an attack would be very unexpected."

"So you're saying they don't expect me to commit suicide?"

"More or less. I think it would not be suicidal, however. And if you do not take his cards away, he will only continue to attack you."

"It still sounds crazy. How are we supposed to face someone who's immortal?"

"Prince Jhodric claims direct descent from the Immortal King who rules the Seven Kingdoms, or in whose name they are ruled. Jhodric himself is not immortal. The Immortal King has been locked in what they call the Forbidden City for over seven hundred years now, completely unseen. I think it would not be unfair to question his longevity. And you would be accompanied by a substantial force. The Seven Kingdoms is Delerian's enemy as well as yours."

Something about this whole plot sounds insane. Even more insane than my life has already been for these last few weeks.

Falorn looked at Zaren, who shook his head slightly. Sera's expression gave no indication of an opinion one way or the other. He sat for a moment and thought.

"You've been very good to me," he finally said, "and I don't doubt that Prince Jhodric is a very dangerous enemy—but he's *my* enemy. I don't think I can ask my friends to face him, even if I have to. I think I need to find someplace safe for Sera and Zaren before I even think about any crazy expeditions against immortal princes and their armies. If that safe place is with General Stennet in Cathan, then maybe I can come back after they're safe and you can explain the reasons to go visit Jhodric then. But until they're safe, I don't think I have the right to drag them on any more wild adventures. I've cost them both enough already."

"I think you are making a mistake," said Danbhe, "and I think it may cost you more than you imagine. But it is not an unexpected mistake. If you do not change your mind, we will of course help you over the mountains into Cathan. Cirque and Ryal have offered to accompany you, to help guard your safety and to assist you in returning after your friends are safe."

"Thank you," Falorn said.

I'm not sure what it is they want me to do for them, or why the Seven Kingdoms is so important to them. But they're willing to take Sera and

Zaren to safety as the price for my help, and given how much I owe to Sera and Zaren, that's probably a price worth paying. If nothing else, it buys me time to learn to get better with the cards, and people who can help teach me to use my sword. After Sera and Zaren are safe and I'm back here, we can talk about crazy hunting expeditions after princes who might be trying to kill me.

"Think on it for a few days," said Danbhe. "When your friends are ready to travel, tell me what your final choice is."

Only after he left the gathering to return to the lodge and his bed did Falorn realize that neither Sera nor Zaren had said a word the whole time he spoke with the Helleinen.

As they grew stronger, Sera and Zaren began to accompany Falorn on his wanderings in the hills which surrounded the hunting lodge. One or more of the Helleinen always accompanied them, ostensibly as a guide should they get lost and an extra sword in case of danger. Usually Cirque or Ryal escorted them, although occasionally Nia came along instead.

It took longer than the few days Danbhe predicted before they felt ready to leave the lodge; even in early summer, a mountain expedition required a great deal of stamina. Nearly three weeks passed before all of them felt ready, and before Falorn asked to speak with Danbhe again. The Hellein wordlessly nodded when Falorn reaffirmed his decision to travel into Cathan.

Falorn didn't see him again before they left, except from a distance at mealtimes.

Three days later, five of them set out: Falorn, Zaren, Sera, Cirque, and Ryal, along with a half dozen pack mules of supplies. Despite his protestations, the Helleinen refused all payment from Falorn. As Falorn had expected, his debt to Danbhe remained unpaid as they began their trek through the forested hills which would lead them toward the mountains, and toward the border of Cathan.

24

Songs in the Night

❖⁘❖

"From the top of this pass you can see into three countries," said Cirque. The Hellein gestured at the rock-strewn path in front of their small mule train. After three days of upward climbing, they had left the thick forest behind. Trees still surrounded them most of the time, but scrub pines had largely replaced the hardwoods of Delerian. "These mountains go on for hundreds of miles, but they form a sort of corner here. The northern spur divides Delerian from the Seven Kingdoms until it fades into foothills and swamp. Where the border is flatter, there is constant fighting."

"Are Delerian and the Seven Kingdoms always at war?" Falorn asked. He and the elven leader walked at the back of the mules, urging them on with sticks when necessary. Zaren had passed out of sight ahead, scouting their path, while Sera and Ryal took their turn at the relatively dust-free head of the train.

"Officially, the two countries have been at war for over three hundred years now. There aren't many big battles, ever since the last Seven Kingdoms invasion foundered. Mostly they raid along the border and seacoast."

"Can't you do anything about it?"

"We raid back, a little. But they have ten times the population we do. Mostly we hold the border, and fight back if they attack, and kill any armies they send into the forests."

"And steal cards from princes?"

"That's a special case. There is a balance of power along the border, and the cards could alter it."

"For them or for you?"

"Either one. The choice is as much yours as anyone's."

Zaren stood waiting for them at the next bend in the mountain path. He leaned against a rock, using one finger to test the blade of the Delerian-made battle axe he now carried.

"Troll spoor up ahead," he said simply.

"What sort of spoor?" asked Cirque.

"Footprints, about a day old—and part of a goat."

"Where?"

Zaren pointed to the ground near his foot. Falorn could see nothing. He focused hard on the spot, until a familiar blue glow appeared. The scuffed ground coalesced into the shape of an odd footprint, more than twice the length of his own foot, and with three clawed toes. Other footprints formed beyond, until Falorn could clearly follow the trail they formed.

"It's up there, in those rocks," Falorn said, pointing.

"Are you sure?" Zaren asked. "I thought it was hiding along the trail ahead of us."

"No, he's right," said Cirque, "Look." He pointed to one of the scuffed spots that now looked so clear to Falorn. "This one's clever."

"Think we can get by him without a problem?" asked Zaren. "I'd hate to take the bastard on here in the rocks."

"I don't see that we have much of a choice," Cirque replied. "It knows we're here. It smells us and the mules. It's just waiting. Our only choice is whether we face it now or tonight when we're camped."

"Has it always been on this trail?"

"It's been eight years since I took anyone into Cathan. It wasn't here then. I take it you've never traveled the mountain route?"

"Never cared for mountains much. Too cold, and too hard to haul supplies through. Terrible horse country, too."

"That's true enough," Cirque replied.

"Can't we just keep moving?" Falorn asked. "I can't imagine a troll would attack the whole group of us."

"Troll'll attack anything," Zaren said. "They'll eat each other if food's short enough. If we keep moving it'll track us, and kill anyone who falls behind, or turns his back. Better we go after it than wait for it to get hungry."

"Are you sure it knows we're here?"

"A troll can smell you from a mile away. Do you think it can't tell when a mule train's coming through its front yard?"

Ryal had hobbled the mules by this time, and he and Sera joined the other three. All of them glanced frequently up at the rocky warren where the troll hid, although Falorn noticed that Cirque and Zaren watched the rest of the surrounding area as well.

"Do you want to watch things down here while we go deal with the troll?" Cirque asked Ryal.

"That would probably be best. If you don't find it, I might be able to hide us tonight."

"If we survive."

"Try to."

"I usually do," said Cirque. He turned to Falorn. "I take it you've never seen a troll?"

"No, never. Don't they live under bridges?"

"Not in real life," Zaren broke in. "They run about twice your height and smell like a sunny day at an outdoor slaughterhouse. Fierce as anything. Don't let it touch you; it'll rip you apart."

"He's right," said Cirque. "A troll is fast, but you have to get inside its guard to hurt it. Don't try dodging in and out too much; it's probably faster than you are. Just pick a spot and attack, without letting it hit you."

With a last wave at Ryal and Sera standing among the mules, Cirque drew his sword and began picking his way upward into the thickening web of rocks. Zaren followed behind, close enough to help, but not so close that both might be hit by a single thrown rock or surprise attack. Falorn unsheathed his own blade and walked after them, trying to focus his mind on the knight card which sat against his chest. He felt a general warmth by way of response.

Cirque and Zaren talked as they worked their way upward toward the troll's hiding place.

"So you like to work inside their guard?" Falorn heard Zaren asking Cirque.

"That's right. It works well, especially with two or more attackers."

"I always preferred to stay at the edge of their reach and harass until

I'd done some damage. Bows and arrows would be nice now. Even a crossbow."

"Bows never seemed very sporting to me."

"Sporting? Who gives a damn? It's a troll. Do you think it's keeping score?"

"We don't keep score among the Helleinen, but appearance and propriety are very important. We live a long time. Slights and insults are not easily forgotten. There is no reason to make enemies through carelessness or impoliteness."

"There's no reason to get killed for being polite to a troll, either. Too much politeness and you're not going to live a long time."

"Should we be making all this noise?" Falorn asked. "Won't it know we're coming?"

"It knows we're coming," Zaren said. "It's getting its napkins and good dishes ready because it knows it's going to have polite company for dinner."

"A little politeness and propriety never hurt," said Cirque.

"They only have to hurt once."

Cirque didn't reply; instead, he halted and put up one arm to stop them. Falorn instantly froze, while Zaren raised his axe and crept forward.

Then the beast burst around the corner at them, nearly flattening Cirque as it thundered over him.

Falorn raised his sword as it charged him.

He ducked under a massive swipe. A huge arm swept over his head; it had patchy gray skin tufted here and there with unevenly clumped hair.

He raised his sword and deflected a second blow. At the same time, Falorn saw Zaren swing at the back of one of the troll's thick, corded legs.

Falorn's sword bit into flesh.

The troll nearly ripped the blade from his hands when it pulled its arm back for another attack. The creature seemed not to notice the bloody wound in its forearm.

Falorn clung to his blade and stepped inward, hoping the troll couldn't swing with as much force at someone close up against it. *Where's Zaren?* he wondered. *Doesn't this thing even notice that there's someone else attacking it too?*

He stabbed at the troll's belly as he stumbled underneath the creature's blows, piercing deeply into rolls of uneven gray flesh. He only just managed to pull his sword out as the troll recoiled.

Red blood and thick yellowish fluid covered the length of the blade. *Finally, it felt something.*

He pushed forward again, swinging too high to hit below the troll's guard, but trying to keep it from hitting him. *Kerion! if it hits me at all, I'm dead. I hope Cirque is all right.*

The troll clambered backward and upward into the rocks, contorting its body in grotesque, inhuman motions.

Before Falorn could do more than open a cut on the creature's shin, it crouched on top of a shoulder-high rock and rained blows down on him. He held his sword high and fended off each stroke, but only the strength from the lion cards kept the creature from beating down his guard.

Its arms seemed to extend impossibly far from its body, allowing it to attack his head and shoulders despite its elevation. He could reach nothing but its arms and hands.

Falorn tried to cut them while at the same time deflecting the force of the creature's smashing hits. Even with all his strength, Falorn seemed unable to do more than nick and scratch the whipcord muscles of the troll's cabled arms, as if its muscles had become so dominant they had driven all the blood from the creature's extremities.

Where is Zaren? Falorn hadn't seen the mercenary since he glimpsed Zaren attacking the creature's legs. Now he could only fight off the troll's punishment for as long as his arms held out. He didn't dare retreat without knowing whether Zaren or Cirque had been wounded, and he couldn't attack the creature up the face of the rock.

Suddenly the troll roared and reared back onto its feet. Blood streamed from a wide slash at the back of its skull. A flap of skin hung down almost to its neck. Falorn saw dull white bone beneath.

The creature turned and swung wildly, just as Zaren leaped back off the rock and beyond its reach.

If it jumps after him, it will kill him, Falorn knew instantly. He dove forward to the edge of the rock and chopped at the creature's feet, the only thing he could reach. He shouted as he swung again and again. With a bowstring-snap, a tendon parted. The troll stumbled as it turned around to confront him.

Falorn thrust at its knee and then jumped back. He retreated three steps, just out of the troll's reach. The creature roared as Zaren's thrown knife caught its shoulder from behind, sinking to the hilt in mottled flesh. The troll turned back and forth indecisively, unsure of which foe to charge after from its high vantage point.

"Damn, what I'd give for a bow and arrow right now," Falorn heard from the other side of the rock.

The noise seemed to make up the troll's mind for it, and it plunged off the rock in Zaren's direction.

"Get over here!" Zaren shouted, and then Falorn could only hear fighting. He rushed forward to the rock and scaled it awkwardly, wishing for the troll's misshapen arms as he did so. In the close-packed rocks on the other side, the troll had Zaren backed against another large stone. The big man caught blow after blow on his axe, redirecting some and using his blade to slice into the creature's arms when he could. Falorn could see the mercenary weakening. His blade came up more slowly each time the troll beat it down.

The troll seemed weaker too. Blood drenched its entire back and pooled on the ground at its feet.

It staggered Zaren with a pounding smash, knocking the mercenary to his knees. The troll reared up to deliver a killing stroke.

Falorn swung as hard as he could. His blade bit into the creature's neck and stopped, with a jarring shock that numbed his hands. The troll turned with a gurgling roar, tearing the blade from Falorn's grasp. He looked at the sword stuck halfway in the creature's neck and gaped for half a second, before hurriedly reaching for his knife and stepping backward.

The troll reeled toward him. Its head lolled on a broken neck. Its legs bowed and swayed from the damage of dozens of sword and axe blows. *It can't still be coming.* Behind the creature, Zaren struggled to his feet. He planted himself and swung the axe with all his strength into the back of the troll's waist, severing its spine. Impossibly, it advanced another step before collapsing against the rock and sliding to the ground.

Zaren walked over to its head, careful to avoid the still-thrashing arms, and chopped three times. Finally, the head rolled free of the creature's body.

Zaren nearly collapsed against the rock himself, clutching its side to support himself. Falorn climbed down and rushed to him.

"Are you all right?"

"Pick up your sword, you idiot! What if there's another one around?"

Falorn hurriedly retrieved his weapon, along with Zaren's knife. "Here," he said as he returned to the man's side.

"Now you can ask if I'm all right."

"Are you all right?"

"Yes, but I'm damned tired. I've been away from this for too long."
He patted his belly.

Falorn looked, and saw nothing but hard muscle.

"Now where's that stupid elf?"

"I thought you might know."

They both cleaned their weapons on the troll's hide and set out to
look for Cirque. They found him around a bend in the rocks, sitting up
and ruefully clutching his swollen right arm.

"Is that all?" Zaren asked. "A damned broken arm and you expect us
to fight a troll by ourselves?"

"Sorry," Cirque said.

"Don't worry about it. The next one's yours."

Falorn helped the Hellein to his feet. Cirque had also twisted one of
his legs, and Falorn had to support him as they made their way back
toward the mules. Zaren walked behind them, watching carefully in case
another troll happened to be nearby.

"That's why you don't just leave trolls alone," Zaren said to Falorn as
they handed Cirque over to Ryal's care. "That thing would have been in
our camp tonight, as soon as one or two of us went to sleep."

"Do you think there are more of them around?"

"I doubt it. Usually they're loners. Sometimes they have mates, but
it would have been close by. We'll have other company tonight if we don't
get farther from the corpse, though."

Nothing bothered them that night except for the wolves. Almost as
soon as they camped, the howling began, rising in pitch and intensity
as the darkness increased in the rocks and thin woods beyond their
small fire.

All of them sat near the campfire, Cirque slightly farther away than
the others. Ryal had splinted the Hellein warrior's arm and placed it in a
sling. As a result, Cirque had endured sarcastic comments from Zaren
throughout the afternoon.

Sera huddled next to Falorn. As the howling increased and moved
closer in the thickening darkness, she began to shiver. Falorn put his left
arm around his shoulder and pulled her closer, first unsheathing his
sword from his left side and setting it on the ground in front of him.

"It's all right," he said to her soothingly.

"They probably won't bother us much," Zaren said from across the
fire. "This time of year, they've got plenty of food. There's no need for

them to go looking after armed travelers. Now, if we were traveling in the winter. . . ."

Ryal threw more branches onto the fire, and the flames jumped perceptibly. Falorn loved the crackle of burning pine, but now the howling overwhelmed it. He held Sera tightly, glad to have her beside him, whatever the reason. He thought he heard her sigh faintly, but a wolf-yelp drowned out the sound.

"Now *that's* annoying," he heard Zaren say. Falorn turned to look. A massive wolf stood about fifty feet from the fire, just at the edge of the circle of illumination. It had a thick, glossy grayish-white coat, with a white splash blazed across its chest. A heavy ruff of thicker flesh surrounded its neck. It looked at the travelers inquisitively out of deep yellow-green eyes, set in a long, thin gray muzzle. Then it sat back on its haunches, turned its head upward to the sky, and loosed a long, mournful wail.

Two other wolves appeared behind the first creature's shoulders. They sniffed around for a moment before joining in the howling. In the rare moments when they stopped for breath, Falorn could hear the padding of other lupine feet in the darkness.

"Damn elves don't have the sense to pack bows," Zaren grumbled.

"They're beautiful, though," Falorn said. Sera pulled away from him slightly.

"They're only pretty when they're not hungry," said Zaren. "And that's not very often. They make warm cloaks, but the eating's not very good."

"Thanks. I really needed to know that." All around them now, the plaintive chorus continued. Falorn thought the lead wolf had remarkable, soulful eyes, but the rest of the travelers clearly disagreed with him.

"How long will they keep this up?" Falorn asked.

"As long as that big wolf does. He's their leader. They'll do whatever he wants until another wolf beats him."

"Hopefully, a less musically inclined wolf," Ryal added.

The wolves gave no signs of stopping or leaving as the night went on. If anything the noise increased as the moon rose further in the sky. Sleep seemed impossible, but Sera gradually slid close to Falorn again and rested her head on his shoulder.

Feeling her next to him exhilarated Falorn in a way that erased all desire for sleep. He would have been happy to stay by the fire all night with her resting against him, even if it meant tolerating the noise. He hated the thought of her getting up to go to sleep.

"Enough of this!" Ryal finally shouted. He stood up and unbuckled his sword belt, letting it fall to the ground. One at a time he pulled off his boots and threw them down next to his sword. Next he slipped off his tunic and close-fitting britches, until he stood naked in the firelight.

"Ryal?" Falorn asked tentatively. Sera's head didn't move from his shoulder. He wondered if she really slept or not.

"Leave him," Zaren said.

Ryal began muttering something and gesturing with strange, circular motions. After a few minutes, the elf's body seemed subtly different somehow, and then the shift became obvious. Black fur sprouted everywhere as Ryal's muttering shifted into a barely vocal whine. His nose lengthened, and absorbed much of his face along with it. His ears, already pronounced, grew longer and thinner. His arms and legs shortened, and melded partway into his increasingly barrel-shaped torso.

The howling from the wolves abruptly changed to curious barking as the transformation continued.

In a moment, an oversized, pure black wolf stood in the Hellein's place.

The black wolf began to stalk toward the silvery creature with the soulful eyes, snarling as it went. The leader of the wolf pack snarled back, although it sounded tentative and confused. The black wolf's growling grew louder as it reached the gray animal. The true wolf looked small by comparison, although it had seemed very large before. It whined slightly, making placating noises. The black wolf snarled again, baring its fangs, and cuffing the sad-eyed creature on the muzzle, twice. The gray wolf gave ground without attempting to resist the larger creature. Within moments, all of the wolves melted back into the trees and rocks.

The black wolf continued growling for a short while, and then returned to the fireside. Falorn expected Ryal to shift back immediately, but instead he curled up by the fire and went to sleep, looking like nothing so much as an oversized sheepdog after a day's work.

After about half an hour, the howling resumed, although from much farther away. The noise seemed to be receding.

"Isn't he going to turn back?" Falorn asked Zaren, when the larger man got up to set up his bedroll.

"I doubt it. I'm not sure he can. Do you see any hands, or a normal mouth?"

"He's just going to stay that way?"

"Until the spell wears off, he will. It'll be a big help keeping the mules moving tomorrow." The wolf's ears perked up suddenly at that, but otherwise it gave no signs of wakefulness.

"Are you planning on sleeping?" Zaren asked him. Falorn didn't want to move Sera, who lay asleep against him.

"No. I'm not that tired."

"Good. You can keep watch then. Wake me or Cirque or the dog if you start to fall asleep. And be sure that you keep your eyes on what's out there," he added, glancing at Sera.

25

The Empty Land

The morning dawned clear and wolfless. A cool breeze blew steadily at their backs as the five travelers continued through the pass. The mules moved much more quickly with the giant black wolf at their heels, and Ryal actually seemed to relish the role. Falorn had carefully stowed the Hellein's clothes and weapons on the back of one of the pack animals.

By afternoon, much of the grade began to slope downhill. Thickening forest encroached on the rocks by the time they stopped to camp that evening. Sometime during the night, the black wolf turned back into an elf, but Falorn slept through the transformation. When he awoke, Ryal was already awake and dressed.

They spent the following days walking through wooded foothills, now and again passing fortified houses. Avoiding the houses, they camped in sheltered areas within the woods. Two more days saw them walking through low, rolling hills, many with growing crops. Castles began to dot the hilltops every few miles. Despite the cultivated fields and frequent fortifications, only a few people could be seen, most of them very old or very young. They found no paved roads.

"Where is everybody?" Falorn finally asked Zaren. "I thought you said this country had *people* in it."

"I said it had Steel Stennet in it."

"He can't be the only person in the country!"

"He isn't," said Sera, from beside Falorn. "Look."

A gate had opened in the nearest castle, and a small troop of cavalry rode forth, cantering across a fallow field toward the mule train and travelers. The riders wore helmets and mail and carried shields and sabers. As the horsemen rode closer, Falorn could see that many of them looked slighter in the saddle than the other cavalrymen he'd encountered.

"They're women," he realized, speaking aloud without thinking. "Some of them are women."

"And what's wrong with that?" Sera asked.

"Nothing. I've just never seen it before."

"I think I've died and been rewarded by the war gods," said Zaren.

"Are you sure they're not going to attack us?" asked Ryal.

"Pretty sure," Zaren replied. "They haven't yet, anyway." He cupped a hand to his mouth and shouted toward the approaching troopers. "We're here to see Steel Stennet. Can you take us to him?"

The soldiers rode closer without replying. They reined in about twenty feet away from the travelers, swords still sheathed. One of their number rode forward—a young women with weathered skin and a stocky build. She wore a green surcoat trimmed with black over a light mail byrne. A half-helmet with no nasal or cheekguards covered the top of her head, and she had tucked her hair within it. She looked over all of the travelers, and then jogged her horse over to where Falorn stood, stopping directly in front of him.

"I am Sublieutenant Risylla Contayne, of Her Majesty the Queen's Own Guard. My troops can give you an escort to the Summer Palace, if you've come to enter service in Cathan." She spoke in his own language, though with an unfamiliar accent.

"We've come to see a man named Steel Stennet. Where would we find him?"

"General Stennet is at the front, of course. But there's no need to see him directly. Volunteers swear their oaths at the palace."

"I'm not sure that we're volunteers, exactly. We had no idea there was a war on."

"Be that as it may, all able-bodied folk within the country who are between the ages of fifteen and fifty are liable for conscription into the Royal Army. And you *are* within the country."

"Of course we are. It's just that the war comes as something of a surprise. We came to see General Stennet."

"I can take you to the Summer Palace. Anywhere farther than that, you'll need royal authority."

"That's fair enough. Do you have horses we can use as far as the palace?"

"A few, if you don't expect much. Most of the best horses are at the front as well. You can use some of our remounts. They're not war trained, but they'll get you to the palace."

"There won't be fighting between here and the Summer Palace, will there?" Zaren interjected.

"Not yet," the sublieutenant answered. "Not yet."

They stopped at the hilltop castle only long enough for a brief meal, during which the soldiers barely talked. Afterward, they found horses saddled and waiting in the courtyard, along with their mules. Four troopers and a middle-aged sergeant had been delegated as an escort to the Summer Palace.

The troopers stayed well clear of them as the journey resumed. The sergeant and two of the soldiers rode two dozen horse lengths in front of the mules, while the remaining two troopers kept a similar distance behind. The soldiers seemed unconcerned about any danger the travelers might pose, as long as all of them completed the journey to the royal seat of power.

Falorn rode between Zaren and Sera on the wide, packed-earth road. Cirque and Ryal rode a horse length or two behind them, chatting in Delerian.

"What do you think's going on?" Falorn asked Zaren.

"I'm not quite sure. Cathan and Calathan are neighboring countries, and they're always at war. And I *mean* always; the two of them have been fighting off and on for generations, and plotting against each other when they're not fighting. But they're well matched, or one of them would have wiped the other off the map by now. The only way Calathan could cause this kind of panic is if they stripped all the peasants from the fields, and that could ruin both countries."

"Is war supposed to be sensible all of a sudden?" Sera asked.

"In this country, it is. They've been at it for a long time, so they've developed a lot of rules. Both countries want to win, but neither one wants to absolutely destroy the other. After all, who wants to conquer a wasteland?"

A nagging feeling had been troubling Falorn. "Could it all be about the cards?" he asked.

"I was wondering about that myself," said Zaren. "I wonder just what it is we're riding into."

"How many cards are there in this country?"

"Not counting ours? Stennet has at least one, the Queen's got a bunch . . . I think that's all, though. I don't know of any in Calathan. How about you, Sera?"

"I'm sure I don't know," she replied. "I've never been in either country, although my father's visited both of them more than once."

"Call it five or six, then. If this whole thing is about the cards, they're not going to be real anxious to let another six cards walk away."

"I guess not," said Falorn. "I hope this Stennet is a good friend, because we could sure use one."

"He is. Or at least he was, and I don't think there's been any reason for him to change his mind."

"Not even the cards?"

"Not even the cards. He's happy with the one he's got, but I don't think he cares much about the rest of them."

"It would be nice if there were a few more cardholders out there like that."

"It would," said Zaren, "but I'm not sure you need to worry. They all seem to be flocking to you. Maybe I should be watching my back."

"Not likely."

"Not likely," Zaren agreed. "At least not until you learn to stop fighting so fair. One of these days giving someone a fair chance is going to get you killed."

"It's all I know how to do."

"He's right, Falorn," Sera said. "You should be more careful. Not everybody out there is as nice as you."

"I think I've figured out *that* much."

"Some days it doesn't show."

He didn't reply, and let the thread of conversation die. They rode in silence for a while, but the unfamiliarity of the country soon got them talking again.

"Are any of the roads paved here?" Falorn asked.

"Near a few of the cities they are, but only for a few miles out. There's not a lot of long-distance trade going on here like in your Free Duchies. The cities are small, and most of the power comes from the nobles and their lands. Even the ones who live in the cities make most of their money from land and peasants; they've all got a castle or two somewhere."

Falorn felt a little uncomfortable at the talk of peasants.

"Do the nobles work at all?" he asked. "They can't just live in the city all the time."

"They'll work now, with a war on. It's about all some of them are good at, but the nobles hereabouts are very good at war."

"I guess they'd have to be good at it, if the country is always fighting."

"No," said Sera, "they *want* to be good at it. They like it, and they don't much care who else gets killed along with them."

"No . . . they don't," said Zaren. "I think you're right, if a little unkind."

"Of course I'm right. I almost married one just like them; don't you think I know the type? I'm not sure you're any different—you're a mercenary, after all."

Zaren seemed to take no offense. "I am a mercenary," he said, "even if I retired for a few years to turn innkeeper. The difference is that I fight other people's battles for them. I don't start battles of my own. And I don't take anyone innocent into battle with me; every other mercenary earns the same blood money that I do."

"I'm not sure I see the difference," said Sera.

"You don't have to. It's my money and my blood. I'll do what I choose with them."

"Sera!" said Falorn. "He saved our lives, and he gave up a lot to do it."

"I know. I'm sorry," she said, smiling but still looking a little miserable. "This place just brings back a lot of bad feelings for me. It's too much like home."

"It's nothing," said Zaren. "It takes more than that to insult me. You'll know when I'm upset."

They first saw the Summer Palace late the next morning, several hours after breaking camp. High, tapering towers loomed above the flat farmland of western Cathan, visible for miles away. The weather remained balmy, and sunlight glittered off hundreds of points of distant metal, from brass-roofed towers to the helmets of drilling troops in the fields surrounding the palace walls.

As they approached, Falorn began to realize the enormity of the Summer Palace.

"That's not a castle, it's a city," he finally said.

"You're not far off," Sera replied. "The whole court moves here in the summer—king, queen, ministers, courtiers, soldiers, everyone. Things happen a little more slowly than in the winter, but this might as well be the capital city of Cathan right now."

"What about the forests?" Two large stands of trees could be seen behind the city, one in neat, evenly spaced rows of level trees, and the other in a state of apparently wild disarray.

"One of them has to be an orchard. I imagine the other is a hunting preserve, stocked with sport animals."

"All that just so people can hunt for sport?"

"All that just so the nobles can hunt. They'll hang any commoner they catch poaching the royal deer."

He looked around in amazement. Ahead, Zaren rode with their escort. At the previous evening's camp, the mercenary and the cavalry sergeant had discovered they shared experience in several battles. Now the two men talked happily about campaigning and weapons, while the four younger troopers listened in respectful silence. The Helleinen remained a few horse lengths behind Falorn and Sera, conversing in their own language.

Low green hedges divided fields of crops, in contrast to the stone walls farmers in the Free Duchies built from the rocks unearthed by their plows. The hedges looked insubstantial, more an aesthetic barrier than a real discouragement to wind or animals. Despite the earlier assurances about traveling conditions, the road remained unpaved earth, rutted and hard-packed by years of heavy traffic. *Aren't there any rocks in this part of the country?* Falorn wondered. *We're not all that far from the mountains.*

Only very young or very old people worked in the fields, just as in the more hilly country they had passed through. The farmland seemed to grow more fertile as it flattened.

Soldiers filled the grounds that surrounded the high, whitewashed walls of the palace. Anything green had been stamped out under the boots of foot soldiers drilling with halberds or partisans. Light cavalry troopers fought with wooden sabers in the midst of a devastated topiary garden. Mailed riders, lances lowered and their warhorses stirrup-to-stirrup in close formation, charged imaginary opponents across a yellowing field of flattened grass.

"They seem well armed," said Falorn, "and there are so many of them. . . ."

"Less than a thousand, "Sera replied. "They are well armed, but there's no use in holding back weapons now. They have to be really desperate before they let the soldiers start tearing up the Royal Gardens."

"I figured that."

"No, I mean *really* desperate. When you rule a country, symbols are important. You have to keep reminding dukes like my father that you're still bigger and stronger and better than them, or else they'll get together and pull you down. That's how my family got to be dukes; my grandfather was a baron who picked the right side in a civil war. Before you let the soldiers start trampling on symbols of affluence and culture, you have to be *really* worried."

"I'll keep that in mind when someone gives me a country to rule."

Sera gave him an odd look. "You shouldn't joke about that. Stranger things have happened."

"Sera, stranger things have happened *to me* in the last few weeks. I'd be happy to find a country where everybody wasn't chasing me. I certainly don't want one of my own. I'm not sure I really even want these cards."

"Don't say that. People would kill for even one of those cards."

"I know, remember? I've met some of them. Some of them have tried."

"That wasn't what I meant."

"I know. Actually, the cards are starting to grow on me. I have to admit, they add a certain amount of excitement to my life."

"You did leave home looking for excitement."

"It wasn't the smartest thing I ever did."

"Really?" She seemed honestly puzzled. "Would you go back if you could?"

"I don't know. I guess not. I was looking for something other than the same life my father had, and everyone else in my family had. I just found a lot more than I expected to, that's all."

"You found me," she said, coyly more interested in teasing than in calling Falorn on his half-truths about leaving home.

"No, *you* found me."

"If you had stayed home, you would never have met me."

"That's true," he said. He reached across the space which separated their mounts to take her hand. "What about you?" he asked, after a pause. "If you could take everything back and start over, would you do it?"

"I'm not sure. I like to think I would handle things a little better. But if I had the cards in my hands again . . . I just don't know. They made me do some awful things."

Falorn thought about Zaren's comments when he'd explained about the cards. *Did they really make you do those things? Or did you have those tendencies inside you all the time?* He didn't really want to believe that. He liked the new, friendlier Sera. *I want to believe that the way she acts now is the person she really is, when her family and cards don't force her to do awful things.* But a part of him still had lingering doubts.

Sera glanced at him quizzically. Falorn realized he'd paused too long in the conversation.

"I'm sorry," said Falorn. "I didn't mean to hit a sore spot."

"There are a lot of sore spots in this country. It's a sore, tired land."

Falorn didn't know what she meant, but he nodded anyway.

While he and Sera talked, the sergeant had sent a trooper ahead. Now more soldiers emerged from behind the walls of the palace to receive them. The new troopers wore the same colors as the escort, and the soldiers greeted each other familiarly.

As they passed through the massive, ornamental gateway arch of the Summer Palace, Falorn thought back to the first gateway he'd crossed, into the festival at Roicenet. It seemed like much longer than a few weeks past, as if he'd lived a lifetime between then and now.

The palace walls concealed dozens of buildings; maybe hundreds if he counted every blacksmith's shed and wainwright's shop as well as the soaring stone cathedral, massive keep, and all the hulking, fortified structures which surrounded them. Everywhere, people scurried along the smoothly paved walkways and broad lawns that covered the scattered grounds between the buildings. Falorn saw a few soldiers, officers mostly, but the vast majority of the insects scuttling around the grounds of the Summer Palace did so unarmed: liveried servants in cloth of silver and the colors of a hundred noble families; ladies' maids in massive, billowing, pastel-colored dresses, their powdered hair heaped in endless artificial ringlets on top of their heads so they seemed more like queens than the servants of nobles; courtiers in clothing that cost more than a suit of armor, with tiny smallswords dangling at their sides in glittering, gem-encrusted sheaths; workmen in leather aprons, spitting at the sight of the courtiers (who in their turn, filled the air with rainclouds of perfume droplets from handheld ewers and crystal decanters, to purify the sweat-soaked air as they walked by).

"Who *are* they?" Falorn asked Sera about the courtiers as the travelers dismounted, under the watchful eyes of their now-enlarged escort.

"Younger sons of nobles mostly, come from the city to attend the summer court. Probably they're here for officer's commissions."

"*Them?*"

"You'd be surprised. Not all officers look like Zaren, you know."

"I'd be a little more confident about this war if they did."

"A lot of soldiers would rather follow a noble. Most of the troops on both sides are probably levies from noble lands, led by their local baron. Besides, most of the courtiers who got commissions are probably at the front already. What you see here are the leftovers."

Falorn wrinkled his nose at the smell of too-strong perfume. "Some days I'm glad I'm not a noble."

"Don't be," said Zaren, walking up between Falorn and Sera and putting a hand on each of their shoulders. "It opens up a lot of doors for you if you're noble, and helps keep your head on your shoulders."

"What do you mean?" Falorn asked.

"If they catch one of these pretty things on the battlefield, what do you think they do to him?"

"I don't know. Kill him, I guess."

"No, never. You, they kill. Me, they kill. These things,they save, and sell them back to their rich parents. Never kill a noble if you can help it, unless you know his family's poor. Hold him for ransom."

"Is that a rule?"

"That's a rule. People who kill nobles are never popular. Not even with their own side."

"I'll try to remember that, in case it ever comes up."

"It will," Zaren said cheerfully. "You have a lot of nobles as enemies."

They walked toward the main keep with an escort of eight soldiers and an officer, all members of the Queen's Own Guard. The officer, a tall woman of about twenty, with a round face and shoulder-length chestnut hair, did not introduce herself. As soon as the horses had been unloaded and handed over to a quartet of overworked stable boys, the soldiers formed up, four in front and four behind, leaving the travelers little choice but to shoulder their saddlebags and walk wherever their escort wanted to take them.

The servants made way on the wide stone path, although many of the courtiers did not, forcing the guards to silently walk around them. Falorn marveled at the towering cathedral, with its polished black marble facing and intricate, fluted architecture. But he had little time to admire it before they reached the entrance to the squat, blocky keep, which dominated the center of the palace grounds like a massive stone bulldog lying head down and sullen in the center of the path, too stubborn to move.

Two guards in blue and cloth-of-gold stamped halberd-butts in salute as the travelers and their escort passed into the gatehouse, which extended for nearly forty feet into the keep. They walked through a central arch the height and width of two tall men. Falorn looked up and caught his breath as he passed beneath iron spikes as thick as his arms. The raised iron portcullis above their heads looked too heavy to hold for more than a moment or two, even with the strongest of counterweights; its metal spikes gave off a dull, oily sheen. Rows of murder-holes pocked the ceiling of the arch behind the portcullis, while thin arrow slits lined the walls at regular intervals on either side. At the far end of the gatehouse a thick, ironbound wooden door stood ajar.

The long, wide hallway into which they passed looked martial in character. A red rug covered nearly the entire width of the floor, showing only a hand's breadth of polished hardwood on either side. The rug extended for the length of the hall, passing underneath the closed double doors nearly sixty paces away. Three long tapestries, separated by branching hallways, hung on either wall, each trimmed in the same blood-colored red as the rug. The tapestries depicted religious and martial scenes, which looked stiff to Falorn's eye. He supposed they pictured significant moments in Cathan's long history. In front of the tapestries stood mannequins and stands displaying armor and weapons. He saw only the first suit of armor clearly; it looked very old, and a dozen unrepaired holes marred the symmetry of its brass rings. A sword hung on the left side of the mannequin, in a tattered sheath of old cloth and cracked leather. At the right side of the armor stood a tall spear with a long, brass head. A tattered blue pennant hung limply from the spear, its insignia hidden in its tears and folds.

Before Falorn could look more closely, the party turned left into the nearest of the halls. They passed a long series of closed doors before the hallway turned to the right. An open door in the corner looked into a guardroom; Falorn saw eight or ten soldiers crouched around the center of the room, and heard the rattle of a dice-cup. Other soldiers worked on their blades, or polished armor with rags. One man sat in a corner reading a small, cloth-bound book.

They walked down the hallway to the right, away from the noise of the guardhouse. Boots clicked on the polished hardwood floors, with no rugs laid down to muffle the noise. Here and there a painting or small tapestry covered a patch of wall, but mostly they walked through a stark white plaster corridor, broken only by identical dark wooden doors at maddeningly regular intervals. Servants scurried around them, rushing in and out of doors like so many marionettes dragged on and off the stage at a carnival puppet show. Everything about the keep seemed square and symmetrical, as if the building had exceeded its allotment of curves in the massive gateway arch. Falorn thought of the Baron of Golden Reeds's impenetrable rabbit-warren castle and smiled. *No one*, he thought, *would have trouble finding their way around the hallways of this place, even if I'm not sure how they tell one room from another.*

The officer stopped in front of yet another unmarked door and produced a long brass key, which she inserted in the unadorned lock-plate and turned easily. The lock clicked open and the door slid silently inward, as if it hung in midair rather than on oiled brass hinges. Falorn wondered how she could tell one room from another with no apparent markings on the door at all. One of the soldiers stepped into the room as if to check for hidden dangers or other occupants. He returned in a minute and whispered something in the officer's ear.

"Go in and prepare yourselves," she said, the first words she had spoken to them. "You will be brought before the Royal Court presently and asked to account for yourselves." She stood aside to allow the travelers to enter the small suite of rooms. None of the soldiers followed. The door closed silently behind them.

Falorn felt no surprise at all when he heard the click of the lock engaging.

26

Feathers, Ruffles, and Ribbons

"Don't bother to unpack. We're not staying here long," said Zaren.

"What do you mean?" asked Sera.

"Look around. Do you see any beds?"

Sera didn't reply. None of the three small rooms in the suite lacked furniture, but nothing suggested more than a temporary visit. Thin strips of dark wood paneled the walls of the central room in which they stood, while the plaster walls of the two adjoining rooms had been painted light brown. No daylight penetrated into the ground floor room, behind the eight-foot-thick walls of the keep, but a dozen oil lamps scattered between the rooms lit the suite almost as brightly as daylight would have.

The central room contained a wide table along the back wall, and several couches and chairs. Platters and bowls of cold food covered the table: sausages, ham, a small half-wheel of cheese, fresh fruit, berries, a bowl of cream, pitchers of wine and ale. Silver mugs and bowls sat in an untidy stack at the far end of the table, as if silver had little value in this place. The wood of the furniture, as well as the silver and brass of the tableware and lanterns, all glittered with an almost unnatural shine, as if someone polished them endlessly. Falorn felt afraid to touch anything, for fear of ruining its marvelous sheen.

Each of the side rooms contained a small table piled with towels and an enormous copper tub. Steam rose from each of the tubs; someone must have changed the water only moments before they arrived. Along the far wall of each room hung a polished brass mirror. A shelf underneath each mirror held a washbasin, brushes, pots of creams, and jars of scented powders. Below each shelf sat several buckets of water, as well as a small empty tub for drainage.

Cirque muttered something that sounded suspiciously like an elven prayer of thanksgiving, and headed into one of the two bathing rooms, closing the door behind him. Falorn gestured for Sera to go first, and she smiled faintly. She dragged her saddlebag into the room with her. Falorn wondered what other clothing she'd acquired in the elven hunting lodge.

Falorn set to work cleaning his boots while he waited for his turn at one of the baths.

"Don't bother with that," said Ryal. "Watch." The Hellein's hands began to move oddly. Try as he might, Falorn couldn't follow the motions. Suddenly, Ryal clapped his hands together. Falorn jumped at the sudden noise.

"The last part was just for effect," Ryal admitted.

Falorn looked at his clothes. They looked exactly as they had when he first picked them up at the bathhouse. All the dust and grit of the trail had vanished, along with dozens of scratches and mars from travel. A smooth, even finish replaced the scuffs and wear on his boots. Even the new scabbards for his knife and sword shone, the dirt gone from their delicately etched leatherwork.

"Thank you," said Falorn. "I feel almost too dirty to be wearing them now."

"You're not," Ryal answered, "I cleaned you too."

"Could've used that a few times on the trail," said Zaren.

"It's not something to waste on the trail. All magic is draining, to some degree, even something as easy as this. It ages you: maybe only a few days for a simple charm like the one I just used, but an added burden of time nonetheless."

"What do you care?" said Zaren. "You're an elf. You live forever."

"We age more slowly, but we still age. You will feel the years long before I do, but I do feel them. I'm glad enough to use my art, but it isn't a toy."

Despite Ryal's words, the Hellein cleaned Zaren as well before going into the bath after Cirque exited.

"What about yourself?" Falorn asked. "Can't you cast the spell on yourself?"

"Of course I can. I'll cast it on my clothes and on Sera's after I'm done. But I like baths, and I've been too long away from the bathhouse. I wouldn't bother with the spell, unless Cirque dirtied the bathwater beyond use."

Falorn thought for a minute and decided the Hellein was right about baths. As soon as Sera emerged, he entered the second bathing room—even though Zaren laughed at his foolishness.

Two hours passed before the same nameless officer came to retrieve them.

"It's time," the woman said. "Leave your packs and weapons here." Four guards walked behind as they followed the officer down the arrow-straight corridors.

They returned to the red-carpeted central hallway, but now the double doors at its far end stood open, revealing a longer, wider hallway beyond. Blue-bordered tapestries lined the second hallway. Dozens of life-sized marble statues replaced the posed armored mannequins of the previous chamber. Again, a number of corridors branched from doorways set between the tapestries, but this time the officer walked straight onward, leading them to a second pair of double doors at the hall's far end.

A pair of guards in blue velvet tunics and silvered armor guarded the door. Their halberds glistened under layers of silver filigree. The soldiers seemed to expect their arrival; they nodded to the officer, and she pushed through one of the double doors.

Only Sera's gentle prodding kept Falorn moving as they entered the glittering room where the king and queen of Cathan held court. Vivid blue light streamed downward through half a hundred stained glass windows set in the high, vaulted ceiling, four stories above their heads. Carved wooden railings edged two upper galleries, which surrounded and overhung the edges of the room on three sides, leaving only the walls behind the twin thrones free of seats and benches. A towering blue curtain covered that back wall, its golden center filled with the lion, goat, and serpent of Cathan's coat-of-arms, each of the animals nearly twenty feet long.

People crowded the lower part of the room, although only a few common soldiers, workmen, and servants populated the upper levels. The chamber glowed with reflected light from acres of glittery gold and silver cloth. Bright colors, giant feathers, ruffles, garish ribbons, long wigs, and a hundred other adornments filled the room. Falorn could barely distinguish the nobles and courtiers beneath the costumes at first. The bright colors and the thick smell of competing perfumes over-whelmed him; he felt as if he'd stepped into a carnival masque, or a mag-ical faerie kingdom, rather than the court of a country at war.

As the officer walked them between the rows of benches toward the thrones, Falorn noticed odd contrasts in the crowd. Mingled among the courtiers, he could pick out a few men and women in simpler clothing, and one or two in battered armor who looked as if they might be old com-patriots of Zaren. He saw monks of a half-dozen unfamiliar orders, pre-dominantly thick-bearded men in dark gray, red-trimmed robes. Most of the monks looked away as he passed by, but a few scowled. Falorn won-dered what offended them until he happened to glance behind, and saw equally dark expressions on the faces of the two Helleinen.

Falorn looked ahead to the thrones as he continued to walk forward. The two massive, gilded chairs, their backs standing twice the height of a tall man, had been carved in the shape of a lion and lioness. The king sat to Falorn's left, beneath the snarling muzzle of a thickly maned lion. He looked small in the great throne, a thin, clean-shaven man with whiten-ing hair, wrapped in a bulky mantle of heavy blue velvet, lined with sleek, silvery fur of some sort. A long-handled gold mace lay across his lap, and he wore the royal seal on a thin chain of golden links around his neck.

The queen sat to the king's left. She wore little jewelry, besides a sin-gle gold necklace and signet ring. She was dressed in a thigh-length white tunic embroidered in blue, which she wore beneath a velvet doublet laced up the front with gold cord. Pale brown hose of soft doeskin cov-ered her legs. She looked very little like the queens depicted in the hall-way tapestries. Her face bore the marks of wind and sun, and her hands looked large, and roughened. As she turned to speak to her husband, Falorn saw long brown hair hanging halfway down her back in a single, five-stranded braid, bound with a piece of blue silk. Both king and queen sat on their thrones bareheaded; neither wore a crown or cap-of-office.

In front of the thrones, an arc of benches faced the audience from behind three long, narrow tables. Ministers and advisers crowded these central benches. Most wore plain, if finely made, clothing. A few wore robes. None dressed in the fanciful clothing of the courtiers who crowded the chamber. Something seemed odd about the lone rank of advisers, and Falorn only realized what as he drew close to their tables. Women filled nearly half of the ministers' benches, but only a few of the hundreds of audience members were women, and those few mostly peered down from the commoners' galleries.

An older woman in gray gestured them forward with a finger; their escort melted away as Falorn and the others stepped up to the ministers' table. Beyond them, the king and queen seemed to take no notice.

"I am Lord Dianeme of Stillwater, Chancellor to Her Majesty the Queen," the woman said in a low, strong voice. "You have been called here to explain your presence to Their Royal Highnesses." The chancellor wore a light gray tunic beneath a darker cape. A silver hawk fastened the cape at her throat. She kept her gray-brown hair long, and bound behind her in a simple horsetail.

"I want you to do exactly as I say. Bow deeply when you are announced. When His Majesty asks who you are, state your name and home country. Do not give any titles or other information. When he asks why you are here, tell him that you came because you felt it was your duty to fight oppression. That's all. Do not say anything more. When he dismisses you, walk backward, without ever turning your back, and take a seat somewhere in the audience. Someone will meet you afterward and take you to your rooms, where your weapons and possessions will be waiting for you. Later this evening or tomorrow morning, you will be sent for, and other matters can be discussed then. That's everything. Now take a step back, and wait for your signal."

She motioned them back a few steps. Falorn realized that the whole time he'd been in the room, one of the ministers had been speaking, his back turned to the audience as he addressed the twin thrones. With all the noise in the room, Falorn could barely hear the man's speech from a dozen paces away, but the queen seemed to be listening, and four scribes positioned just behind the array of advisers frantically took down every word, their quills shaking and dancing across wide sheets of thick paper.

The speech went on for another half hour, although Falorn made out only a few of the words, and none of the meaning. Finally, the minister bowed deeply to each of the thrones before him and resumed his seat. The hall fell eerily silent as the king scratched his face and responded.

"Wise words, and well spoken indeed, Duke Southwell. Your erudition and articulation do honor to Our court, as always. We will not neglect the ways of prudence and caution, but nevertheless, We shall take your bold proposal under consideration. You have Our thanks for your fine words, and for your noble spirit, which do credit to one of the noblest lines in Our land."

The audience exploded into raucous cheers when the king finished speaking. The ministers cheered as well. Even the scribes had put down their pens when the king began speaking. Falorn wanted to turn and ask Sera what the king's words meant, but he didn't dare while in front of so many noble and royal eyes. Lord Dianeme gestured for them to move forward slightly even before the applause quieted. When the hall quieted again, the king looked around, and seemed to notice them for the first time.

"Who comes before Us?" he asked, not unkindly.

Falorn bowed, as deeply as he could without falling over. "My name is Falorn, your majesty, from Tidewater in the Free Duchies." The king nodded, and continued to nod as each of the others introduced themselves, although he looked a little puzzled at the Helleinen faces.

"Those are honorable names all. And why have you come before Us, traveling from such great distances to visit Our court?"

"Your majesty, we felt it was our duty to fight oppression," said Falorn.

"Fine words! Fine words indeed! It is every man's duty to fight oppression. I wish all of Our own subjects shared your ardor. You will find much to fight for here, and manifold glories to be fairly won on the fields of honor. Be welcome, all of you, to Our court." The king nodded again. Falorn began walking backward carefully as the king's attention shifted to one of his ministers. He saw the scribes pick up their quills again as the adviser stood to speak.

They found places near the back of the audience. No one seemed to pay much attention to them; few courtiers' eyes left the king, not even for a moment. Falorn tried to listen to the ministers as they spoke, but he could understand very little over the noise of the crowd. When the king spoke he could hear clearly, but understood even less.

He felt a light touch on his shoulder and looked up. He expected to see Sera, but instead found an unfamiliar young blond woman standing next to him. He glanced around hurriedly, but saw none of his companions. *Where did they go?* he wondered. *Why didn't they say anything?* His hand dropped reflexively to his belt before he remembered leaving his sword and knife behind. He could still feel the heat of the cards against his chest.

"Excuse me," the young woman said softly. "Could you come with me, please?"

"Who are you? What happened to the others?" He asked quietly so as not to disturb the Royal Court, but he felt an edge in his voice.

"They are probably in their rooms now. You will be too, if you come with me."

"Come where?"

"Please, I'll answer all your questions in a few minutes. Just come with me now."

She turned and walked a few steps, and Falorn followed. The woman looked back over her shoulder; when she saw him close behind she continued walking, not toward the main door, but around the back edge of the room, under the overhanging gallery. She opened a small door, nearly invisible against the shadow-covered side wall of the audience chamber. Falorn walked silently behind her, watching their route as closely as he could; he hoped the blue thief card might give him a few seconds' warning if someone waited in ambush up ahead.

He found himself in a much narrower corridor than the ones he had traveled previously. Dents and wide scratches marred the unvarnished wooden floor. The wall lamps sputtered and smoked, fueled by fat or tallow rather than smooth-burning oil. Doors and trapdoors spotted the walls like a pox. The hall seemed to be a servants' corridor of some sort, to allow quiet access to and retreat from key points in the keep.

After several twists and turns his guide opened another door, this one leading onto a larger corridor. Blue rugs covered much of the floor. Here and there a brightly painted shield or a pair of crossed greatswords broke up the symmetry of the white walls, but mostly they walked through bare hallway and past closed doors of darkly stained wood. A few open doors hinted tantalizingly at the wonders that might lie behind them. Falorn saw a wall covered from floor to high ceiling in leatherbound volumes through one cracked door, while another revealed a glimpse of a clear crystal globe the width of his arm, housed in an elaborate frame which glittered in the lamplight like the purest gold.

They seemed to be walking toward a wide set of double doors where the hall ended.

"That's the main dining hall up ahead," the woman said over her shoulder. "We won't be passing there now, but you'll probably eat there sometimes. Come this way." She turned left into a branching hallway.

Falorn followed her into a guardroom, where a pair of men in chain-mail sat on a bench polishing a pile of tarnished helmets. An open side door revealed a small armory, where another soldier worked on a broken shield. Falorn could see several racks of spears in the weapons-room, but little else except battered or damaged equipment. A heavy wooden door bound with iron filled much of the far wall.

"Hello there, Elise," one of the armored men looked up and said.

"Hello, yourself," answered the blond woman. "Is everyone else upstairs?"

"Have been for a while. They're about the only ones in the tower except the guards, with all the wizards and generals off at the front."

"We'll all be at the front soon enough, No need to hurry it."

"S'pose you're right."

The woman walked over to the door and tugged on the great brass ring at the center of the door. It swung open reluctantly, slow and silent on oversized brass hinges. Within, a wide staircase of unadorned stone curved gently upward. A thick wooden bar leaned against a wall, ready to be placed on the matching rings set into door and wall in case the tower needed to defend against invaders attacking from the guardroom.

The staircase wound lazily around the inside of the broad tower. They walked up only a single level before passing through an unlocked door and into a short hallway, which ended in a round room at the tower's center. Like spokes from a cartwheel's hub, six doors led from the unpainted stone chamber, including the entrance to the hall.

"These rooms are for you and your friends. I thought you might want to see that they were safe before I explained what's going on. Take a few minutes if you like, and then meet me here."

"Thanks." Falorn walked to one of the thick, oak-bound doors and knocked.

"Who's that?" he heard from inside, in Zaren's voice.

"It's me. Falorn."

"Oh, come on in then."

Falorn pulled the door open slightly and slipped into the room. Zaren and two soldiers sat at a table, its top an irregular slab of polished black marble. An odd collection of mismatched coins filled the center of the table. One of the soldiers cursed and dropped a small stack of playing cards onto the table face down in front of him. The second guard ruefully put his own cards down as well, shaking his head. Zaren nodded to them both, said something Falorn couldn't quite make out, and scooped up the pile of coins, depositing it somewhere off the table. He looked up at Falorn as the first soldier gathered all the cards together and began to shuffle.

"I hoped you'd show up soon. Tersse and Khirel here were just showing me how to play a few of their country's games. I've had a bit of beginner's luck. Care to join us?"

"Sorry. Next time maybe." *Beginner's luck. Right. Didn't he say he fought in this country for years?*

"Anytime is fine. See you later tonight."

"I hope so." Falorn glanced around the room briefly before leaving. A tall, narrow window looked out onto the fields and ruined topiary in front of the Summer Palace. A comfortable-looking mattress covered with white sheets sat in an undecorated wooden frame. Zaren's saddlebags and weapons lay on top of the mattress, next to a folded quilt. A washbasin and bucket sat against opposite walls, but the room contained no other furniture.

Falorn found Cirque and Ryal together in the next room, together with an unsmiling guard, who stood stiffly against the wall as far as he could from the Helleinen.

"We had a second guard, too," Ryal explained, interrupting a conversation in his own language when Falorn entered the chamber, "but he left as soon as I came in here to talk to Cirque. I don't think they like Helleinen much. This one won't even talk to us."

"I think the other one is in with Zaren. There were two men playing cards with him."

"I hope they're enjoying themselves immensely."

"Zaren is."

"That's even better. I think the guards are supposed to be telling us something, but it's hard to tell when they won't speak to us."

"I think they are, too. The woman who brought me here said that she had to tell me some things. I just wanted to make sure everyone was all right first."

"We're fine. Comfortable beds, nice rooms, good company to stand in the corner and ignore us. Whatever it is we're supposed to know, tell us what it is later."

"I will. We can all meet in the central room or something."

"I don't think we'll all fit, if we each have a guard. Maybe each of the guards could take turns standing here and ignoring us, while the others waited downstairs. Then we'd have plenty of room."

The Helleinen resumed their conversation as he turned to leave. The guard glowered at Falorn.

An unfamiliar woman's voice answered when he knocked on the next door. He entered, and found Sera sitting on the bed next to a tall, lithe, black-haired woman with piercing blue eyes. The woman wore thigh boots, a black tunic, and dark blue hose. A long, thin rapier hung at her side.

"Hi, Falorn," said Sera. "Is everything all right?"

"I think so. I was just coming to ask you the same question."

"I'm fine. But I'm in the middle of talking. Do you think you could come back later?"

"I can't stay anyway. I have to go do some talking myself."

"Oh. Enjoy it, then. And I'll see you before dinner." She blew him a kiss as he turned back to the door.

27
The Rapist and the Wraith

Elise waited for Falorn in the hall. She stood facing away from him when he exited Sera's room, as if trying not to pry. Her broad shoulders showed prominently even beneath the light cloak she wore. Blond hair hung down only as far as the nape of her neck, where most of it had been cropped off raggedly. A single, very thin braid hung a third of the way down her back, slightly off center to her left side.

She didn't look like a servant, and she certainly appeared unlike the nobles he'd seen wandering the halls and paths of the Summer Palace. He wondered who she was.

She turned around, as if sensing someone watching her. She smiled when she saw his eyes on her hair.

"It's a mess, mostly," she said. "Lord Dianeme is always getting angry about the soldier's cuts I give it any time it gets in my way."

"I think it looks nice," Falorn said.

"Thanks, but it *is* a mess. You probably just got distracted by the rattail."

"The braid? I've never seen anything like it."

"I've had it since I was a little girl. I never let the rest of my hair grow, but I always keep the rattail this way."

"Is it a family tradition or something?"

"No. My mother and sister both have long, straight hair. I just decided to braid a little piece of my hair one day, and I never stopped."

She pointed toward an unopened door. "That's your room. We can talk in there."

"Sure, if you'd like."

"Actually, I've been ordered to. But I'd be happy enough to tell you what's going on anyway. Or at least as much as I can before dinner. You've all been invited to dine with the King and Queen tonight."

"I'm honored," Falorn said, pulling the door open and stepping inside.

"You should be," said Elise. She closed the door behind herself as she followed after Falorn.

The room resembled the other tower chambers he had seen. The marble-topped table might have been a twin to Zaren's cardtable, and the unadorned bed looked the same as well. His belongings sat on the bed, seemingly intact. Late afternoon light poured in from a wide window bay with a high, arched window.

"I like the light," he said. "Why is the window so much wider in here? The other rooms just had arrow slits."

"Look through it. It looks down on the inside of the walls. This room's not in any danger of being shot at during a siege."

He walked over and sat in the window seat. Looking downward, he saw a section of the paths within the palace walls, now nearly empty except for servants and workmen. He looked around for the cathedral, but it lay out of sight, beyond his angle of view.

"I guess all the people in the fancy clothes are still at the audience?"

"I hope so. Lord Dianeme asked that all of you be brought here before the audience ended, with as little fuss and attention as possible. If any of those courtiers started to think you might be important or might be able to talk with Her Majesty, none of you would ever get any peace. A lot of them are spies, anyway."

"Spies? In the court?"

"Why not? Nothing important ever happens in court, so Her Majesty doesn't much care. She knows who they are."

"Why doesn't somebody do something about it?"

"They may be spies, but they're still of noble birth, mostly. You can't just kill them. It's easier just to keep them here, where they can be watched. When the fighting starts . . . people have been known to die during wars."

"Even nobles?"

"Even nobles. Not as often, but even nobles."

"What's so important about us that the king and queen of a country the size of Cathan would give us personal attention?"

"I don't know. I think *you* probably do, but that's between you and Her Majesty. My job is to keep you safe, to let you know what's going on, and to get you to wherever Her Majesty and Lord Dianeme want you."

"I guess I do have an idea of why the queen wants to see us," Falorn said, unconsciously fingering the pouch at his chest.

"She may just want to know what you've seen. Information is important, especially on the eve of a war."

"We didn't know we were walking into a war. The first we heard about it was when we came down out of the mountains."

"There hasn't been very much fighting yet, just skirmishing between cavalry troops and scouts. The real war is still coming, as soon as the armies finish gathering."

"But hasn't there been fighting between Cathan and Calathan for years?"

"This isn't just between Cathan and Calathan. Calathan's army isn't much bigger than ours, and they're not as good, to my mind. But this year, we captured soldiers from the Seven Kingdoms in raids as soon as campaigning season started. The queen has her own information sources, and they've told her for certain what every trooper already thought was true: There's an army from the Seven Kingdoms on its way, along with every soldier Calathan can put in the field. We've got everyone who can handle a sword or spear heading for the border defenses, and there will still be twice as many of them."

"So why not attack now, before all of their army is in place?"

"Because we'd lose. Calathan's border is fortified too. We'd lose so many soldiers taking their castles that we'd have nothing left to fight the armies off with. Our only chance is to hold the border castles and the ground between them with every soldier, wizard, and peasant spearman we can put in the field."

"And women too, I guess."

"No, not really." Elise sighed. "Women fight in the Queen's Own

Guard, but that's the only unit under Her Majesty's direct control. Most of the army won't fight beside women soldiers, much less recruit them and train them. The women you see around the palace, and on patrols in the queen's personal lands—those are the only armed women you'll see in this country. If we lose this war, the Seven Kingdoms will kill the lot of us, or worse."

"Why?"

"The Seven Kingdoms is a funny place. Or maybe it's Cathan that's funny. If you give a serf a weapon in any of the Seven Kingdoms, they'll hang you. But if you give a woman a weapon, even if she's of noble birth, the inquisitors will impale you on a spike in the nearest public square and leave you to die. If they catch a woman with a weapon, no matter who she is, they scourge off her skin with hot combs."

"How can people live there?" Falorn wondered about the Hook in Roicenet, or the inquisitors in Windford. *How can people live anywhere?* he thought to himself, without saying anything aloud. *How can people live anywhere at all?*

"The same way they live everywhere else."

Elise leaned back in the chair she sat on, and shook her hair in an unconscious motion. She had taken off her cloak and hung it on the chair back; she wore a loose blue tunic, slightly faded, that looked like dyed silk. It gapped open slightly as she sat, revealing a thin gold chain with an enameled rose pendant. The shiny blue cloth molded around her wide-set shoulder blades, and hinted at the outlines of small breasts beneath. Green britches of soft-looking deerskin loosely covered her muscular legs; polished black riding boots gripped her calves, with the britches tucked into the boot-tops.

Falorn caught himself staring and turned away, looking out the window once more.

"We need all the help we can get, Falorn," Elise said. "If there's something you can do that will help us in this war, you've got to tell the Queen."

"I'll do what I can," Falorn said, wondering what she expected from him, "but you understand I didn't come here to fight in a war."

"No, I don't understand that. You're here, you're armed, and you've walked into the middle of a war. Why else would you be here?"

"I'll be happy to tell the queen about everything I've seen that might help her. But I don't know what else I can offer. I can't offer you my friends' lives."

"No, of course not," she said, although she sounded uncertain. "We all do what we can. It's just that the stakes are higher for some of us than for others. They'll never let the Queen live if they win this war. They might leave her husband on the throne, but they'll won't leave Her Majesty alive for a moment after they enter the palace."

"Elise?"

"Yes?"

"What was it that Lord Dianeme asked you to tell me?"

"I have to prepare you for dinner. You need to know where to sit, what to say and not to say, the orders of precedence, that sort of thing."

"Can we do that now?"

"Of course. My apologies. I'm afraid the war's weighing too heavily on my mind."

"I understand. But I don't want to embarrass you at the table tonight, either."

He only had a few minutes to talk with the others in the central hall, before Elise and the other guards insisted they begin walking back down the tower stairs toward the dining room. Sera seemed to like whatever her dark-haired guard had told her; she wore a satisfied expression as they walked the stone corridors, like a woman returning home after a long absence.

The loudness of the dining hall astonished Falorn. A dozen or more long tables crowded the smoky room, dimly lit despite hundreds of torches in wall sconces and additional illumination from silver candelabra on the tables. People filled every empty space in the room. Overdressed courtiers packed the benches of the center tables so closely that there seemed to be no room left for food. Soldiers and skilled workmen sat more easily at the outer tables, while everywhere servants milled about, bringing things and taking them away again with seeming randomness.

One had to shout to be heard over the clanking of dishes and hundreds of moving people, so everyone shouted at once.

Falorn turned to say something to Zaren behind him. He changed his mind quickly when he realized he couldn't make the mercenary hear him without shouting loudly enough to be heard at the surrounding tables.

Elise led them unerringly through the shifting eddies of people and food. In the middle of the room, at the centermost table, a wide empty space had been left—enough to hold all of them and their guards, and not a dozen feet from the king and queen. The rest of the table held ministers, high-ranking nobles, and a wide knot of the gray-clad monks, including one who wore a robe trimmed in gold instead of red.

The din continued as they reached the table. The meal had not yet begun, although half-eaten loaves of bread already littered the wooden surface, and many tankards of wine had already been filled more than once. Falorn looked to Elise as he stepped toward the bench. At her nod, he and the others all sat.

The room fell quiet as death. Falorn looked up, and saw all the gray-robed monks at the end of the table standing. Their leader—the man with the gold-trimmed robe—threw back his cowl, revealing a thin, shaven head and angry blue eyes. The priest turned sharply to where the king and queen sat, and raised his arm to gesture. He must have thought better of the motion before any words emerged, however. The arm dropped back to his side. With a furious, withering look toward the Helleinen, the old priest pulled the hood back up over his head and walked away from the table. The rest of the monks followed behind. Unnatural silence continued to grip the hall until the gray-clad procession filed out the door, and for a long time after.

Even then, the noise seemed forced; nothing above the low rumble of half-muted grumblings rose from the table until the king, as if nothing untoward had happened, gestured to a quartet of musicians standing in a balcony above. The minstrels began playing a lively reel, and the servants brought meat and more wine to all the tables, but the noise still paled beside its previous level.

"What happened?" Falorn asked Zaren, who sat beside him, after enough food and wine had been served to distract other listeners nearby.

"It's a religious thing. They worship different gods here than we do. All the countries around here—Cathan, Calathan, the Seven Kingdoms—worship the same gods. That archbishop and those other monks you saw are all priests of Sart, the leader of their gods. Sart had a son named Bretek. A lot of the soldiers worship Bretek; He's a sort of war-god.

"A long time ago, Bretek came across a beautiful mortal woman named Fianna. He raped her, and beat her when she didn't submit willingly. Bretek left her in the woods for dead—only she didn't die. She lived to bear a son, named Hellein."

"The Helleinen!" Falorn barely kept his voice down.

"Right. The elves all claim descent from Hellein. But you can imagine the priests around here don't much like to talk about the products of their gods' rapes. Especially when there're too many soldiers who're all too willing to follow their god's example."

Falorn watched the king and queen closely during the meal. The king delighted in the food, the music, and the conversation of the nobles nearest him. He laughed constantly, and roared out stories of his own which drew applause from around the table, even though Falorn felt certain that most of his tablemates heard no more of the king's tales than he did. The king seemed to take no notice of the empty seats at the end of the table, as if the monks had withdrawn from his mind at the same time they had left the hall.

The queen, by contrast, looked frequently at the vacated bench. She wore a grim smile on her face, as if the scene had played out in exactly the manner she wanted. Falorn wondered if the incident had been planned on both sides, and suspected it had. Not for the first time, he felt like a marionette, a participant in events controlled by unseen forces, who never thought to explain their choreographies to the puppets who acted them out. *Just what's so important about us that the queen is willing to offend her own monks by seating us at the high table? Or was offending the monks the whole point? Maybe the queen is trying to send a message to them, and we're just an easy way of doing it. Or maybe the cards have something to do with it. They seem to be involved with everything else.*

The combination of the huge, rich meal; the endless cups of deep red wine; the noise, which seemed to assume a rhythm of its own as the meal went on; and the smokiness of the room made thinking almost impossible. Falorn felt groggy long before the last meat course emerged from the hidden, cavernous kitchens. Though he remained awake, and drank very little, he felt his alertness fading as the evening slipped onward.

Elise seemed anxious to get Falorn out of the dining hall as quickly after dinner as possible. He agreed with her; after the long day's events he wanted to rest, and to put off dealing with all the questions the cards seemed to be leading him into. He thought he saw the queen catch Elise's eyes and nod slightly, just before the guardswoman touched his shoulder. He touched the pouch at his chest instinctively, and glanced around at the others as he stiffly pushed himself to his feet.

A short distance down the bench, Sera and her dark-haired escort seemed fascinated with each other, as they had throughout the evening. Every time Falorn looked toward them, he saw the two women in deep conversation, their eyes locked together like new lovers, or circling cats. He wondered what they talked about so raptly, what sort of bond they had found on such short acquaintance. *Not that I've known Sera for very long, either,* Falorn realized. *There's no point in getting jealous just because she gets along well with her guard. This is her element, in with all the kings and queens and castles and nobles. I should be glad she's happy to be back in it.*

Still, he felt uneasy about something, although he couldn't think of what it might be.

Next to him, Zaren had found ready conversation, as always. The mercenary chatted amiably with a bushy-whiskered nobleman, discussing horses and cavalry tactics. The Helleinen talked only to each other. No one else even sat near them; the nobles beside them had shrank away over the course of the meal, leaving the bench immediately on either side of the two Helleinen bare.

Falorn's head felt thick as he walked from the table. Elise took his arm as he staggered slightly. *Why am I so tired?* he wondered, but somewhere amid the rich food and wine, the fatigue and strain of the journey and their precarious position seemed to have caught up with him. Even with Elise's help, he barely made it up the stairs into the tower. He supposed the others followed, although he heard no one walking behind. Inside his tower room, Elise let go of him, and Falorn all but collapsed onto the bed. He started to protest feebly as she began to undress him.

"You don't have to . . . I'll do that. . . ."

"Don't be silly," she said, with the air of a cat grooming its kitten. She stripped off his boots and clothing, leaving him naked except for the pouch he wore around his neck, which she did not touch. A cool breeze blew steadily from the open, wide window. Goosebumps appeared on his arms, and he began to awaken slightly. Without a word, Elise unfolded the thick quilt at the base of the bed, and spread it over him. She tucked its edges around him carefully, leaving him warm and cocooned. He heard her speaking faintly, but could make out no words; she was humming a lullaby, he finally realized. A fog seemed to spread gradually over him, beginning at his feet and stealing gradually over his body like a wraith in search of his soul. He didn't hear Elise leave the room. Long before she finished her lullaby, the wraith crept into his heart, and he slept.

28

The Hunt

∴∵∴

Falorn's eyes opened when he began to feel uncomfortably warm. Sunlight streamed into the room through the enormous window. Dust motes played in the wide shaft of light which spread across the bed.

Someone pounded on the door; not for the first time, Falorn realized.

"Coming," he said.

A thick brown robe sat next to the bed, neatly folded. Falorn thrust his arms into it and pulled the rough cloth around himself. He rubbed his eyes as he walked to the door. The cards felt secure and warm against his chest.

"Who's there?" he asked, but opened the door before anyone could answer from the other side.

Elise stood in the hall, looking awake and fresh. She wore a red velvet doublet belted over brown hose and tunic. A short broadsword hung at the left side of her belt, and a knife at the right. Her hair looked slightly tousled, but Falorn noticed fresh polish on her boots.

"Time to get up. You've got a long day ahead of you," she said.

"I have a long day behind me, too."

"You can sleep later if you want. The Queen wants to see you before her hunt."

"All of us?"

"Just you. She's already talking to Zaren now, and she met with the elves while you slept, last night."

"What about Sera?"

"Sera's going on the hunt with the Queen. Lady Tirya invited her."

"Who?"

"The black-haired woman you saw with her yesterday. She always hunts with the Queen. Lady Tirya's the best trailfinder in all of Cathan. They say she can track a trout in a river, and that all the hounds in Cathan couldn't find her if she didn't want to be found. She and Her Majesty have been friends from childhood."

"Oh," Falorn said, a little put out that Sera had been invited along while he hadn't. *She's a noblewoman and you're an innkeeper's son. What did you expect? Just because they respect your cards doesn't mean they respect your breeding.*

"You'd best get ready. We have to go in twenty minutes. There are new clothes on the chair."

Falorn hurriedly scrubbed himself as Elise retreated into the hall. The new clothes looked far too much like the courtiers' costumes: an abundance of velvet and cloth-of-gold, crowned with a thick, ruffled collar. *Will the queen be angry if I don't wear them?* Falorn wondered. *Do they have a Hook in Cathan? It doesn't matter. I can't bear the thought of wearing them.* Finally, he pulled on his Helleinen clothing again.

Ryal's changes seemed to have endowed the garments with remarkable resistance to dust and stains. They felt clean and new against his skin. Falorn left his baldric and sword hanging from one of the bedposts, although not without some reluctance, given his previous castle experiences. He opened the door before Elise had to knock again.

He hadn't realized how early in the morning it was at first: only an hour or so after dawn. Servants and a few soldiers stirred around them as he and Elise walked the halls of the keep, but most of the Summer Palace's inhabitants probably still slept.

A cathedral bell started ringing as they passed onward, tolling a long, low melody. *I guess that's to wake people for the morning prayers,* Falorn thought to himself. *I wonder what the prayers are like here. What could it be like inside a huge church like that cathedral, filled with all those angry, gray-robed monks?* He had never cared for the circuit priest's outdoor services in his home village, but he felt a little loss in their absence now. Quietly, so Elise wouldn't notice, Falorn mouthed as much of the Morning Supplication to Mara as he could remember.

Elise walked briskly, only stopping when they came to a door with a pair of women guarding it. Both guards wore gold-on-blue colors, over silvered chain mail. The two women held swords out and ready, although they relaxed slightly at the sight of Elise.

"You're to go right in," the first guardswoman said. "The mercenary left a few minutes ago; they're preparing for the hunt now."

"That means we'll only have a few minutes," Elise said to Falorn. One of the soldiers rapped twice on the door with the pommel of her sword. A moment later someone pulled the portal open from within.

"Come in. Be welcome," he heard the queen's voice say.

"Your Majesty," Falorn said, as he stepped into the room and knelt.

"Welcome, young Falorn. Stand up, by all means." Falorn looked up. The queen wore riding leathers and a pale blue cloak, like a storybook huntsman. A short hunting sword hung at her side. The other women in the chamber—he only saw women in the room—were dressed likewise. "Your friends have been telling us all about you. I was becoming very anxious to talk with you, after hearing their stories."

What did Sera tell her? Falorn wondered anxiously. *I know the queen has cards herself; did Sera tell her about mine? Is she still angry about the Helleinen?*

His fear must have shown on his face. The queen laughed as she looked at him.

"Don't look so scared," she said. "You came by your cards fairly, and we won't ask you for them. Not now, anyway. But we have a war to win, and would like your help."

"My help? What could I do?"

"You are a cardholder. You may be able to do quite a lot, with some training. You may not owe the people of Cathan any loyalty, but we share the same enemies."

"You mean the Seven Kingdoms?"

"Do you think they will leave you with your cards if they win? They are trying to take them from you now, to turn them against the armies and people of our country. Your country could be next, or Delerian, or the world. But if you stay, and fight here, there are great rewards to be had."

I'm not sure how this all fits together. I don't know what she wants, or what she's offering me, and I don't think I should ask. I'm not sure I believe her when she says she won't take the cards. But I'm also not sure she'll let me leave the country without giving them to her.

"May I think about it?" he asked, avoiding the queen's mention of rewards. "I want to do what I can, but I have to talk with my friends first."

"Of course. Talk with them all you like. I'd like the *Helleinen* to help too, if they would." She emphasized the word, as if she was unused to it, and trying to remember to say it. "You have the run of the palace, and one of our best knights to guide you." She gestured toward Elise. "Go and do what you must to decide. We will talk again when the hunt is over."

She turned to talk to Lord Dianeme, also dressed in hunting leathers, and Falorn knew the audience had ended. He backed out of the room as unobtrusively as he could. No one seemed to take any notice of him.

Zaren shared none of Falorn's worries.

"Of course I'm going to stay!" he said. "The queen's offering money, a captaincy, troops to command. I'd be a fool not to take it. I was never much cut out to be an innkeeper anyway. The only thing I really enjoyed was breaking up the fights. But this—this will be glorious. And if we win, there's talk of lands, maybe even a title."

"Glorious? I thought you were the one who told me never to fight fair."

"Glory doesn't come from fighting fairly. It comes from winning."

"Or dying."

"There's plenty of time for dying later, when I'm back at the front with Stennet. *There's* a man who knows how to be in the thick of the killing, and I'll be glad to be with him again."

The conversation turned to bloody reminiscences. Falorn found himself feeling a little queasy, although the feeling embarrassed him. He'd always loved stories of war and battle as a boy, but they'd never contained the gritty realism that Zaren's tales held, even when he suspected the mercenary of exaggeration. Now, after seeing real bodies and real fights, he no longer felt the romance of the stories. Part of him missed the feeling, while another part could only think of the dead Helleinen warrior, and of Zaren and Sera unconscious in the bottom of a doomed lake-boat.

After an hour or so, Falorn excused himself. Zaren seemed a little glad to see him go, he thought, as if the old warrior craved a more attentive audience, perhaps among the soldiers down in the guardroom.

He found Cirque's and Ryal's rooms empty. Falorn wondered where they might have gone. For a moment he feared they had left the country entirely, disgusted by the monks' and guards' reactions to them, but he saw packs and neatly folded clothing in Ryal's chamber, and his initial panic faded.

"Where do you think they've gone?" he asked Elise.

"They could be anywhere. They have the run of the palace, just as you do." Falorn glanced out the window. At the foot of the tower beneath Ryal's window huddled a small, walled garden, nearly overgrown with thorns and long, trailing vines.

"There they are," he said. He saw the two Helleinen sitting together in the garden talking, although no sound reached him from the ground. The guards appointed to Cirque and Ryal were nowhere in sight. "Can we go down there, Elise?"

"I suppose. That garden's overgrown and full of thorns, though. The gardeners all joined the infantry; I can't imagine anybody but an elf would want to sit in there now."

Hellein, he corrected automatically in his mind. But he knew better than to correct her. *Still, saying nothing seems disloyal.*

"Elise?"

"What?" She turned around; she had already started toward the door.

"Please, no remarks about the H . . . the elves. They saved my life. Everybody I meet seems to hate them, but they've never been anything but kind to me."

"You and the queen seem to be the only ones who feel that way. If they can help in the war, I won't say anything about them. I couldn't imagine liking them, though. I'm sorry, but I just couldn't."

"I don't understand them sometimes, Elise, but they're not what you seem to think. The bravest and best swordsman I've ever seen was Helleinen. I saw him die for no reason at all, just because someone hated his kind."

"Sometimes there's a reason for hate."

"And sometimes there isn't."

"You're probably right, Falorn. Besides, there will be plenty of killing to go around, soon. I'm sure everyone will have enough of it."

"I'm not sure some people ever have enough of it." Falorn's vision swam. He wondered about the people who chased him for the cards. He saw Zaren's face in his mind, describing past battles to young soldiers.

What's the fun in it? Where's the glory? I don't see it. I have every-

thing I thought I ever wanted and I don't see it. I could never kill any-
body who wasn't attacking me. I just couldn't do it. I wonder if Zaren
started that way. I wonder if everybody starts that way.

"I hope it never gets easier for me," he said, not meaning to speak
out loud.

"It will," Elise said, a little sadly, "I'm afraid it will."

Elise waited outside the garden while Falorn gently opened the wooden
gate and passed through the mortared stone walls. The two surly guards
stood outside as well; they and Elise quickly fell into conversation as
Falorn passed beyond their view.

Walking inside the walls felt like crossing once more into the forest.
Young trees competed with unkempt bushes for the air above his head.
Purple and white wisteria grew everywhere, covering walls and climbing
trees. Tiny violets carpeted the trails beneath his feet. The brush rustled
wildly, as squirrels rushed back and forth, far busier than the servants
within the walls of the keep.

He found the Helleinen sitting together on a sheltered bench,
amidst a grove of thin beech trees.

"Falorn," Ryal called out when the Hellein saw him, "we hoped you
would make it. Come here, we have wine."

He walked to the bench and greeted the two of them. Their eyes
looked guarded, although no concern showed in their voices. He told
them about his meeting with the queen and later conversation with
Zaren. He wanted to mention his misgivings about the queen, but something held him back. Cirque seemed to sense his uneasiness.

"Best not to discuss hosts when you're staying in their house," the
Hellein said softly. "Someone could take unintended insult, or unintended harm."

"Of course," said Falorn. "I don't want to seem ungrateful."

"That's best."

"You'll stay, of course," said Ryal, as if Falorn had made the choice
freely. "We'll stay as well, as long as you're here. Danbhe would be very
unhappy if you came to harm because of human carelessness when we
might have been helpful."

"Human carelessness?"

"Swords, arrows, poisons, that sort of thing," said Cirque.

"Humans are always leaving them around where someone might get
hurt," Ryal added helpfully.

"I think I understand. I hate to ask an impolite question, but after it's all over, how am I expected to return the favor, seeing as I'm already in Danbhe's debt? By helping you kidnap Jhodric?"

Neither of the Helleinen looked offended.

"Why not see what happens after events are done here?" Cirque answered him. "We may want to travel the same way or we may not. For now, we're here because the Seven Kingdoms are enemies of Delerian, even if the queen's people are hardly our friends. If the Seven Kingdoms want your cards, that's reason enough for us to help keep them safe with you. You owe us nothing. Anything you do to help us later is your own choice."

That was an evasion worthy of my father, Falorn thought, *even if it as politely worded. I suppose I should respond in kind.*

"I appreciate the help," Falorn said. "I don't know what will happen later. I'd like to help; your people helped me without asking for anything. I just don't know what's in the future. When the spring started I was just an innkeeper's son; I have no idea where I'll be by winter."

"That's promise enough for me," said Cirque. "Whatever you were, you are more than an innkeeper's son now—though there's no dishonor in running an honest tavern. I think by winter you will be more than you are now. I only know a little about the cards you carry, no more than you do, but you are at the center of great events, for better or for worse. Did you not say you left home to find adventure?"

"Yes, I guess I did," said Falorn. *Even if it wasn't quite the truth.*

"Then you should have no complaints. When your heart's dream comes true so quickly in life, either you have been blessed by the gods or you are their pawn. Either way, all you can do is give thanks."

"Thanks. I think you're right. And I have enjoyed your company, and Sera's and Zaren's. I have a lot to be thankful for, I guess."

Ryal laughed. "Don't be too grateful, though. I don't think you have to give thanks for the men trying to kill you, or for the food they serve in the swamp."

"I wouldn't even know how to begin," Falorn said, and laughed along with him.

When he left the garden along with the Helleinen, Falorn felt much better. His face tingled a little, perhaps from the skin of wine they'd drunk while watching the sun climb slowly over the garden walls. The Helleinen had brought several small loaves of bread and a cheese as well, so they'd all eaten breakfast. Now, a warmth filled him, starting at his chest where the cards touched him, but spreading outward through the rest of his body as well.

Elise and the other guards still stood just beyond the walls, their faces as serious as chanting priests. Elise smiled slightly when she saw him emerge, but the other two guards only scowled.

"Is there a practice yard we can use?" he asked Elise. "It doesn't have to be anywhere other soldiers are using, if you'd rather we stayed away from them. Anyplace with a floor and some wooden swords or staves would be fine."

"I'm sure we can find something," she said, and glared the other guards to silence before they could protest.

He practiced most of the day, trying to force himself toward exhaustion, as he had in Delerian. The Helleinen remained with him for the rest of the morning. Cirque sparred with him and explained points of swordsmanship while Ryal watched, and occasionally joked with both of them.

Falorn had worked with Cirque on the trail through the mountains as well, and occasionally in Delerian. Usually he could block the Hellein's blows through his own speed and strength, and he managed a few return strokes, but Falorn felt years away from matching the smoothness and elegance of Cirque's motions, or the ease with which the Helleinen blade skimmed and flew through the air.

He practiced doggedly, fighting to absorb all he could of what Cirque taught. *I don't want to depend on the cards for everything*, Falorn though to himself. He found he could think and fight at the same time; swordwork no longer sapped his entire attention.

Heat blazed against his chest. *They help me fight, but I hate not knowing how to fight without them. I hate being a fraud of a knight.* Falorn redoubled his attack, forcing Cirque to give way before him.

It feels like cheating somehow. I have to use them, as long as people are chasing me, but I don't like to owe everything to anyone else—man or magical card. Besides, the cards might choose to leave me as quickly as they came. If I don't learn to really use the sword I'll be dead.

Early in the afternoon, the Helleinen left in search of a library. Their guards left along with them—somewhat reluctantly, Falorn thought. The two soldiers had been gradually drawn into the sparring, at first watching only because there was nothing else worth looking at in the small, dusty courtyard. Eventually they watched with real interest.

Falorn hoped to continue working out after the Helleinen left, perhaps practicing form and movements alone, or running along the walls. A tapping noise made him turn around. Elise held one of the wooden prac-tice blades.

"Well, I wouldn't be much of a knight if I left all the teaching to elves, now, would I?"

"I guess not," he said, still surprised. "You don't mind?"

"I swore an oath," she said. "It's part of my duty to instruct."

Her style differed markedly from Cirque's, although both she and the Hellein depended more on speed and finesse than strength. He found himself more easily able to match and follow Elise's movements, and even to emulate some of them. He went through each new motion again and again as often as he could get her to repeat it, trying to learn all he could. He never knew when he might get another lesson, or even another chance to work out; he felt like he had to get the most out of each day's practice.

I wonder if this is how those lizard soldiers felt, trying to learn all they could from their doomed Hero before the prophecy killed Him. Falorn's mood turned sober. *I wonder how many of them died. I wonder how many of them followed me to their deaths. I know I fulfilled their prophecy, complete with the tragic fall and disappearance afterward, but I hope some good came out of it for them. At the very least, I hope they got their swamp back.*

By late afternoon, Elise looked worn out. The warmth in Falorn's muscles had deepened, but otherwise he felt little fatigue.

"We can stop if you'd like," Falorn said.

"Only if you want to. Don't you ever get tired?"

"Yes, I do. But I have a lot to learn."

"True," she said, gasping for air, "but you don't have to learn every-thing right this minute. Leave a little bit for tomorrow."

"If you say so."

"I do say so. It's almost time for dinner, and neither of us has eaten since this morning. You'll want to bathe and change."

"Will there be a feast tonight?"

"I don't think so. The Queen is likely to be late at her hunt. She and the King will probably eat in their chambers. There will be plenty of food in the dining hall, though."

"Do you think we could eat in the tower, if we don't *have* to be down-stairs?"

"Why would you . . . oh," she said, remembering the previous night's feast. "That might be best, actually. I'll have someone see to it."

She stopped a servant as they walked back through the wide halls of the keep, and smiled with satisfaction after the boy scurried off toward the kitchen.

"There will be plenty for all of us brought up," she said, "although I think your friend Zaren might prefer to eat downstairs."

"I think you're right. The Helleinen would rather eat in the tower, though"—they'd said as much to Falorn after they'd finished avoiding each other's questions in the garden—"and honestly, so would I. I didn't grow up in a castle, and it takes some getting used to."

"I suppose it must," said Elise.

She looked like she wanted to ask more about his upbringing, but she held back. Falorn volunteered no information. He wondered if she would be quite as anxious to teach an innkeeper's son, even one who was the momentary guest of the queen.

29

Night Visitations

∴∴∴

Sera returned to the tower just as they started dinner. Dirt and grime covered her clothing and skin, as if she'd spent the day riding through mud, rather than forest.

"Did you have a good hunt?" Falorn asked her as she opened the door. From outside in the hallway, he could hear the guards muttering. "Here . . ." he pointed to an empty spot at the table, "take Zaren's place."

Falorn and the Helleinen sat together at a medium-sized plank table in Cirque's room, the largest table in any of their rooms. Zaren and his guard had gone to eat in the main hall, while the Helleinen's guards preferred to eat outside the room. Elise had accepted Falorn's offer to loan her his room and bath while he and the others ate; duty forbade her from leaving the tower, but she didn't need to be immediately at his side.

"I am never, ever, *ever* doing that again, no matter *who* asks me to come along."

"Does that mean you didn't have a good hunt?" Ryal asked innocently. Sera glared at him.

"I'll be back," she said. "I'm going to go to my room and scrub off whatever dirt hasn't permanently adhered to my skin. If there isn't *a lot* of food left, I *will* kill all of you." She stalked out of the room, slamming the door behind her.

"I think she had a bad day," said Ryal.

When Sera returned to the table half an hour later, she downed her meal like a wolf. Periodically, she looked up, as if to prevent anyone else from taking the food away from her.

Sera knocked at his door later that night, as he practiced by candlelight, stepping through each of the sword movements Elise had shown him again and again until they started to flow reflexively.

"Are you busy?" she asked. "I'll go if you are."

"No," said Falorn, sheathing his sword and leaning it against the bedpost. "Please stay," he said, when she looked like she might leave anyway.

"All right. I feel like I've barely seen you since we've been here." They both sat down at the black marble table, with the candle flickering between them.

"I feel the same way. You and Tirya seem to have made friends."

"She's been very nice to me, and helpful. What about your guard? She's very pretty, isn't she?"

"I suppose," said Falorn, "I hadn't really thought about it." *I really haven't thought about it*, Falorn realized. *She really is pretty.*

"I thought that was all men thought about."

"Not here. Not me, at least."

She looked at him disbelievingly. "After the way you looked at those elf-waifs?"

Falorn shrugged.

"What makes you think you're any different from anyone else?" asked Sera.

"I'm not sure I am. I've just been busy trying to stay alive, that's all. I guess she is pretty. Not as pretty as you, though."

"Thanks. That's very nice. It's not true, but it's very nice."

"Sera . . . I mean it."

"That's very sweet of you. You really shouldn't say things like that. Not here. Not to me."

"Why not? What are you talking about?"

"I don't know." She wrung her hands helplessly, as if unsure what to do with them. "I'm very tired, I'm probably not making much sense. I've been riding through the woods all day. It's just . . ."

"Just what?" he asked, when it didn't seem as if she would go on.

"Oh, I don't know. I should really go." She stood up from the table. He caught her arm gently as she moved toward the door.

"Please don't go," he said softly. "Please?"

She shook slightly, as if trying not to cry. Turning back around, she wordlessly put her hands on his shoulders.

"We don't have to talk anymore," he said. "We can talk in the morning if you want." She kept on shaking. He saw a lone tear escape from one half-closed eye. He stood up and took her in his arms, holding her close against his shoulder while she trembled.

"Hold me," she said. "I don't ever want to leave you."

"You don't have to," Falorn whispered, stroking her back gently with one arm while he held her close with the other. "You don't ever have to."

She continued to shiver against him. "Just hold me tonight," she said, trying and failing to hold back tears. "I need you tonight, just to hold me."

"I will," he said. She snuffed out the candle with her fingertips and shuffled backward to the bed. Sera trembled while she undressed. The moonlight which shone through the wide, open window reflected the tears on her face.

He held her close against him, just held her and stroked the smooth skin on her back and legs softly while she shivered against him, her body pressing as closely against his flesh as she could.

After a long, long time, her breathing evened out and she slept alongside him, shifting so that she still touched him, though not quite as closely. He lay on his back awake, thinking of the smooth skin of the woman who lay beside him, and hoping to dream of her instead of lions.

The moonlight had faded by the time he heard the scratching. It sounded like rats squeaking on the walls outside his window. He opened his eyes. Sera had shifted again in her sleep, and now lay on her stomach. He saw the curve of her breast where it touched the sheet beside him, and then he heard the scratching again.

A hand appeared at the edge of the window, gloved in black.

Falorn reached quietly to the edge of the bed, and felt his hand close on the hilt of his sword. An arm followed the black hand in the window, as someone pulled himself into the room from the wall outside. Falorn closed his eyes to the barest squint so the whites wouldn't show as the man climbed through the window. *Just like being back at home and pretending to be asleep.* The man glanced around the room briefly, his eyes passing over Falorn's unmoving form quickly, lingering a little longer on the pale skin of Sera's back and legs. He turned and reached out the window, and quickly a second man clambered into the room as well. The first man put a finger to his lips and pointed to Falorn. Then both of them drew long, thin-bladed knives, their edges black in the moonless dark of the room.

Falorn flung himself from the bed and shouted, pulling his sword from its sheath. The two assassins reacted instantly, throwing themselves at him as if they'd expected just such a move from the naked man in front of them.

They couldn't move fast enough.

Falorn slashed the first man across the eyes before he could block the heavy sword with his slender knife blade. He collapsed as his partner just barely avoided a second blow.

The assassin tried to fight his way inside Falorn's guard where his knife could be of use. Falorn blocked each attempt, stepping smoothly into one of Elise's routines as if he'd practiced it for years, not just this one day. The man plunged forward, aiming his knife at Falorn's eyes. Falorn stepped aside and countered the blow. His own swing shattered the blade of the assassin's knife and carried into the man's neck. Blood spurted everywhere as the man dropped to the ground.

The door burst open. Elise and Tirya ran into the room. Behind them, the elves' two guardsmen carried torches. Sera bolted up, awakened by the slam of the door. She pulled the sheet over her breasts hurriedly. Falorn suddenly remembered his own nakedness. He looked at the two assassins to be sure neither moved, then reached for the robe next to the bed. The thick cloth felt sticky against his skin as he pulled it around himself. The second assassin's blood covered his chest.

"Are you all right?" Elise asked.

"Fine," said Falorn. His head suddenly swam, and he concentrated to focus his eyes. Something blue and faint danced around the two bodies. He reached down and removed the pouches from each man's belt. From behind him, where Elise, Tirya, and the other guards stood, it looked as if he had merely stumbled.

Elise motioned one of the guards forward, and he knelt by the two bodies, checking each in turn. "They're both dead," the soldier said. "That was good swordwork." Falorn didn't reply, and the man continued to check the assassins' bodies. He pulled aside their black cloaks to reveal the green colors beneath. "Ha!" said the guard, "Ever seen these before?"

"I have," Falorn replied. "They're from the Seven Kingdoms. They belong to a nobleman named Jhodric of Northfall."

He felt suddenly tired, and wondered how long they would keep him awake with questions. The pouches in his hand gave off a low, steady warmth.

Two hours later, they finished asking all the questions. Lord Dianeme herself had come up to talk with him about the men in green, before ordering guardsmen to haul the bodies away. No signs of other assassins could be found, nor accomplices or horses waiting outside. If the two men had any fellows, they'd long since fled.

Falorn and Sera went to bed in her room, with the narrow window shuttered. Elise and a handful of guardsmen waited in Falorn's chambers in case anyone else returned, while Tirya stood watch outside of Sera's door.

"What did you find?" she asked him once they were alone together, after she'd sponged the stickiness from his chest. "You did find something on the bodies, didn't you?"

"These," he said, setting the two cards on the table. A crimson glow gradually rose up from the flat plaques, welling upward and outward until it overshadowed the light of the flickering yellow candle. The first card held a scarlet match to the blue thief which warmed against his chest. A sinister-looking, red-cloaked man peered at something from a dark corner. A carmine mask covered the upper half of his face. Maroon shadows nearly hid him from view, even on the card's framed surface. It clearly matched his own blue thief in theme, though the red thief in the picture looked very different.

The second card Falorn had seen before. A sinister woman reclined on its face, her red flesh suggesting something deeper than desire— something more haunting. Once again, the crimson temptress looked at him with sultry eyes, the same sultry eyes that had seemed so real when they gazed at him from his hiding place in Sera's secret closet. *I wonder why he let two of the cards out of his hands, instead of just giving he assassins one to track me by. Maybe he thought they'd need both to accomplish their mission?*

In a way, I suppose I've done part of what the Helleinen wanted me to do for them by coming here and depriving Johdric of two more of his cards.

From behind him, Sera let out a little cry.

"What's wrong?" he said.

"What . . . what are you going to do with them?" she finally asked.

"I don't know. I'm too tired to think about it right now."

"Then come to bed."

This time, she held him.

Something felt wrong when he awoke in the morning. The bed felt wrong, the dim light coming through the shutters' slats seemed different. Gradually, he remembered where he was. He heard a pounding at the door, almost the same as the one which had woken him the previous day. He smiled, and wondered when Sera would answer it.

A fist hammered on the door again.

"Falorn? Are you in there?"

He looked around for Sera, but didn't see her anywhere. he didn't even see her pack; he wondered if she'd stowed it under the bed. Then he looked to the table, and saw nothing there except for the guttered-out candle.

He suddenly felt very, very cold. He reached for the pouch at his chest, and found it in its place. It still warmed him, but he felt little reassurance in the presence of his cards.

He heard the pounding on the door once more.

"Falorn? Where are you?"

"I'm in here," he said. His voice sounded strange to his own ears. He reached for the robe where he had left it by the bed and pulled it on hurriedly. Dried blood flaked off against his skin. He walked to the door and opened it. Elise stood outside, her eyes wide and reddened.

"Sera's gone, isn't she?" he asked.

"She and Tirya. We don't know when they left, but they're long gone now."

I wonder why she left? By now, after all the turmoil they'd been through together, it felt like she had just abandoned him to cause emotional pain, but he supposed she had a reason that didn't have anything to do with him. *Like getting her cards back.* He hoped there was more to it than that. *There has to be more to it than that, or Tirya wouldn't have gone with her.* Falorn wasn't sure if he really believed that.

He and Elise rode out immediately, at the head of dozens of searchers dispatched by the queen, but Falorn really didn't expect to find them. Sera had the crimson thief as a companion to her recovered temptress card, and the best tracker in the country accompanied her instead of chasing her. He focused on his own thief card, hoping to sense the presence of its mate. The card betrayed nothing; either Sera knew how to mask her card, or she and the trailfinder had already passed beyond the range of his own blue thief.

He mentioned her cards to no one, not even Zaren and the Helleinen. At first he didn't plan on keeping them secret; the subject just didn't come up amid the confusion and the assassination attempt. As the next few days passed, however, he thought better of telling anyone about them at all.

He didn't know where Sera had gone, or why, but he didn't want her brought back against her will either. If the cards helped keep her free, he wanted Sera to have them. Falorn hoped they brought her less trouble than his had brought down on his own head. *They haven't so far*, he knew.

I just wish she'd trusted me enough to tell me where it was she felt she had to go.

He missed her, and her image crept into his thoughts and dreams, when he couldn't bury it with endless hours of sword practice and exercise.

Elise and Cirque took turns teaching him swordwork when they could. As the spring days lengthened into summer, the palace took on even more of a frenzied atmosphere. Newly mustered units assembled on the lawn for training before being sent to the front. Everyone with any skill at all was pressed into service helping to instruct the levies, even Falorn. When he could, he practiced with the more experienced soldiers, learning what he could about combat on horseback, or fighting in tandem with other soldiers.

His chambers had been moved to a less exposed room, with the Helleinen in one adjoining room and Elise in the other—Zaren had left for the front a few days after Sera's disappearance, in command of the new infantry levies Falorn had seen drilling.

Ultimately, Falorn had agreed to help the queen's cause. With Sera gone and Zaren enthusiastic in support, it felt like the right thing to do. It wasn't his war, but it was a war for the homes of people who had helped him, regardless of their reasons, and that seemed like a much better cause to fight for than the cards themselves were.

The queen had long since decided it was pointless to assign guards to Cirque and Ryal. The Helleinen could evade them almost at will when they wanted privacy, and most of her soldiers had a reflexive dislike for all things Helleinen. Instead, three troopers guarded the door outside their chambers against assassins while they slept, but during the day the

Helleinen went where they wanted. Cirque worked with Falorn and a few others willing to listen to him on swordsmanship. Ryal spent much of his time closeted with several of the royal wizards, who seemed to care little for race or religion—at least where a fellow practitioner of magic was concerned. Eventually, the monks reappeared at the evening feasts, although they sat as far from the Helleinen as the queen permitted.

Elise surprised him one night by offering to teach him to read. He'd said as little as possible about his background, afraid she would look down on him as an innkeeper's son. She seemed genuinely to want to help, however, and he gratefully accepted. He could already puzzle out a few words and write his name, but she put him to work just as arduously as he pushed himself on the practice fields. Ryal and Cirque helped as well, and for once, Elise and the Helleinen seemed to see eye to eye on something. It had never occurred to the Helleinen that he couldn't read, although Elise, more attuned to a culture in which education levels varied dramatically, had noticed quickly.

Reading came less easily than swordsmanship, no matter how hard he worked at it. Some nights he wished he had stumbled on a card bearing a scribe on its enchanted face, rather than a lion, thief, or knight. He thought often of Sera's room in Roicenet, with its full shelf of books, or of the book he'd found in the dead knight's pouch and then lost again, still unread.

In a funny way, he thought he wanted to learn to read as much for Sera as for himself, although he couldn't say if it was to prove something to himself or to her memory.

He wondered if he'd ever see her again, and stayed up late many nights, thinking about her and their last, sad night together.

"Try it again," Elise said, gently.

"My eyes hurt."

"Just a little while longer, Falorn. Your eyes will feel better in the morning."

"So why don't we wait until morning?" He looked down at the elaborate flourishes on the page again. The table swam a little in his vision.

"We may not be able to tomorrow. It's almost midsummer."

"So? What happens at midsummer?"

"The battle, probably. If they wait much longer, the Seven Kingdoms won't be able to get its soldiers back home in time for the harvest. We'll be leaving for the front soon."

"Do you know when?"

"As soon as the Queen thinks this last batch of levies is ready. The Queen's Own Guard and these levies are about the only units left that haven't been sent to the front yet. A few days from now, I think, we'll all be marching for the Calambria."

"The Calambria?"

"The river that divides Cathan and Calathan. There are forts and castles guarding the hills on both sides. That's where the battle will be."

"Everybody decided in advance where the battle will be? Isn't it usually supposed to be a surprise?"

"Not after months of waiting. I'm sure the queen still has a few surprises left, but the battlefield won't be one of them."

Falorn looked down at the page, blinking his eyes until the curly black lines sharpened in his vision.

"Well, I guess I'd better get reading, then," he said.

30

The Taste of Blood

Falorn stood next to Elise on top of the hill. He wished he had a horse, but the queen's army had none to spare; he and Elise had given theirs up to unhorsed cavalrymen when the remounts ran out, on the second day of the battle. A hundred spearmen stood or squatted behind the low stone wall on the hill behind him. None of the men wore more than scraps of armor; nor had they ever fought before. After three days of battle they remained untested, guarding the low hill which overlooked the approach to the Cathanese army's right flank.

"I think they're going to charge the center again," Elise said.

"Again? Don't they ever do anything else?"

"They won't, as long as they think they can break Stennet's footmen by throwing enough troops at them."

"Are we throwing anything back?"

"I don't think we have anything left to throw. The wizards are worn out or dead, and the archers are out of arrows."

"Maybe they'll run out of men."

"I hope so. Sooner or later, they have to."

"I wish Zaren wasn't in there."

"We all have friends in the center. All we can do is hold our place in the battlefield, and hope they hold theirs, somehow. The queen put us here for a reason."

"What reason is that? We should be in there with Zaren and Cirque and Ryal. You're a knight; you should be in the heart of the battle."

"Falorn, let me explain something to you." She glanced back to make certain that none of the spearmen behind the wall could hear her. "Someone has to hold this hill. You know that. They probably won't attack here, but if they do, they might break all the way through and hit the army on its side. You and I have fought in battles before. None of these men ever has. If the queen put a commoner in charge—or a woman— these peasants would run at the first sign of a fight. They want their leader to be a traditional knight, a warrior they can rally behind. The queen needed someone she knew she could trust here, so she sent me. But they won't listen to me; they'll only listen to someone who looks like a knight."

"But I'm . . . "

"Don't say it. As far as they're concerned, you're a foreign knight who came to fight for their cause. They want to follow you, and you *are* a pretty good swordsman. Don't give them any reason to doubt you. They're fighting for their homes and their lives here. They need all the support they can get."

"It just feels like I'm lying."

"Only you know the difference. They need you here, so you're just going to have to live with the lie."

Falorn nodded reluctantly, and looked toward the center of the battle. The Seven Kingdoms footmen streamed back toward the river in retreat, battered once again by Stennet and Zaren's wall of shields. A few dozen Calathanese horsemen protected the soldiers' retreat and harried the Cathanese lines, but they need not have bothered. The Cathanese cavalry remained out of sight, no threat to the Seven Kingdoms footmen trying to regroup at the river's edge.

"How long can they hold out, do you think?" he asked Elise.

"As long as it takes. With the cavalry run off the field they're all alone now. If most of their cavalry hadn't gone chasing ours, they would have punched through the lines by now. Some cavalry general is going to lose his head over that chase."

As the Seven Kingdoms troops reached the safety of the river's edge, some of the horsemen began to drift away. In ones and twos the riders moved away from the re-forming infantry lines. A few of them rode toward the hill where Falorn stood.

One of the horsemen pointed, and called something; Falorn couldn't make out any sound over the clatter of metal and the shouts of injured men from the infantry lines. Several other riders joined the first, and they cantered in the direction of Falorn's position.

Soon, he heard bugles from below, and the trilling noise of Seven Kingdoms cavalry horns. At the base of the hill, a troop of cavalry began forming up for a charge, a mixture of Seven Kingdoms and Calathanese and a few mercenary guardsmen, men left behind in the running fight when the Cathanese cavalry was driven from the field. Many of the cavalrymen carried long, curved sabers, while a few men still held light cavalry lances—designed for throwing or stabbing rather than a charge in force. Others held broadswords, axes, or maces. Armor of one sort or another covered most of them, even the light horsemen. Falorn fingered his own light chainmail shirt. Elise wore a mail hauberk and leggings, but the men behind the fence would fight unprotected.

Looks like our luck's run out, he thought to himself. *I wanted to be in the middle of the fighting with Zaren and the Helleinen. It looks like some of the fighting is coming to me instead. I wonder if these poor levies will hold.*

"They've got to hold," Elise said, as if reading his thoughts. "There's no cavalry behind us to stop a breakthrough. They could hit Stennet from the side and wipe him out. All that would be left is the two castles, and the Calathanese could just go around them with the whole army gone. We have to hold until the cavalry gets back."

If it gets back, Falorn added to himself. *If it hasn't been wiped out completely.* He nodded, however, and turned to face the spearmen behind.

"Get ready," he called out, "It's time to do what we came here for. It's time to fight for your homes. Company's coming to visit." He tried to sound confident as the soldiers shifted nervously, looking at each other and at the barely-familiar weapons in their hands.

The image of his father's inn came to Falorn suddenly. He wondered what it would have felt like to have to defend it. He wondered if his father missed him, whether word would ever reach his father about the way Falorn had risen in the world so briefly before falling in a foreign land for a nebulous cause.

The men behind him, at least, would be fighting for their homes.

It's not really any different for me, Falorn realized. *We're all of us fighting for our lives, that's all.*

Elise followed closely as Falorn walked back up the hill a few steps and jumped to the top of the low wall, which reached to the hips of most of the soldiers. Maybe the sight of him and Elise fighting in front of them would embolden the spearmen; he wondered what else he could say to inspire them. He glanced over at Elise, who just shook her head slightly.

From below he heard the sound of bugles and horns again. He couldn't see the riders from this far back on the flat hilltop, and he realized the spearmen could see nothing either.

"They're just playing those horns to scare you," Falorn said. "There aren't that many of them. Stand fast with me and we'll throw them back." Before, he'd fought to keep the nervousness out of his voice; now, the fear had vanished. In its place, a surge of heat and energy flowed through his chest. He looked at his feet and found himself standing in a perfect fighting stance.

The bugles pealed again in a loud flourish, and then hoofbeats began to drown out the constant trill of the horns. The horsemen topped the edge of the hill in a long, single line. Then every one of them yelled, and charged for the wall.

"Hold fast!" Falorn shouted, but he could hear the clatter behind him as men dropped their spears and ran. He dared not turn around as the charge bore down on him.

"Guard my back!" Elise cried out beside him. He sensed her sword swinging as the fastest horsemen reached the wall. Falorn thrust forward at a light horseman, catching him in the throat before the man could plunge his upraised lance downward. The man fell backward as the horse leaped the wall. Several other riders followed, not bothering with the pair of defenders. They rode the fleeing spearmen down instead; Falorn heard loud screams from behind, but dared not turn his attention to look.

A trio of heavy cavalrymen reined in while most of their fellows jumped the wall and rode onward. They wore thick mail hauberks, with linked hoods protecting their necks and heads. Only one of the three wore a helmet. Their shields and surcoats bore the same device: a gold falcon on a royal blue field.

"Well, look here," the first rider said, in oddly accented Denbar. "We found 'usselves a pair of deathwalking knights."

"Rich 'uns, fra' the clothes an 'em."

"Whall, what are ye waiten' far?" The first man raised his broadsword and spurred his horse forward toward Falorn. A second soldier followed after, while the third turned his attention toward Elise.

"Hey, thissun's a girl!"

"Whall, don' kill her than. More's the loot!"

The first rider came straight at Falorn, swinging a sword high above his head. Falorn deflected an overhand blow, and felt his own strike turn on the soldier's shield, notching the golden falcon's head. The second knight couldn't maneuver past his companion as Falorn and the soldier traded blows. After a few seconds of trying, the man backed his horse a few steps so it could leap the wall and come at Falorn from the other side.

The first soldier tried to knock Falorn from the wall with the strength of his horse. He used his sword to keep Falorn occupied while he pushed forward, hoping to throw Falorn off balance, or at least keep him occupied until the second warrior entered the fight. The man seemed to anticipate everything Falorn tried, effortlessly turning aside each sword-blow, or shedding them harmlessly off his shield.

What would Zaren do now? Falorn wondered. *This guy knows everything I do. If his friend's just as good, they're going to cut me into table scraps.*

He slashed outward suddenly, instead of upward. The horseman's blade darted downward, to deflect a blow toward his leg or his horse's flank. Falorn let his sword slide along the soldier's blade, catching the edge of the man's boot and neatly severing one of his stirrups.

"Hey! Wha' kind've trick are ye tryen' there?" The man swung, and his blow went wild as he nearly slid from his horse. Falorn slapped the man's sword aside and thrust under the man's arm, piercing the gap in the hauberk. This time the man did fall down. He screamed; his left arm gave a sickening crack as he hit the ground. The riderless horse reared above him, trampling the man. The soldier gave one more scream, choked off in the middle as sharp hooves crushed his lungs.

Falorn swiveled to meet the second attacker. At his back, he still heard Elise fighting. The horseman galloped at him, broadsword leveled at his face. Falorn held his ground, ducking under the blow at the last second. The man's horse barely cleared the wall. He thrust at the soldier's leg as the man brushed by; his sword slid under the hauberk and drew blood.

The man cursed as he pulled his horse to a halt. He pivoted his mount around to face Falorn once more. His eyes widened suddenly as a thrown knife split the space between them. He remained completely still for a moment, then sank noiselessly to the ground.

Falorn glanced to the side in time to see Elise lower her right arm from the throw. In front of her, the third man slumped in his saddle, her long, thin-bladed rapier still protruding from his face.

"*Well, don't kill her then. More's the loot.*" Elise imitated the man's voice as she twisted her sword to free it from his head. "Grab a horse," she said to Falorn. "Let's get these cretins out of my country."

Falorn quickly recovered the second soldier's horse, pulling out Elise's knife from the dead man to give back to her. He looked around, but the battle had passed onward. Dead spearmen littered the hillside, most cut down from behind. A pair of armored bodies showed where a few of his men had stood to fight, but the rest of the horsemen had vanished.

"We have to go after them!" Elise said. "We can't let them get to the lines without a fight." Falorn looked back at the empty hill, now completely undefended, and followed behind her. She knew what the queen would want a lot better than he did, and he did want to ride toward the fighting. He could feel the lion cards against his chest, anxious to spring into battle.

Some knight, he thought to himself. *First time I lead men in a fight, and every soldier runs away and gets killed. I've got a lot to make up to the queen before this battle's over.*

Elise seemed to know the way, so he followed after her. As they rode up the second hill, they heard the trill of horns. Falorn spurred his horse over the rise. As he crested the hill, the whole battle opened before him. Thousands of men fought in the front of the little valley, so many that they choked off the grass and the sight of everything but steel, blood, and death. Falorn smelled blood and sweat on the wind, and acrid smoke left over from the last wizards' duel. Behind the assault, a sparse line of horsemen rode toward the rear of the Cathanese troops. A few mounted knights turned to try and stop them, but every other reserve of soldiers had been thrown into the fight against the massive assault on the center.

"For the Queen!" screamed Elise, pointing her sword and charging at the riders. Falorn followed right behind her, trying not to let her open up distance between them.

His blade raked the back of a rider's neck before the man even turned around. Falorn felt a twinge of guilt, despite all of Zaren's teachings about not fighting fair. Two other horsemen turned their mounts just as he overtook them. Falorn rode as if to charge between them, then wheeled his mount at the last moment, so only one of the soldiers could reach him. They traded blows, and the horseman's sword shattered. Falorn slashed at the man's face and took him from his horse before he could recover from his surprise.

The second rider threw a knife as Falorn approached. He ducked as it passed over his head, and the man rode at him. Falorn barely parried four quick blows. He countered, cutting the horseman's wrist.

Trumpets belled from the hills behind. For a moment he hoped the Cathanese cavalry had returned to the field, but the tune sounded unfamiliar. Had the Seven Kingdoms or Calathan horsemen ridden around the army? If so, few of them would live through the day; already, the force of the attack on the center had literally begun to push the footmen backward, their line bulging toward him in a convex bell shape.

The horseman suddenly shouted and dropped his sword. Elise appeared behind the man, wiping her blade clean on the dying man's leg. They found themselves momentarily clear of the fighting, with the rear of the queen's army in front of them, and the horns blowing in the hills behind.

"Thanks," shouted Falorn, trying to be heard over the din of battle and the flourish of trumpets. "That's twice today you've saved me."

"You were doing all right," she said. "You were just taking too long, and I didn't want to get separated from you."

"What are the trumpets? I've never heard them before."

"Damned if I know. They're not ours, though, so they must be theirs. I think we're about to get swamped."

"That's what I thought. I'd hoped it wouldn't turn out like this."

"It's not over yet. Let's fight together while we can. If the battle is totally lost, we can try and fight clear. Maybe between our swords, we can make our way out of the country. But as long as the Queen is still fighting, I'll fight on."

"I'll be right next to you." He reached out and touched her hand. "And thanks for everything, Elise. I never really thanked you for helping me learn to read, and for all your help with my swordsmanship."

"You've got a way to go still on the reading. Let's both live through it so I can keep teaching you." She kissed him lightly on the cheek. "Let's see what we can do to help the infantry out, now that those horsemen have all gone away."

"Just keep an eye out behind you."

"What's a trumpet or two? Those horsemen are pretty far off yet. I don't know why they're going so heavy on the trumpets, though; you'd think they would want to surprise us."

She spurred her horse to a walk and began toward the rear of Stennet's lines. The front of the lines had disappeared, its soldiers washed away by the wave of attacking men. Falorn could see men fighting in small, isolated clumps, which one by one were pulled under by the onrushing tide of the Calathanese attack. Further back the lines still held, but the Cathanese soldiers had already begun to waver as attackers cut their way through their lines. The few knights still mounted rode back and forth behind the line, shouting encouragement and slapping retreating soldiers back into the lines with their swordflats.

In the midst of the Seven Kingdoms attackers, knots of Cathanese men fought on with swords and axes. Zaren's wall of shields had disintegrated; its battered survivors rallied desperately around Stennet's banner.

Gradually, the momentum of the attacking force began to slow. Both sides now looked more like armed mobs than disciplined formations. Men fought alone, or in small clusters grouped around the knights who still lived.

Everywhere, tendrils of Calathanese or Seven Kingdoms soldiers reached out to envelop groups of the queen's soldiers. One tendril reached nearly to the rear of the lines, and threatened to break through entirely, clear of the swirling individual mobs.

"We can't let them break through," said Elise. She raised her voice to a shout. "This way! To me! Push them back!"

She rode straight for the closest group of Seven Kingdoms soldiers, grim men in black armor who fought beneath a shredded gray and black banner. A few other knights joined behind her as she cantered forward. Cathanese troops moved to the sides or followed behind where they could. A thin wedge formed, with Elise at its head, increasing slowly in speed as it moved toward the leading edge of the encroaching troops.

"Rally! Rally and push them back!" Elise shouted. "Push them back for the Queen!"

"For the Queen!" others echoed. "Kill them for the Queen! Cathan and the Queen!" Falorn shouted with the rest as the wedge struck.

His sword hit with shoulder-numbing force, nearly throwing Falorn from his mount. Around him, horsemen hacked at foot soldiers, who countered with swords, spears, and pole-axes. Pulling his blade from a dead heavy footman, Falorn quickly looked around. Two footmen rushed at him, and he raised his blade to defend himself.

His chest burned. Falorn slashed hard, cutting through the first man's mail hood. The second soldier fell just as quickly, but then three more attackers came at him before Falorn could do more than draw a breath. Heat ran through his blood, spreading through his body. Falorn felt his arm speeding up, as if the lions wanted him to swing more quickly, to attack more fiercely.

Something dripped across his eyes, but Falorn barely needed to see anymore. He fought by smell, chasing the scent of enemy sweat and blood across the field. Nothing could stand before him, Falorn knew—although he knew little else.

When his eyes focused, Falorn found himself in the middle of a wall of swords, threshing like mowers among the hayfields. He wondered how anyone could stand in it, how anyone could last longer than a stalk of hay. Warm, salty blood filled his mouth. He smelled more blood around him, enemy blood. Falorn swung almost blindly, giving the lions their head as his blood roared and sang.

Like a drowning man, he rose fleetingly above the surface of the surging blood, only to sink instantly back into the ecstasy of the thick liquid which pulled him under.

Now he knew how the Helleinen warrior had felt.

At one point, he found himself standing in the saddle, waving a gray-and-black banner above his head on its broken staff while he swung his sword at the helmets below him, crushing with all his strength when his now-blunted weapon refused to penetrate the iron caps. Everything faded into a swirl of blood and noise and colors. He smelled blood and the sweat of his horse as its mouth foamed and frothed, but he sensed nothing else; his sword found its own targets.

The haze lifted again and he saw a few armored men defending Stennet's Red Anvil banner. Piled dead surrounded them, corpses in all colors. He recognized none of the soldiers, but he cut his way to their side anyway.

Falorn fought on foot now, his horse long dead. He stood on a pile of dead and he killed and killed, even after all of the other men who fought beside him fell.

A knot of men with spiked maces advanced on him, their banner a black tiger on an orange field. The red fog descended once more. Blood watered his hands. His clothes were soaked. He smelled the tang of his own sweat. Despite the salt taste in his mouth, he felt no fatigue at all.

When he could see again, he was still standing on the mound of bodies, with a dozen or more fresh corpses scattered around like so many heaps of mown hay. The tiger banner lay at his feet. He no longer stood alone on the little hillock. He glimpsed the edge of a bloody sword in the corner of his eye. Familiar blue tinted the blade for an instant and he knew it for Cirque's weapon.

His hearing returned as the madness began to fall away. New war cries filled the air at the rear of the lines. "Alex!" he heard men call out, "Alex of Rohn! We're saved!"

Falorn wondered if he had died in the fight, or lay somewhere half-conscious and delirious. The name sounded like one he had heard before, in the half-conscious dream of the woman he had lost.

Falorn looked around at the field of corpses, where no enemies remained. The shouts continued unabated, calling out the lost name, mingled with cries for the queen and Cathan.

Falorn fell to his knees among the dead piled around him, sword held before him like a crutch, and began to cry.

"Quite the hero, your son."

"It was the worst moment of his life, I think."

"Bah. If he still lives, after all that followed that battle, he'll be proud of it someday. Perhaps not now, but in years to come, when people whisper about him and give him special seats at the theater, and when his children are accepted at the University without initiation or sponsorship." Something sounded a little unreal about the interrogator's remarks, as if the words came secondhand, rather than from personal experience.

"He's a long way from that, Councilor."

"Not enough pride, that's all. He comes from a fine bloodline; it's to be expected that he'd be a great warrior. Don't you think?"

The interrogator received no response.

"Pity he's probably dead now."

Still no response. Night had long since fallen. Lamps illuminated the parlor.

"Perhaps we should take a break and you can continue your story when you're feeling more talkative."

The parlor remained silent, except for the occasional noises of gulls outside on the moonlit docks.

The interrogator got up to leave. As he reached the door, he turned to ask a final question.

"So tell me, what did he get out of all of it? He didn't care about the money or the titles or the battles. So what did he accomplish?"

"Nobody lies to him anymore."

The interrogator laughed at that: He seemed genuinely amused.

"Everyone gets lied to."

"Not in the same way. Some people chase after their destinies, or let the world rule them. My son came to make his own choices. Slowly, to be sure, painfully at times. He may have started out as my pawn, or someone else's, but now no one rules him. Here you are with all the wealth of the University behind him, and you have no more control over him than I do. You haven't even figured out where he is."

The interrogator nodded. "That's true. But of course, that's why you are here. Good night, captive. We will speak of this again tomorrow."

The door closed on the parlor, with its velvet cushions and barred windows.

Outside, noises rose from the docks: fishermen unloading, and always the gulls.

Tomorrow would be time for more lies, and another day of freedom for his son.

About the Author

Leigh Grossman teaches science fiction, fantasy, writing, and book publishing in the English Department at the University of Connecticut. He is the author of twelve published books, and has edited many others, for a variety of publishing houses. He lives in northeast Connecticut, in a big old house with a computer programmer fiancee, four cats, and a robot. Visit him at www.swordsmith.com or www.wildsidegame.com.

www.ingramcontent.com/pod-product-compliance
Lightning Source LLC
Chambersburg PA
CBHW030021180626
46810CB00001B/153